THE DARKEST SIDE OF A STAR

The Darkest Side of a Star

Olivia Ocran

To those who have searched for themselves in literature, your search is now over. And to those who fight to be seen in the world, I see you. And for those who choose to ignore the world around us, take notes.

Preface

This book contains instances of violence, death, blood, murder, discrimination, and family trauma

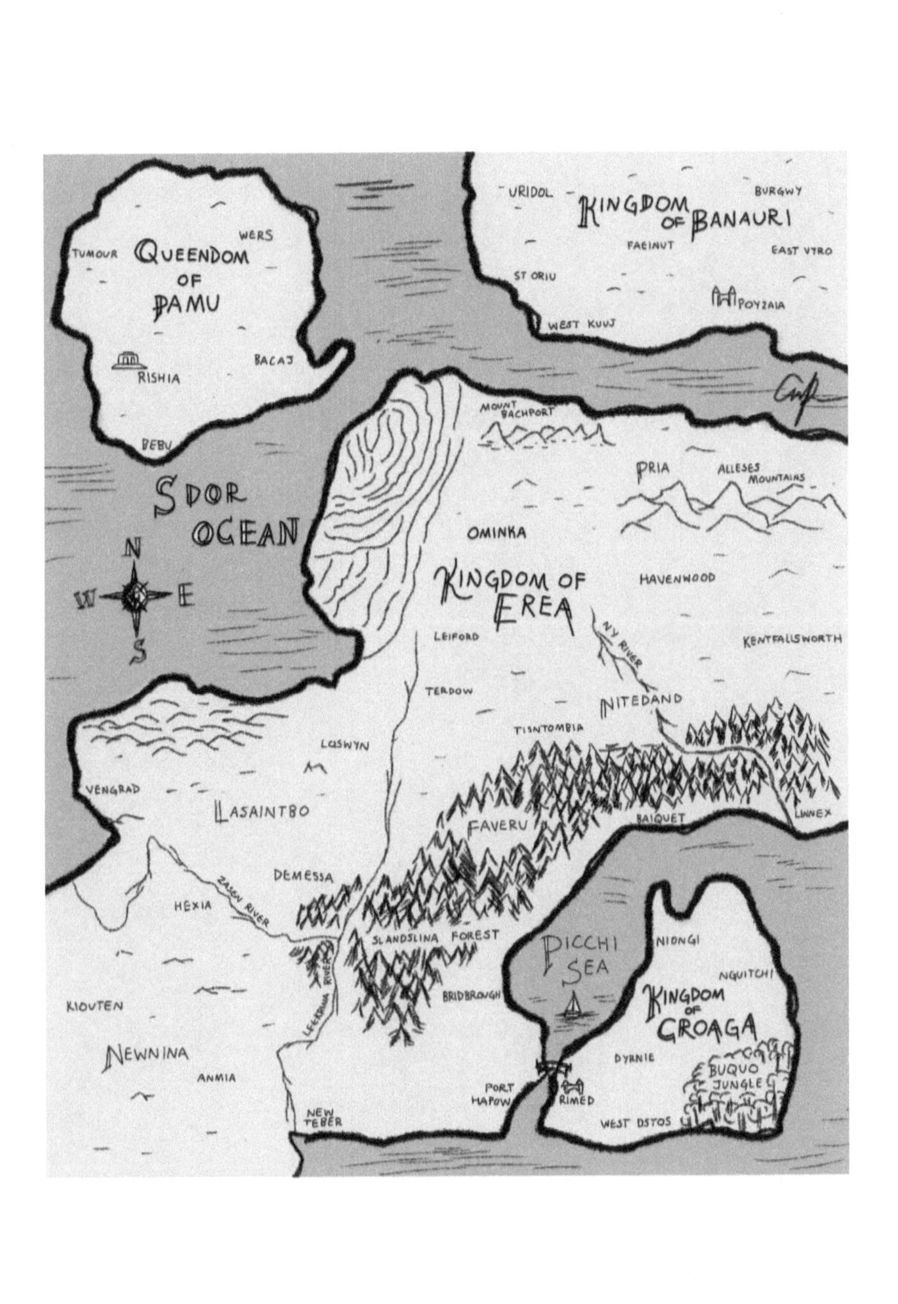

QUEENDOM OF PAMU
TUMOUR
WERS
RISHIA
BACAJ
BEBU
SDOR OCEAN
N
W E
S
URIDOL
BURGWY
KINGDOM OF BANAURI
FAEINUT
EAST VTRO
ST ORIU
WEST KUUJ
POYZAIA
MOUNT BACHPORT
PRIA
ALLESES MOUNTAINS
OMINKA
HAVENWOOD
KINGDOM OF EREA
KENTFALLSWORTH
LEIFORD
NY RIVER
TERDOW
NITEDAND
LOSWYN
TISNTOMBIA
VENGRAD
LLASAINTBO
FAVERU
BAIQUET
LINNEX
DEMESSA
HEXIA
ZAION RIVER
SLANDSLINA FOREST
PICCHI SEA
NIONGI
NGUITCHI
KINGDOM OF GROAGA
KIOUTEN
LECERINIA RIVER
BRIDBROUGH
DYRNIE
BUQUO JUNGLE
NEWNINA
ANMIA
PORT HAPOW
RIMED
WEST DSTOS
NEW TEBER

Chapter 1

Ilise

Noble couples twirled around each other as the summer ball was in full swing. It almost looked fun. I even took a step forward, causing my dagger hidden under the folds of my dress to press into my skin, a solid reminder—that's not what I was here for.

Draped over the golden chandeliers were garlands of orange tulips, like raindrops frozen mid-air. My gold heels clicked against the marble floor. Guards and guests—including myself—wore red roses or tulips to adorn our outfits, paying homage to the Fire Spirit. I'd chosen to also craft a crown of red roses, pinning it to rest atop my afro.

Flowery scents warred with sweat. I wrinkled my nose the deeper I pushed into the crowd, trying my best to blend in. My eyes darted around the room, waiting, studying, watching. The chorus of voices swelled, drowning out the grating melodies of the orchestra. Tonight's music painted a harsh picture. Dissonant melodies clashed together like nails on a rough stone. I supposed the nobles thought it to be some deep, beautiful story. To me, it sounded like an ensemble of irritated cats. I bet if the Fire Spirit were here, their face would turn sour.

I pushed towards the edge of the crowd to find a better vantage point. People gawked at me as I passed, eyes drawn to the tulle sleeves I'd added to my dress. But not having them would only draw more unwanted attention, even though the heat of the room glued the light silk to my skin.

Attention was the last thing I needed. The small part of my brain I was never able to rid of fear kept my eyes also scanning for the monarchs. What would become of me if I were to be discovered was almost too horrific to imagine. But the fear kept me alive, it kept me prepared. It kindled the fire in my belly that appeared when I thought about how the monarchs stood by as my, and so many others' lives were forever altered. The golden pendant under the neckline of my dress warmed on my chest like a second brand—another reminder.

I found an empty spot in the far corner of the room, half hidden by the marble staircase. Although, I didn't fully know what I was looking for. Messages from the Union were limited to avoid interception, but the last message Kass had sent could've won first prize for being cryptic.

Have fun at the ball tonight. There's been gossip about some new guests, and I'm curious about who they are. In the deep crevices of the envelope, she'd added another note, uncoded.

Keep a close eye and don't attract attention. Everyone here's on edge.

She had added the second note as if I hadn't been a spy since I was fourteen, in charge of keeping track of anything the royals are up to, occasionally the opinions of certain nobles to see if we could sway them to our side and help us with funds. I scanned the room, taking special note of the at least a dozen and a half guards clad in Erean black and gold. They paced the perimeter of the room between the towering tan columns, hands rested on the broadswords sheathed at their hips. It was as if they were waiting for something to jump out of the shadowed corners.

The faces I could see were familiar, regular guests of the balls and the court. Lady Ebony and her husband Lord Fion of Faveru mingled with Duchess Aimee of Lasaintbo. Every part of their bodies sparkled with jewelry specifically chosen to match the color of the crystals tied around their necks. The children of the Lords and Ladies of the court huddled together in a dance circle, laughing while they clinked flutes of champagne. I hadn't taken the time to learn many of their names. They seldom attended any court meetings, and I wasn't supposed to talk to them anyways. Or any noble for that matter.

And I bet if they knew I was a Primis servant they'd do their best to keep their distance from me if I was lucky, look upon me with disgust if not. That was the deal with Imperium, with the nobles especially. Their wealth, power, and control over the elements seemed to come at the price of empathy. Any compassion I could have shown towards them had died five years ago with everything else I held dear.

My best friend Aerilyn, however, with her preternatural charm, managed to wiggle her way into their group, her periwinkle dress sparkling under the dazzling candlelight. I could hear her bubbling laughter from my corner, whether she was actually entranced by one of the Water Imperium transforming his champagne into floating bubbles or just being polite, I couldn't be certain.

I paced in my corner, craning my neck to look for unfamiliar faces. Across the room I spotted the King and Queen in deep conversation with Duke Oskar and Duchess Zakira of Pria. A bitter taste coated my tongue and I made a mental note to stay far from that side of the room.

The hairs on the back of my neck rose, my hand immediately resting on my hidden dagger.

"Excuse me, miss? Have we met before?" a soft voice asked. I whipped around in the direction of her voice. Her forest green ball gown was covered in white lace vines, wrapping around her shoulder. *What is with this kingdom and vines?* Red roses were pinned to her glistening gold belt, matching the glittering jewels throughout her long curls. And I could swear the candlelight shone just slightly brighter on her heart-shaped face. I guessed her to be about my age. And I couldn't shake the sickening feeling in my stomach. Who was she? She carried herself with the grace of a fox, probably someone with power. But she wasn't the daughter of any of the Lords or Ladies. I had observed the last court gathering after days of begging Ms. Kira to assign me to work there. I would have seen her.

"Who are you?" I asked. She outstretched a perfectly smooth brown hand, flashing a radiant smile. My face fell as realization dawned on me, my gut clenching with alarm. The few times I had seen her were from too far away to really see her face. And usually, a golden crown adorned her head, identifying her as one of the most powerful people in the kingdom.

Princess Yorena.

My back stiffened into a rigid pole as I dipped into a low curtsy. "I apologize, Your Highness. I didn't recognize you." She waved her hand, taking my silence as an invitation to step closer. I managed to stiffen more.

"I saw you from across the room and thought you looked familiar." Familiar? In the five years I'd been here, I never once ran into the Princess. I'd made sure of it. Until last year, she'd been attended to by her ladies in waiting, rarely leaving the library where she had her lessons.

As I opened my mouth to respond, the orchestra's melodies grew louder. I could hardly hear the words coming out of my mouth, the sounds getting lost in the music and cheers of the guests. *Ugh, nobles.*

The Princess leaned in, her rosewater scent filling my nose. My skin bristled from her proximity but I forced myself to remain still. *Don't react.* The less interesting I made myself seem, the quicker she would leave me alone. I hoped. "Can we talk outside," she shouted over the music.

I nodded. I couldn't very well say no to the Princess, I had studied *basic* court etiquette. If the royal family requested something of you, there wasn't much of a choice for you. Kass and Val could survive a few minutes without me searching for the "special guests".

I swerved away from her hand as she tried to place it on my shoulder. I didn't think she noticed. The Princess led me through the long, empty halls of the palace, through the golden arches lining the corridor, and taking a right into the garden. I inhaled the fresh air, perfumed with the smell of lavender and roses. The silver water fountain glistened under the light of the full moon, and small torches lined the cobblestone walkway.

The Princess gestured to a gray stone bench in front of the fountain. "What about me is familiar? I'm a servant so you may have seen me walking through the corridors," I said. Although, I knew we never once passed each other. She sat down within a few inches of me. Panic spiked through my blood as my eyes locked on the orange fire crystal around her neck. I could almost hear the sizzle of skin, smell the burning of flesh, feel the burn that felt like hugging the sun. I fought a shudder and widened the space between us.

She tilted her head as her dark brown eyes bore into mine. Golden flecks were scattered in the sea of brown, one of the defining traits of Fire Imperium. The same golden flecks that kept me in this prison of a palace.

"Your Highness?" I said, snapping her out of her daze. I needed her to leave. All it would take was one slip-up for her to see right through me.

"Sorry. I must have been mistaking you for someone else. I should return to the ball." I could have told her that inside. I watched her walk back inside the palace, her head held high. Ugh, she even *walked* with an air of superiority. Finally, I let the scowl I'd been suppressing surface on my face. Anger was good. Anger kept the fear in check. It helped me stay motivated.

Relief flooded through me the farther she went. Royals made my skin itch like a persistent rash that refused to leave no matter how much salve or remedies you used. Her careful smiles were even more infuriating than her parents'. I'd like to see her try and keep the same smile outside of her glistening palace, away from her army of servants to do her bidding, away from freshly cooked meals most could only dream of, and away from a life without worry. A smile returned to my face as I imagined how she would react to her kingdom outside the lines of New Teber.

Petite footsteps crunched the damp grass as Aerilyn strolled towards me, her intricate blonde curls blowing in the warm, soft breeze.

"What are you doing out here?" she asked, joining me on the bench and resting her head on the crook of my neck as I wrapped my hands around her slim shoulders.

"The Princess thought she recognized me. Why're you out here?"

She shrugged. "The usual. The noble sons kept asking if they could court me. They're a persistent group." Like clockwork, at least three of the noble sons would try to court Aerilyn. Avoiding courtship was the whole reason she was working here in the first place, but I guess it was hard to escape it when you were the embodiment of a peaceful summer day.

"Want me to come in there and share a few words with them?" I offered. She chuckled. Many of the boys would back off when I showed up with Aerilyn. I towered over many of them, intimidating them too much to approach. Not exactly what Val had in mind when he'd told me to not attract attention, but scaring them away worked just as well. Aerilyn's personality attracted people like magnets, while mine tended to repel them away.

"If you want," she said, standing up from the bench. "But I still want you to come back inside."

"I'll come inside in a minute," I said. She shrugged and walked back inside. I strolled through the garden, not in any rush to go back inside. I ran through the list of guests I knew in my head at least three times. Unless the mystery visitors arrived late, I didn't think I was missing much. Not one person inside had been much of a surprise to see.

My fingers brushed the newly planted hummingbird mints, my personal favorite. Sometimes when I closed my eyes, I could imagine I was a child again. Skipping through the fields beyond my family's farm with my brother and sister, inhaling the flowers' perfume scent without a care in the world. A twinge of longing shot through me, sharp as an arrow. Remembering my childhood would only bring more pain. And more images of charred fields and scorching buildings. The anger I'd felt around the Princess returned, settling deep in my stomach. *Push it down. Sweep it under the rug to never be seen again.* Val had told me that when I first joined the Union, and since then, it's the only way I've been able to keep myself together out here.

I returned to the ballroom, scanning the room for Aerilyn. She stood by the buffet table, chatting with one of the daughters of the court—Lady Ebony's daughter, I determined. Something resembling a grimace formed on her face before promptly leaving Aerilyn as I approached. A few years ago, that would have stung, but it was a regular occurrence by now.

"Took you long enough," she said, not even having to turn around to tell it was me. "I could only talk about the latest court fashions for so long." The daughters of the court were a bland bunch. I toyed with the thick, white tablecloth, half-listening to Aerilyn fill me in on her experience of the ball.

My mind was still captured with thoughts of who the mystery visitors could be. The seasonal balls typically drew nobles from all over the kingdom, even from the most northern reaches of the Alleses Mountains in Pria, to the most isolated parts of the Slandslina Forest in Faveru. The mystery visitors could be nobles who haven't been to one in the last few years, but that wouldn't cause Kass to want their names and make me watch them. Unless they were a Progression member. The Progression wasn't anywhere near here, yet, so that eliminated anyone from Lasaintbo, Pria, Ominka, and here in Newnina. So I should be looking for someone Faveru or Nitedand-born.

The Air Imperium announcer began to speak, his white crystal glowing bright enough to take everyone's attention. "Attention honored guests. Please make your way to the eastern courtyard for the elemental demonstration." People filed out the towering oak doors. Aerilyn pulled me by the wrist to one of the nearby servant doors, closed off to the general public. We could get anywhere in the palace much quicker. And I could get anywhere with much less interference.

"Who do you think is performing?" Aerilyn asked. I shrugged. The King and Queen hand-picked nobles to demonstrate their elements for every seasonal ball. I placed my bets on it being whoever had done the best job of boosting their oversized egos. We walked through the empty, dark servant hallways because, of course, we weren't allowed to have matches to light any of the torches unless we gained permission. I picked up the bottom of my dress to prevent it from dragging in the black puddles, and ducked to prevent my head from bumping on the low ceilings.

Warm air blasted our face as we opened the door to the eastern courtyard. Noble couples mingled in front of the massive stone stage, illuminated by the full moon and stars. Flaming torches lined the perimeter of the courtyard, revealing the posted guards. *Several more than last season. Interesting.* Through the thick trees to the right, guards lurked, visible only by the golden rose crest stitched on their uniforms flashing in the torchlight.

Aerilyn and I stood at the front of the stage as the rest of the guests trickled outside.

"The order of tonight's events are as follows," the air announcer began, quieting the growing chatter. "Princess Yorena Schaefer demonstrating fire, Queen Saskia Schaefer demonstrating air, Mx. Oliver Li demonstrating water, and Mr. Nikos Vikander demonstrating earth."

And Kass's mystery guests finally reveal themselves. Neither of them were nobles as far as I knew, and their last names weren't ringing any bells. *And why are the royals performing?* In all my time here, they'd always watched the show from the balcony overlooking the courtyard. I rose to the tips of my toes to spot the mystery performers, but their faces were shrouded by the dark, too far away for me to decipher.

And it appeared Oliver was "One with the Spirits" as we called them. My friend Rori back at the base was One too. The four Spirits were more than just a "he" or "she", they encompassed all aspects of life. Hence why we referred to them as "they". Some were born with this sense that they also encompassed multiple aspects of life. Which is why we called them "One with the Spirits".

The Princess stepped onto the stage when forceful winds blew through the courtyard. I was knocked to my knees, wincing from the impact as piercing screams rose in the crowd. Aerilyn crouched onto the ground, covering her ears. I wrapped an arm around her, tucking her close to me. Others in the crowd covered their heads from flying torches.

The wind howled, making my eyes burn with tears. There weren't any clouds. It was impossible for a storm to come together this quickly. Unless... Air Imperium.

Guests still able to walk trampled over people to escape to their carriages, only to get knocked down by another forceful gust. *Selfish bastards.* Trees were ripped from the ground, soaring above our heads. Some swirled around each other in an elaborate dance before raining down on the crowd.

"We need to crawl back," I shouted to Aerilyn. Her lip quivered as she nodded. I stayed behind her as we crawled back to the servant hallway door. Good thing I had made us stand in the front. *Always position yourself to make for an easy escape.*

The wind clawed at my face as if it were comprised of actual nails. We finally made it to the door. Slowly, I pushed myself to my feet and opened the door. I pulled Aerilyn in after me, slamming it shut behind us. Even through the thick oak of the door, I could hear the wind howl, muffling shrill screams.

"What in the four Spirits was that," she panted, still shaking. I clasped her hand in mine, giving her a reassuring squeeze. I could've said it was an attack from Air Imperium, but she only knew me to be a servant, not a spy, and she looked shaken enough already. Lying to her constantly hurt like none other, but I'd forced those feelings away a long time ago.

"It was probably just a freak storm. Go on without me, I need to catch my breath," I lied. She nodded, clearly too spooked to question me. I waited until the entrance door closed behind her before trying to open the outside door again. Those Imperium wouldn't get away from me again; I needed to know who was doing this.

Yanking on the door, I threw myself back into the storm. Sharp slices of wind and dust tore at the sleeves of my dress. I kicked off my unnecessarily tall heels for better balance, not feeling the rocks digging into my calloused feet. Dust and darkness limited my field of vision. And at a snail's pace, I forced myself through the wind. The best way to find Imperium in action was to follow the glow. Air Imperium used white crystals, and those always glowed the brightest.

I pushed against the winds for what felt like years before I saw it, a pinprick of white light. Air Imperium. No guests lingered in the debris-filled courtyard, already escorted away by guards.

I shielded my eyes and pushed in the direction of the light. Then, quick as it came, the wind stopped. I almost fell forward from the absence as dust and debris settled to the ground. I strained to find the glow of the crystal, my eyes meeting nothing but gray darkness. Dammit, I was too late.

Goosebumps rose on my arms as I heard footsteps behind me. *Hells.* My eyes landed on one of the only remaining pieces of shrubbery. Picking up the bottom of my dress, I bolted for it, keeping my footsteps soundless, and crouched low behind it. Thorns stabbed through the delicate silk, and I bit my tongue to keep myself from wincing.

Footsteps stopped a few feet into front of the bush and I froze, forcing my breathing to slow to quieter than a whisper. *Become invisible.*

"Couldn't we have struck tonight instead of this pitiful attack," a hoarse voice said. Pitiful? If this was pitiful, I would hate to see their true definition of an attack. Just one of those flying trees could have easily killed a dozen people. But I wouldn't have felt much remorse for the nobles anyways.

"Have patience, we must follow his orders and give them time to pre-pare," a masculine voice said. *Prepare? Prepare for what? Who is "him"?*

"Let's go before the other guards get suspicious," the first voice said. I waited until their footsteps receded before standing. Taking one last glance for more of them, I scurried towards the door. I opened the door and shut it behind me, the slam echoing off the stone. I exhaled deeply, trying to calm my frazzled nerves.

I left the servant hallway and walked down the steps to the ground floor. Soft snores echoed from other servant's rooms, the only sounds in the vacant hall. I opened the door to my boxy room and flopped onto my small bed. It creaked noisily under my weight. Moonlight streamed in from the one small window, brightening the dingy stone walls.

There was no way those two men were real guards. They were fearful of the other guards suspecting them of something, So they could've been the ones who attacked the palace. They seemed to be stupid enough to try. But that strong of a storm couldn't have been done with only the two of them. There had to be at least a dozen Air Imperium to generate a storm that powerful, possibly more.

No. I shook the thought away. I wasn't here to play detective, I was here to spy for the Union, and gather any information I could about the *royals'* plans. No suspicious guards, and no windstorms unless I had clear evidence that The Progression was behind this. That's all I had to do. Then I could leave this prison, go back to my friends, and get my revenge. I looked down at the golden pendant around my neck. I would avenge them, no matter how long I had to be stuck like this.

But I had a sinking feeling that would be the last thing on the Union's mind. They were much too busy dealing with The Progression.

Chapter 2

Ilise

MY HEAD POUNDED LIKE a second heartbeat in my skull as six bell tones rang from the clocktower. Sunlight poured in through my beige patchwork curtains, blinding me as I sat up. As I rubbed the drowsiness from my eyes, the events of last night flooded my brain.

Wind storms, mystery performers, possible Progression members, and I was only supposed to be there to find names. Why did my life have a habit of turning upside down in a matter of hours? But at least no one died this time.

I rose from the bed and peeled off the ruined gown. *There goes three months worth of coin.* I pressed a hand over the bandage on my right arm. It stung like fire after not changing it before bed. Slowly, I unwrapped it, sighing as the air cooled the wound, and threw the soiled bandage in the wastebasket. I had to keep the upper part of my arm wrapped, or else it would get an infection.

We hadn't been able to heal the burns until it was too late to save the skin. And the rest of the skin on my arm was covered in dark brown patches, shades darker than my own skin.

I grabbed a rough towel from the old dresser and wrapped it around myself. Servants had to use communal baths, and the water was always either dirty or frigid. I rummaged through the tiny drawer and grabbed extra bandages and healing salve, and slipped into a pair of slippers. Before I left, I slipped a small silver dagger under the towel to take with me. *Never go unarmed.*

I left the room and hurried down the hall. It was still early enough that no other servants traversed through the hall. I pushed open the swinging doors to the communal baths. Metal basins of water were scattered throughout the room, separated by a system of curtains. The few torches lining the walls were dim, close to burning out.

I chose a bath in the back corner of the room, giving me a perfect view of the entire room. I stepped behind the yellowing curtain, leaving a small crack so I could still see outside the bath.

I dropped the towel outside the bath and stepped into the chilling water. *At least it's clean this time.* There was a discarded bar of soap on the edge of the bath and I lathered it onto my dirt-caked skin. I carefully rinsed the dirt off my arms and dried them with the towel.

I then scooped out some of the minty salve and spread it over the scars. Footsteps echoed from outside the doors. I quickly wrapped the bandages around my arm and jumped out of the bath. Not sparing another second, I wrapped myself in the towel and rushed from the room. I hated being in here with other people. It felt too vulnerable, too exposed.

Water dripped from my hair as I scurried to my room. I shut the door behind me and rubbed the remaining water from my skin. I grabbed my yellow servant uniform from the hook on the door and put it on. The honey-colored dress just brushed the top of my feet, with a white apron tied around my waist. Although it was summer, I still wore long-sleeves.

Bandages were even more conspicuous than the scars themselves. I left my afro out. I didn't have the energy to do anything more with it.

Then, I tucked a small, silver parrying knife into the sheath I strapped to my thigh, perfectly hidden by the folds of the dress. I left my room to find something to eat.

I still had to find a way to get a message to Kass and Val. Based on the conversation I had heard, I could only assume whoever those people were receiving their orders from were planning to attack again. And only one group of people would be bold enough to attack the palace—The Progression. But they'd never dared to step foot in Newnina, let alone the royal palace.

I pushed open the kitchen doors and was greeted by Seth's smiling face. He was one of the assistant chefs in the palace, and was always willing to cook me food since I typically woke up early. His food was better than what most servants got from other chefs.

"Good morning, Ilise," he sang. He rolled up his white sleeves and bent over the titanium countertop. The kettle whistled on the stove, steam shooting out of the spout. "What can I get you?"

"Just a coffee. Black." He retrieved a mug and poured boiling water over a filled coffee filter.

"Bad morning?" he asked.

I shrugged. Good morning, bad morning, it all blurred together after a while. "I have a feeling it might be." He set the steaming mug in front of me with a small plate of strawberries. I downed the contents of the cup, not caring as it burned my tongue. I pushed the empty mug back towards him. "Thanks, Seth," I said, the sound muffled as I stuffed the strawberries into my mouth. They burst on my tongue with the type of sourness they only had when they weren't in season.

"Don't come crying to me when you get blisters on the inside of your throat," he mused. I shook my head. He never failed to make people smile.

The seven o'clock bell hadn't rung yet, so I paced the halls.

I cracked each of my knuckles, needing something to do with my hands. I almost wished the leader of The Progression would come here and stop playing their games. All I needed was an opportunity to drive my knife into their chest, end this once and for all. But no, I had to be a spy in one of the worst places for me to be. The one place where I would get executed if the royals found out who I was. And *I* was the one who had to stay isolated from everyone.

Sometimes I wanted to sprint out of the nearest exit and never look back. But it was much too late to run. I'd run away from my family, then I had to run from their corpses. Running wouldn't solve anything this time. I gripped the gold pendant around my neck, the same pendant my mother and sister should've been wearing.

Other servants gave me side-eye glances as I walked past them, mumbling as many threats to The Progression leader that I could come up with. Most of them involved my dagger piercing their heart, and it brought me the smallest amount of joy.

Lost in violent daydreams, I almost didn't notice the seven bell tolls booming through the halls, which meant I needed to go, *now*. The last thing I needed on my plate was another lecture about my "lack of punctuality".

I raced up the twisting staircase to the second floor. I would never get used to how different opposing parts of the palace were. One second, I was in a dark, stone stairwell, dripping wet from random leaks. Then the second I left the stairwell, towering tan columns wrapped in carved oak vines lined the walls, gold chandeliers hanging from the ceiling. As if they needed this much light in one place.

I slowed my pace as I watched the other servants file out of the servant's office. *Spirits help me.* Ms. Kira tapped her foot as she waited for me outside the door, arms crossed over her chest.

"I thought you'd forgotten you had a job," Ms. Kira scolded. She was the one who coordinated where every servant in the palace was needed. I always thought the job created more silver streaks through her brown hair, along with more wrinkles.

"Sorry, I lost track of time," I said with a slight curtsy. She narrowed her eyes as she circled me, scrutinizing my attire.

"Sure you did," she said, stopping in front of me. For a woman at least a head shorter than me and frail enough to look like she could blow away with the slightest wind, she had a talent for being intimidating. Her brown eyes shot poison in my direction. And her white crystal swung on her neck with each dramatic turn of her head.

"Since you insist on being late, I'm sending you to inspect the marked visitor apartments to make sure they are in acceptable condition. Then go help out in the gardens, maybe a little dirt under your fingernails will teach you a lesson."

I forced a smile on my face. "Yes, ma'am," I said. She sighed and waved me away, her clear annoyance bleeding from her face. I crossed the hallway into the stairwell and climbed to the third floor.

This floor was even more ornate than the rest of the palace. Any visitors were sent to these rooms, and they were decorated to impress. In addition to the over-the-top oak-wrapped columns, a giant mural depicting the four elemental Spirits covered the ceiling.

Of course, nobody knew what the Spirits truly looked like. This mural depicted them as colossal figures made of sparkling crystal. They loomed over my head, as if they were looking down on me from above, or from wherever it was they disappeared to. Many legends said they ran after the fifth Spirit, the Soul Spirit. Although, many refused to acknowledge them as a true Spirit. Mainly because they were the whole reason sorcerers existed. A chill shot down my spine just thinking about it.

The symbols of the four Spirits also adorned the painting. For Fire, two vertical overlapping waves with three slashes. For Water, two overlapping horizontal waves. For Air, a circle filled with criss-crossed lines. And for Earth, four triangles crossing in the middle with four lines shooting out from the corners. I always thought it looked like a rigid flower.

I reached the first apartment with a marker. A simple black ribbon hung from the door handle and I pushed open the gilded door. Yellow light shone through the tall windows, making the tan tiles of the room sparkle. It appeared other servants had already come through; not a speck of dust was to be found. All apartments had the same layout: a small kitchen right across from the living room, and a long hall with five bedrooms for the guest and their team of servants. I did a quick once-over of the five bedrooms, deeming them acceptable. As I left the last room, my thoughts wandered to the identity of the mystery guests.

Two of the apartments could be for the mystery performers from last night, but who was the third one for? Two unfamiliar people lingered in front of the door across from this one. *The mystery performers.* Keeping my head down, I walked to the marked room they weren't blocking next door. *Become invisible.*

"Why are you going into my room?"

I whipped around, startled by the venom in the man's voice. The loud green and gold vest he wore demanded attention. I would've recognized him if he were a regular of the court. I dug my fingernails into the palm of my hand.

"I'm checking to make sure your room is in order, sir," I said in the most polite voice I could muster. He crossed his arms and took a step forward, towering over me. I forced myself to not step back. I wouldn't be bullied by this cocky, entitled man. I was not a very short person. Most would say I was quite tall, so having to look up at this man was not something I particularly enjoyed. It only added another thing on my growing list of reasons to dislike this man.

His pale skin and sharp jawline make the green of his eyes stand out like emerald daggers. The other visitor put a hand on his shoulder.

"Come on Nikos, leave the poor servant alone," they said. If the blond was Nikos, then they must be Oliver. Nikos knocked their hand away.

"Whatever. Let's go," he sneered. Oliver ran a hand through their spiky black hair, looking after Nikos.

"I apologize for his behavior," they said before running after him. The moment their footsteps receded, I dashed into the room. Running into Nikos again was not on my agenda for today. Punching a royal guest wouldn't help me stay invisible. I looked into the five bedrooms in his apartment and was about to deem them acceptable when something I hadn't noticed before caught my eye.

My heart dropped into my stomach. I knew precisely what the fabric hanging from the wall meant. It was what would live in the nightmares of every Primis citizen if the Union failed. Much like the Erean flag, it had four colored rings covered in winding vines to represent the Imperium, but instead of a yellow diamond in the center to represent Primis, it was painted black. Almost every rendition of the flag was drawn by people who had been dispatched in rescue missions. But, even then, they were rarely flown during attacks. If they did, those ignorant royals would have to admit they existed.

The Progression.

I fled from the room. Anyone who proudly hung a Progression flag was not someone I wanted to be around. Unless, of course, they were on the business end of my sword. Part of me yearned to confront Nikos, but he wouldn't complete my mission.

Flustered as I was, I didn't see the point of making sure Oliver's room was spotless. The prospect of helping in the gardens, surrounded by plants, was more enticing. The things, if I had any less dignity, I would call my friends.

I dashed down the stairs to find a pair of garden gloves. My eyes took a few seconds to adjust to the darkness as I opened the door to the storage closet neighboring the kitchen. The gardeners always had a calming presence. Or maybe they just reminded me of Mama, taking me back to the days she helped me and my little sister Aline plant flowers in front of our small house. And she'd always saved one of the flowers to tuck behind our ears.

My eyes roamed over the stacks of towels and napkins until I found a pair of thick gloves on the bottom shelf. My fingers fumbled as I struggled to put on the slightly too small gloves. But even tight-fitting gloves couldn't dim my eagerness to get outside.

I felt a tap on my shoulder and tensed.

"Can you help me," Seth begged. I relaxed to see it was only him, with what looked like soup staining strands of his wavy brown hair. *What did he do this time?*

"You spill something again?" I asked. He nodded quickly, pulling me towards the laundry room.

"I'll give you extra dessert later if you help," he said. I mulled it over. Gardens, or soup? He stuck out his bottom lip, clasping his hands together. "Please," he pleaded.

I sighed. "Fine." A smile broke onto his face and he snatched towels off the shelf, throwing them into my hands. I followed him into the kitchen and immediately understood why he was so frantic. There was not just one overflowing pot, but three of them, the broth on the brown tiles pooling like a giant puddle of mud. "You said there was only one pot," I said as I kneeled on the ground.

"If I'd told you it was three pots you wouldn't have come." *Fair enough.*

"This'll cost you an extra dessert for Aerilyn too." He nodded and waved for me to start soaking up the broth. Seth was known to be generally laid back, even during a disaster like this. Which happened more often than not. But he seemed ten times more stressed about this spill.

"Calm down. The world isn't ending because you spilled some soup." He scrubbed the floor with his towel, focusing on the mess in front of him. *Why is he so high-strung?*

"Today is the start of Heircestrial. Everything has to be perfect," he said. Heircestrial? I thought they'd stopped doing that centuries ago. "The other nominees are already here, and the King himself told me everything has to be perfect." He leaned close to my ear. "The King sounded nervous. He *never* sounds nervous."

I couldn't blame him for that. After meeting Nikos, I could tell he was the type of person to run you over with a cart and make *you* feel guilty. But he couldn't be any worse than half the sons of the court were. There were multiple occasions where I was one more snide comment from pulling my dagger on them. Sometimes, the threat of getting executed for being a spy paled in comparison to how some of the nobles treated servants.

"Seth, I'm sure everything will be fine," I said, trying to calm him down. We managed to soak up half of the broth before the doors flew open, allowing an air message to fly in. I caught the fluttering note just before it landed in the broth. Air messages were what Air Imperium used to send notes over short distances. Or sometimes, they could carry their voice with the wind, making people able to hear them from impossible distances away.

Report to the servant's office immediately. Forget any current assignments.

-Ms. Kira

Spirits help me. What could have I done in the short time I was gone? "Sorry, Seth," I said as I stood. "Ms. Kira is summoning me to the servant's office. I'll see you later." I leapt over the remaining broth and scurried out of the kitchen.

I sprinted through the hallways and up the staircase, pushing my way through other servants traveling on the staircase. Many of them carried baskets of laundry or cleaning supplies. My job would be much easier if I wasn't the type of servant who could get assigned to anything. Most others had one job they had to do for the full thirty years our contracts required. I slowed my pace as I neared the servant's office and opened the oak door to see Aerilyn leaning against the wood paneling on the wall.

"Haven't seen you today," she said, trying to hide a smile as I fought to catch my breath. It didn't matter how many years of intensive training I had, running was not one of my strong suits. You could only run so much in an underground cave.

"I had an early summoning time. Not all of us get to sleep in until after eight," I said. My head turned as someone coughed. Two boys sat in the chaise lounge pushed into the corner. "Who are you guys?" I asked.

"I'm Mathias," the short one said. Brown curls covered his forehead, and his dark freckles and tanned skin told me he worked as a gardener. "That's Chafik," he said, pointing his head in the direction of the boy next to him.

"I can speak for myself, you know," said the boy. He ran a hand through his loose black curls, and the orange torchlight gave his brown skin a warm glow. My eyes lingered on his gaze. One eye was blue and the other brown. *Interesting.* Two-colored eyes was generally a sign that one of your parents were Imperium while the other was Primis. Quite uncommon.

"You were taking too long," Mathias said. I shared a look with Aerilyn, trying to clamp my mouth shut. I could already tell these two would be a handful.

Ms. Kira strode into the room, fiddling with her beaded bracelet decorated with the symbols of the four Spirits. Her eyes scanned over the room before speaking. "Alright everyone, as you should know by now, Heircestral is about to begin." But what did *we* have to do with Heircestrial? My history lessons as a child had been quite limited, mainly because we focused our studies more on money-making skills. I may not have known much about it, but I was certain servants had no place in it.

"Each of the nominees are going to be given a team of servants, and you four have been randomly selected to attend to Princess Yorena for the next month."

A whole month? Could her ladies in waiting not attend to her? My skin crawled to think I would be living with her until the end of Heircestral.

The Princess had infinitely more power than me, yet she did nowhere near enough to help protect Primis people. But I guess some never realize how bad it is until they experience it for themselves. At least three possible Progression members were in the palace, and I was expected to wait on a spoiled Princess? I was finally getting some *action*, there was no point in being fully trained if I couldn't use it.

"And when you're not attending to her, you'll all come back here for another assignment," she said, taking the time to meet each of our eyes.

"Ilise, you'll be in charge of cooking for the Princess." She paused. "And for the others I suppose." She added that last part as if she'd forgotten the rest of us had to eat too.

"Aerilyn, you'll be the Princess' handmaiden. And try to keep the rest of them in check." Aerilyn dipped into a slight curtsy. Some part of me knew it would be rational to feel a slight twinge of jealousy that Aerilyn was Ms. Kira's favorite, but it was merely amusing to me.

"Of course, ma'am," she said. She moved behind my chair, pure pride on her face.

"Chafik, you'll be in charge of keeping the apartment clean. There better not be a speck of dirt."

He gave her a tight-lipped smile. "Yes, ma'am," he said.

"And Mathias, you'll be in charge of doing everyone's laundry."

Mathias tilted his head, blowing a stray curl from his face. "Can't I switch with Chafik? You gave me the worst job," he whined.

Ms. Kira stepped closer to him, meeting his nervous gaze. "Maybe I will give you a better job when you learn some respect, young man. You are all dismissed. Go wait outside the ballroom door," she said, waving us out of the room.

We filed out of the office and walked down the steps to the ballroom. "Since we're gonna be stuck with each other, why don't we introduce ourselves," Aerilyn suggested.

Mathias groaned as we exited the stairwell. "Blondie, no offense, but I'd rather not," he said. Oh, this was going to be an interesting month. We stopped in front of the closed ballroom doors, and Mathias dropped to the floor in one fluid motion, almost horizontal save for his head and shoulders, which were propped against the wall as if it were a pillow.

"What are you doing," Chafik hissed. "We're supposed to act properly."

"I get the feeling this is going to be my last break for a while, and I intend to enjoy it."

Chapter 3

Princess Yorena

LESSON NUMBER ONE FROM my etiquette teacher: a Princess must not show her nerves under any circumstance.

I rubbed my sweaty palm along the beads of my red dress. The candle chandeliers flickered as my thoughts continued to run wild. My eyes were glued to the oak ballroom doors, and I was hardly able to contain my anticipation. Nikos and Oliver—the other nominees—had yet to arrive for our kickoff brunch, leaving my brain all the time to come up with every possible way this could go wrong. They could act hostile towards me, or they would try to get close to me only to stab me in the back later.

Would they be better monarchs than me if I lost my crown? I'd been training to be Queen my whole life, it was what I was made for. But if two provinces already saw me as a failure, what did that say about me? I was only nineteen. I had only started to shadow my parents last year, and most of the court only saw me during the seasonal balls. What could I have done to warrant the revival of a centuries-old tradition, long forgotten?

When my parents would let me sit in on court meetings or help them receive the citizens, I couldn't have messed anything up. I could barely interject, let alone anger two provinces. And it was only recently that they had allowed me to come to strategy meetings with the Commander.

Father's fingers thrummed on the circular oak table, barely containing his nerves. At least he wouldn't have to deal with the other nominees as much as I did after today. Father dabbed a cloth on the sweat beading on his coppery brown skin.

"Yorena, stop picking at your dress," Mother chided. She was the one who had suggested I wear this, but it was too tempting to not pick at it. It was better than bouncing my leg. The maroon tulle ended before my knee, and it wouldn't hide the bouncing. Mother took her cold hand in mine, giving me a reassuring squeeze. "Remain calm. If you want to be Queen, you need to control your nerves."

Remain calm? Control my nerves? The one thing I was destined for was being threatened, and she wanted me to be *calm.* My heartbeat rose in my ears, pounding like a drum. I took slow breaths, trying my best to calm myself and my still shaking hands.

"Are you sure they were informed of this meeting?" I asked Mother.

"Yes. The notice was sent to their rooms last night," she said. I ran through what I knew about each of the nominees. Neither of them were prominent members in court, which was quite peculiar. Although, they both came from influential families. Nikos' father—Wayne Vikander—was an advisor under Duke Leonard of Nitedand, but Nikos had never been reported to be seen in Nitedand's court. And Oliver's mother—Nadia Li—was in charge of the largest exporter of wood from the Slandslina Forest. But I wouldn't say that made them monarch material. And the rest of the information I knew was from the meager report Father had handed to me when I entered the room.

Nominee: Nikos Vikander of Nitedand, Earth Imperium, age 21
Nominee: Oliver Li of Ominka, Water Imperium, age 18

Not exactly helpful.

Surprises made me nervous. I didn't know enough about the nominees. With the nobles, I could study them, craft a plan for anything they could throw at me. Prominent court members could have records tracing where they've stood on issues, or any problems they'd caused. I always read through them before a court gathering. Even for those I couldn't study, they followed similar patterns to other court members. These nominees were unpredictable and left too much up to chance.

Finally, the doors to the ballroom swung open. Three guards marched behind Nikos and Oliver as they strode into the room. After last night, more guards had been assigned for this week to ensure the threat was gone. But I didn't get the mentality behind surrounding two Imperium with Primis guards.

Father motioned for all of us to stand and I tried to put on my most welcoming smile, ignoring the way I wanted to crawl under this table and avoid them. Both of them kept a cold look in their eyes, making chills travel down my spine. *Going great already.*

"Welcome nominees," Father said as he outstretched his hand. Oliver took it while Nikos remained motionless next to him. "It is an honor to welcome you to the royal palace for this monumental occasion." The pair sat in the chair across from us and suddenly, the table felt infinitely too small.

Mother clapped her hands, and servants poured in from the back doors carrying brunch on a silver platter. Steaming vegetable omelets with freshly baked biscuits were set in front of us, along with an assortment of butters and sauces. And my personal favorite, blueberry butter.

"Is there a real reason we were called for brunch today? Because I can think of a list of things I would rather be doing," Nikos said. Father muttered something under his breath. "What was that, Your Majesty?" he asked, batting his lashes.

"Nothing, Nominee Nikos," he said. *Why isn't he reacting?* I'd seen him yell at servants for less. Nikos was clearly mocking him, yet he'd said nothing. I spread the blueberry butter on my biscuit and placed it on my tongue. Usually I would be craving more of the tangy sweetness, but today it covered my tongue in a thick cloying layer. I forced myself to swallow and put the biscuit down. A thick silence settled over the table, weighing on my shoulder like a tangible heaviness.

"You know most people eat with a fork and knife, *Princess*," Nikos sneered. Well, it looked like he was choosing the openly hostile option. I'd spoken to him for less than five minutes, and his dislike rolled off him like crashing waves. I wiped my fingers with the cloth napkin.

"Only the most pretentious would eat a biscuit with a fork and knife," I said. We settled into silence again, the clanging of our utensils the only sound in the room. Out of the corner of my eyes, I studied the two nominees.

Reading people's faces had always been a skill of mine, and most lacked the skills to mask their emotions. Taking Oliver for example, they hunched over their half-eaten plate, taking extra care to avoid eye contact with any of us as they shoveled food into their mouth. They wouldn't be too much of a problem unless they were the manipulative type. The quiet ones tended to bite the hardest.

Just a few months ago, I'd fallen prey to someone like that. He'd made me trust him with his easy smiles and shared feelings of boredom during court meetings. Turned out that he'd been toying with me to convince me to back his father when he fought to gain permission to build a new manor on Primis lands. But he was only one of many examples.

Moving on to Nikos, he lay back in his chair, elbows on the table. Clearly trying to take up more space, maybe to overcompensate for the power he wanted. And the smug yet cold smile he wore was the kind that took practice to master. But if I had understood correctly, he'd never been a prominent member in his court. So where could he have learned it? A moss-colored crystal swung from his neck, covered in white etchings of the Earth Spirit's symbol. Most Imperium kept their crystals hidden when possible. And those who didn't tended to hold themselves with the air of superiority. I would have to watch out for him.

"I almost forgot," Mother began. I jumped at her voice. "The three of you will meet with the Council of Sorcerers tomorrow afternoon. Do *not* be late." I fought back a laugh at her obvious jab at the other nominees' tardiness.

Oliver looked up from their plate for the first time since they sat down. "Oh good. I was hoping we wouldn't have to wait to begin the tests," they said. *Eager to meet with sorcerers? Interesting.*

Heircestrial was one of the topics I had studied most. My tutors had tried to convince me I'd never had to worry about it, but my nerves wouldn't let me rest unless I learned as much about it as I could. Though not much information was left about it. The last time it had occurred was before Anora Schaefer took control. She'd been the first in my royal line, and the person who led the revolution for equality for Primis people. Heircestrial only happened when a province didn't want the current line to continue. And the Schaefer line was the longest ruling in history.

The Council of Sorcerers seldom made an appearance outside of their home, Mount Bachport. And they were only seen outside the mountain when they had to carve the symbols into crystals so we could use them. Or in this case, Heircestrial. Sorcerers were born with power over earth, air, fire, water, and control over souls. It was the reason they resided far from other towns. Nobody trusted them. Even though they were no better than banished, having five crystals gave them a superiority complex. I bet Nikos was the type to worship the ground they walked on.

"So, Nikos. Why do you want to become the heir?" I asked.

Father dropped his fork to stare at me, a cold, warning smile spreading across his face. "Now Yorena, let's not bother our guests with silly questions."

Nikos leaned forward on the table. "No worries, Your Majesty. Personally, I think Her Highness would be much too soft a leader. And the kingdom would benefit from leaning away from the *ideals* of the Schaefer royal line." I quirked an eyebrow. *A Progression sympathizer?*

I drummed my fingers on the table. "Well I can assure you, Nominee Vikander, being a compassionate leader is not the same as being soft. I think the kingdom would prosper in my hands." He narrowed his eyes at me.

"Time will tell," he put simply. *Time will tell?* This was the fate of Erea we were talking about. A mixture of anger and annoyance simmered in my veins. Nobody with an ounce of self respect would want him to represent Nitedand. I somehow found the strength to look at my parents' reactions, and neither looked amused, the promise of a lecture burning in their gazes.

Looking back at Nikos, he took a long, slow sip of his juice. "We will see who will be a better heir soon, *Princess*."

Mother sighed, shifting in her chair. "Allow me to introduce you to your teams of servants," she said. She stood up from her chair, practically jumping out of her seat. I wished I could do the same.

The doors to the ballroom swung open, and three groups of servants marched in. "Has Ms. Kira told all of you who you're assigned to?" A servant with mismatched eyes stepped forward.

"Yes, Your Majesty," he said as he bowed to her.

Mother walked back towards the table, taking Father's hand in hers. "Wonderful. Yorena, Nominee Vikander, and Nominee Li, you are dismissed until your meeting tomorrow." Hand in hand, Mother and Father left the ballroom. I could almost see the relief flooding through their faces the farther they got from the other nominees.

They seriously left me with the nominees? I wished I could say I was surprised. But they were just teaching me valuable skills I would need as Queen. They wouldn't leave me alone for no reason.

Nikos pushed his empty plate away and stood up to leave. "All of you attending to me follow me back to the apartment," he ordered. He strode through the oak doors, servants in tow.

Oliver quickly wiped their hands, rushing after Nikos. "I'll be fine until lunch. My servants can go wherever," they said. Their servants scurried into the servant hallways, already affected by the thick atmosphere.

I walked up to the remaining four. "I guess you are my servants. I'm Yorena." They dipped into bows. I waved my hands. I never was a fan of bowing and curtsying. It seemed like a tedious thing to do. "You don't have to bow to me."

"That's kind of rule number one," the blonde girl said.

I shrugged. "Then I'm making it a royal order for you to ignore that rule." My eyes caught on one of the servants. She was the girl I had seen at last night's ball. I never did catch her name, and she still looked familiar. Who was I mistaking her for?

"What are all of your names?" I asked.

"I'm Ilise," the mystery girl said. "She's Aerilyn, the freckled one is Mathias, and that's Chafik." Mathias looked appalled by her introduction.

"So I'm 'the freckled one' now?"

I fought a chuckle.

"To be fair, you called me blondie when we met," Aerilyn said.

I waved my hands, forcing their attention back to me. "Hey guys, before you argue each other's heads off, have you moved into the apartment yet?"

Ilise shook her head.

"Well how about you guys move in, and then we can get to know each other a little. We'll be spending a lot of time together." Hopefully, they wouldn't be as dull as my ladies in waiting. They only ever talked about the latest rumors in court. Mostly who was courting who and who was having an affair with who. It became repetitive after a while.

"Yes, Your Highness," Chafik said. They filed out the door behind him, leaving me in the empty room.

The meeting could have gone much worse, but Nikos was proving to be an issue. Nowadays, when someone said they wanted to lean away from the ideals of Anora Schaefer, it meant they preferred the ideals of The Progression's inspiration—*Letita.* Just thinking of the name sent a shudder through me. Letita had built this kingdom on the back of other Primis, with Imperium at the top of the social and wealth ladder. And it would've stayed that way if not for my ancestor Anora. Letita's vision for Erea was not one I ever wanted to see. But if Nikos won, I'd likely have no choice.

The Progression was the group of people who wanted to do precisely what Nikos said. Could he be a member of The Progression? Or was he just a sympathizer? The difference was minor but destructive.

Fighting for my crown was never in the plan.

Chapter 4

Ilise

M Y FINGERS MET CRACKED wood as I searched my drawer for the old letters from my family. There weren't any other places they could be. Aerilyn was practically bouncing from where she waited in the door frame, having already packed. But I couldn't leave without the letters. They were some of the few things I had left of my family.

I had first come to the palace when I was thirteen. Mama and Papa had ordered me not to go, but I couldn't stand to watch them suffer. A drought was destroying our farm, taking away our primary source of income. I'd even tried taking odd jobs around Demessa—my village—to earn coin, but I had only managed to earn a few coppers. Jobs like cleaning houses, delivering mail, fetching water for people who couldn't make the energy-depleting journey to the nearest pump, and it still hadn't been enough.

So, while everyone slept, I had packed my clothes and used the little money I'd earned for a cart ride to New Teber. And for my first year here, I'd sent them all my wages. From the few letters I'd received, they were glad for the money. But it had been a lonely year, especially since Aerilyn hadn't even arrived at the palace yet.

The palace gave every worker a week-long break every few months, but I hadn't wanted to go back until my family was back on their feet. And once I'd received a letter saying things were relatively back to normal, I'd finally left for my break. And it was that moment when I'd been set on the road that would forever change me. For better or worse, I'd yet to find out.

"Aren't you excited?" Aerilyn asked, plopping herself onto my bed. I finally found the letters half hidden by a broken plank of wood. I carefully folded them into a protective cotton pouch, pausing to look at her blankly.

"Excited for what exactly?"

She gave me an incredulous look. I ignored her and returned my focus to packing. Most of my belongings were mementos, and they needed to be packed with care: an old rusted hair clip I was certain belonged to my mother, a wooden horse that was supposed to be for my younger brother Sam, and of course, the letters.

"Excited for change," she said as she sat on my rickety bed. "Heircestrial hasn't happened in ages. And I think it'll be interesting to watch." Interesting? I'd describe it more as stressful, a pain in the butt, and a waste of my time that I could be using to plot against The Progression.

The last thing I packed was my childhood princess doll—the oldest friend I had. I settled her on the top of the basket and waited at the door. "I thought you were ready to go?" I said. Aerilyn jumped from the bed and looped her free arm in mine.

"I've been ready," she said. I walked with her through the halls and up the stairs. Her excitement was contagious, but it settled like dread in my stomach. Nikos and Oliver were the other two nominees, and I already suspected Nikos to be a Progression member. The weapons tucked between my clothes felt like carrying around a target. I would have to take extra care when I hid them in the apartment.

"You're way too excited for this," I said. She turned to me, her blue eyes sparkling with joy.

"I'm the normal amount of excited. You're just being a stick in the mud."

I opened my mouth in a fake gasp. "Who? Me? But as my best friend you should know how much I *adore* watching spoiled nobles compete for a ring of metal."

"Very funny," she said with a smile. I fought a shudder as we passed Nikos' room and Aerilyn pushed open the doors to the Princess' apartment. Mathias and Chafik lounged in the living room chairs.

"What took you two so long?" Mathias asked as he fiddled with the strings of a violin. A violin? Didn't peg him for the musical type.

"This one was being slow," Aerilyn said, bumping me in the shoulder.

"I wasn't being slow, I was being methodical," I said.

"Well, you two left me to be subjected to this one's violin," Chafik said.

I snorted.

"Hey, I was serenading you. You should be thanking me," he said. Chafik sat up in his chair, cutting Mathias a look.

"Thanking you for single handedly insulting every music composer dead and alive?" Chafik shot back. I clamped my lips shut, smothering a laugh. At least these two would offer me some entertainment for the next month.

Crossing the room, I took the first empty servant bedroom. This room was probably twice the size of my old one, with a full-sized bed and a desk pushed into the corner. The tan stone was covered with matching rugs, scattered throughout the room. Light glinted off the gold foil etched into the walls, shining from the tall windows. There weren't any curtains, and I hated being watched. One could never be too careful in the palace. That needed to be fixed immediately.

My window overlooked the south wall of the palace, a towering travertine structure at least two stories tall. At least six guards marched on top of it, watching both sides of the wall like hawks. Any of them could easily watch me through the windows and the thought made my skin crawl. At the very least it provided me with a better vantage point to see anything happening near the gate. At this height, I could even see the Picchi Sea in the distance.

I set my basket on the plush bed, no doubt stuffed to the brim with cotton and imported goose feathers or something equally absurd, and left the room. I would unpack later. Aerilyn sat cross-legged on the floor in front of the boys. At least Mathias had put away his violin, and yet the boys still argued about something stupid.

They reminded me of Rori and Cain. Rori and Cain were two friends who contributed some much appreciated levity during my training with the Primis Defense Union—the organization founded to stop The Progression. We could be talking about which route to take when we were about to leave for a mission, and those two would manage to argue about it until Val had to scream at them to stop. Hearing Mathias and Chafik argue was like getting a small glimpse of home.

There wasn't a day that went by that I didn't wish I was waking up in the small room I shared with Rori and we would spend the day training with the rest of our friends, or plotting against The Progression. But I would see them soon. I had to.

The Princess strode into the room, sitting on the couch next to Mathias. I dug my nails into my palms as my eyes fixed on the orange crystal around her neck. It took carefully trained amounts of self-control to not move as far from her as I could.

"Hello everyone," she beamed. "I thought we'd do some quick introductions." Her eyes landed on me and I could've sworn her smile wilted, just a bit. "Maybe just say your name and where you're from. I don't want to take up too much of your time. Also, I would prefer if we did away with the formal titles. Just call me Yorena." If she wanted to play at being fun and innocent, she could just let us go. Being in the same room as her made every hair on my arms stand up. "Ilise, why don't you go first."

I sat on the couch behind Aerilyn. "Ilise. From Newnina."

The Princess leaned forward in her chair. "You are? Which town?" *What is this, an interrogation?*

"Demessa," I said, not offering any more explanation. Demessa was a small village, just on the outskirts of the Slandslina Forest. It was the type of village where you only knew about it if you lived there. *But even that wasn't enough protection from The Progression.*

She didn't ask more questions after that. The other three introduced themselves. I already knew Aerilyn was from Pria, in the snowy northern peaks of the Alleses Mountains. It's what gave her a moonly complexion.

Chafik said he was from one of the larger villages in Faveru, the province east of Newnina. I chewed on my lip when the Princess didn't pester him with more questions. She went just as easy on Mathias, who said he was from the northwestern city of Vengrad in Lasaintbo. *Why is she so interested in where I'm from?*

"Yorena," Aerilyn began. "Was that blond nominee as terrifying as he looked?" Not needing to contribute to the conversation, I tuned out whatever answer the Princess gave. If you looked past Nikos' smugness, he wasn't all that scary. Just another power-hungry Imperium who saw himself as superior to everyone. I'd dealt with people like him before. Most were harmless. While others...

The burns on my arm tingled at the memory. I could almost feel the Imperium's hands on me, so desperate for control that he would come after a child. I snapped out of my daze when Aerilyn called my name. "What?"

"I said, can you believe the Council is coming here?" The Council? Did she mean the Council of Sorcerers? The Council was supposed to stay in Mount Bachport and train other sorcerers. Unless they were carving the elemental symbols into crystals.

"Why would the Council be coming here?" Mathias asked.

"Because they oversee Heircestrial," the Princess said as if it were common knowledge.

"It's a tradition," Chafik added.

If my life depended on my knowledge of Heircestrial, let's just say Kass wouldn't have to stress over my impulsiveness anymore. I had come close to giving her likely multiple heart attacks.

"How do you know?" Mathias asked Chafik.

"I was tasked with helping my adoptive father in the Faveru Archives."

"Quite an honor for someone so young," the Princess said.

"If by helping you mean hiding in a corner and reading a book I'll bet," Mathias teased.

"Reading *a* book? I believe I read every book in that place."

I tuned out the rest of their conversation as my mind kept wandering back to Nikos, or rather, the flag in his room. A nagging voice in the back of my head wanted me to tell the Princess about the flag. Personal feelings aside, the royals hated The Progression as much as they did the Union. And she could think I was sticking my nose in business that didn't concern me.

A few years back, the royals had denounced the Union, claiming we were the same as The Progression. It was why I had to be so careful about everything I did. The last spy of ours they found had been executed for treason after they aroused too much suspicion showing off some knife-throwing tricks. Servants weren't supposed to be trained fighters.

And the Princess seemed to have a habit of asking me too many questions. But it was clear the royals still didn't like The Progression. They *were* the ones who disagreed with everything about their royal line. But would she brush it off as nothing, like her parents did for the ball? I made a split second decision I hoped I wouldn't regret. I could tell her but play dumb about it. She didn't need to know *everything* I knew.

"Um, Princess," I said. She ceased her conversation, eyes open to me. "I had to check all of the rooms earlier, and Nikos had an interesting flag in his room."

She tilted her head, questioning. *So far, so good.*

"What kind of flag?" I opened my mouth and shut it promptly. I couldn't say The Progression, that would lead her to ask how I knew about them. Val's words from when he taught me how to withstand interrogation echoed in my mind. *Give them the minimum. Let them draw their own conclusions.*

"It looked like the Erean flag. But inside of the overlapping rings, the diamond was black instead of yellow."

She blanched. So she did know what it was. "Princess?" She drummed her fingers on the arm of the couch as her eyes stared at an invisible point. "Princess?"

She took a deep breath. "The rest of you are dismissed. Ilise, I need you to stay for a minute." Aerilyn shot me a sympathetic look before leaving with the boys. *Dammit.*

She waited until the door slammed shut, sealing my fate before speaking. "Ilise, what do you know about that flag?" I challenged her gaze as it bored into mine. Val had taught me different ways to make interrogators think you knew nothing. All it required was to make people think you were dumb, an innocent person who had no idea what they were talking about, someone a little in over their head.

It was easier to do when dealing with nobles. Even the nicest of them tended to see Primis people as a charity case, someone who was beneath them and couldn't possibly know as much as them.

"I don't know anything. That's why I was asking you." *Dial it back on the sass, Ilise.* I was supposed to be innocent, not overconfident. The Princess was clearly more sly than I would give her credit for, so I couldn't talk to her like I would a lesser noble.

"No. I think you know more than you're letting on." This girl just didn't quit, did she?

"What do you want from me?" Her heart-shaped lips curled up in a smile. Was she enjoying this?

She leaned forward in the chair. "I'm gonna let you go now. But you're a curiosity. Most people would have thought the flag was nothing more than a sewing mistake. You could just be playing dumb for all I know." Spirits, she was good.

I stood up from the chair and walked to the door. Taking one last glance back, she waved me away, an innocent smile plastered on her face. I forced my face to smile.

The moment I opened the door, Aerilyn and Chafik jumped back. I raised an eyebrow at the two of them. "Were you two trying to listen through the door?"

The pair looked away. "Of course not," Chafik said. His two-colored eyes looked everywhere but my face.

If the Princess was good at one thing, it was taking me off guard. Between her confrontation at the ball and my latest interrogation, I had a feeling I would have to watch out for her as much as I did Nikos. Just one more person to put on my list of people who could mean my downfall.

Aerilyn started to pull me down the hallway, trying to distract me from Chafik's meekness. "We should get to the office," she said. After a few seconds of silence, Aerilyn spoke again. "So what did the Princess want to talk to you about? You know, because we *weren't* listening." I toyed with the golden pendant at my neck.

"She wanted to know what I knew about some stupid flag in Nikos' room. It was nothing important." We continued our walk in silence.

I needed to get a message to Kass. My first thought was that the Princess suspected me of being a Progression sympathizer or member. They rarely flew the flags, so the only people who knew what they looked like were either in The Progression or survivors of their attacks. Not like there were many.

But if she was choosing to put her energy into questioning me rather than address the issue of the flag, then I would have to tackle the problem of Nikos on my own.

CHAPTER 5

PRINCESS YORENA

I WATCHED THE SUN rise over the south wall as I massaged the crick from my neck after hunching over my desk all night. I had awoken in the middle of the night after an air message was delivered. It was an overflowing envelope filled with recent incident reports from Nitedand and Faveru. The two provinces had always had a history of minor skirmishes and disagreements, and the latest incident happened after a Progression riot on their shared border.

I had tried to sleep, attempting to ignore them. But I couldn't help but look. The border skirmish wasn't the only thing in the reports. More Nitedand Progression members and sympathizers attacked guards and destroyed Primis villages, and citizens against The Progression attacked sympathizers and members in response. Half the province was fighting while the other half was barely making it by and I wanted to yank my hair out just thinking about it. It would only be a matter of time before I had to start reading casualty reports instead of just incidents.

I forced myself to step away from the desk. A warm bath would calm me down. I pushed the chair out, crushing discarded balls of paper. At first, I almost didn't believe my parents had given them to me. They usually handled any military decisions with the Commander. In addition to mulling over the reports, I had tried coming up with solutions. If I was going to be Queen, solving problems like this would be my new normal.

I needed to clean this mess. No one could see me like this. I could barely stand to see myself like this. A future Queen was supposed to be the epitome of strength, an unwavering front. I hardly wanted to admit I was lacking that strength to myself, let alone to any of my servants. Slowly, I gathered the balls of paper. The world swayed under my feet; days without sleep were finally catching up to me. I held the crumpled paper balls in my arms and dumped them into the wastebasket, along with the burnt-out stub of the candle I'd been using these past nights.

A knock sounded at the door. "Come in," I said. Aerilyn walked into the room with Ilise, carrying metal tubs of steaming water. I opened the door to my bathroom and they filled the standing tub. Ilise curtsied before hurrying out of the room.

"I'll lay out some clothes for today on your bed," Aerilyn said as she sprinkled rose petals into the soapy water. "Would you like me to come back and help you after your bath?" She dried her hands on her apron and turned towards me. I shook my head and she curtsied before closing the door behind her.

I stripped off my clothes and lowered myself into the steaming bath. I grabbed the fluffy sponge and lathered soap over my body and face, filling my nose with the scent of roses. But even the relaxing steam couldn't clear the pestering thoughts from my mind.

If I was going to be Queen, I needed to be able to come up with solutions. But every solution I thought of had at least a thousand ways it could go wrong. We could send more guards, but that would make both sides angrier. No one enjoyed having soldiers breathing down their necks all day. Or maybe we could close the borders of Nitedand to handle the problem without any outside trouble, which would only give the people of Nitedand more reason to riot. We could also try talking to them to solve this diplomatically.

But diplomacy had gone out the window weeks ago. The leader of The Progression had stopped responding to any letters or representatives we sent. And without so much as a name or face, we couldn't go looking for them. They'd cut The Progression off from the rest of the kingdom. Any spies we sent anywhere close to where we thought they were hiding out in Nitedand and Faveru either came back injured, or not at all. It was like trying to invade a completely different kingdom.

I dipped under the water to rinse off the soap suds and wrapped myself in my towel. Stepping out of the bathroom, I noticed that a green silk dress was laid out on my bed. My eyes caught on a note sitting on top of the dress, stamped with Mother's seal. I quickly put on the dress and returned to the bathroom to sprinkle some water from the sink on my tangled curls, combing them through with my fingers. After another once-over in the mirror, I thought I looked awake. Aside from the dark circles marring my under-eyes, and the dulled glow of my skin. Hopefully, nobody would ask any questions.

I paused at the door frame, feeling like I'd forgotten something. *Mother's note.* I ran back to my bed where I'd left it, breaking open the seal.

Report to our room after you get dressed. We have much to discuss.
-Mother

Someone knocked on the door. "Come in," I said. Aerilyn stepped into the room.

"Ilise wanted me to tell you breakfast is ready," she said.

"I'll be out in a minute." She waved goodbye before closing the door behind her. My parents wouldn't mind if I ate breakfast before going to their room. If they needed me right away, they would have sent one of their servants to wake me up.

I banished any thoughts of the incident reports and The Progression to the back of my mind and put on the best smile I could. I walked into the kitchen, the buttery scent of omelets filling my nose. "Good morning everyone," I said. The boys looked up from where they sat on the couch, blessedly not arguing. Mathias was folding a basket of clothes, displeasure clear on his face.

"Good morning Ms. Yorena," Chafik beamed.

"I hope you all slept well," I said. Spirits knew I hadn't.

They gathered around the small table next to the kitchen as Ilise set down plates of breakfast.

"How can you people generate this much dirty laundry in one day," Mathias grumbled. Ilise caught my eye, and her lip twitched downwards before she looked away. Maybe I shouldn't have questioned her yesterday, but it was necessary. Two times already, we'd discovered spies in the palace. One of them had worked for The Progression, while the other was from the Primis Defense Union. It was unnerving to think spies had managed to infiltrate the palace. Both of those "organizations" were a plague within Erea, and I hated to think they would have infected the palace as well.

And most people wouldn't spare The Progression flag a second glance. It was too similar to the Erean flag. I guessed that was the point; maybe they assumed it would give them more anonymity when they flew the flag. I sat down at the table with the rest of my servants.

"Thank you for breakfast, Ilise," I said. I took a bite and practically melted. The food tasted better than anything the royal chefs had ever made. I shoveled bites of the omelet into my mouth.

"This is better than the meals my mother cooked at the seasonal feasts," Mathias said. I gulped down my cup of water to wash the food down.

"I'm sure your mother's cooking was just as good," Ilise said as she joined us at the table. I could tell she was purposely avoiding my eyes. Yeah, she definitely hated me now.

"Nope," he said. "In fact, one time my father fed the cat pieces of food under the table to avoid eating it." I fought back a laugh. I wondered what it would be like to celebrate the seasons with a simple feast. All the balls blurred together in my mind after going to them for my nineteen years of life. Mingling with other nobles, extravagant feasts, dancing with every noble son the court threw at me, even after I'd made it clear I preferred women. They wanted to ensure I would be matched with someone I could create heirs with. It was all tiresome and headache-inducing. What would it be like to sit around a table and share a meal with my parents instead?

Running a kingdom didn't leave much time for family meals. Unless I counted the time we shared during balls. But I was sure they would spend more time with me if they could spare it. "Future queens don't whine about not receiving their parents' attention," is what my old tutor had told me. Back then, it had sounded harsh, but now I saw she was merely preparing me for the absence of help from my parents. I would survive without a family dinner. No matter how nice it would be to just have the three of us together, with no nobles or palace staff fighting for my parents' attention, and we would be able to just... talk.

"Ms. Yorena?" Chafik said. I shook my head, snapping myself out of my daydreams. "Will you tell us what the sorcerers tell you after the meeting today?" Everyone but him visibly shuddered. Couldn't say I blamed them. Sorcerers not only had control over all four elements but also control over souls. If they were powerful enough, they could basically control your every action. No one trusted them, and with good reason.

"Of course. But I do not think much will happen. They are just supposed to go over the rules of Heircestrial."

Chafik shrugged. "I'll take what I can get." A thought nagged the back of my head. Did I forget something? Wait, I was supposed to meet with my parents. They would be furious if I made them wait any longer. I wiped my hands on the cloth napkin and pushed away from the table.

"I thought your meeting wasn't until this afternoon," Ilise said. Those were the first words she'd said to me since yesterday.

"I forgot I had a meeting with my parents. I shall be back shortly." I rushed out the door and ran down the hall to my parents' room. Their room—and my old one—was on the opposite side of the floor. My parents always said it was essential to be close to your guests, even if they rarely talked to them outside of parties and planned meals.

As I rounded the corner, two extra guards stood watch outside their door. They bowed to me as I approached and opened the door for me. "Thank you," I said. Mother and Father looked up from the stacks of papers they were hunched over. I recognized the stamp of the Erean Royal Guard. They must also be reading the reports that had come in last night.

"Yorena, do you know why we summoned you here?" Father asked. I could think of at least twelve reasons, but I didn't think they wanted to hear me ramble about them.

"Is it because of the semi-disastrous meeting with the nominees yesterday?" He paused. I feared a lecture after I'd spoken to Nikos with such a flippant tone. My perceived "disrespect" of so called "esteemed" guests was a frequent conversation I had to have with them.

"To an extent," he said.

"What do you mean by 'to an extent'?" He motioned to an empty chair next to them. I sat down and almost sat on one of my old practice daggers. I picked the blade up from the chair, the metal glinting from the candlelight above. "What's this doing in the chair?" I ran my fingers along the black floral etchings in the metal.

"We'll get to that," Mother said.

"I am sure you have received the newest reports about the situation in Nitedand," Father said.

"Yes. I read over them last night and have yet to think of a possible solution. But I should be able to think of something soon—"

Mother waved her hands. "Don't worry yourself over finding solutions. We will handle that." *If they don't want my help, then why did they give me the reports?* Mother walked over and put her hand on my shoulder. "Your only job is to win Heircestrial and keep your crown," she said with a weak smile. I touched the top of my still wet head, bare without my usual tiara. One of the Heircestrial traditions was not to wear it until the end of the competition. My head felt lighter without its constant weight; I wasn't sure if it was a relief, or if I missed it.

"That is a given, but it seems like there is something else." They glanced at each other uneasily. "What?" I asked warily.

"You see the practice dagger we put in your chair?" Mother asked. I glanced back down at it, resting beside me. "Well, your Father and I think it is time for you to restart your combat training." I shot up from my chair.

"Why do I need to restart my training?" I fumed. "I am a Fire Imperium. Anyone who tries to hurt me would be charred in an instant."

Father slammed his hand down on the table. "Using fire only works as long as your crystal lasts, and if it died, you would be no stronger than a common Primis villager." Technically true.

"But—"

Father's eyes burned in a warning. "And if someone got close enough to take it from you, what would you do then, huh?"

Much to my dismay, he had a point. While Imperium were stronger and had power over an element, we still needed to pull the energy from a power crystal. Crystals could last from a day, a few months, or even over a year, depending on how much you used them. They could only be mined from the Alleses Mountains, and after they were mined, a sorcerer had to carve the corresponding Spirit's symbol into the stone. So even someone scratching out one of the symbols would make the crystal no more helpful than a rock.

Running out of crystals during a battle would mean almost certain death without any combat training. Someone managing to take them from me would mean certain death. But who would want to hurt me?

"I wouldn't be surprised if one of the trials involved combat considering our current *environment*," Mother said. "You will begin again with Instructor Fowler tomorrow. *Without* your crystal."

"But Mother—" She shot me a look; I shut my mouth.

"Our decision is final. Sit back down," Father said.

I sat back down and twisted the dagger in my hands. I had not picked one up since I was fifteen. I'd begged my parents to start training and was sorely disappointed when all I gained was basic defensive skills and more bruises than I could count. On top of that, I hated Instructor Fowler. He would scold me for taking any breaks during his lessons, and the man was plain rude; I was a child, not a battle-hardened soldier.

"The Progression gains new followers every day. It's only a matter of time before they start spreading outside of Nitedand," Father said. My fingers scratched the inside of my arm.

"They might already have," I said.

Any frustration drained out of both of their faces, replaced by terror. They gulped. "What are you talking about, Yorena?" Mother groaned.

"One of my servants yesterday said Nikos had a Progression flag in his room." Father's jaw tensed.

"We already have informants investigating Nikos and Oliver. But how would your servant even know what the flag looked like?" Father asked.

"Technically, she did not *say* she saw a Progression flag, but she did notice the difference. Most people would have overlooked the black diamond in the middle. And when she'd brought it up to me, I felt like she wasn't telling me everything when I tried to question her, she played dumb. And you know how good I am at reading faces? It was almost as if she practiced deflecting questions."

Mother sighed. "Are you one hundred percent sure she was lying?" Was I? I could be reading into this too much, but that nagging feeling in the back of my head wouldn't stop replaying the conversation on repeat. I nodded.

Father rubbed the graying stubble on his chin. "What's her name?"

"Ilise. Ilise Obrien," I said. "I already looked her up in the palace files. She came to work for the palace a few days after turning thirteen and has been here since. Her file said she sent her first year's wages to her family, but they mysteriously stopped, and nothing in the file said the reason why. Nothing about it was enough to incriminate her of being a Progression member or a Union member."

"Get closer to this servant and see if she tells you more about herself," Mother said.

I gaped at her. "I think Ilise hates me after my miniature interrogation, she would never want to get close to me."

Father sighed. "Yorena, you will do as your Mother tells you," he ordered.

"But Father—" Mother blew a burst of wind in my face, springing tears in my eyes. Okay, that wasn't necessary. The last time she did that had to have been when I threw tantrums as a child. Nothing could shut someone up faster than a gust of wind to the face. "Fine. I shall try to be her friend, although I doubt it will work."

"It does not matter what you think will work, we are the King and Queen," Mother said. "We know what to do. You are dismissed." I couldn't believe they'd saddled me with a nearly impossible task.

I hurried out the door and headed back towards my apartment. I thought they were finally allowing me to help them with their job. I thought I was going to receive a more Queenly task. Is it not what they trained me for my whole life? I stopped myself before I could find more inane reasons to blame them. They'd been doing this longer than me. I just had to trust their judgment and everything should fall into place. But I couldn't tell which would be more difficult: Getting close to Ilise, or keeping my crown.

Becoming close with one of my servants didn't seem like the best use of my time. There was already a growing list of challenges being added to my plate for the next few weeks. And now I had to think about combat training for the first time in four years. Nobody in the kingdom besides the sorcerers would know if the trials ever involved combat.

Nothing I ever read as a child, or recently, spoke of what any of the tests were, and my old tutors would practically ignore me when I asked about Heircestrial. The only information I knew was that the last Heircestrial took place before Anora Schaefer took control. Noble kids who were allowed to go to boarding schools whispered tales about Kings and Queens who'd tortured anyone who dared defy them. And how the dungeons were so full, there had been more prisoners than people who lived in New Teber.

There was even one story I'd heard about how Anora had worked as a palace servant to secretly rally support from other workers and prisoners, right under the monarch's nose. That was likely the only story that was true, however, I wouldn't put anything past the previous monarchs. It still amazed me how Anora had so much support, they were willing to put a commoner on the throne. Why couldn't I rewrite the way our kingdom worked for the better like Anora had? Sure, it may have meant she had to live in fear that the next time she woke up would be in a dungeon, and going against some of the most powerful people in the kingdom.

But I'd still rather have to do that than become friends with Ilise. I ruined any chances I had with her already; it would take a miracle for her to warm up to me. But what else could she know? She may be right about Nikos, but she'd grown up in a small village in Newnina, most likely far from anyone in The Progression. So far, all I could tell was she couldn't be trusted. But if dealing with Ilise would help the kingdom, then I would do it. It was like learning about any other noble, and limited information never stopped me before.

But maybe we could be friends. There had to be something we had in common I could use to bond with her. Maybe I could find something to compliment her on, that tactic always worked with other noble children. But what could I compliment her on?

I admired how easily she seemed to be able to wipe her thoughts from her face, but that was only another reason not to trust her. And she was a servant with barely any records about her, and she would probably rather jump out the nearest window than talk to me long enough for me to find something to compliment her on. So maybe this would be harder than I thought.

Chapter 6

Ilise

Soap suds coated my hands as I washed this morning's dishes. We couldn't leave until the Princess came back to dismiss us, and the others were already done with their jobs. Chafik had offered to help me, but I'd declined. Sometimes it was nice to not be stuck in the middle of a conversation. Thinking through every word that came out of my mouth got exhausting after a while.

"All I'm saying is Yorena is the best candidate," Mathias said from the couch. Since the Princess left, we'd been debating who would be the best heir out of the three nominees. Aerilyn, Chafik, and Mathias were placing their bets on the Princess. "Nobody has even *heard* of these other two nominees," he added. I didn't have the energy to argue too much, but I still felt the need to give my opinion.

"How do we know she'd be a good Queen, it's not like she's been in court all that long," I said. Aerilyn sighed. I scrubbed the dishes harder and water soaked the bottom of my sleeves.

"Be careful Ilise, your hatred is showing," Mathias said with a grin. My hatred?

"I have no idea what you could be talking about." I rinsed off the last dish, pausing to stare at them. The three of them raised an eyebrow before locking eyes with each other and bursting into laughter.

Aerilyn wiped tears from her eyes. "Ilise, I love you but you are the *least* subtle when it comes to your dislike for Yorena."

"It's practically bleeding from your eyes," Chafik said.

"It's not hatred, more of a strong dislike."

Aerilyn stared at me. "You couldn't even look her in the eye for more than two seconds at breakfast, and you put less cheese in her omelet just to spite her," she said.

Mathias snorted. It'd seemed like the best revenge I could think of at the time. It wasn't like I could do much else.

The Princess walked back into the room with a beautifully engraved dagger clutched tightly in her hand. Even Mathias straightened his posture on the couch, and Aerilyn took a step back. I, on the other hand, was more intrigued. It looked like it was straight out of the royal armory, gleaming in the morning sunlight. It made the dagger under my uniform seem no better than a dull kitchen knife. *What does she need with it?* I dried my hands with a towel and joined them in the living room.

"Um, Ms. Yorena," Chafik said. She turned to him with a look on her face that could wilt flowers in seconds. He took a step back. "Is there a particular reason you're holding a dagger?" She looked down at her hand as if she didn't recall holding it.

"It is just one of my old practice daggers," she said with a wave of her hand. If that was a practice dagger, I'd love to see the palace's normal daggers. Then, without realizing it, I was in front of her, taking the blade in my hands. I ran my finger along the delicate edge, sharp enough to cut through skin like water.

"I never knew practice daggers were so sharp." She yanked the dagger from my hands, eyeing me curiously.

"I have to resume combat training, my parents gave this to me." Combat training? Since when did the Princess have to do combat training? Even back at the Union base, we had only trained those going on missions, such as myself. And the Princess rarely left the confines of New Teber, if at all.

"Is something wrong, Ms. Yorena?" Chafik asked.

"No... it's just something all heirs have to do," she said quickly, a bit too quickly. I thought royals mastered the art of hiding what they were thinking, yet she wore her emotions on her face. My eyes landed on her hands as they fiddled with the fabric of her dress.

"Since when was that a thing, Princess?" I said. Aerilyn elbowed me in the stomach, the warning clear in her eyes. *Be nice.*

"It is not public knowledge, do not feel bad for not knowing," she said nonchalantly. I pressed my mouth into a thin line. I hated being talked down to, even if she was *technically* a royal and she's *technically* taller than me. When I'd first joined the Union, it was the only way people talked to me. To them, I was a heartbroken, traumatized child, but I'd proved them wrong. I never would have become a spy if I hadn't. Even if I still had to live with the consequences.

It had been on the mission Kass had forbidden me to go on. The Progression members were overpowering our small group of fighters, and the Union hadn't been able to stop Progression members from attacking the residential section of the town. Being the overconfident child I was, I'd gone after the members and tried to stop them myself.

Most had already fled, but there was this one household that was unable to escape before The Progression members broke into their house. Somehow, I'd managed to subdue the two members long enough to allow the family of four to escape. I'd even taken The Progression members' crystal so they couldn't use the elements against me. Long story short, my friends in the Union were a mix of proud and mad that I'd gone against the members on my own.

"Have you done combat training before?" Chafik asked. I joined Mathias on the couch.

"I did a few years ago, but it was too hard for me back then." Too hard? I fought a scoff. I started training when I was just fourteen, and I pushed through every bruise, every mistake. It couldn't have been that hard. The Princess whirled on me, and I forced myself to not shrink under her gaze.

"What was that, Ilise?" the Princess asked. Did I say that out loud? Oops. An unappreciated wave of confidence, or really just stupidity, coursed through me.

"I said it couldn't have been that hard, Princess."

Mathias covered his mouth to muffle his laughter. Aerilyn hid her face in her hands, clearly done with me. What else did she expect, for me to give the girl a kiss?

"How would you know? Have you had combat training before?" I bit my tongue to prevent me from exposing myself more. If I pushed any further, the subtle amusement could easily veer to suspicion. A smirk spread across her face. "That's what I thought." Our stare-down was broken as two letters slid under the door. I stood up to retrieve them. One was addressed to Chafik, and the other was addressed to me. *Kass.*

"Hey Chafik, you got a letter." He jumped from the chair and took the letter.

"Who's it from?" Aerilyn asked as she took my seat beside Mathias.

"My family back home." As he scanned the letter, his expression darkened, haunted.

"Chafik, is something wrong?" the Princess asked.

"The guards are starting to pull out," he said absently. The guards were pulling out? The Princess crossed her arms.

"What do you mean they are pulling out? I do not remember reading that." Reading? Was one of her Princess perks getting official incident reports? I'd have to get my hands on those. We had a few Union people undercover in Nitedand and Faveru, and all they could tell us was the more recent attacks. Infiltrating The Progression ranks was almost impossible. My heart clenched to think about the one person who was able to infiltrate The Progression. My friend Orla had volunteered herself months ago and we hadn't heard from her since. I was terrified to think what might have happened to her. Royal guards had been sent to the border to try and keep it contained, but I guess The Progression overwhelmed them.

"I will have to discuss this with my parents. The guards should not be pulling out, that leaves people in danger, and people in danger is the last thing we want. Don't worry Chafik, I'll get to the bottom of this." She paused. "I need to think," she said, breezing past us and shutting the door to her room.

"Who's your letter from, Ilise?" Aerilyn asked. I'd almost forgotten about the letter I was crushing in my fist. The thick envelope was stained with dirt, scents of earth wafting from the paper. Kass must have arrived back to base after her mission in Nitedand.

"It's from an old friend. We don't talk that much." Mathias cleared his throat from where he waited at the door.

"Are we going to the office yet? I highly doubt Yorena needs anything from us anymore," he said, gesturing to her shut door.

"I'll be there in a few minutes, I just need to read this letter." The three of them waved goodbye and left for the servant's office. All letters from the Primis Defense Union had a decoy in case they were intercepted. I removed the fake letter, tossing it into the wastebasket in the kitchen. Then, I pulled the actual letter from the almost seamless flap in the envelope. I smiled at the cramped letters of Kass's handwriting. Everything was written in a way that wouldn't be too incriminating if a letter were to be intercepted.

I,

I know you'll be disappointed, but I won't be able to visit—not now.

She can't pick me up for my leave from the palace.

Things are getting more hectic by the day. Nitedand is getting busier by the day after the ball, and it may be the same once I start traveling.

The Progression is growing in strength, and they may be spreading to other provinces. *Spirits.*

Most of us are returning home to help V with the chaos.

Everyone's returning to the base in Hexia to help Val form a new plan.

One of my friends near you said you're closer to Ava now, correct?

One of the Union's temporary spies has reported I'm working under the Princess now. We referred to any of the royals by their middle names. The Princess' first middle name was Ava.

I hope you two are doing well, I remember how much you despised each other when you first met.

She knows how much I despise the Princess and her family, but she wants me to get close to her.

And while you're at it, tell Rayhan and Laskeisha I'd like to hear from them soon. I hope they're doing well with all the mess going on in the kingdom.

The Union wants to know how the King and Queen are reacting to the recent spikes in violence in Nitedand and Faveru.

I also have some new friends delivering a few mementos of mine. You'll look after them, won't you?

She wants me to keep an eye on the palace visitors—the nominees.

I may not be able to visit, but I'm sure you'll have fun these coming weeks. And don't do anything stupid, I'm not there to help you if you have too much fun, and I doubt you want to be on the receiving end of R's wind storms.

Some more action should be coming my way soon and she doesn't want me to do anything too reckless. A sharp stab of loneliness spiked through my heart to think of Rori. Spirits, even the thought of being on the receiving end of one of Rori's wind storms made me miss the Union.

With love,

K

They were moving. If what had happened to my village was any indication, they would spread their message while leaving a trail of destruction in their wake. Rage flooded my blood. If they were getting closer, why weren't they calling me back to the base yet? I wanted to be in on the planning; they weren't the only ones who'd lost something to The Progression.

Did none of them understand what it was like to be kept so far from them for all these years? I thought this would be the letter telling me I could come home. Kass even said everyone was going back. I should be allowed to as well.

But no, I had to be the Princess' friend. The thought of it made my breakfast want to make a reappearance. Just yesterday, she'd acted as if I was a Progression member because I recognized the spiritsdamned flag.

I looked to the Princess' door. How was I supposed to earn her trust? If only the letter had been delivered yesterday, then I would've known to keep my mouth shut. What was the quickest way to earn someone's trust? From past experiences, bribes usually worked. But I didn't think bribing one of the wealthiest people in the kingdom would end very well.

And I couldn't tell her much about me without attracting *more* suspicion. *Don't do anything stupid.* But maybe a little stupidity was what it would take to earn her trust.

I forced my feet towards her door and took a deep breath before knocking. She opened the door almost immediately. "Do you need something, Ilise?" My mouth became parched. *Why am I scared? I can do this.*

"You asked about what I knew about combat," I said, raising my chin slightly. "Thought I might show you." The Princess opened the door wider, inviting me in. I'd never seen a room so put together. Not a single wrinkle marred her crisp white sheets, and a thick stack of paper rested neatly on the desk. *Papers. That must be what she was referring to earlier. Would it really be that easy?*

I focused my eyes back on hers. "Are you challenging me to a match?" she said as she paced around me in slow circles. Her eyes burned on my skin wherever she looked. I mean, I was thinking more along the lines of showing off some knife skills. But a match could work too.

"Yes," I said. The corner of her mouth turned up in a smile.

"Let me get you something first." She walked into another closet of the room, pulling out a mop. A mop? *Is she going to fight me with a mop?* She held the mop in both hands, raising it above her head. Involuntarily, I stepped back as her crystal glowed a deep orange, and she brought the handle down on her knee, snapping it clean in half. It never ceased to amaze me how strong Imperium were with their crystals. The muscles in my body stayed tense until the light died down. I took a breath of relief as she unclasped it from her neck, chucking it onto the bed.

She removed the mop head and tossed me one of the halves. "We're going to fight with sticks?"

"Yes. Now see if you can beat me, though I highly doubt you will," she said. She was baiting me. Unfortunately for her, I was in the mood to bite.

We circled each other as if we were two lions sizing each other up. The Princess struck first, quite sloppily, trying to sweep me off my feet. I leapt back right before her foot could trip me. She already had an advantage over me with her height, and her dress allowed her to move more freely than mine could. But she was pushing her hair out of her face every few seconds. I would just have to use that to my advantage. I attempted to hit her half of the mop out of her hand, but she grabbed my half and knocked me over.

I rolled onto my upper back to soften the fall and sprung back onto my feet. Our makeshift swords continued to clash in an elaborate dance, both of us deflecting the other before one was able to get the upper hand. I would've been impressed if I wasn't holding back.

I pushed harder against her stick, forcing her against the foot of the bed. I could end it right there, subdue her with a quick attack on her torso before knocking her down. But I couldn't unveil all my tricks yet. Sure, I was reckless, but I didn't have a death wish. I needed to tire her out a little more, making it more believable that I was able to best her.

Both of our swords became locked in a standstill, her arms quivering with the effort to push back against me. I felt the pressure of her stick lighten; she must have already been getting weary. *Finally.* Seizing the opportunity, I led the offensive attack, using my half of the mop to hit her exposed side. She half-crumpled in surprise. *Never leave your side exposed during battle.*

Using the bedpost for support, I jumped back from her next strike and hit the mop half out of her hand. It skidded across the room, far from her reach. I rid myself of my mop half as well to keep the fight somewhat fair. She tried using a spinning kick to knock me to the ground. But her curls swirled around her head, blocking her view of me. I used the small moment she was blinded to grab her foot from the air and knock her off balance, pushing both of us closer to her desk.

She fell hard onto her back, and before she could get up, I dropped on top of her, pinning her down to the ground. "Do you yield?" I said. She attempted to squirm her way from my grip but eventually gave up and relaxed with a groan.

"I yield."

I leaned close to her face, leaving only a few inches of space. Her panting breaths warmed my face. "Told you I knew a thing or two." She let out a low laugh. Spirits, even her breath smelled like roses.

"Guess I stand corrected."

"Technically you're lying corrected," I countered. I was suddenly very aware of the fact I was still on top of her. My face burned before I rolled off her. Double checking she wasn't facing me, I leaned against the desk, feeling for the stack of papers behind me. A smooth paper envelope graced my fingers. Painstakingly slow, keeping eyes forward, I folded the envelope and tucked it in the back of my dress.

"You're different from the other servants. Who are you, really?" she said as she pushed herself off the ground.

"A friend, hopefully." I curtsied to her before turning to leave. Was that a stupid idea, yes, but did it also pique her interest in me, also yes. She was curious about me, and she wouldn't want to accuse me of anything before she figured me out. Val once told me that curiosity was just as dangerous as suspicion. The line between them was too fine. But if I wanted to succeed, I would have to walk that line.

Was I finally one step closer to my goal, one step closer to getting my revenge?

Chapter 7

Princess Yorena

A FRIEND? I DIDN'T realize friends were the people who could defeat you with a stick and a two-second warning. The servant girl, Ilise, if that was even her real name, moved with confidence, with purpose, as if this was a walk in the garden for her. And her uniform hid her true strength. She wasn't even Imperium, yet trying to push against her was like trying to beat Kieron. And Ilise was smaller than me, granted not by much, but shorter still.

A few months back, a servant had shown off his knife-throwing skills, and we'd investigated him. Turned out, he had been part of the Primis Defense Union. But was Ilise also a member? Or she could be a Progression member since it would explain how she knew the flag was not a misprint. Both were equally dangerous. My fingers thrummed against the metal bedpost, matching the pace of my racing thoughts.

Figuring Ilise out would have to wait, I had Heircestrial to worry about. I stood up from the bed, pacing. Heircestrial hadn't occurred for almost a thousand years, and no one alive had seen it happen. Except for maybe some of the sorcerers. The information about it I *was* able to scrounge up was limited. Hours I'd spent combing through every shelf in the library, only to find a paragraph or two. And most of them had droned on about how it was a sacred tradition and the consequences for the royal families that had been dethroned.

The Sparkson family, for example, had been shunned and forced to live isolated in the Ritker Desert to the north after Prince Emmanuelle had lost Heircestrial to Cressida Somerset of Pria. The Sparkson monarchs had been so upset with Emmanuelle, they'd even thrown him out of the family. Stories say that he'd died not long after that from heatstroke in the desert sands. I would like to believe that wouldn't happen to me and my parents if I lost, but it was a sickening motivator for me to win.

I stopped pacing, an idea itching the back of my brain. I constantly searched in the library, but I had a much older source right here in the palace. The Royal Archives. They contained the recorded history of our kingdom dating back thousands of years. There had to be at least a few old scrolls about Heircestrial.

I clasped my crystal around my neck, about to leave, but paused. The archives were too extensive to search on my own. If only I'd thought of this earlier, I could have asked one of my servants to help. But I wanted them to think of me as a friend rather than an employer, and making them inhale decades of dust wouldn't be much of a bonding activity.

I could ask Kieron, I decided. My parents had always tried to teach me that royals didn't need friends. Strong political allies were the better option to them, but that was one thing I would never agree with them on. After years of being friends with Kieron, they'd backed off. But it still irked them that I'd chosen to be friends with a royal guard.

Kieron and I had been friends since the day he'd caught me sneaking into a court gathering, even though I wasn't supposed to be there. He was my closest friend and the youngest Lieutenant in history at only twenty years old. And he was always looking for a way to get out of work.

A few years back, he had begged for me to get him out of patrol duty on one of the hottest days of the year, and I'd requested to have him hold my umbrella while I went peach picking in the palace peach grove. Let's just say it wouldn't take much convincing to get him to help me.

I needed to find the Commander; he was the one who coordinated the guard schedules. He was like an uncle to me. When I was younger, I would skip out on tutoring sessions to help him make the guard schedules. After the first few times, he had started leaving a pile of schedules for me to lay out. I was sure he wouldn't care if I stole Kieron for a little.

I left my room in search of him. His office was on the second floor, so I should start there. I dashed down the staircase, exiting on the second-floor landing. I slowed my pace when I stepped on the floor. A Princess was not meant to look hurried at any time, always walk with purpose, not with haste. Lesson number three from my etiquette teacher.

My heels clicked against the marble floors, echoing down the empty hall. Save for a few guards on duty, clad in the black and gold uniforms. I reached the end of the hall where the Commander's office was. I knocked on his open door.

"Commander?" He sat in his leather desk chair, talking with one of the guard captains. They bowed to me.

"Your Highness, what can I do for you?" the Commander asked. He waved away the guard captain, and he left the room with a bow. Worry lines marred the Commander's porcelain forehead. *He must also be stressing over the Nitedand/Faveru situation.*

"I need to find Lieutenant Flores." He quirked an eyebrow. With a huff, he stood up from the chair, rummaging through the drawer in his desk. He ran a hand through his salt and pepper-colored hair, taking out a manilla folder.

"What do you need with him?" He flipped through what I assumed was today's guard schedule. He glanced at one paper before putting it back in the drawer.

"I need his help with something," I said. He shot me an amused look.

"Define 'something', Your Highness. I cannot just remove my guards from their posts without reason." I rubbed the smooth silk of my dress between my fingers.

"I need his help to look through the Royal Archives. They are too extensive to do on my own," I said, leaning closer. "And I think Ms. Nettie would fall asleep within seconds if asked for help." He let out a husky laugh.

"I will let you pull him away just this once," he said. "But next time, you're dealing with the old crone. We already have extra guards where he is anyway. He's at the front palace gate." Yeah, Kieron would jump at the opportunity to get out of the sun.

"Thank you, Commander," I said as I turned to leave.

"You're welcome, Your Highness." I took the other stairs to the first floor. Servants milled about the hall, carrying all sorts of yellow decorations. Garlands and honey-colored rose centerpieces spilled from their hands, while others held overflowing baskets of amber tablecloths. Was there about to be another ball? The summer ball was only a couple days ago, and we usually held off on hosting another so soon after.

Two guards bowed to me before they opened the front door of the palace. I always loved these doors. It was a towering oak door, but it was the gold foiling that I loved. Mother had hired artists to create a mural of the four Spirits in all their glory, floating above the rolling hills of Erea.

A thick blanket of air washed over me as the doors opened. Summer in Newnina could be described with only two words: sweltering and heavy. Sweat already beaded my brow after a few steps. I spotted Kieron standing guard at the outside gate, talking with another guard. "Kieron," I called. He flashed a full-toothed smile as I approached.

"Yorena," he beamed. The stoic guard beside him cleared his throat at the informal greeting. Kieron elbowed him in the side. "The last time I called her 'Your Highness', she threw a ball of fire at my head." I looked back on the moment with joy. It had been quite entertaining to watch him try to pat the fire off his hair.

"Being stuck with this one for two hours, I could see why you did that," the guard said. I stifled a giggle. The shadows of archers marching along the top of the wall passed over me.

"Kieron, I need your help with something," I said.

"Does this mean I get to go inside?" he said.

I nodded.

"Thank the Spirits. Let's go." He looped his arm through mine and led me back inside. Typical.

He sighed a breath of relief as we crossed into the shelter of the palace. "So where are you taking me today?" A large smile spread across his face. "Are you using me as a cover to meet with your secret lover?"

I shot him an incredulous look. "Is that the latest gossip the guard has come up with about me?"

He nodded. "Rumors say you had a connection with Lady Ebony's daughter."

I snorted. "That girl is as shallow and self-centered as they come. Could they at least create a make-believe relationship between me and someone *decent*?"

He shrugged.

"Don't worry, if I happen to have a secret love affair with someone, you'll be the first to know," I joked.

He pointed his chin towards the ceiling and crossed his arms over his chest. "I better."

"Unfortunately, we're just going to the Royal Archives. I need information on Heircestrial."

He halted.

"What?" I said.

"The Archives are creepy. And they smell like death and decay."

I rolled my eyes. The Archives weren't *that* bad. Sure, they were in the underground level of the palace with no windows. But that was so the books, scrolls, and documents weren't damaged by the sun. Or to protect them in case the palace was ever under attack.

"And I have to escort the sorcerers to the gardens at noon," he said. I glanced at the grandfather clock against the wall. We had a good two hours until then. That would be plenty of time if we hurried.

"All the more reason to do this *now*. And would you rather go back outside?"

Kieron scoffed. "Spirits no."

"Then let's hurry," I said, grabbing his arm so he would walk faster.

We hurried to the only staircase that went down to the Archives. Kieron was transfixed by my glowing crystal as I lit a burnt-out torch hanging on the wall. Using my free hand for balance, I walked down the spiraling staircase. Our footsteps echoed off the rough stone.

"I bet you five silvers ghosts will appear," Kieron said.

"We're going to the Archives, not a crypt."

"But ghosts also love libraries."

My laugh echoed down the dark stairwell.

"You're laughing now, but ghosts love libraries and creepy basements. And we're about to be in both." I tuned him out for the rest of the walk down.

We finally reached the door to the Archives, and I snuffed out the torchlight, pushing open the door. It creaked open from little use. Massive shelves lined the high walls, jammed with ancient-looking books. Most of these had to be older than the palace itself. Our shoes kicked up dust as we ventured farther into the room. Stubby candles hung from the ceilings, casting an eerie glow over the room. I couldn't blame Kieron for thinking this place was haunted.

"Ms. Nettie?" I called. No response.

"She's probably asleep somewhere," Kieron suggested. We continued deeper into the room, coughing as we kicked up more piles of dust. It felt as if the walls were closing in on me. The amount of shelves in here left little space in between. Kieron's broad shoulders left him no more than an inch between him and the nearest shelf.

"Old lady," Kieron bellowed. His silver eyes flashed with mischief. I smacked him in the stomach. "What? If she wakes up to scold me, we'll find her faster." Fair enough. We walked to the desk in the back corner and found Ms. Nettie asleep at her desk, face-down in a book. As per usual. I placed a hand on her shoulder, lightly shaking her awake. When she didn't wake up immediately, Kieron leaned into my ear. "Is she dead?"

"Kieron!"

She shot her head up, momentarily dazed until her weary gaze landed on me. "Hello darling," she said in a small voice. "What can I help you with?" Ms. Nettie was the Archives keeper. She spent so much time down here her wrinkled skin looked as white as the ghosts Kieron was so sure lived down here, almost translucent from the lack of sunlight.

"I need to find information about Heircestrial." She put a shaking hand on her chin.

"Heircestrial? For what reason would you need to know about that?"

"Because it's about to start." I knew she was isolated down here, but not *that* isolated.

"I always wondered if it would ever happen again. Follow me sweetie." She grabbed my hands to pull herself up and Kieron and I followed her as she led us to the smallest bookshelf in the room. It was only half my height, but it still overflowed with yellowing scrolls and books. "This shelf has all the Heircestrial information. Let me know if you need anything else." She walked back to her desk for another nap, I assumed.

"Are you telling me we have to read through all that?" Kieron grumbled. I removed the first book from the shelf, placing the dusty hardback in his hands.

"Yup. Better get to work." He sighed but settled on the floor, flipping through the pages. I grabbed a few of the scrolls and started to comb through them. Quite a bit of the text was in the old language, but I could translate most of it. The words had a similar structure to the ones we used today, but some of them I'd never seen before. It was like a slightly more complicated puzzle.

For the next two hours, Kieron and I skimmed through every book and scroll on the small shelf. My eyes began to ache after staring at the tiny lettering for so long. And it was all for nothing; all the information here said the same thing, droning on about how sacred the competition was and how it was the most important tradition in the kingdom. Although it clearly wasn't, considering no province had wanted it to occur in so long.

"This is pointless," Kieron said finally.

I sighed. "I'm starting to realize that. There's just one more pamphlet I need to read. Then we can go." He stretched out on the floor, letting out a loud yawn.

"Thank the Spirits."

I rolled my eyes. The paper of this pamphlet felt thicker while all the other scrolls felt flaky, almost on the verge of disintegrating. I flipped open the paper, and my jaw dropped. Blank. It was purely blank. Faded ink was smeared across the page, but every page had no legible writing. *Why is this even here?* I groaned and put the pamphlet back. Guess this was a waste of my time, and Kieron's.

I stood up and kicked his side. He peeled open one eye. "Get up, sleepy head. Time to go." He pushed himself up.

"Did you find anything you were looking for?" I shook my head. He rubbed the top of my head, causing pieces of my hair to frizz. "Maybe you'll find out more at the meeting you have today."

"Hopefully." Wait. The meeting. I glanced at the mechanical clock hanging on the wall. Twelve o'clock. I was late. "Remember when I said we would have plenty of time?"

He groaned. "Are you about to tell me that we're late?" he said.

I nodded.

"Hells," he said. He grabbed my arm and we bolted to the door. "If Commander yells at me for being late, I'm blaming this on you."

I let out an empty laugh. "If my parents find out, I couldn't care less about what the Commander would have to say to me."

I was the Princess, and I was about to be late to our first meeting with the Council of Sorcerers in almost a thousand years. I should've paid more attention to the time instead of staring at unhelpful pages for hours. I didn't bother with a torch as we bounded up the steps.

I ran all the way to the gardens, my breaths coming in pants as I slowed.

"And the Princess finally arrives," Nikos taunted. I ran all the way to the gardens, my breaths coming in pants as I slowed.

"Technically the Council is not here yet so I am actually early."

Nikos scoffed. Light reflected off the silver stitching of his navy vest, blinding me for a few seconds. I suddenly felt severely underdressed in my simple green silk dress. But at least Oliver wasn't as dressed up as Nikos. They'd chosen to wear a simple white tunic, decorated with several pins I assumed they'd earned while working in Ominka's court.

The usually busy rose garden was empty of gardeners. I supposed news of the Council's arrival had scared them away for this meeting. My skin itched in anticipation. The only sorcerers I'd ever met were quite rude, basically worse versions of Nikos. They were a very secluded people that rarely left Mount Bachport. But they couldn't all be like that, could they? What was the worst that could happen? Wait, no. The moment I asked myself that question was the moment my thoughts would run wild.

Kieron marched a group of guards into the garden with the Council in tow. My back stiffened as they approached. No one alive had seen the Council face to face. The six of them wore somber, almost unreadable expressions. I was able to catch Kieron's eyes before he left, shooting me a sympathetic look.

The Council wore matching floor-length black robes, rimmed with silver. Half of them had short salt and pepper beards, unruly and wild. *How old are these guys anyway?* One woman stepped forward, probably the oldest one. Her coiled gray hair was pulled into a tight bun atop her head, and her coppery skin was more wrinkled than the rest of them. Despite her short stature, her presence reeked of authority. I shot a quick glance at Oliver and Nikos, watching their faces light up in admiration.

Of course.

"Greetings Nominees. I am Imogen, eldest Council member," she said with a bow. I stepped forward, clasping my hands behind my back to hide their shaking.

"Welcome to the palace, Council. We are delighted to have you. I am Yorena, current Erean heir." The Council nodded. "These are my fellow nominees," I said, waving them forward. "May I present, Nikos Vikander, and Oliver Li."

Nikos bowed to Imogen. "It is an honor to meet you," he said. *Kiss up.* Imogen smiled at him and began to pace.

"Today's meeting will be short. I only need to go over the rules you must live by for the next month," she said with a smile. A *month?* "There are three tests you will go through that can start at any time and you must pass two out of three to be named Heir. You will get no prior warning, and if you are suspected of sabotage or using outside help, you will be disqualified." *Not as bad as I thought.* Passing two tests would be easier than passing all of them, and I aced any test I was given.

"Do we get to know what the tests are at least?" I asked. Tests were fine; tests were predictable. But I still needed to know what they were to prepare. Imogen halted in front of me. Her bright violet eyes bored into mine.

"No," she said sternly. "Leaders need to be able to think on their feet. Do you think you'll get more than a few moments warning if someone were to attack the kingdom? Hmm?" I casted my gaze downward. I should've been able to see that. "That is all for today. And remember, we will be watching you." *Watching us?* What did she mean by watching us? I didn't realize keeping my crown meant putting my life on display. How could my parents have allowed this?

"Your Highness, will you please retrieve the guards so we can be escorted to our rooms?" I nodded to her and tried not to look like I was running from her. Once I rounded the corner, I let out a breath of relief. I'd forgotten how alive the air felt around sorcerers. The fine hairs on my neck and arms still stood up. It was like something about their powers made the air want to compress around them. I spotted Kieron leaning against the palace wall, his tan skin slick with sweat. I bit back a chuckle as he tried to fan himself with a broadsword.

"One, I don't think fanning yourself with a sword will be very effective. Two, where are the rest of your soldiers?" He blew a stray piece of hair out of his face and retreated farther into the limited shade.

"One, it's sweltering out here and the uniforms are not exactly breathable. Two, I have no clue. They dispersed back to their posts. And I'm the Lieutenant, so I had to stay." He picked at the collar of his black and gold guard jacket.

"Then maybe you should cut the mop on top of your head you like to call hair." His brown curly hair went past his shoulders, always tied into a low ponytail with a piece of string.

He put his hand over his heart in a dramatic fashion. "But then I'll lose my title as the most swoon-worthy guard in the palace."

I pretended to study my nails. "I thought you were named the laziest?" He stuck his tongue out at me. "And the Council meeting is over. You need to escort them back to their rooms." I could see the reluctance clear on his face, though he tried to hide it.

"And try not to look like I told you to put your hand on fire."

"I make no promises," he said as he left for the gardens.

One obstacle down. I made it through the meeting, and it didn't turn out for the worst. Now, all I had to do was keep a close eye on Nikos and Oliver, find a way to keep my crown, and figure out who the hells Ilise was and if she was a friend or foe. This was a headache waiting to happen.

CHAPTER 8

ILISE

*B*LEND IN NO MATTER *what.*

I'd stashed the Princess' envelope in my pillowcase before I left for the servant's office, and it was as if it was calling to me from across the palace. I wanted nothing more than to abandon my assignment of scrubbing the ballroom floors. My knees were numb after kneeling on the hard marble for almost three hours. Ms. Kira said the floors had to shine so much they could be used as mirrors. Personally, I thought she was punishing me for being late, *again.* Who needed a mirror-like floor, clean was clean. But at least three others were helping out.

I finally finished scrubbing my quadrant of the floor and left my bucket of dirty water with the others. If I wasn't mistaken, the Princess should be meeting with the Council of Sorcerers, meaning I had time to look through the envelope and her room. I waved goodbye to the others I was working with and walked to the staircase. My feet wanted nothing more than to bolt to the apartment, but I forced myself to walk with leisure. *Stay invisible.*

I slightly picked up my pace when I arrived on the third-floor landing, keeping my head down. The rotating guards nodded to me as I passed. I got to our apartment door and creaked open the door, listening for any sounds of life. Silence.

I slipped inside and bolted to my room. Shutting the door, I retrieved the thick envelope from my pillowcase. Pouring the papers onto my bed, I started to sift through them. They were stamped with the official seal of the Erean Royal Guard. *Why does she have these?*

Half of the papers were incident reports of different violent interactions between Progression members of Nitedand and people in Faveru, along with which interactions involved any of the royal guard. Kass wasn't kidding when she'd said The Progression was putting down roots elsewhere. I just didn't think it would be this soon.

Another large chunk of the papers laid out the living conditions in Nitedand and near the border. The paper crunched in my hand as I read down the page. Half the province was starving and without homes after The Progression had destroyed their villages, yet the report listed the cause of destruction as "inconsequential". These weren't mere accidents, these were planned attacks by The Progression. And of course, all the listed destroyed villages were mostly Primis. I'd bet if it were Imperium towns getting attacked, the problem would have been fixed before it got nearly this bad.

I'd seen too many people break down as they watched their entire lives be ruined by these people, myself included. Even the thought of The Progression flag in Nikos' room brought back the tear-jerking smell of ash and charred flesh, the sight of my village reduced to nothing when it should've been sprawling with activity in preparation for the summer feast, and the feeling of my family's cold skin from where they'd lain on the floor in a pool of their own blood. I forced the painful memories back to where they belonged. So deep in the back of my mind that they could never resurface.

How'd getting more information end up making me madder? Nothing in here talked about what they were actually *doing* about it. I saw a whole lot of problems, all lacking solutions. I put my hand in the envelope, searching for anything else. My fingers brushed a rough paper, and I pulled it out. It looked like a letter, but the receiver's name was smeared away. And the longer my eyes skimmed the parchment, the harder it was for me to not crush it in my grip.

Our village is all Primis people, most of which can barely wield a small knife, let alone a sword. They grow stronger every day. We need help. Please. Before they come to our village next. Protect us. Protect us against the soulless ones. Before it's too late.

This was a plea for help, and they put in with incident reports instead of on the desk of the Duke and Duchess of Nitedand. The Dukes and Duchesses were supposed to be in charge of province-level problems, and yet they sent the letter to be mixed in with reports. I could only assume the "soulless ones" were Progression members. I'd be shocked if any of them had souls. But why hadn't the Duke and Duchess of Nitedand sent them help? The capital wasn't even that far from this village; they could have easily protected them.

I needed more. The Princess hadn't returned yet, so I still had time to search her room for anything else. Was this a slight invasion of privacy? Yes. But was I looking for personal information? No. I packed the papers back into the envelope and left my room. If she didn't notice it gone already, she would definitely notice if I didn't put it back now.

I walked further down the hall to her room and tested the gold handle. Locked. I sighed and pulled a metal pin from my hair. After a few seconds of maneuvering it inside the lock, I heard the soft click and pushed open the door. I returned the pin back to my hair and closed the door behind me. It was just as spotless as it was this morning, but now I could take a closer look at it. *Don't do anything stupid.* I'd thrown that piece of advice out the window a while ago.

Only blank papers rested on her desk. I sat the envelope on top of the papers, so it looked the same as it did this morning. Now, if I was a Princess, where would I hide useful information? I started with the desk drawers, finding nothing but unused candles and fountain pens. I was about to close the door when my eyes caught a piece of paper at the very bottom of the drawer.

I almost wanted to laugh. It was an old report about the Primis Defense Union.

The ones who call themselves the Primis Defense Union are a plague upon this kingdom. If any of them try to recruit you or reveal their identity, it is your responsibility as a subject of Erea to report them to the nearest guard. They can often be found in the same vicinity as The Progression and are not to be approached except by guards. They are armed and dangerous.

According to the King and Queen, we were no better than The Progression, but this was just comical. The only information they had on us was that we were often in the same places as The Progression, and we were armed. Of course we were armed. How else would we get Primis people out of their villages safely during Progression attacks? But it put me at ease to know they didn't have much else on us. The less they knew, the better.

Although, after they denounced us, the little information they had on us made it next to impossible to recruit anyone else into the Union. And on some missions when we came face to face with The Progression, villagers couldn't tell the difference between us and The Progression.

The look of terror when we'd try to approach them would never be erased from my memory.

I remembered one of the families I'd tried to help escape threw rocks at me. Hot tears had rolled down the mother's face while she tried to get her two kids away from me. It'd stung. It still stung. But I'd helped them get out in the end, it hadn't matter if they wanted to attack me the whole time or not.

I put the paper back in the drawer and shut it. I moved to the bed, feeling in the sheet and pillowcase for any hidden documents. Nothing. I even scoured the armoire against the wall, finding nothing but an overly extensive amount of silk dresses and heels.

Why didn't she have anything? I rubbed my temples as I sat on the edge of her bed. Wouldn't a Princess be privy to at least *something?* Generic reports could be obtained by anyone, even the Union. But it still stung to read about villages meeting the same fate as mine. It sent an unending amount of rage through my blood. They would pay. They would all pay.

I stood to leave when my eyes caught on her overflowing wastebasket. I bent to pick up one of the crumpled paper balls. I uncrumpled it and attempted to read the Princess' crossed-out frilly handwriting. It looked like she was trying to think of... solutions?

- Find and reason with Progression leader

- Send a battalion of soldiers to surround Nitedand until Progression leader reveals themself

- Close Nitedand border

- Send spies to infiltrate Progression

- Find and capture Progression member for information

The page was filled with her ideas, albeit horrible thoughts. But it wasn't helpful to the kingdom if they were thrown out before attempting at least one. I scoffed. And I had hoped she would be better than her cowardly parents. I balled up the paper and left it on the floor.

Doing one more once-over of the room, I shut and locked the door behind me. Without anything left to look for here, I decided to return to the servant's office for my next assignment. Better to seem busy. I opened the front door a crack and froze at the sound of two distinct voices.

Nikos and Oliver.

I spied through the crack in the door as they spoke to each other in hushed voices while leaving Nikos' room. Once they rounded the corner, an idea came to mind. If the Princess didn't have helpful information, where better to go than the room of the man with the nerve to hang a Progression flag. And since Nikos was gone, his servants were most likely gone too.

I looked in the hallway for anyone else before I sprinted into Nikos' apartment. I quickly shut the door behind me, taking a few seconds to calm my nervous heartbeat. I had to be careful here; I had no justification for being inside his room. I rubbed my sweat-slicked palms on my dress and tried to not look at the flag but utterly failed. Most would see it as a harmless piece of fabric, but I knew it for what it was. A threat and a promise.

I fought back a shudder and walked to Nikos' bedroom. Of course, his door was locked. I pulled out my hairpin once again and moved it around until I heard the soft click. The room barely looked as if someone was living here. His desk in the corner was bare of any reports or letters to give me any information. I searched all the drawers, only to find a few dust bunnies. I even looked under his bed for anything he might have hidden, and to no avail. There were only so many places he could have hidden something. I stuck my hand in the cases of his pillows, once again finding nothing. The last place to check was the bathroom. I opened the shutters, washing the bathroom in sunlight. I searched every nook and cranny in the vanity, once again, nothing.

I was certain he was in The Progression. But where was the proof, where was the evidence of his contact with The Progression? Anyone who went through the trouble of locking their *bedroom* door must have been hiding something. My heart lurched as I realized my novice mistake. Here I was, a spy, and I had put myself in needless danger coming here, when I should have known better. Of course he wouldn't have evidence lying around. The letter from Kass was still in my pocket, waiting to be burned. If I were to be caught with it, the letter wouldn't be the only thing getting burned. I shuddered at the thought, the scars on my arm tingling.

As long as I was here, I should make sure there was nothing else incriminating. My eyes raked over the room, taking in every minute detail. I stopped on a picture frame sitting next to the bed and crossed the room, taking it into my hands. It was a small painting of a little blond boy, probably a young Nikos. Flipping it over, I removed the back of the frame. A folded note fluttered to the ground. *Aha!* I replaced the back of the frame and picked up the note.

I'm watching you. Always watching you.

Oh, wonderful, more cryptic messages. But this one sent a chill down my spine. It wasn't meant for me, but it was effective nonetheless.

I was wasting time standing here. Nikos could come back at any moment, and I had to report to Ms. Kira anyhow. I did a quick once-over of the room and locked the door behind me.

I bolted to the office, the black soles of my shoes squeaking against the floors. I opened the door to Ms. Kira with her arms crossed over her chest, jaw clenched.

"Is there a reason you've arrived here almost fifteen minutes after the others came back from the ballroom?"

"I was helping the Princess prepare for a meeting, ma'am." The lie came quickly. She sneered, moving back behind her desk.

"Your next assignment is to help finish setting up the rest of the ballroom. The Heircestrial ball is in two days, and the other servants are already there working."

"Yes, Ms. Kira," I said with a bow. *What is it with this kingdom having balls for everything?* I hurried through the hallways to the ballroom.

The tall oak doors were thrown open, the room full of servants. Aerilyn and Chafik were bringing in small tables and waved to me. I looked up to see Mathias on one of the ladders replacing the candles of the chandeliers. "Hey, Ilise," Mathias called down to me. "Can you help me with these candles?"

I hated candle duty. Climbing fifty-foot ladders while balancing a twenty-pound box of candles was not one of my favorite activities. If I hadn't been training for as long as I had, falling would've been inevitable. I grabbed some of the candles from the box and climbed up the other side of his ladder. "Do we have to change all of these?" I asked.

He nodded. Great. I had pent-up rage and frustration after a fruitless search, and I was rewarded with replacing candles. One of the most futile, and never-ending jobs one could be assigned to in this palace. Most of the candles we were replacing weren't even burnt out. There was still at least half of the wax left, but no, the palace could only use full ones. I could remember times when one candle would cost my family a week's worth of money. *Wasteful.*

We moved from chandelier to chandelier, finally getting through the whole room after a couple of hours. My arms ached from holding them up for so long, and candle wax coated my fingers. Half the servants who were here earlier already left, having finished their jobs. We climbed down the ladder and walked to where Aerilyn and Chafik waited for us.

"I thought I was going to have to grow a beard waiting for you two to finish," Chafik said. Aerilyn stifled a laugh.

"Why don't you try replacing a thousand candles on over fifty chandeliers with only two people?" Mathias said. Chafik clamped his mouth shut. "Yeah. You're doing candle duty next time."

The four of us left the ballroom to go back to the servant's office. On the way, we crossed paths with Nikos, moving as far from him as we could, practically pressing against the wall, earning a sneer.

"I bet it'll be only a week before he snaps at someone," Mathias said once Nikos rounded the corner.

"Make that a few days," Aerilyn countered.

I hadn't seen much of either of the two other nominees. Nobody even knew what they would do if they were to become Heir. Nikos, I could easily guess, would give The Progression all the power they wanted to mold this kingdom the way it was a thousand years ago. The lives of Imperium would stay relatively the same, but Primis people would be treated no better than dirt. And all anyone knew about Oliver is they shadowed their province representative for two years, and they were born in the northern kingdom of Banauri. Not helpful.

We arrived in the servant's office to find a head of long curly hair sitting across from Ms. Kira. The Princess stood up from her chair and settled her gaze on me, wearing the same fake smile she used in court.

"Ilise, can you come with me for a moment?" she said in a soft voice. Had I given myself away? Was I about to be executed for being a Union member? No, I couldn't start spiraling. If I was about to be killed, it wouldn't be without a fight.

But what could I have done? I thought I'd piqued her interest without any suspicion. I hadn't suffered here alone for five years just to get cut down now. My heartbeat pounded in my ears, and I forced my voice to remain steady when I said,

"Of course, Your Highness."

She led me out of the office down to one of the lowest levels of the palace. Spaced-out torches flickered in the dark hallway as we passed, and water dripped from the stone. She opened the door to an unfamiliar, windowless room.

"One moment," she said. The fire crystal around her neck began to glow orange as she simultaneously lit all of the candles along the walls. I stepped back.

Rows of daggers, swords, and metal staffs lined one of the walls. Practice mats were rolled up in every corner, as well as a few practice dummies.

"Is this an old training room?" I asked. It was like they had a whole armory for this one room. Some of the weapons gracing the walls were ones I'd never had the pleasure of using. The Union only used weapons we could swipe from shipments and what we were able to find for cheap.

We would either have to raid weapon shipments to royal outposts, or dig in landfills for scrap metal to create our own weapons. A very small percentage of our weapons were actually bought. Even the knife under my dress was something we'd found during a landfill raid.

"Yes," she said.

I jumped when she suddenly appeared beside me. "It hasn't been used in years." I walked over to one of the walls, grazing my fingers over all the beautifully sharp daggers. Probably sharp enough to sever someone's limb with almost no resistance. I could imagine a few people I'd like to do that to. "Do you like those?"

"Is there a reason you brought me here?" She stood a mere foot away from me, forcing me to look up into her eyes.

"I start training tomorrow and I want you to help me when the instructor is not with me." I gave her an incredulous look.

"Me?" I crossed my arms, making her take a few steps back.

"Yes, you. You bested me within minutes without breaking a sweat. I need to learn to fight like you." I pondered her for a minute. On the one hand, I *would* get out of seeing Ms. Kira as I do now. And it would give me an excuse to keep my skills sharp while I can't train in the Hexia base.

But on the other hand, I would be helping out the girl whose parents wanted to stomp the Primis Defense Union into the ground and continue The Progression's torment on the kingdom. *Get closer to her.* But this *would* help me get closer to her.

"Give me one reason why I should," I said.

She studied her nails, as if bored. "Well, if you choose not to help me, then I would be inclined to have you investigated. It is not everyday a servant knows anything about fighting." She was blackmailing me? I'll admit, I didn't think she had the capacity to do that. Was she bluffing? Would I be willing to risk exposure? My eyes drifted to her hands, and despite her efforts, I could see the way they shook. She was nervous, but I couldn't risk her exposing me if she wasn't bluffing. I flashed her a fake smile.

"Fine," I gritted out.

She jumped with excitement. "Thank you, Ilise," she said in a voice so high-pitched, I was surprised glass didn't shatter.

I started to leave the room, hoping she would stay here. After a few seconds, I heard her footsteps running to catch up with me. We walked in silence until we heard a scream after reaching the first floor. My instincts kicked in, and I bolted towards the sound. The Princess followed me, earning confused looks from passing servants. We turned right and almost collided with a servant staring at the wall. A horrified expression was plastered on her face.

I turned to the wall to see what she was scared of. I wish I could say I was surprised, but then I'd be lying to myself. I couldn't quite hear anything going on around me. The world was muffled, my heartbeat was a booming bass in my stomach.

The phrase was in dripping, red letters. It must have been done in haste because many of the letters were smeared together, but I could read it all the same.

Rise from your shackles, and regain your rightful glory.

CHAPTER 9

ILISE

AND THEN, I WASN'T in the palace anymore. I wasn't a spy. There was no graffiti in front of me.

I was fourteen again, visiting my family for the first time since I'd left. I'd just met Kass one day prior, and she was taking me to Demessa. I could barely sit still, barely containing my excitement. A week before I'd left, I had bought gifts for my family from the market. For my baby brother, Sam, I'd bought a hand-carved wood horse. And for Mama, my younger sister Aline, and I, I'd bought us all matching necklaces with a gold pendant. Each engraved with the symbols of the four Spirits. And lastly, for Papa, I'd bought him a lavender and honey-scented candle we rarely could buy at home. Unless he traveled halfway across Newnina to find some in Kiouten.

I had taken naps for most of the journey home because I wanted to be wide awake when I arrived home. I'd woken up as we were cresting the last hill before reaching Demessa. I'd always loved the fresh pine scents that blew in from the Slandslina Forest. It had been the turn of the season, and my village traditionally held a huge feast around this time.

All of us would come together, bringing braised lambs, fresh okra stew, and all sorts of treats to celebrate the Fire Spirit.

But instead of the warm, decadent scents of the feast, I had been greeted with smoke. I'd thought the smell was simply a bonfire that had grown too strong too quickly, or maybe it'd been the smell of someone burning the giant hog. In my eyes, nothing could have gone wrong on such a wonderful day. I was supposed to see my family for the first time in a year, and we would have danced the night away.

But the first face I'd seen was the old lady in the town square who would always give me loaves of bread for free. Her face had been nearly unrecognizable. Parts of her charred flesh had been peeling away in the wind, and I'd just stared at her, unbelieving. My hands had been shaking, and my knees were weak. What had my village done to deserve this? Was this my punishment for leaving them? Maybe if I had never left, they would still be here. Maybe I wouldn't have been stepping over the blackened remains of my fellow townspeople.

Fires still burned as I ran through what was left of my village. The town square that was once a hub full of life, teeming with the outdoor market and stores, had been reduced to piles of rubble.

I had run for ten minutes to my house while Kass could barely keep up behind me. My house still stood, even the flower garden my siblings and I had planted for decoration. And I'd believed for a second that maybe, just maybe I hadn't damned my family too. My hand was on the doorknob, and I opened the door, expecting the smiling faces of my family. But the inside told me a different story.

Furniture laid in pieces, still smoldering. I walked to the room I'd shared with my brother and sister. It had looked like they were just taking a nap on the floor. I remembered a distant voice calling my name, it might have been Kass. But all I'd seen was their pale brown faces. My knees hit the floor. I'd brought my hand to Sam's face, my baby brother, still no bigger than a toddler. His face had been frigid. He was a child. And they'd killed him.

And all that had been left of the attackers was a single note nailed to the door. I remembered my tears soaking the little slip of paper as I read it, barely grasping who would do this.

Rise from your shackles, and regain your rightful glory.

-The Progression

I was thrown out of the memory and stood frozen in front of the graffitied wall. My body was not my own. I knew the Princess and the other servant were calling my name, but their voices were muffled to me. My chest was erratic, with breaths coming in pants.

I told myself Nikos must be part of The Progression. New visitors, a Progression flag, a wind attack at the ball, and now this. There was no denying Nikos was part of The Progression. I knew they were already here, yet this one sentence was enough to strip me down to the Ilise I was five years ago—nothing more than a scared little girl with a village to avenge. Images of blank, charred faces flooded my brain. *No. Not now.* And their faces forever frozen in fear of who had killed them. I didn't even get to bury them.

Hot tears ran down my cheek, but I couldn't find it in myself to wipe them away. Hairs rose on my neck as someone approached me.

"Ilise, are you okay?" the Princess asked. More servants flocked to the wall holding cleaning brushes as guards rushed past, looking for the perpetrator. They wouldn't find them. They would be long gone by now.

"I will be. If you'll excuse me." I brushed past the Princess. Where to? I didn't know. My fist tightly clenched the golden pendant I still wore. I needed to distract myself, stop dwelling on the past. What happened cannot be changed, and nothing I did would ever change it. I needed to focus on moving forward and making up for the past in every way I could.

I ran up the stairs to the servant's office. I needed to go into the gardens; they would calm me down. I pushed open the door to see Ms. Kira talking with another servant. Her eyes shifted to me, only mildly annoyed.

"I see the Princess is done with you. I have your next assignment." She waved away the other servant, and they left with a bow.

I wiped my puffy eyes. "Please let me help out in the gardens," I said, my voice shaking slightly. Ms. Kira paused, studying my face. Her eyes were filled with an emotion I'd never seen on her face, concern. But quickly as it came, it hardened into an indifferent expression.

"There are already plenty working there," she said in a stern voice. I couldn't do this right now. I had thought someone even as prickly as Ms. Kira would show some sympathy.

I sniffled as snot threatened to drip down my voice. "Please. I need to work in the garden for the rest of the day," I said firmly. Tears began to blur my vision. It took every ounce of self-control to keep them from falling. "I know I'm always late, and not the kindest, but I never ask you for anything else. You probably need help in the gardens, even if you don't want to admit it because I'm the one asking."

Ms. Kira sighed. "Fine. You're lucky I'm in a good mood." I curtsied to her before leaving. I bolted down the stairs to the first floor. I couldn't even see where I was going, but my feet knew the way like the back of my hand.

A thick blanket of heat washed over me as I walked into the garden. It was days like this that made me wish I didn't have to wear long sleeves all the time, as most of the gardeners wore short sleeveless dresses or short trousers to combat the heat.

I searched the royal garden for the head gardener. I always loved spending time with her. I found her crouched in a rose bush, digging new holes for new seeds. Dried dirt clung to her curling hair. She wiped away the sweat beading on her tanned forehead as she looked up at me. "Hello Ilise, did you want to help us out today?"

I nodded, not trusting myself to keep a steady voice. She pushed herself up from the ground, brushing the dirt from her knees. A single tear slid down my cheek, but I wiped it away before she could see.

"The only thing we need help with is clipping the flowers off the yellow rose bushes. We need them to make crowns and more decorations for the Heircestrial ball." She tied her gray hair into a bun as she led me to the far side of the garden. I took one of the giant baskets and a pair of shears piled near the bush. "Try to fill as many baskets as you can. Thank you, sweetie," she said. She walked back to plant the rest of the new roses, leaving me alone.

This was perfect. A monotonous task I could throw myself into.

I clipped the yellow flowers from their stems, tossing them into my basket. Thorns poked my fingers, but I hardly noticed them. Before I knew it, I'd clipped every flower from my bush. I moved on to the next one, repeating the process for about an hour. I tried not to think of doing this with my family. *Snip.* I tried not to think about the field of flowers that would never grow again. *Snip.* My clothes stuck to me like glue from the sweat.

I heard the crunch of footsteps behind me and turned to find Aerilyn approaching me. "Did Ms. Kira send you to the gardens too?" I asked. Aerilyn hated garden duty during the summer. It was too energy-consuming. And Ms. Kira actually liked Aerilyn, so she was rarely assigned out here. Why would she be here now?

"No, but Ms. Kira did send me. She said you didn't look too good earlier."

I paused.

"I'm fine," I said, resuming my clipping. She placed a hand over mine, taking the shears from my hands.

"No you're not. You always try to get Ms. Kira to send you out here when you're upset." Her blue eyes drifted to my hands. "And you're not even taking the time to remove the thorns." She pulled me to a nearby bench and started plucking the thorns from my hands. I winced after each one she pulled out.

"So here's the plan. You're gonna tell me why you're so upset, and I'm gonna help you come up with a solution." She took my chin in her small hand, forcing my eyes to meet hers. There were no solutions. The only thing that would fix this was my knife piercing multiple people's hearts, but even that would be too merciful.

"I can't," I choked out. I felt the tears welling in my eyes, threatening to spill. And I didn't think they would stop if I let them free. Aerilyn tilted her head.

"Why not? I'm your best friend, it's in my job description to help you," she said as she pulled out the last of the thorns. I shook my head. I couldn't tell her. If I told her the real reason, it would only bring more questions I didn't want to answer. Or even know the answer to.

"Well, is there anything I can do?" A sob managed to escape my mouth at the sincerity in her voice. She pulled me into a hug, squeezing me tight. Normally, I would squirm my way out, but I couldn't bring myself to this time. "Do you just want me to hold you until you stop crying?"

I nodded.

"Okay. Take all the time you need." My body shook as I was wracked with sobs. As I suspected, the tears didn't stop. And Aerilyn rocked me back and forth, not saying anything else.

It reminded me of the way Mama used to rock me. No matter how stupid the reason for my tears, she never hesitated to rock me until the tears ran dry, and a smile returned to my face.

I felt pathetic. A few measly words were all it took to push me over the edge. My tears soaked the sleeve of Aerilyn's shoulder. I needed to move the memories away; I needed to focus on my task now. I pushed every image, memory, unhelpful emotion to the back of my mind, never to resurface. Steeling myself, I forced my tears to stop falling and brought my head up.

"Do you feel better?" Aerilyn asked as she wiped away the last of the tears on my cheeks.

No. "Yes. I think I want to go back inside now." She nodded and held out her hand to help me up. "Thanks for letting me soak your shoulder."

Aerilyn smiled. "Anytime."

Chapter 10

Princess Yorena

I LANDED ON THE firm mats of the training room, wincing as a sharp pain shot up my spine. "If this were an actual battle, you'd be decapitated by now. Try again," Ilise ordered. I had assumed she would be a much easier teacher to deal with than Fowler; clearly, I was wrong. Today was our first training session, and only one hour in, I was already exhausted.

She paced around me, her mouth set in a hard line. "Can I please take a break? We have been at this for over an hour." She rubbed her chin, considering.

"Fine. You get two minutes." Too weary to stand, I crawled to my silver canteen of water and chugged it down. Strands of hair were plastered to my forehead with sweat. After being stuck in this small room, Ilise also fanned herself. She may have felt hot in this room, yet she was hardly breaking a sweat from fighting me. My parents had never displayed any interest in their servants, but I naturally was curious about the stories of those who helped, and spent so much time around me. Ilise, however, was a tough nut to crack. The long-sleeves in a sweltering room were just one of the many things I was realizing that I might never understand about her.

"Why do you insist on torturing yourself by wearing long-sleeves?" She walked up to me, leaning in close to my face. My heart pounded at an accelerating pace from her proximity, close enough to smell the cocoa butter from her soap. That was another thing I didn't understand about her. Anytime I asked a question about her, she would get defensive.

"I thought I was here to train you, not be subjected to irrelevant questions. Break's over." I groaned but pushed myself up. Could this girl lighten up even a little?

"I imagine men are just lining up to court you, aren't they? You know, before you inevitably scare them away," I remarked. She looked unimpressed.

"They don't have the guts to approach me, let alone court me. And besides, I find that most are more observant than you seem to be, Princess. They can tell my interests lie with women, not men." Well... I was not expecting that response. I lowered my gaze to the floor and shuffled back to some semblance of a fighting stance.

Maybe I shouldn't have blackmailed her into helping me, then she might have gone easier on me. I wouldn't have reported her no matter her answer. She didn't peg me as a member of the Union or The Progression as I'd previously thought. If she were a spy for either of those organizations, she would have tried to pry information from me by now. And I highly doubted a Progression or Union member would want the Princess to have more combat knowledge. Our entire conversations consisted of her breaking down everything I was doing wrong with a simple punch. Who knew there were so many ways to accidentally break your fingers?

I planted my feet and raised my shaking fists. Within seconds, she struck out her fist, aiming for my stomach. I spun to the right and attempted to knock her off balance with a kick to the shin. As if reading my mind, she caught my leg mid-swing and flipped me onto the mat. The pain felt like fire racing up my back. Ilise grimaced at my fall.

This morning, Fowler had spent three hours re-teaching me the proper stances, defensive attacks, and evasion. And, as usual, he'd chosen running laps as my punishment for messing up. I almost preferred that to being thrown around like a sack of rice. "One more time and then you can go," Ilise said, her mouth pressed into a thin line.

Slowly and painfully, I returned to my feet. This time she swung out with her leg, and I jumped over it. But I didn't bend my knee to absorb the shock of my landing, and my ankles threatened to give out under me. I bit my tongue against the pain. If only I was allowed to wear my crystal, I would be able to move faster than even Ilise. I hated how slow I was without it, how much even the smallest of punches could hurt.

Again, she threw out a fist aiming for my stomach, but I was ready for her this time. I blocked her punch with my forearm and tried to punch her back. She caught my arm and twisted it hard. I landed on the mat, groaning with pain.

Ilise knelt beside me. "Are you okay?" she asked.

"Just fine," I grunted out.

She rubbed my back where I'd landed on it. "First of all, you were supposed to focus on defense today. Secondly, if you're going to land on your back, land on the upper part so you can get up faster and it hurts less." My hands shook as I gave her a weak thumbs-up. She hoisted me up from the ground, and I limped to the table with my crystal. I clasped the gem around my neck and sighed with relief as strength flooded through me.

It was difficult to describe the sensation. It was like being doused in cold water after a week of braving the Ritker Desert. Being an Imperium without a crystal sometimes felt like missing an appendage.

"Why'd you take off your crystal?" Ilise asked.

"Because my parents said I need to decrease my dependence on it."

"Why would you need to do that? Most Princesses wouldn't spend their days falling on their backs when they have a royal guard to protect them," she said with a grin.

I followed her out the door as we left for the apartment. "Because it is important to be prepared for anything," I said. She fell silent at my answer. I smiled at the servants as we walked into the dim stairwell. I wondered what'd put Ilise in her sour mood. I knew she was still upset about the blackmail, but I felt something else was bothering her.

My mind went back to the other day when we saw The Progression's graffiti on the walls. That was the only time I'd ever seen a crack in her armor. She had frozen, staring at it as tears threatened to spill from her eyes. And when I'd tried to talk to her, she'd run away to Spirits knows where. It was as if she'd seen one of those ghosts Kieron insisted were here.

"Did they find who graffitied the wall?" Ilise asked in a small voice. *Bingo.*

"It was only a cruel prank. Nothing to worry over." At least that's what we told anyone who managed to hear about it. The only other people who'd seen it were the servants who'd cleaned it, and they'd sworn not to tell anyone about it. She turned to face me, eyes narrowed, clearly not believing me. I placed a hand on her shoulder, and she stiffened. I didn't think Ilise would go around and spread panic, but the less it was spoken of, the better. "Is there something else bothering you?" I couldn't tell if she bought it as her eyes were glued to my hand. I quickly removed it, and we continued to the third floor.

"I remember how spooked you were after we found the graffiti. Are you okay?"

She kept her gaze forward, ignoring my question.

The graffiti marked the second time The Progression had attacked this week. And it was getting harder to hide this from the rest of the kingdom. If we told the people what was happening, kingdom-wide panic was almost certain.

I felt like Ilise didn't appreciate that. For some reason, she knew more than most would about The Progression. And lying to her wouldn't work in my favor if I was going to get her to tell me about herself, but I couldn't admit the full truth. Not even to her.

We exited the stairwell, and I moved to Ilise's side. "So...where did you learn this?" I said, trying to break the silence.

"Learn what?"

"All of these skills. How can you fight so well? I know you can't be much older than me, yet you fight just as well as, if not better than, Instructor Fowler. And I know you said you were just from a village in Newnina, but you must have learned this from somewhere else."

"My grandfather was in the royal guard and he taught me a few things," she said, not bothering to turn and look at me. *Is she telling the truth?* It was impossible to tell with her. But that was such a small detail, and there was no reason to lie about that.

I opened the door to the apartment and started for my room, needing a long bath. "Lunch should be ready soon, Princess."

I nodded.

"Aerilyn, would you draw me a bath?"

Aerilyn stood from where she waited for us in the living room. "It's almost ready. Chafik just needs to bring in the last bucket of hot water." She hurried out of the room with Chafik in tow to retrieve hot water.

I walked to my room, putting thoughts of Ilise aside as I stripped off my sweat-drenched clothes and grabbed a silk robe from the armoire. Chafik opened the door holding a metal bin of water. Aerilyn trailed in after him, the steam spreading throughout the room. I opened the bathroom door and they poured the last of the water into the clawfoot tub. "Thank you," I said as they bowed and left the room.

I grabbed the sponge and soap from the edge of the tub, and tossed my robe to the side. A sigh escaped my lips as I lowered myself into the steaming water.

As I lathered the rose-scented soap on my skin, I thought more about Ilise. Every question I asked about her past was answered with half-truths and lies. Unless I was in the wrong and she *was* telling the truth. But I could usually read people correctly, and the files would have mentioned if she had a grandfather in the royal guard.

But a mistake could have been made. Maybe the records keeper forgot to list a grandfather down in her file. Or perhaps she had a different last name than him. Sometimes the man took the woman's name once they married. Nothing was adding up. Village-born girls wouldn't be able to afford a weapon, let alone know how to use one.

I winced as I brought my hands up to comb through my tangled curls. Training must have taken more out of me than I thought if I wasn't healed by now. I dipped below the water to rinse off the soap and stepped out of the bath, drying myself with the towel hanging on the back of the tub. I walked out of the bathroom to find a pink silk gown resting on my bed.

I slipped it on and left for the kitchen. Savory scents filled my nose as Ilise stirred the giant pot on the stove. My other three servants were already waiting at the table, and I joined them, sitting next to Aerilyn. "How did training go today?" she asked. The boys halted their conversation, also interested.

"Long, painful, tortuous, and any other horrible adjective you can think of."

Aerilyn winced. "Well, it's only the first day. You'll get better," she said. I hoped so. Otherwise, the next month would be the most painful of my life. Ilise brought out five bowls of steaming stew on a silver tray.

"Why'd you make stew, it's sweltering outside," Mathias groaned. Ilise slowly turned towards him with a blank expression. Another thing I couldn't figure out about her: her ability to hide every shred of emotion.

"Says the person whose only skill is running his mouth," she said. The table broke out into laughter.

We were interrupted by a knock at the door, and Aerilyn stood up to answer it. Mother's lady in waiting curtsied upon entering. "Your Highness, your mother has requested the presence of you and one of your servants."

"I will be right there," I said.

Aerilyn grabbed Ilise and brought her towards me, mischief painted on her face. "Ilise can go with you." Ilise's eyes widened as she shook her head.

"I'm not dressed to meet the Queen," she said quietly. I looked her up and down, surveying her fitted training clothes. Her black leggings looked worn, and the matching black shirt clung to her still sweating skin. Mother would disown me if I ever wore something like that, but she looked at home in it. She seemed ten times more confident in this than in her servant uniform, and if I was being honest with myself, since the morning she'd challenged me, I hadn't been able to take my eyes off her. A strange emotion was stirring in my chest, and I couldn't quite figure out what it was. It was something stronger than admiration, but I couldn't place it.

"And I have to wash the dishes," Ilise said. She rubbed the back of her neck, as if nervous. Could she be nervous to meet my mother? I never imagined she could be nervous about anything.

"Chafik and I will clean up after we eat if you go," Aerilyn offered. Ilise stared at Aerilyn and crossed her arms. Aerilyn did the same.

"For Spirits sakes, would one of you go before I have to break up a fight," Mathias said.

"Fine. I'll go," Ilise said.

We followed Mother's lady in waiting through the hall towards Mother's room. The guards stationed in front of the doors bowed and opened the doors to her room. "Mother?" I called.

"Come, Yorena." She was admiring a dress the royal tailor must have brought in. "The tailor just delivered your dress for the Heircestrial ball this evening." I had nearly forgotten about the ball. After the last two attacks, I'd thought they would cancel it altogether. Mother spun around to face Ilise and me. "Have your servant help you bring it to your room. You are dismissed." She waved us away with her hand but paused, her eyes narrowing on Ilise, studying her. "Have I met you before?" she asked Ilise.

"I don't think I've had the pleasure, Your Majesty." My mother stepped closer to her, and Ilise stiffened. *So she is nervous to meet Mother.*

"You resemble someone I once knew." So I wasn't the only one who thought Ilise looked familiar. But I still couldn't put my finger on who she reminded me of. "Where are you from?"

Ilise clasped her hands behind her back, hiding how she twiddled with her fingers. "Just a small village north of here," she said. *Why isn't she saying the name?* Mother stepped closer to Ilise, leaving less than a foot between them. I almost missed Ilise's small gulp.

I grabbed Ilise's wrist and pulled her away from my mother. "I think you're making her uncomfortable, Mother," I said.

Mother shrugged. "I was only asking the girl a few simple questions." Her gaze flicked back to Ilise before settling back on me. "You may leave."

We curtsied and Ilise picked up the dress, and I held the bottom to prevent it from dragging on the floor. She didn't spare another glance to the room, nor did she say anything of my mother's comments. Thoughts churned beneath her brown eyes. Thoughts I was still unable to decipher, but I hoped I would be able to soon.

From the little knowledge I had of Heircestrial, everyone was meant to wear yellow—signifying the sun rising over our land with a new heir, assuming any of the nominees won. It was why one of our kingdom colors was gold. Anora Schaefer had been the light that lit our kingdom out of the dark ages.

"Does the dress have to be this massive?" Ilise asked as I struggled not to trip over the fabric of the dress.

"According to my mother, yes."

Aerilyn must have heard us, since she opened the door. "That is the most beautiful dress I have ever seen," she said in awe. We threw it onto the couch, our arms tired already from carrying it. Chafik and Mathias came over to look at it.

"Have fun wearing that," Mathias said. I ran my hand along the delicate silk and tulle.

"You sure you don't want to trade with me?" I joked.

"Respectfully, I would rather be stuck doing all of your laundry for the rest of my life," he said. "We have to go see if the ballroom needs any more decorating. See you all at the ball." He and Chafik walked out the door.

"Oh, Aerilyn and Ilise," I said. Another reason I was not a fan of balls was it usually led to me ordering around my servants. Granted that's what I was supposed to do, but it still made guilt sit in my stomach. I would get myself ready for the ball, but that dress would be nearly impossible to put on alone.

"Yes, Yorena," Aerilyn said.

"I will need assistance from both of you before the ball, meet me back here at the seventh bell toll."

"Of course." Aerilyn curtsied and left the apartment.

"Ilise, one more thing." She stopped walking towards her room. "During our training sessions, could you go easier on me? It's been years since I've done any of this." She crossed her arms, expression bland.

"I *have* been going easy on you." That was easy? Then what would her going hard on me look like? If she went any harder on me, she would have to throw me straight onto the battlefield. Without a crystal, weapon, or armor.

"Please Ilise? You're ten times more skilled than me, and I can't even wear my crystal during training to give me strength."

"You'll get used to it, eventually. And I'm not that skilled, I only know the basics."

I clasped my hands together, my smile strained. "Is being stubborn another one of your hidden talents?" The corner of her mouth lifted slightly. I let out a frustrated sigh.

"Ilise, I just want to be able to protect myself and my kingdom. And I can't learn if you insist on not letting me catch up."

Her face softened.

"Do you promise to stop whining every five minutes?"

"I do not whine."

"Yes, you do."

I held my hands up. "Fine. I solemnly swear there will be no more of this non-existent whining. And no more blackmail."

She exhaled. "Then I *guess* I can go a little easier on you."

"Thank you." She started walking back towards her room but paused with her hand on the door. "If I slow down our pace, this means you're not touching a weapon any time soon."

"But those are more fun than falling on a mat for an hour." She gave a light laugh. The sound was foreign but pleasant in my ears, like the bubbles in a glass of champagne. I wanted to hear more of it. I wondered what it would take for her to do it again.

"You're not going anywhere near those until I know you won't poke your eye out...or mine for that matter." I had faith I wouldn't poke anyone's eye out if she let me use the weapons. But considering I couldn't stay upright for more than a minute while fighting her, I could see where she was coming from.

"Fair enough."

Chapter 11

Ilise

The rest of the day passed in a flurry of activity. Every servant in the palace ran to and fro, setting up for the Heircestrial ball. Aerilyn and I were stuck with one of the worst jobs—removing thorns from yellow roses and turning them into crowns. Thorns were stuck in my fingers, numbing them to the point where I didn't feel the stab of pain anymore. Others milled around us in the ballroom, shooting sympathetic looks.

Aerilyn watched me trim the thorns and stems in awe. "How are you not removing those thorns? I think I've pricked every finger by now." She hissed when she pricked herself, again.

I grabbed a stray rag and tossed it to her. "Honestly, my fingers are numb at this point. And keeping the thorns in keeps the blood in. Unlike what's going on with you. I suspect the nobles will have a fit if they receive a bloody crown."

She threw one of her half-finished crowns at me and wiped her bloody hands on the rag. "How many more do we have to make?" she asked, picking up another bouquet of roses. I looked into our basket of finished crowns. The basket was already full, but we still had another full basket of fresh roses.

"We need about a hundred, and I counted seventy, so thirty," I said as I split up another bouquet for us to turn into crowns. According to Ms. Kira, it was an Heircestrial tradition for every guest to wear flower crowns. It just seemed like a waste of these beautiful flowers. We even had to pin a rose to our dress uniforms for tonight.

My parents had always taught me to treat plants and animals as we would people. Picking them apart like this felt like a betrayal to their memory. But if they could see me now, they would have felt that I'd already betrayed them in more ways than one.

I cracked off the end of one of the stems. *Treat the Spirits' gifts as you would your kindest neighbor.* Oh to hells with it, the amount of people I wanted to treat worse than these flowers was beyond extensive.

I was tempted to leave a few thorns on the crowns, a little surprise for the nobles. Most of the guests coming were the most powerful families in every province's court, including the Dukes and Duchesses. Spirits knew there was a long list of things I'd like to say to the Duke and Duchess of Nitedand, none of which I think they would appreciate. I didn't take a liking to people who ignored their citizens' pleas for help. I would have to take extra care to avoid all of them.

The bell tolled seven booming tones, telling me it was time for us to help the Princess get ready for the ball. I tied off the last end of a crown and placed it into the basket of finished crowns. "Come on Aerilyn, we gotta go help the Princess."

She stood up, brushing stray thorns and stem pieces from her dress. "Who's going to finish the crowns then?" I called over one of the other servants and she gladly agreed to finish making the crowns.

Aerilyn and I hurried up the stairs. "Why don't you ever call Yorena by her name?" she asked after a long moment. I picked up the pace to the apartment, and she pumped her short legs faster to match my pace.

"Because she's the Princess," I put simply. The only people you addressed by first name were your friends. And she may think I was her friend, but there was no way in hells she was mine.

"But even Chafik calls her 'Ms. Yorena'."

I stopped in front of the door. "Does it matter?" I asked, struggling to hide my exasperation.

Aerilyn put her hand on the handle, blocking me from entering. "It does. You act like her name is poison." *Because it is.*

"I do not. Move."

She stared at me with her cool blue eyes, smiling. "Yes, you do," she teased.

"Aerilyn we need to help her get ready, please drop it." She blocked the door with her whole body. If I really wanted to, I could pick her up and move her aside. But I knew avoiding answering her would only prove her point. I knew she was right, but I didn't need to admit that to her.

"You need to start getting along with her. I can't sit through another tense meal."

I let out a sigh, giving in. "Fine."

Finally, Aerilyn opened the door. "You know I'm right," she said.

I huffed.

"Maybe we can also tone down the attitude a little." I threw my rag at her, earning a giggle from Aerilyn.

"There you are," the Princess said. She motioned for us to hurry. "Come on, I will need as much help as possible." We entered her room, and my eyes immediately landed on her monstrosity of a dress. Aerilyn started undoing all of the buttons on the dress and unknotting the laces, and the Princess pulled me aside, a jar in hand. "I need you to put this salve on my back to help with the pain. And probably my arms too."

"Yes, Your Highness." I didn't see why she couldn't do this herself. I've had to stitch myself up on multiple occasions while on the run. But I guess it would be unseemly for a Princess to have bruises all on her back. I spread the salve along her back and arms, and fresh lavender and peppermint filled my nose. She flinched when I started applying the salve, and a pang of sympathy went through me. I must have gone harder on her than I thought, but a little pain during training never hurt anyone. Her crystal should help her heal, and it was weird it hasn't already. Was she not wearing it enough? Maybe taking it off as often as she was for training was slowing down the healing process. *Since when have I cared about how the Princess uses her crystal?*

"I've unbuttoned the whole dress, we'll help you into it now," Aerilyn said. I spread the last of the salve on the Princess' back and wiped the excess on my apron. The Princess stripped down to her undergarments, walking to the full length mirror next to her desk, and stepped into the dress. Since it was the summer, this dress was strapless with a low back. Despite myself, my eyes slowly trailed up her body. The Princess smiled as she surveyed herself in the mirror. It was the bewitching type of smile that could bring even a noble to their knees. My eyes trailed the snug silk as Aerilyn tightened the laces so the bodice hugged the slight curve of her waist. I shot Aerilyn a guilty glance, wondering if she could somehow read my thoughts, but she was focused on tying the last of the laces.

The dress was the color of the sun first thing in the morning. Sunflower petals adorned the neckline, and the bottom was coated with glitter, resembling a shower of stars. Finally, a belt of diamonds was tied at her waist, making her look more regal than ever. Seeing the dress on its own, I had thought it was awful, but the Princess managed to make it magnificent.

Why was I thinking like that? That's not what I should be thinking about. I should've been focused on the possibility of The Progression making a move on the ball and how I would stop them. Hopefully. The Progression liked dramatics, and never operated in the quiet. Any place they attacked, they left something to signify they were the ones who did it. Usually it was a flag or that spiritsdamned motto. The more places they successfully attacked, the more they grew in power, and the more likely simple sympathizers would go on to become members. Crashing a second royal ball would be their next most likely move.

We moved the Princess to the vanity in the corner to do her hair and makeup. Aerilyn began smearing and powdering the Princess' face while I started on her hair. "Would you like your hair up or down, Your Highness?"

"Down please." Easier for me. Her hair was a long mess of curls that went down to her waist. It was softer than anything I'd ever felt before, almost what I imagined clouds to feel like. My fingers lingered in her hair longer than they needed to.

I took the front section of her hair, pinning it to the back with a diamond clip. Then I detangled some of her hair with my fingers, making her curls pop more than ever. Aerilyn stepped back, done with doing the Princess' makeup. She had painted her eyelids and lips deep gold, complete with an aureolin blush. The yellow theme was to signify the sun rising over the kingdom, and the Princess' makeup surpassed that idea.

"Do you have a flower crown for me?" she asked. Aerilyn held one up; she must have brought it with us. I placed the crown on her head, finally finishing her look. Aerilyn and I stepped back to survey our work. The Princess looked radiant, the embodiment of sunshine.

"How do I look?" she said, twirling in circles.

"Beautiful, Yorena," Aerilyn said, a beaming smile plastered on her face. When I took too long to answer, she elbowed me in the side.

"Amazing, Your Highness." We heard a knock at the door, and I opened it to find one of the royal guards.

"I'm here to escort Yorena to the ball," he said. *First name basis with a guard?*

"Coming, Kieron!" The Princess hurried out of the room and linked her arm with his with a smile. I wondered what it would feel like for her to smile at me like that.

"We should get dressed too," Aerilyn said.

I nodded.

No elegant dresses for us. As servants working the ball, we had our uncomfortable formal uniforms to wear. The new ones we'd been provided with to match the theme of the ball looked even more ridiculous and scratchy than the usual ones.

The uniforms consisted of a deep yellow formal vest to put over a white dress shirt. The vest was more like a corset based on how tight a fit it was. And the pin from the yellow rose on our chests poked me every time I moved too quickly. If I never saw a yellow rose again, it wouldn't be soon enough. But at least we got to wear trousers for once, even if I look like a banana. Trousers could always hold more weapons than a restricting dress.

I quickly got dressed, making sure to tuck my dagger under the vest, and met Aerilyn at the door.

As we walked to the ballroom's kitchen, my eyes scanned the hallways as we passed more guards than usual. There had to be at least one guard every few feet. *So Their Majesties are being cautious for once, good.* Unless The Progression brought a whole army, I didn't think they would try to go against all this security. We entered the ballroom kitchen and spotted Chafik and Mathias. They waved us over.

"Am I the only one who thinks we look like walking bananas?" Chafik said.

"Not a chance," I said. Seth started showing us how to fill up our platters. There were small plates of fresh shrimp, whole tilapia doused in a peppered sauce, bowls of vegetable soup all the nobles seemed to love, thin slices of goat and lamb that smelled like pure heaven, and many other appetizers and entrees.

Through the door, we could hear light string music beginning to play. Guests must have started arriving. "All right everyone, start making rounds on your assigned sides of the ballroom," Seth said. "And remember not to talk to them, they don't like that," he added.

All of us lined up into two lines corresponding to the side of the room we were assigned, tray in hand, and marched out into the ballroom. Saffron banners with the royal crest were on every wall, strings of yellow roses were strung on the chandeliers. And everyone was wearing their crowns of roses. Guests started to sit down at their assigned tables, the room became a yellow sea of every possible shade. I began passing out their soup as an appetizer.

The nobles paid me no attention while I dropped off the puny bowls of soup. I told myself being this invisible didn't annoy me, but I knew it was a lie. Not even a thank you or a mere *look* in my direction. At least it was helpful for listening to any secrets passing through these careless nobles' lips. It was how my life had to be. Well, at least the half-life I'd been living in for the last five years. But it would all be worth it once we took down The Progression.

The only person who even truly knew me were my friends back at the base. Aerilyn only knew the version of me I'd created for her and our friendship based on lies. She didn't make me feel seen. But that wasn't fair of me to think. Aerilyn tried her best, but I could never share enough of myself to be true friends with her. Maybe if I was someone else we could've been real friends. Which definitely didn't help with my assignment of trying to get close to the Princess. I could share even less with her than I could Aerilyn.

Sure, I was able to be myself, whoever that was, around her more than others. And she knew better than anyone the amount of danger this kingdom was in, despite rarely leaving these walls. But I couldn't start listing the few good things about her. They did nothing to make up for the pain her family caused, no matter how much she claimed to want to help this kingdom.

Trumpets blared, and the room fell silent. Every head turned towards the balcony entrance. An announcer stood in front of the doors.

"Presenting Their Majesties, King Adil and Queen Saskia." Guards opened the doors, and out stepped the King and Queen. Applause quickly filled the silence. The Queen's dress was even more ridiculous than the Princess', and the Queen lacked the natural beauty to pull it off. The deep yellow ball gown was covered in an assortment of yellow flowers, complete with a tulle cape trailing behind her. The King wore a brass colored suit to match, also covered in flowers.

"Presenting the Heircestrial nominees. Nikos Vikander, Oliver Li, and Princess Yorena." The guards opened the doors once more, and the Princess entered, followed by Oliver and Nikos. The King tapped his golden rings against his glass, grabbing everyone's attention.

"Welcome honored guests to the first Heircestrial ball in almost a millennium." He paused for the smatterings of applause. Burying my pride, I tucked a now empty tray underneath my arm and joined in on the applause. *Don't be different, mimic the crowd.* "We are gathered here today to wish good luck to this generation's nominees." The three nominees stepped forward, scattered applause filling the room once more. The King held up his hand, silencing the applause. "The ball has now officially begun, you may now resume your conversations." He linked his arm with the Queen's and sat down at their table on the balcony. The orchestra rose again, filling the room with soft melodies.

After a quick refill in the kitchen, I made more rounds around the room handing out flutes of champagne and snacks as the party went on. I weaved through dancing couples, narrowly avoiding collisions. Half my brain was focused on handing out food, and the other half was focused on the rest of the room. The security increase may make a Progression attack less likely, but the prospect of attacking a second ball might be too big for them to pass up.

A woman with perfectly curled blonde hair and enough diamond jewelry to feed an entire village for at least two years, stepped into my path, and I was one second too late to veer out of her way. It was like watching everything happen in slow motion. The flutes tipped off my tray, the bubbling liquid flying toward the woman. Other nobles' mouths opened in pure horror, and the now empty glasses fell to the ground, shattering into large pieces with a delicate crash.

"You wretched child! You've ruined my dress!" Her pale skin reddened from her screaming. I scrambled to pick up the glass shards.

"I apologize, ma'am. I was not paying attention." A crowd of spectators gathered around the woman and me. *Hells.*

"You refer to me as 'Your Grace' and nothing less." Hells. Now I recognized her, the Duchess of Nitedand, Isla Vance. I felt my stomach drop. I curtsied.

"I am so sorry, Your Grace. I meant no harm."

"You have ruined my dress," she yelled, gesticulating violently. *I need to get away from this woman.*

"Allow me to retrieve some towels for you, and I promise it will look good as new." She huffed and narrowed her eyes. What was her problem? I had made a simple mistake, and I had not been rude in responding to her.

"How dare you." She raised her hand to hit me, and out of instinct, I caught it. *Spirits, what have I done?* Fighting back against a noble was punishable with time in the dungeon. *Blend in with the crowd.* A bit too late for that piece of advice.

Duchess Isla's jaw dropped. "Do not touch me," I said. The jaws of multiple onlookers were wide open while others began whispering among themselves.

"How dare you? You dirty little Infirmi, trying to rise above your station? Don't think I couldn't tell what you were with those dull eyes." My lips curled into a sneer and a bitter taste stained my tongue. The guests seemed more appalled by me catching her hand than her use of the slur. I'd never been referred to with that word before. It was what Imperium had called Primis people before the revolution. *Infirmi.* I could almost feel the word wrapping around my throat, keeping the words I burned to stay locked in my throat. It was rare to hear the word in Newnina, but I suppose Nitedand had yet to let go of it.

I felt a hand on my shoulder pulling me away from the Duchess. "I am so sorry about her Your Grace, I will take care of her." One of the servants pulled me away from the room and into one of the smaller corridors. I turned my head and smiled at the sight of long red hair and a freckled face.

"Rori?" I said, in full disbelief that they were here. They almost never visited the palace, it was too risky. They turned around and let out a breath of relief. I finally had a friend with me, I wasn't alone in this prison anymore.

"How are you here?" I whispered. They put a finger to their lips and led me into one of the smaller hallways. The firm grip they had on my hand was grounding, familiar. We were far from where the guards were and they stopped us. I'd expected to be greeted with a smile, or an "I missed you", or a hug. But instead I was greeted with one of Rori's famous glowers.

"What in four hells were you doing talking back to Duchess Isla?" I crossed my arms. The happiness I'd felt moments before, died.

"I wasn't 'talking back', I was merely having a conversation."

They raised their eyebrows.

"What kind of conversation involves her yelling at you in front of the entire ballroom?"

"The kind that happens when you mess up her eyesore of a dress." Rori started rubbing their brow.

I realized I might have been going slightly mad when Rori's glowers didn't bug me the same way they used to. "I came here to give you more direct orders from The Head." *No happy reunion for me I guess.*

"Why couldn't you tell me in a letter? Though I do appreciate the visit."

They didn't even crack a smile. "Because all of them have been getting intercepted and we've yet to find out by who. We don't want to risk anyone finding out about you."

If they haven't found out about me by now, they never would. It'd been five years of being a spy, and not one person has accused me of anything. Nobody ever would. At least not before I was able to escape this place. "What does The Head need?"

They took a deep breath. "I'm gonna need you to stay calm when I tell you this, okay. Just take a deep breath." I stared at Rori furiously, but did take a deep breath. I already had to act buddy-buddy with the Princess; there weren't many other assignments I could get that would upset me at this point. "We need you to act as the Princess' protector, a—like a secret bodyguard of some sort." They had to be joking. A secret bodyguard?

"Just last month every last one of you would spit on her name without question. But in the last week, you've asked me to be her friend and now I'm supposed to protect her?"

"I know you're upset but she might be our only chance at taking down The Progression."

I looked at them questioningly. "What do you mean?" They shushed me at the sound of footsteps. I pointed to a storage closet behind them, and they opened the door. We stayed silent, ears pressed against the aging wood, until the sounds retreated.

"Okay, we should be fine to talk now. This room stays empty most of the time," I said.

I leaned against the wall, trying not to snap at them. "Now. Tell me why I need to protect little Ms. Pampered Princess when she lives in a place full of guards who would gladly throw themselves in front of a sword to protect her."

Rori stood beside me. "Orla finally got back to us and said—"

"What? Orla is alive?" I could feel my features softening, a hint of a relieved smile on my lips. All these months, I had feared the worst. Sweet Orla. She wasn't much older than me, and from the moment I'd first met her, it was like I had a sister again. Her short blonde hair and deep brown, blue-flecked eyes always made her look more innocent than she truly was.

Paired with her short stature, people always underestimated her. But she was one of the strongest of us. But I didn't have time to rejoice yet. I had a job to do.

"What did she say?" A heavy weight lifted off my heart to hear she was alive. I'd been imagining the worst, fully believing The Progression has taken another person from me. I hoped I could see her again soon.

In the dim light, I could see Rori twirling their fingers through a lock of red hair, tugging at it. I had known Rori long enough to know what that meant. They were nervous. They were *never* nervous.

"They've started placing their people within the palace and if the Princess gets too close to winning Heircestrial they'll come after her. And they always say the enemy of my enemy is my friend." They said that last part with a shrug.

I put my head in my hands, trying to absorb what I was hearing. More of The Progression, in the palace? I might be able to discover more of their plans, but I couldn't waste my time keeping track of that girl. Hopefully, with the extra training, I wouldn't have to keep my eye on her 24/7. And she had her crystal; she should be fine enough without my help. But an order straight from The Head was not to be taken lightly. Val was only in charge of a base, but The Head was in charge of the base leaders, and everyone in the Union. If they said it was best, they were probably right. "Fine. I'll be her 'bodyguard', but I'm not gonna pretend to enjoy it."

Rori brought me in for a hug. "I would expect nothing more from you. I know how Fire Imperium make you feel." Their eyes dropped to my arms, my scars hidden by the shirt. They tingled under their gaze.

"And I know you don't like the Princess but—"

"Hate. I *hate* the Princess."

"Don't like, hate, loathe, whatever word you wanna use. I'm proud of you for taking one for the team. You've grown from when you first started."

"Will I have to be here much longer?" I woke up every morning, hoping for the letter that would tell me to come home. And every morning I woke up with bitter disappointment coating my tongue. They sighed and broke off the hug.

"I don't know. But you won't be away much longer." I brought them in for another hug, clutching onto the back of their vest.

"One more hug before you go." I didn't know how long we stayed like that. Rori, along with Orla, has been like the older sibling I never had. I missed them and the others more every day I was here.

They broke away, leaving a cold space in their absence. "You need to go back now. But I suggest staying with the kitchen staff for the rest of the night." Probably a good idea.

"Bye, Rori." They waved goodbye to me as they walked out the door, out of my reach for who knows how long. This next month might be the most painful one of my life. But I was sure I'd been through worse at this point.

A few minutes after Rori left, I peered out the door crack to watch for anyone coming. The only sounds came from the faint dance music emitting from the ballroom. I closed the door behind me and briskly walked back to the kitchen.

Seth looked at me with concern. "What is wrong with you? Is it true what I hear about you talking back to the Duchess of Nitedand? Like *the* most high-ranking, meanest Duchess?"

"I didn't talk back, I just spoke words she was not entirely fond of."

He put a hand on his hip. "Is that what we're going with tonight?"

"Yup," I said, patting him on the shoulder. I noticed a bowl of fresh strawberries and jumped on the counter next to them. I picked one from the bowl, hoping for a burst of sweetness. But the juice burned like acid in my mouth. Seems like my new job from The Head wouldn't even let me enjoy a strawberry.

"Hey hey hey, those are not for you."

"Then who are they for?"

He jumped onto the counter beside me, taking a strawberry of his own. "Planning and cooking for a ball is not exactly easy. They are for *me*."

"You can spare one."

He glared at me but didn't object.

"I'm gonna let you hide here but if Ms. Kira comes in… you're on your own."

I let out a short laugh. "Fine, but we'll see who helps you clean up another bisque disast—" I was cut off by the sound of multiple screams, all originating from the ballroom. Our heads whipped towards the door. I jumped down immediately, and Seth grabbed my arm.

"I know I don't have the best judgment but usually you run *away* from screams." I yanked my arm from his grip. "I'll be right back." I opened the door to complete blackness. Before, the room was brilliant, with the light of a thousand candles gleaming off the gold decorations scattered throughout the room. Every light had been extinguished. Only one thing could do that so quickly.

Air Imperium.

This was too similar to what had happened during the summer ball. My eyes took a few moments to adjust to the eerie darkness. Couples grabbed onto each other, terrified of what could have caused this. Some hid under their tables. Out of the corner of my eye, I saw a blip of light. Red light.

Fire Imperium.

My instincts told me to find Aerilyn and protect her. But most of the servants knew about all sorts of doors and hidden entrances. Against my true desire, I had to get to the Princess. This very well could be what Rori warned me against. They wanted to take her out of the running before the race even started. Last I saw the Princess, she was on one of the upper levels. I squeezed through people, slowly making my way to the staircase.

That was when the first arrow came.

The uncanny sound of arrows slicing through the air was suddenly close to me. I dropped down to the floor as fast as I could, continuing my trek by crawling. One woman screamed, her voice reverberating off the walls. I squinted my eyes and saw an arrow sticking out of her shoulder. The people around her sprinted from her as if she was poison, trampling over each other to get away from wherever the archer would strike next.

The nobles' horror-stricken faces told me they weren't used to seeing things like this. The woman yanked the arrow from her shoulder. *Rookie mistake.* Crimson blood gushed from the wound, not slowing no matter how much she pressed on it. Tile crumbled behind me as Earth Imperium tried to shield themselves from flying arrows.

I crawled between people, using them as my shield. I narrowly avoided being smothered by a large man collapsing almost on top of me. His eyes stared straight ahead and half a dozen iron-tipped arrows protruded from his neck. Dead.

"Everyone remain calm. The guards will protect us," the King announced from the highest balcony. *Easy to say for someone surrounded by at least six guards.* The cacophony of screams kept rising, accompanied by the sound of more arrows whizzing through the air. I resisted the urge to cover my ears. Most were paired with cries of agony as arrows sank into flesh.

My finger finally brushed the bottom step. I hurried up the stairs as fast as my feet would carry me. Forgetting the fact I couldn't see more than two feet in front of me, I tripped on the last step, slamming my head on the hard marble tiles. Spots danced in my vision and I gritted my teeth against the pain. I had to keep going.

"We have come to make you pay for the havoc you have caused," a dark voice announced. "Surrender now and we will keep most of you alive." I scanned the room, searching for the source of the voice. All I could see were waves of guests trying to run out the doors. People banged with both their fists. Crystals gleamed with all different colors from people attempting to blast open the doors. *Something locked the doors.*

Crystals glowed white from Air Imperium trying to blow open the doors. Green light from Earth Imperium shone as they attempted throwing chunks of tiled stone as them. Fire Imperium tried to burn down the door, but the palace made as much of the building materials as possible fireproof. Even blue light shone from Water Imperium trying to open the doors with streams of water. All futile.

"Guards! Seize this intruder," the King ordered.

The faint gleam of guard armor began rushing towards the direction the voice came from. I forced my head forward; I had a job to complete. I scanned the length of the balcony, searching for the bright yellow monstrosity that was the Princess' dress. My eyes locked on the orange glow of a fire crystal. The light revealed a dress the color of sunshine, covered in sunflower petals. She must be preparing to use it if one of the intruders came for her.

She was on the opposite side of the second-level balcony, and I started sprinting. "By resisting to surrender to the Primis Defense Union you have lost your chance at mercy." I stopped in my tracks. *What.* We would never stage something like this. Unnecessary violence was the exact thing we were trying to prevent. We were being framed.

My hands fisted tightly. The Progression already had the power, the resources, the man-power, all without having the monarchy breathing down their neck. But they still felt it necessary to blame us for this, and paint an even larger target on our backs. I took a few deep breaths, although they did nothing to cool the simmering in my veins. I picked back up my pace and grabbed the Princess' shoulder.

"Princess," I said, panting for breath. The world swayed around me, as if I were on a rocking boat. I couldn't pass out now, we needed to escape.

She whizzed around, hands ready to attack me. I jumped back at the sight of her still glowing crystal. Well, at least she learned something.

"Ilise?"

"You need to come with me."

"Why?"

"So I can keep you safe," I said.

The glow of her crystal died down, and I let out a quiet breath.

"I can take care of myself," she said in the most princessy voice I had ever heard.

I grabbed her arm and started dragging her back towards the kitchen entrance. "Now is not the time to argue with me."

"But I can—"

"No," I said sternly. I paused before continuing. I tore off some of the sunflower petals off her dress and ripped off the bottom of her dress.

"What are you doing?" she exclaimed, slapping my hands away.

"Helping you run easier and making your dress a less recognizable target." I grabbed her arm again before she could argue with me anymore.

We made it to the staircase leading back down when *they* began to come out of hiding. At least a dozen midnight black figures stepped out of various hiding places. At the bottom of the stairs, one of the figure's crystals glowed a blinding white light. Air Imperium. I pulled the Princess by the waist onto the ground and winced at the sound of her grunt in my ear. Not even a second later, they unleashed their power. Other people, too slow to react to the glow of the crystal, were thrown up to the third-level balcony. From here, I could hear the sickening thud of their bodies landing, the sound of cracking bones and organs being ejected from the sheer force of them being thrown. Tables and chairs flew through the air, shattering as they hit the wall.

The Princess' quickening breaths flooded my ears. "Ilise, let me lead," she shouted over the rising shrieks.

"I know a place we can go," I yelled back.

"Just trust me this once." We didn't have time to argue. The black figures were scattered throughout the room, thankfully not attacking us. But the word "yet" still lived in the back of my mind. I reluctantly nodded. I would agree with her only so we could get out of here quicker. And in the end, she was Imperium. She had a better chance if we came face to face with any of the figures. She grabbed my hand and pulled me up. I chose to ignore the subtle comfort it brought me. We quickly ran down the stairs and were finally in the midst of the attack.

Some of the guards on duty were in fierce duels with the figures. Others formed circles around the guests, attacking anyone who came too close. It was pure chaos. The Princess pulled us straight through the middle of the crowd. *Is she thinking straight? She's about to get us killed.* One of the figures approached me, hands outstretched. I caught their hand mid-swing and twisted it back until I heard them gasp in pain. Their leg swung towards me slowly enough I was able to kick their other leg out from under them. With their arm still in hand, I twisted it until their arm was completely behind their back. They laid on the floor writhing in pain. Normally I wouldn't be this cruel, but these were not normal times.

The Princess pulled on my arm, almost tripping me. "I'm coming. You're welcome for saving you by the way."

She looked back, still pulling me. "I didn't ask you to." With a less recognizable dress, we didn't get intercepted by many attackers. We were forced to run over the bodies of the unlucky victims. Many of which had faces frozen in fear, probably from the excruciating pain they experienced in their last seconds of life. I swallowed the bile rising in my throat. *They look just like my family's faces.*

One figure decided to come barreling towards us, crystal glowing bright green. I tried stepping in front of the Princess, but she kept a firm grip on me. She wrapped her hand around my waist to keep me behind her as her crystal started to glow bright orange. *"This will teach you not to meddle in other people's business."* The unwelcome memory heated my arms as if it was happening all over again.

I jumped back on instinct when she released a powerful stream of fire, but the figure ducked just quick enough to avoid the flames. The ground beneath us began to shake, no doubt because of them. The Princess fell on the ground at the sudden shake. I hoisted her up, but the figure used the opportunity to remove a chunk of the tile floor. "You must pay," they shouted above the noise. Floating it above their head, they released it in our direction.

I scrambled to drag the Princess away from the figure behind another couple running away. Dust filled the air on impact. She tripped over a broken piece of tile and brought me down to the ground with her. Pain shot up my arm from her weight. The Earth Imperium towered over us, hovering another chunk of stone above their head. I had few options.

Either push the Princess away and "disable" this person, possibly getting crushed in the process. Or grab her and run.

There was no running.

I moved myself to my feet and pushed the Princess away from the Imperium. Good thing I always kept my dagger on hand. And no one would notice a dagger-wielding servant in this chaos. I unsheathed it from under my uniform and charged the Imperium. They released the stone, and I ducked to avoid being decapitated. It grazed my forehead, warm blood dripped down my face. But I didn't let it slow me down. These people were pinning this on the Union, on me. If anyone needed to pay, it was them. Before they could get more stone, I threw my dagger towards them. It sailed through the air, straight into their chest, and they fell to the ground in a heap. Kass would be proud of that throw.

Just as I turned around, pain shot through my stomach. Another figure was on me, their dagger lodged in my stomach. Tears welled in my eyes, and my legs shook, but I couldn't fall, not yet. "You must all pay," they seethed before running back into the chaotic crowd. I bit back a scream as the dagger began to burn like a brand.

The room around me began to spin. It was a miracle I was still standing, but I needed to move. My stomach roiled as bile rose in my throat, threatening to empty the contents of my stomach onto the floor. The blade must have been coated in poison. *Spirits.* Gritting my teeth, I yanked the dagger out, letting loose a waterfall of blood. The poison would kill me faster than blood loss would.

Clamping my hand over the gushing wound, I limped to the Princess' side, and she pulled me until we reached the wall. I kept my hand pressed over the wound. My fingers were sticky with blood. My limbs felt like impossible weights. The walls looked like they were swirling, as if I were looking at the world through cracked glass. *I won't faint. I won't fall. I can do this.* Half the gold embellishments were destroyed, as well as chunks of the wall itself. The Princess started feeling along the wall. We were far enough in the corner that it would be almost impossible to see us in the darkness. I glanced over my shoulder to survey the room. The floor was littered with debris and the bodies of the dead or dying. Yet, the fighting had not slowed.

"We don't have time for this," I said, swaying on my unsteady feet. She ignored me. I started shaking her shoulder with my non-bloodied hand, albeit weakly. "Princess, we need to get out of here." She let go of the wall and grabbed my hand once again. Her hand was surprisingly soft and also covered in sweat.

"I am." She pushed on the wall, revealing a hidden door. I gaped at her as a triumphant smile appeared on her face. She pulled me inside and shut the door behind us. She retrieved a torch from the wall and lit it with a spark. I could finally see her face. Her makeup was melting, it was streaked with dust, and the crystals I had put in her hair had matted into it, but she was relatively okay. *Mission accomplished.* "I told you I could handle myself." I would have believed the false confidence in her voice if not for her shaking hands.

I took the torch from her and hung it on the wall. The sounds of fighting were muffled by the thick stone. "We need to go," I said in a weak voice.

"Shouldn't we stay here until the fighting subsides?" she said. I felt myself beginning to tip forward, but she caught me in her arms before I could hit the ground. "Ilise, what's wrong?" she said in a panicked voice. I removed my hand from the wound, eliciting a wince from her. Even though it pained me to say it, bruising my pride in every way possible, I said in a parched voice, barely above a whisper.

"Help me."

CHAPTER 12

PRINCESS YORENA

ILISE'S EYELIDS FLUTTERED CLOSED, and her body went limp in my arms. The blood from the wound in her stomach flowed freely, like a rushing river. I needed to get her help quickly. Sweat began to bead on her forehead, but stab wounds didn't do that. Unless... poison.

Why didn't she tell me she was stabbed? I could have helped her or at least gone faster while looking for the tunnel entrance. What if she died because of the poison? I would never forgive myself if I let that happen. Especially after she ran through the middle of an all-out battle to help bring me to safety, even though I was certain she disliked me.

No, I couldn't start spiraling now. Ilise needed my help, and I was the only one here who could help her. The only place I could bring her would be the infirmary, but the doctor might not be there. I stared at the growing bloodstain on Ilise's white shirt. I still had to try and get her there, and maybe find the antidote to her poison.

Using my crystal to light the way and provide enough strength to carry her, I ran down the stone passageway as fast as possible with Ilise. She needed an antidote and stitches if she was going to make it through the night. The sounds of fighting diminished the farther I ran from the ballroom. Ilise let out a pained moan in her sleep. "It's okay, I've got you," I said into her ear.

I took a sharp left, bounding down the stairs to the underground floor, and kicked open the exit door. The dim torches flickered above my head, casting a sickly glow over the brown stone, my heels echoing down the empty hallway as I ran to the infirmary. Kicking opened the door, I lit all of the torches.

The doctor wasn't here.

I gently set Ilise down on one of the three cots and brushed stray hair from her face. Her skin was now drenched in sweat, and even in sleep, her body trembled. The normal dark brown of her skin had taken on a gray pallor, looking even more ghastly under the torchlight.

Okay, so the doctor wasn't here, and Ilise was still slipping away. The first thing I needed to do was stitch up the wound to prevent her from losing more blood. I rummaged through the white cabinets lining the walls for a needle and thread. I'd watch Doctor Mendoza work some-times, and stitching a wound wasn't too hard if you had a strong enough thread. I prayed to the Spirits it wasn't too different from stitching clothes. I finally found a clean needle and thread buried under gauze in the back of the third cabinet. I pulled out the materials and rushed to Ilise's side.

I didn't think someone could lose this much blood, and the crimson river still flowed. I ripped away her vest and shirt, wincing as I beheld the wound. It wasn't as big as I thought, but it still looked awful. Dried blood was on the perimeter of the slash going right through her chiseled stomach; some of it solidified into a jelly. What kind of poison was this? Grabbing a bottle of alcohol from the bedside table, I doused the wound, needle, and thread. I was surprised the sting didn't wake her up.

Pushing together the two sides of the wound, I began stitching. I used the same running stitch I had been taught a few years back. My hands still shook from the shock of the events over the last few minutes, but I managed to not mess up. I quickly tied off the stitch and ripped off the excess thread. The wound might scar horribly from my inexperience, but it would heal. Ilise moaned again, her eyelids fluttering open.

"Ilise, are you awake?" Her eyes darted around the room as she took in where she was.

"The poison is getting worse," she said, her voice hoarse. She clutched her stomach as vomit shot out of her mouth. I ran to retrieve the nearby wastebasket and held it in front of her. I held her up as she emptied the contents of her stomach into the basket. Giving her a pat on the back, I put down the wastebasket and helped her lie back down.

"Do you know what poison this is?" I asked. I used the corner of the sheet to wipe off the excess vomit off her face.

"It's from the Beniniara plant," she mumbled. "I think it looks like a rose... or something." Her eyes fluttered closed again. Now I remembered. Beniniaras grew everywhere in this kingdom, and we even used to have some in the royal garden. Many people ingested them accidentally because they looked so similar to the roses we used to make rose water. For a plant that common, there should be an antidote already here.

If I was remembering correctly, the poison caused delirium, hallucinations, nausea, burning when it came in contact with skin, and muscle weakness. And not long after exposure, it eroded your organs from the inside out.

Ilise let out a traumatized scream and I jumped. She thrashed in her sleep, gripping the sheets so hard they were beginning to rip. "Ilise! What's going on?" I said, trying to shake her awake. Even in her sleep, her strikes were powerful. Her fist made contact with shoulder and I stumbled away from her. *Is she having a nightmare?*

"Get away from him!"

"There's no one here," I said. Though it was pointless, I knew she couldn't hear me.

"You monsters killed them! You killed them all!" My heart broke for her. I didn't think this was a made-up delirium from the poison, she must've been having a nightmare. A scream ripped from Ilise's throat and it took all of my willpower to not try to wake her up. I needed to find the antidote before I could wake her up. But guilt settled in my stomach nonetheless as I returned to searching the cabinets.

I didn't see any antidote in the cabinets I already looked through, but there were still two more. I opened the small door and a creeping sense of hopelessness settled over me. There were dozens of bottles, all holding different antidotes from the one I needed. I looked in the last cabinet and still didn't find it. Panic settled in my bones.

"I'm sorry, Mama. I thought I was helping," Ilise said in a scratchy, broken voice. *Are her nightmares over?* "I never should have left." Maybe this was a memory. Her file had said she sent her wages to her family for a year. Did her parents not want her to leave? I shook the unneeded question out of my head. I needed to find her an antidote, fast.

The ingredients for the antidote were not things I could find within the next five minutes. I yanked on the matted strands of my hair. What could I do? I ran through my knowledge of plants; some plants were so similar, we could use their antidotes interchangeably. Beniniaras were another species of roses, but most roses were completely harmless.

I scoured through the vials of antidote, still listening to Ilise's sleep-talk, praying to the Spirits one would jog my memory.

"Miel rof em ym sra. Ilth eh yaw rof I aev olt mesfl ot oy. Ot oyru adkrenss, ebuatilu ni et yaw lla civisuo hisg era. Oyru adr ised of et sra, ym sra." Was she speaking Old Croagi? I didn't know much of the nearly-extinct language, but as the cryptic words spilled from Ilise's mouth, I couldn't help but be entranced. The words flurried together in my mind, trying to find some translation, but none came. Just another mystery from this girl I intended to solve. I wished I knew what she was saying, but that was a problem for another day. She fell silent again, and I turned around to see her thrashing finally stopped.

I pulled out a small vial filled with a pink liquid. I read the label; it was an antidote for the Harrisania. I wanted to squeal, but it didn't seem appropriate at the moment. The Harrisania was another species of poisonous roses. If any antidote was going to work, it would be this one.

I popped off the cork and returned to Ilise's side. I leaned in close to her ear and tried to shake her awake. "Ilise. Please. Drink this." Her eyes peeled open into thin slits. I brought the opening of the vial to her lips and helped her drink it down. There were only a few sips, so I gave her the whole thing. She drained the bottle, and I threw the empty glass into the wastebasket.

Chapter 13

Ilise

I T WAS A WEEK after the attack on the ball, and the stab wound had already healed quite a bit. I didn't know what magic the Princess did on me, but I was grateful for it, even if I couldn't bring myself to admit it. She even teamed up with Aerilyn to make sure I stayed in bed instead of working after almost dying.

The sun shone through the thin curtains I'd had installed in my room, waking me up from another nap. I wanted to leave; I needed to see if there was any talk about the attack. The Progression was playing dirty, blaming the Primis Defense Union. I lifted up the shirt of my nightgown to look at my wound. I got out lucky. Even though I hated just about everyone in that ballroom, they didn't deserve to die because of The Progression. My wound was now a thick, pink line, running across my stomach.

I had few memories from my delirium after being stabbed. But I could have sworn I heard the Princess begging for me to wake up. But it must have been my imagination. The last full memory I had of that night was right after the Princess gave me the antidote. I remember her squeezing my hand, and I think there was a tear in her eye. Out of fear or out of relief, I couldn't tell.

Chapter 14

Princess Yorena

THEY'VE INFILTRATED THE PALACE. Those four words echoed in my mind while Ilise watched me practice my punches.

That was what the Spymaster told me. He was our eyes and ears outside of the palace, he informed us of *everything*. Even the trivial passing of pure court gossip. And the Primis Defense Union was anything *but* trivial. Half of their forces weren't even Primis, but Imperium, constantly attacking innocent people and villages. The Spymaster had intercepted dozens of letters to their members in the palace. But none of them had matched the names of anyone staying or working in the palace.

If they'd gotten into the palace, they could have been the ones who staged the wind attack during the summer ball. And it may have been them who painted the wall to throw us off their trail in preparation for the Heircestrial Ball.

"Are you going to stare at the wall the rest of the night?" Ilise asked. I remembered where I was, another training session with Ilise.

"Sorry, I am just tired."

Her face remained impassive. "Break time is over, we aren't leaving until you can subdue me in a match." I rubbed my eyes and stood from the floor and prepared to fight. Ilise stayed on offense while I focused on defense.

The last week had almost completely drained me. I'd been sitting in constant meetings with my parents to figure out what to do about The Progression *and* the Union in light of the most recent attack. I would never forget the faces of the nobles who had lost loved ones to the Union monsters. Almost a third of the guests had been killed. It was a miracle Ilise and I even made it out alive. Ilise's stab wound had mostly healed, along with the cuts on her face. A large pink scar graced her forehead from the Earth Imperium she'd fended off, but it could have been worse. A sense of dread went through my stomach at the memory of how close she had been to dying.

I was beginning to enjoy our training sessions. She didn't expect me to complete impossible tasks like my parents did, or drain my emotional energy on damage control. Not that I hated giving my condolence to those who lost someone, but I was only one person. All Ilise expected of me was to stay on my feet for as long as I could, and attempt to knock her down. She even occasionally let me vent to her after an especially stressful day.

Deep in my thoughts, I didn't notice Ilise shifting her weight for a kick. She knocked me hard in the side, and I fell over. Her judgmental gaze burned holes in my back, but it was normal. Although I enjoyed her company, it was still next to impossible to coerce a smile onto her face. "You should have seen me shifting my weight. That would have given you plenty of time to avoid my attack."

I groaned standing up. "Sorry, my head is everywhere right now."

Pain laced through my side, and I clutched the fabric of my black tunic. I felt her calloused hand on the bare skin of my shoulder. I froze. "Are you ok?"

I winced as I rolled up. Her brown eyes churned. "I will be fine. We can go again." I started to stand, but she guided me back down, her fingers resting on the bottom hem of my tunic.

"Can I make sure you aren't injured?" With one sentence, she made my sweat-drenched face heat more.

"Um, ok," I said, barely a whisper. She lifted the bottom shirt, wincing as she examined my side. This morning, my reaction was the same. Purplish splotches decorated my tender side. If I were to move too much, the bruises would throb like a second heart. Imperium needed to wear their crystal at all times to be at our normal strength level. Taking it off everyday for training sessions had slowed my healing down to a crawl. But there were more important things to worry about than a few bruises.

Her fingers brushed the bruises with a feather-light touch. My breaths hurried, I hoped she wouldn't notice. "How long has it been like this?" Her gaze returned to me, a rare softness in her gaze.

"Um... since I started training."

She ran a hand through her thick curls, annoyance painted clearly on her face. "You can't ignore something like this for that long," she chided. *Says the person who tried to hide a whole stab wound and poison.*

She stood from the ground and dug through her bag in the corner. "What are you looking for?" I said.

"I remembered the bruises I saw on your back the night of the ball so I decided to bring the healing salve with me to our lessons."

No one ever paid that close attention to me, and I wanted to hide in a corner when her eyes stared at my side, her gaze burning a line of fire wherever she looked. Like there wasn't anything I could hide from her.

She came back to my side, lifting my tunic again. And with careful fingers, she spread it over the bruises. I sighed with relief as she spread the cooling paste on my burning skin. "If you don't mind me asking, what has you so stressed?"

"Do I get to go to bed after I tell you?"

She snorted, the sound was adorable. "Sure, Princess."

"I will only tell you this because I know you already know more than most. And I feel like I can trust you won't repeat this."

She nodded, her hands still moving in small circles across my side. My nerves were aflame by her touch, and it took longer than normal to remember what I was going to tell her. "You already know about The Progression, but have you heard of the Primis Defense Union?" I tried to ignore the slight waver in my voice, hyper aware of her hand.

A muscle in her jaw twitched. "I've heard about them in passing." She peeled her eyes from my bruises, staring into my eyes. How had I never noticed the shining flecks in her eyes, the sparkles dancing in the dim light?

"Well, it appears some of their members have made their way into the palace."

"They have?"

I nodded solemnly.

"Why would that be causing you stress?" Her hand slowed, still glued to my waist. My stomach fluttered. *Fluttering? What?*

"Because they're no better than The Progression." I saw the impassive mask fall back over her face. Did I say something wrong? She should be agreeing with me, especially after what happened at the ball. Knots formed in my stomach at the memory of what had almost happened to her because of them.

"What makes you say that?"

"They attack innocent Imperium under the guise of attacking The Progression."

She stared at the ground for a few moments and removed her hand, leaving a cold absence behind. "Well, what's the palace doing about it?"

"Besides trying to weed out any members, I don't know. My parents aren't letting me know much." Ilise stared at me. Was she seething with rage? Her fists clenched so tightly I was surprised her nails didn't break the skin.

She leaned in close to my face, holding my gaze captive, eyes churning like a restless sea.

"Do you feel better now?" I gulped at the intensity of her gaze, her face mere inches from mine, and I averted my eyes to the ground. I was close enough that I could tuck back Ilise's stray strand of hair if I wanted to. I wanted to, but I thought against it.

"My side or my head?" I said with a weak chuckle.

"Both."

"Yes. Thank you."

She rose from the ground, lending me a hand. "Get some rest Princess. You're working yourself a bit too much." I gave her hand a squeeze before grabbing my crystal and walking out. I paused at the door.

"What will it take for you to call me by my name?"

She crossed her arms, a smirk playing on her lips. "Are you not a Princess?"

"I am. But my name is Yorena, not Princess."

"I prefer to call you Princess."

I crossed my arms. "What if I made it a royal order for you to call me Yorena?"

She raised an eyebrow. "Is that a royal order?" she asked.

"No. But I know I'll grow on you eventually."

She scoffed and turned away from me. "Grow on me like what? A piece of mold?" I turned and left the room until Ilise started speaking again. "Princess, I know I don't act like it, but you're doing better than I expected. You don't have to overwork yourself just to get better." Pride filled my chest. I was improving. I was one step closer to being able to protect myself and the kingdom.

"Thank you," I said.

"Don't think this means I like you now."

I laughed and left the room.

It must have been past midnight. The underground level was empty of anyone else, and the only noise was the quiet tap of my boots. I hurried up the stairs, ready to crawl into my bed. A few guards were posted while I made my way to the door of my apartment.

"Help... is anyone there?" a quiet voice said. I turned my head around to scan the corridor. Empty.

"Ilise? Was that you?" No response. "Guards, did you hear that?"

The three guards shook their heads.

Nikos and Oliver stepped out of their rooms. "Princess, it's past midnight. What do you think you are doing?" Nikos asked.

"Did you not hear the voice?"

Oliver rubbed the sleep from their eyes. "Are you sure it wasn't your imagination?" they said. I was pretty sure I heard someone, but it's possible my exhaustion was catching up to me. The guards said they didn't hear anything, so it could be possible. Unless...

"What if this is the first test?" I said.

Nikos scoffed. "I don't think chasing an imaginary voice counts as a test." My ears strained to hear the voice anymore. "Wait," Nikos said. "Do you hear that?" I did. The faint sounds of shouting. I clasped my crystal back around my neck and started towards the sound, Nikos and Oliver trailing behind me. Even with the strength from the crystal, my body still felt like jelly.

"Hello," I called. "Is anyone there?"

Nikos gave another annoyed sigh. "This is stupid," he said. I ignored him.

We followed the sounds to the side of the garden facing the Leekrina River. I scanned the area and found no one. Crickets chirped as the river rushed past us, splashing water onto the bank. "It's late, we should just go back inside," Oliver said.

"I know I heard something."

"HELP US!"

"The scream came from the river," I said. I ran to the edge of the water, Nikos and Oliver close behind. The only light available was the half-moon, making it hard to see much of anything.

"Over there," Oliver said, pointing to a fallen-over tree. Half of it was in the water, with three little girls hanging on for their lives.

"We need to help them," I said.

"I'm gonna wring your neck," another voice yelled. We whipped our heads around to at least twenty royal guards, in the midst of fighting each other. Half of them had their crystals of all colors glowing full force, this would not end well.

Goosebumps rose on my arms as a familiar heaviness returned to the air. "Welcome nominees," Imogen said, appearing suddenly and making me jump.

"I told you it was our first test," I said to Nikos. He gave me a bored look. Imogen started pacing in front of us.

"This test will challenge your decision-making. Obviously, this is on a much smaller scale than if you were the actual monarch... but it should suffice," Imogen explained.

"Can we start now?" Oliver asked.

Imogen's face turned into a warm but frightening smile, unnaturally white teeth nearly glowing in the moonlight.

"Of course. And remember, no helping *or* sabotaging. You will have five minutes to save who you choose. We'll be watching you." At that she strutted away, cloak trailing behind her.

Five minutes? That wasn't enough to save all the girls *and* stop the guards from seriously injuring each other. I crouched and covered my ears to give myself enough silence to think. The hardest thing to do would be to save the girls. This part of the river was one of the strongest and most dangerous. But having twenty injured guards would be detrimental to palace security. But the guards were least likely to die in this scenario so the best course of action would be to save the girls first. And the guards were grown men, they should know better than to get wrapped up in silly disagreements.

I looked up to see Oliver parting their way through the river to get to the girls. Nikos must have chosen the guards. My crystal wouldn't be much help to deal with a strong river. And Oliver wasn't going to help me. I scanned for something that would help me get across. One tree had a low hanging branch... low enough for me to grab on. And with the strength from my crystal, I would be able to jump onto it after grabbing at least two of the girls.

I took a deep breath and sprinted towards the branch to gain enough momentum, leaping onto it. My arms burned and it creaked under my weight but it held. My hands were immediately filled with splinters and I blinked away tears of pain. I swung on the branch once, twice, a third time. Once I let go I landed on the trunk of the fallen tree. It was slick with water but I was able to balance myself. Ilise's voice popped into my head. *"Foot placement is the most important part of your landing," she said, circling me. She placed her hands on my shoulders, pushing down on me so my knees bent slightly. "And you need to keep your knees loose and bouncy to absorb the shock from your fall."* Ilise's training had helped me so much, and I was sure it was only thanks to her that I hadn't lost my balance now.

Oliver was still only halfway across the river. The girls looked up at me with wide eyes and tears streamed down their faces. All of them had a white knuckle grip on the tree.

I held out my arms to balance me as I slowly walked over to them. Once I got close to them, I had to yell to be heard over the sound of the rushing river. "I'm here to save you! I can only carry two of you at a time. Just try to crawl as close to me as you can."

They nodded. The closest two started to crawl across the tree. The first one reached me and I put her on my back.

The ground began to shake, causing the next one's hand to slip on the wet bark and she fell over the side, barely clinging on. This was definitely Nikos' doing. "Hold on! I'll come get you!"

The bark was becoming more slippery the closer I got to the edge. I held out my hand to her. "Grab on." She grabbed onto my hand and I picked her up. "I'll come back for you," I yelled to the last girl.

I slowly walked to the other side of the river and put them down on the other side. "Stay here, okay?"

They nodded, whimpering. Almost all my energy was drained out of me. My clothes became an extra weight, soaked, but I still had one more to go. I looked to see Oliver's position, but I couldn't see them. *Where are they?* I didn't have time to ponder over where Oliver went, I needed to save the last girl.

I began to walk across the tree again. The ground quaked again and I fell over the side of the tree, but I clung onto the bark. What in four hells was Nikos doing? My arms strained to hold on.

They were beginning to slip.

I tried pulling myself up, my muscles screaming in protest. My nails dug into the thick bark, and then, a large wave of water hit me and I fell into the river.

The water swept me away from the tree. I tried to keep my head above the water, but another wave came before I could fill up with air. Against my will, I inhaled a mouthful of water. This couldn't be how it ends. Bested by a river during only the first Heircestrial test. Half of my vision went black.

A strong pair of arms wrapped around my waist and pulled me out of the water. As soon as I felt the wind, I coughed up all the water. Oliver's face came into view. *They saved me?* The sound of the guards fighting had ceased. The three girls were carried over the river and through the air by the sorcerers. It took a few more seconds before I could see clearly again.

"Are you ok, Your Highness?" I squinted my eyes at the blue light of their crystal as they formed a dry path for us to walk. Using them for support, we walked back ashore.

"Times up," Imogen called. Had it been five minutes already? I was only able to save two of the girls. "Your Highness and Oliver, don't worry about the other girl. We've got her." Oliver removed my arm from around their neck and went to stand with Nikos.

"The six of us have conversed and determined the winner to be... Nominee Vikander." What? Nikos' face was beaming with pride. I almost drowned trying to save the girls. Keeping some guards from sporting a few bruises was hardly comparable.

"Wait. How is he the winner?" I fumed.

Imogen turned to me. "Because he chose to break up the guards from fighting and prevent them from hurting each other."

I gaped at her. "But I saved two of the three girls from death." She gave me a tight-lipped smile and shook her head.

"But imagine if this were on the scale of the whole kingdom."

I tilted my head. "I'm not sure I am following."

"Imagine if this were the decision between saving one village or the entire kingdom. What would you choose?"

"The kingdom," I said quickly.

"Then why did you choose the village over the good of the kingdom?" She was making no sense. How was I supposed to see the girls were a village while the guards were the kingdom. I saved the people who were closest to dying, it makes more sense than a group of guards. Hells, *I* could have drowned along with them had it not been for Oliver.

"Oh," Oliver began. "I once spoke with the Duke of Ominka about this same scenario. Sometimes you have to sacrifice the few for the good of the many."

Imogen nodded approvingly. "Very good Nominee Li." She joined the rest of the sorcerer council. "Nikos is now in the lead. Until we meet again." The council walked out of the garden, the little girls trailing behind them.

"You seem so shocked, *Your Highness*," Nikos said.

"You know good and well what we had to do for this test was nowhere near similar to what Imogen was saying."

He gave a mock gasp. "Or maybe *I'm* just better at one of the most vital parts of being King. And also, the test was about saving people, not drowning in a river."

I stepped up to him. "I wouldn't get so confident calling yourself King yet," I said in a low voice.

His smile turned sinister. "Whatever you say, waterbug." He clapped Oliver on the back and started walking away.

"Oliver," I called. They broke away from Nikos and jogged to me. "Why did you save me? Imogen said no helping." They put their hands on their hips, a confused look in their eyes.

"So I was supposed to let you drown?"

I paused. "I mean, the sorcerers would have saved me." They threw an arm around me. I stiffened.

"Just because we're competitors, doesn't mean we can't be friendly towards each other." *They should try telling Nikos that.* "I should retire for the night," they said. I watched them walk back inside, leaving me alone.

I couldn't tell if Oliver was truly trying to be kind or not. They could've only saved me so I would trust them, and then they could betray me later. But their tone wasn't laced with deceit. They actually sounded genuine. And I had other things to worry about.

I needed to become Queen. It was what I'd been training for my entire life. And frankly, neither of the other nominees have done or said anything that showed they would be a good monarch. Though Oliver had shadowed in Ominka's court, so they might be decent.

But no one could love this kingdom as much as I did. I wanted to be the one to reunite its people. If I couldn't do that, then what else was I good for?

After a few minutes, I walked back into my apartment, careful to keep my wet footsteps quiet. I already failed one of the tests. I fought back tears, there was no time for that. I needed to strategize. How could I ensure I get ahead in this race? A dark thought popped into my head. What if I couldn't? What would happen to my kingdom if I failed?

CHAPTER 15

ILISE

THE PRINCESS FOCUSED ON her plate, absently scraping her fork through the eggs. I couldn't determine what'd made her so upset. Did I give myself away when she was talking about the Primis Defense Union? It had taken nearly every bit of my self-restraint to keep my mouth shut when she talked about the Union as if we were no more than common criminals. Somehow, I had expected better. But any expectation I had of her would never be met, and I needed to get that in my head.

I'd been here far too long to get caught now. I was walking on eggshells trying to choose the correct words. I had gone over the conversation in my head dozens of times last night, and she hadn't looked suspicious of me. I wiped my sweaty palms on my apron under the table.

Aerilyn looked at me, nodding her head towards the Princess. I shrugged. She looked at Chafik and Mathias; both of them shrugged too. I'd never been good at comforting people, Orla had always been better at it. Chafik was the one to finally break the silence.

"Um, Ms. Yorena?" She looked up from her plate. Dark circles were prominent under her eyes. "Is something wrong?"

"Was Mathias keeping you up with his violin playing?" Aerilyn joked in an attempt to lighten the mood. The Princess gave a weak smile.

"I'll have you know," Mathias began, "My violin playing was breathtaking." I raised an eyebrow at him.

"If you call a cat giving birth breathtaking," I countered. Chafik spat out his drink, and Mathias crossed his arms, sticking his chin in the air.

"Don't write to me when you want free entry into my concert once I'm famous." Aerilyn was gasping for breath in a fit of giggles.

"I share a wall with you, I don't think that'll be a problem," she said.

The Princess put her face in her hands. "I failed the first trial," she confessed. *She failed?* I'd never seen her look more defeated than she did in that moment. But the whole thing was stupid anyway. Although, I didn't think she wanted to hear that.

"I'm so sorry," Chafik said.

Mathias spoke up. "Then who passed?"

"Nikos." *Of course he did.*

"Don't worry," Aerilyn said in a soft voice. "There are still two more left, you just have to pass those two."

The Princess let out a harsh laugh. "It would help if I actually knew what they're going to be," she said.

"I actually know quite a bit about Heircestrial," Chafik said.

"You do?" the Princess said. A large smile spread across his face, his two-colored eyes almost twinkling.

"History is one of my guilty pleasures. And after we first met, I decided to do a little research."

Life finally returned to the Princess' face. "Where did you find out about it?"

"Books of course."

"You have a book?"

"In my room." Chafik shrugged as if this were a matter of course.

"Can I borrow it? The more I know about this process, the better."

"Of course," he beamed. "Let me go get it."

"I think that's the most excited I've ever seen him," Mathias said. All the tension left my body. At least I didn't compromise myself last night.

"So what was last night's test exactly?" I asked.

"It made less sense than all the etiquette rules I've had drilled into my head." She paused, rubbing her eyes. "We had to choose between saving three girls from drowning in the Leekrina River or stop a large group of guards from tearing each other apart for Spirits know what."

"Did you choose the guards?" Aerilyn asked. I didn't think her *that* stupid as to choose the guards. Palace guards tended to be as stupid as they were strong, which wasn't the best combination. The amount of times Ms. Kira would have to send a group of servants to clean up the debris from the latest guard brawl was more than I could attempt to count.

"No. I chose the girls, but *apparently,* the girls were supposed to represent saving a small village and the guards were supposed to represent saving the entire kingdom." I pondered for a second. That had to be the most inane, convoluted analogy I'd ever heard. It's like the Council was *trying* to make a joke out of this—a joke out of the decision that could be our downfall.

"How were you supposed to know?" I said. I had the sudden urge to put my hand on her shoulder, soothing her worries. Or just do something to wipe the distressed look off her face. The reason why, I wasn't sure.

"Exactly."

"That made about as much sense as all of the backlash my violin skills have gotten," Mathias said.

I should say something to her, try to make her feel better. *Act as her protector. Become her friend. Blend in.* She was confusing me. I had one mission: keep her safe. Nowhere did anyone say I had to keep her happy. I didn't need her distracting me. To keep myself from saying anything, I began clearing the table of dirty dishes.

Chafik came back into the room, carrying a book larger than his head. "I found it!" he called. His two-colored eyes were lit up with sparks of excitement. "This book focuses mainly on Erea's broader history, but there is a pretty large section on Heircestrial." He flipped through the thick yellow pages to the middle of the book and pointed to a section. "Here it is."

I had to suppress my annoyance. History was never one of my favorite things. It seemed to always be a group of stupid people making the same stupid mistakes another group of stupid people made a century earlier. What was the purpose of learning history if you were just going to watch the same thing happen again.

He started reading a passage.

"Heircestrial was put in effect in order to ensure the sanctity of the monarch. Once the new generation grows of age, each province may put forth one nominee to compete for the title of Heir. The Council of Sorcerers will oversee all events taking place. Each nominee will undergo three tests to determine their right to rule. The tests include: sound decision-making, diplomacy, and a test of loyalty. A nominee must pass two out of three tests to be named Heir."

"Well, that was a mouthful," Mathias said. Chafik put the book down.

"Yeah. And the rest of the section talks about every single Heircestrial in Erean history. Even all the past nominees' names and the tests they passed."

The Princess placed a hand on his shoulder. "Not even the Royal Archives had something like this. Thank you Chafik."

"Don't thank me, thank the Faveru Archives," he beamed.

"So I guess you could say the first test makes some sort of sense," I said. The Princess set her gaze on me. Much softer than usual.

"Well technically. But when you have to choose between saving children from *dying* and stopping guards from acting *like* children, there is one obvious answer of what to do."

"Fair enough." I guess the ideals of a test from a thousand years ago weren't applicable anymore. Or ever.

Chafik stood up from his chair. "You can look through the rest of the book, I think there is another passage later in the book. But I think we should head to the office before Ms. Kira bites our heads off."

Aerilyn scoffed. "She isn't a monster," she said. Mathias put his hands on her shoulders, looking down at her.

"Oh, never-made-a-mistake Aerilyn. If you've ever seen her mad, it wouldn't seem too far-fetched for her to bite your head off."

"I'll be there in a minute," I said to them as they left the room. The Princess and I were the only ones left.

"Before you go," she began, "Just a random question but wh—" I put up my hand, ceasing her speech. She had a way of making me want to tell her everything, and I didn't know how much longer I could push my secrets down.

"You're doing the 'I'm prodding into Ilise's life voice'." She crossed her arms, mouth pressed into a thin line.

"That voice does not exist." I stepped closer to her.

"Every time you try to ask me about my life your voice goes up a full octave."

"Does not," she said, her voice shooting up an octave.

"I thought Princesses were supposed to be truthful," I said flatly.

She crossed her arms with a huff.

"Fine. For every time you can take me down during our training today, which you've yet to do, you can ask me one question." What was the harm in a little game?

"Deal." She held out her hand, a broad smile on her face, and my heart fluttered at the appearance of her spiritsdamned dimples. I shook her hand, our hands lingering together a few seconds after. I released my hand from hers. "I'll see you later today."

"Yeah... see you later," she said.

"Got something on your mind?" Aerilyn said with a smirk on her face.

"Huh?" I said. Ms. Kira let us help out in the gardens today, but I felt like the assignment was more Aerilyn's doing than Ms. Kira acting out of the kindness of her heart. We were trimming hedges and pulling out all the weeds. Many of the gardeners were taking a vacation as they always do after balls. Couldn't say I blamed them, my fingers still tingled at the thought of having to make those flower crowns for every ball. I enjoyed working in the gardens anyways. It always kept me calm, and well... sane.

The singing birds, rustling leaves of willow trees, the sounds of the rushing river behind us, and fragrant flowers of the royal gardens have always felt like a second home. Or, more likely, it reminded me of home. The days I'd spent playing outside, running through the stone streets of Demessa, and picking flowers on our family farm. I'd always felt like the Princess of my own small kingdom, with all the barn animals as my loyal subjects.

This could never feel the same as home, but it was closer than anything else right now enough. Even if I was drenched in sweat and my limbs felt heavy from the dense air. My fault on account of my insistence on covering my arms. I slightly envied Aerilyn, humming to herself while pulling weeds, barely breaking a sweat. She had opted to wear the much lighter and cooler version of our servant's dresses.

Watching her work with that carefree expression made me wonder what it would be like to not have to hide. Who she was, her past, even something as trivial as her arms.

"You've had that small smile all day. And usually, you're brooding like it's your *job*."

I gave a mock gasp. "I do not brood."

"Yes, you do. You're like 'I am Ilise, my life is pain, Aerilyn is the only person I mildly tolerate, brood brood brood,'" she said in a monotone voice.

I slapped her shoulder. "You just might lose your place on my list of people I tolerate." She sighed and settled into the grass, foregoing her task of pulling weeds.

"We both know you couldn't hate me even if you tried." I allowed myself a small smile and joined her on the ground.

After a while, Aerilyn started talking again. "I have a theory," she said.

"A theory about what?"

"Why you look happier than you were weeks ago." I propped myself up on my elbows.

"And what is this reason you've invented?" Her smile somehow grew wider.

"You listened to me for once and stopped acting like Yorena was a vial of poison."

"Okay, so *maybe* I tolerate her mildly now."

"Oh, you more than mildly tolerate her," she said mischievously. I narrowed my eyes.

"What are you implying?" She rolled up to a crossed leg position, facing me.

"You like Yorena."

I scoffed at her. "Not a chance." I wasn't supposed to like her, I was supposed to protect her, train her, and keep her at arms-length.

"Oh really? Then why were you staring at her the *whole* time during breakfast? And not one eye roll was to be seen."

"I was not staring at her, I was *looking* at her. There's a difference."

I'd never told Aerilyn my actual role here—a spy for the Primis Defense Union. As far as she knew, I was only here because my family needed money. Granted, she knew they died, but it would be too dangerous to tell her the full truth. She didn't deserve to be dragged into my mess of things. But if she teased me one more time, I might be tempted to.

"Believe whatever you want to believe but it doesn't make it true." Aerilyn stayed on the ground, humming to herself. I stood up and picked up my garden shears again to continue trimming the bushes.

I had only been staring at her to determine if I had compromised myself. The only feelings I had for the Princess were a constant burning hatred and overall annoyance. But I could admit she even had me fooled for a short time, just like all the other two-faced phonies in this palace. Hearing her talk about the Primis Defense Union as if we were no better than The Progression killed any kindness I might've felt towards her.

And so what if I wanted to make her feel better about failing the trial? We *all* needed her to focus on passing the others. And so what if my heart skipped a beat every time her smile grew large enough for me to see her cute dimples? She was the daughter of my enemies, the beautiful embodiment of everything I was supposed to loathe.

The only reason I was playing nice at all was to fulfill my role. Which hadn't been doing anything useful lately. It was almost comical how easily the Princess danced around her words like she was doing the world's most complicated waltz, one only she knew the steps to. But soon enough, I would know them just as well.

"Well, you seemed pretty sympathetic towards her when she told us she lost," Aerilyn said.

"Obviously. I may only mildly tolerate her, but I still don't want either of the other nominees on the throne."

She shrugged. "So you say," she sang. I finished with the row of bushes and moved on to the roses.

"Are you just going to lie here the rest of the time?"

She groaned. "I'm tired and it's too hot to be picking weeds." A mischievous grin spread across my face. It was time for payback. If there was one thing Aerilyn was most afraid of, it was bugs. Growing up in the snowy areas of Pria didn't lend her much experience with them. And because Newnina tended to be warm, we had them in never-ending quantities. But even the idea of a bug being near her was enough to make her freak out.

"Then I guess you'll have to deal with all the crawling spiders in the grass."

Her eyes shot open. "There are no spiders, you're just trying to scare me into working."

I only shrugged. "Then don't come crying to me when all the little spiders crawl up your dress and cover your whole body."

"Ilise..." she said, her voice wavering.

I started towards her slowly and lowered my voice. "And they start to cover you in all their little webs."

"Ilise... don't you say another word."

I came up beside her, ready to strike. "And they make a home out of your long hair, they would definitely like that."

"You're not gonna make me get up."

I jumped on top of her, tickling her. She laughed so hard half of them came out in snorts. "Fine fine fine... I'll get up... just stop... tickling... me," she pleaded in between giggles.

I let go of her and let her stand up. "You have now been demoted to *my* 'mildly tolerate' list."

I stood up slowly, racked with laughter. It felt good. She started picking out the rest of the weeds, and I moved on to the rose bushes.

"Next time you're getting weed duty," she grumbled.

"Whatever you say. And you're almost done anyway—"

A sharp slice of pain exploded in my chest. I heard the clang of the garden shears hitting the ground. My heart felt like it was in my throat. My limbs were not my own. I clutched my chest as I fell to my knees. The pain from the fall hardly registered when every nerve in my body was already aflame.

"Ilise, are you alright?" Aerilyn said, panic lacing her voice. I didn't even hear her come to my side, but there she was.

"Where are you?" The toneless voice echoed loudly in my head. Aerilyn? *"I've finally found you." What is going on?*

"I'm going to get help, just hold on." Aerilyn's voice sounded distant then. The pain felt as if I was being stabbed repeatedly by a flaming blade. I didn't know when Aerilyn came back with help. All I remembered was the sensation of being lifted before my eyes drifted closed. And I was finally graced with unconsciousness.

Chapter 16

Ilise

My eyes were anvils as I peeled them open, and my head pounded like a second heartbeat. I took in a deep breath of musty air. Yellow candle light cast a sickly glow over the room...wherever I was. I scanned the room, vision still blurred, and cabinets full of vials and jars lined the walls. Other small rickety beds were scattered through-out the room. Judging by the gray stone wall, I must have been on one of the lower levels of the palace. Aerilyn was dozed off against the wall on one of the chairs.

Slowly, I sat upright. More spots danced in my vision but cleared after a few moments. Aerilyn blinked her eyes open as the paper-like sheet rustled beneath me. "Aerilyn?" I said in a thick voice.

"Ilise," she said with a sigh of relief, rushing to my bedside. "How are you feeling?" She handed me a cup of water. I downed the whole cup, and it felt like heaven on my parched throat.

"I'm feeling better now. But what happened? How long have I been out?" I hadn't felt pain like that in years. But at least that time, I knew it was happening.

"Well, you were perfectly fine one moment and the next thing I knew you were on the ground in pain mumbling nonsense." She rubbed my shoulder in small circles. "I was scared for you, you've been asleep for a few hours." A few hours of my life, gone. A few hours where I was completely vulnerable in a palace probably infiltrated with Progression members. The thought sent chills down my spine and I suppressed a shudder.

"What was I mumbling?"

She waved her hand. "Just a bunch of gibberish. I'll go get Doctor Mendoza and tell her you're awake." She patted my shoulder and then left to go find the doctor.

I tried to think what could have caused me to collapse like that. Was it the heat? I never had much of a problem working in the heat. But I didn't think a heat stroke would make me feel like I'd been stabbed. And I had no pain anywhere else. Although the chest pain had gone away by now. Did someone do something to me?

A sharp pain exploded in the back of my head. I shut my eyes, trying to make the pain stop. I felt as if someone was smashing my head in. *I was thinking of something. What was I thinking about? What am I forgetting?* "Ilise?" Aerilyn returned with Doctor Mendoza.

"Is something wrong?" Her eyes were widened.

"No, why?" Her brow lowered in confusion. "You just had your eyes closed... and your hands were grasping your head." I tilted my head. Was I?

"I think I would remember if I did." She waved her hands in the air.

"Maybe I imagined it with all my worries."

Doctor Mendoza sat on the edge of my bed. "How are you feeling, Ilise?" Her voice was like a soft lullaby.

"I'm doing fine now."

She nodded. "That's good. You were probably getting too hot wearing that long sleeve uniform in the garden. Today was one of the hottest days of the summer. Way too hot for what you're wearing."

I lowered my eyes. "I guess so."

"I already talked to Ms. Kira to let you off the hook for tomorrow. Try to rest for the rest of the day and see how you feel then."

I shook her hand. "Thank you, Doctor Mendoza."

"Anytime. And if you start feeling worse, you know where to find me."

"Goodbye," Aerilyn waved.

I rose from the bed, and Aerilyn immediately ran towards me. "Calm down, I'm not gonna collapse again."

She linked her arm through mine. "Not taking any chances." In the back of my mind, I felt a thought trying to surface. What was I forgetting? I ignored the feeling. It was probably nothing anyway.

I expected us to go straight back to the apartment, but Aerilyn led us in the direction of the kitchen. "Why are we going to the kitchen?"

"Because," she said with a large smile, "What better way to ensure you are perfectly healthy than a snack?"

"Aerilyn, I'm not hungry." I hardly thought I would be able to eat anything after that ordeal.

"Not even for doughnuts?" she sang.

"Well... I *guess* I wouldn't object to doughnuts." She jumped with glee.

"Come on then, Seth just made a fresh batch." The sugary scent already wafted from the kitchen, making the hall smell like a bakery.

She half-pulled me down the hall to the kitchen. My nose was filled with the sweet aroma of fresh dessert. She pushed open the swinging doors and Seth's head perked up from where he hunched over the bowl of doughnuts, lightly dusting them with powdered sugar. "Ilise! I heard what happened and figured you would want something to make you feel better."

I put my hand over my heart. "Aw, thank you, Seth." He put a hand over the bowl of the still steaming doughnuts before I could grab one. He'd puffed the spherical dessert to almost the size of my palm. My mouth watered.

"I hope you share some with your roommates. My baking deserves to be shared."

I did a sarcastic pout. "I make no promises."

He chuckled.

Aerilyn covered the bowl with a napkin to keep them warm, and we hurried up to the apartment. Now that I was above ground, outside the windows, the sun cast an orange glow over the landscape. *Asleep for a few hours, yeah, sure.* We opened the door to see the others—minus the Princess—already inside. Everyone turned their heads when we entered. "We come bearing dessert," I said.

"Don't you usually eat dessert *after* dinner?" Chafik said.

"Are you turning down dessert?" Mathias said as he jumped up. "Just 'cause he wants to be a stick in the mud doesn't mean I don't want dessert early."

Chafik huffed. "I am not a stick in the mud. Right guys?" All of us avoided his gaze. "Traitors." We laughed and sat in the living room and dug into the bowl of doughnuts. Eventually, the Princess came out of her room and joined us.

I started to stand up to start cooking dinner, but Aerilyn stopped me. "I'll cook dinner tonight. Relax."

I shrugged and let her go into the kitchen. Not like I particularly enjoyed cooking anyways.

"Aw, I wanted Ilise's cooking," Mathias said.

"Well, Ilise collapsed in the garden earlier and is on doctor's orders to relax."

Chafik and the Princess dropped their doughnuts mid-bite. "You what?" The Princess said. She moved closer to me, her brown eyes wide with worry. It was almost like the gold flecks in them were spinning, energized by the pure power in her gaze.

I finished chewing before explaining. "I probably got too hot while working in the gardens earlier. But I'm fine now." I locked eyes with the Princess.

"Are you sure?"

"Yes." *Why is she so concerned?*

"Well, why are you wearing the winter uniforms? I *just* did the laundry so you should've had plenty of clean summer uniforms." Mathias said.

I couldn't tell them the real reason. "I was in a rush this morning and threw on the closest clothes to my bed." I took another bite of the doughnut, letting out a silent sigh as the vanilla and nutmeg spread across my tastebuds.

"Well maybe it wasn't such a good idea to dress like you were traveling through the forest in the dead of winter when it's hot enough to cook an egg outside," Chafik said.

"Hey," Aerilyn said from the kitchen, "Since you have time to make jokes, boys, why don't you come to help me set the table." They both groaned but left for the kitchen. I heard paper fly underneath the door and turned to see a letter had been delivered.

My heart skipped a beat. Maybe Kass had managed to get around all the intercepted letters. I stood up and picked up the letter as fast as my tired feet would take me, only for it to be addressed to Chafik. It was in a fancy and loopy handwriting Kass would never use. Hers always looked like she wrote it while riding a horse at full speed. My shoulders sagged.

The only contact I had with them was when Rori had visited me during the Heircestrial ball. The silence was unbearable.

"Chafik, you got a letter," I said, trying not to sound disappointed. He came out of the kitchen carrying two steaming bowls.

"Just put it on the table, I'll read it in a second." Mathias came out carrying two more bowls and placed them on the table.

"Why did you make steaming hot soup for dinner? It's been sweltering all day," he said.

Aerilyn poked her head out of the kitchen. "It's the only thing I can make."

Mathias put a hand on my shoulder. "Ilise, never let this girl cook dinner again."

"Hey, at least it tastes good," she countered.

"You have to admit it probably tastes very nice," I said.

The Princess walked over to the table. "Okay, stop complaining and eat the wonderful dinner Aerilyn cooked, " the Princess said.

Aerilyn pointed the dirty ladle at her. "See, Yorena agrees with me."

We all sat down to eat, and Chafik opened his letter. His face brightened. "It's from back home." *Guess that makes one of us.* Home. The last home I had was miles away, too far out of my reach to even imagine being there. No Progression members, no princesses, no bothersome jobs, and no having to hide my arms wherever I went. A place where I could work towards my one true goal. Revenge. Rori had said just a little longer, then I could forget about this place, forget about the Princess, and stop The Progression.

Chafik scanned the letter, and Mathias read it over his shoulder. I watched both of their faces harden the longer they read the letter.

"What's wrong?" Aerilyn asked.

"It's gotten worse." He put his spoon down. "My family lives near the border of Faveru and Nitedand so anything bad that happens in Nitedand easily affects them."

The Princess nodded.

"For quite a while the protests, rallies, and riots were confined to Nitedand. But now they've started moving closer to the border and the border guards in Faveru are barely holding them back from spreading. They wrote they were planning to move somewhere else to avoid all the violence."

My appetite became nonexistent and I pushed away the bowl. "That's awful," the Princess said. I bit my tongue before I could scoff. The tone of her voice sounded as if she'd had lessons on fake sympathy. Now that I thought about it, she probably had. What was the point of having power if you weren't going to use it? Half-hearted words of sympathy could only do so much, if anything.

"I'm supposed to be meeting with my parents in the coming days to discuss our strategy." She set her gaze on Chafik. "Don't worry, we'll make sure your family and everyone else will be perfectly safe." This time I did roll my eyes. Aerilyn saw and kicked my shin under the table.

"Ow."

"Something wrong?" Mathias said, trying to suppress a snicker.

"Nothing," I said through gritted teeth, "Just bumped my knee on the table."

"Well I think I've had enough impending doom talk for one night, I'm gonna head to my room," Mathias said. He lightly punched Aerilyn's shoulder.

"Thanks for dinner, it wasn't too bad."

"Told you so," Aerilyn said.

Chafik also went to his room half an hour later after cleaning the mess from Aerilyn's cooking, his usual upbeat demeanor squashed. He shuffled his feet to his room, hunched over, staring at the floor. I wished I could help his family. But they were in Faveru, and we barely had any permanent bases in Faveru. The province was mostly dense forest that was either populated by large animals, or was the site of a lumber farm. Building a base there would draw too much attention.

Aerilyn and I finished the doughnuts on the couch. Both of our faces were coated in a layer of sugar. "You eat like a child," she said.

"Your face isn't much better." She wiped the sugar from her face. It was moments like this where I could easily pretend my friendship with Aerilyn wasn't fake. I could just be a normal girl from a small village eating a batch of delicious doughnuts. I wasn't a spy. There was no Progression, and there was no Union. My family hadn't been killed in a brutal attack, and my village still stood. I didn't have to lie about basically everything about myself and Aerilyn knew everything about me. It was a nice fantasy, but I couldn't live in it for too long. Returning to the real world would only hurt the more I thought of it.

"I need to clean myself up." She stood to leave and rested her hand on my shoulder. "Are you sure you're doing alright?" Concern was etched into her furrowed brows. I didn't want her to worry about me. The only person who needed to worry about me was myself.

"I'm fine. I didn't mean to scare you."

She exhaled slowly. "Okay. Goodnight." She walked into her room, leaving me alone.

The Princess walked back into the room and I stared at her dark silhouette leaning against the wall. "Are you just going to stare at me like a stalker?" I said. She said nothing and walked to the couch.

"Why do you always wear winter clothes?" she said, still staring at me. I was done with this girl. No answer I gave was ever enough to satisfy her.

"I told you, I was in a rush. And I like them better." They were my armor against curious souls and any unwelcome memories that tried to make an appearance.

"You passed out in the garden. And during all of our training sessions, you look uncomfortable. Why don't you just wear more breathable clothes?"

I started to leave the room before she could try digging into my life any longer. To hells with protecting her. I was one more question away from making her stay quiet.

"Running away from me does not count as answering."

I bit my tongue and gave her a forced smile. "In my book it does."

She motioned for me to sit on the chair across from her. "Well we're going to be playing by my book tonight. Sit." I was almost taken aback. She never used a commanding tone with me. My brain told me to leave, but my gut told me to stay. It'd never led me astray before, but around her, I couldn't trust it. Against my better judgment, I sat down.

She moved, so her head hung off the front of the chair, long curls falling to the floor. "You are a curiosity to me," she said. I rarely got to see her like this, acting like a normal human being rather than *Princess Yorena Schaefer Heir to the Erean throne*. The smile on her face reached her eyes, and I could see one dimple making an appearance.

It was almost cute. Wait, why was I thinking that? She was everything I was supposed to hate. I shouldn't have thoughts like that. I pushed them to the back of my mind, burying them as deep as I could.

"Curiosity, why?" I asked.

She shrugged. "Everyone's shared at least something about themselves. But you keep a curtain draped over your life. I want to see what would happen if I ripped away those curtains, finally revealing the true Ilise."

"Well, maybe I like my curtain." My curtain kept me safe. Alive.

"Ilise, can I ask just one question?" I rubbed the tiredness out of my eyes. I'm surprised I was even tired after sleeping for half the day. Answering one question wouldn't do any harm. And I was still keeping her at arm's length... or maybe an arm and a leg.

"Fine one question and then I'm going to bed."

She squealed, and I covered my ears. She sat up. "When was the last time you spoke to your family?"

Well. I didn't expect that. "Why do you ask?"

She moved so she was sitting next to me, subjecting my nostrils to her sweet, rosy scent. "When you were poisoned, you were talking in your sleep." *Talking in my sleep? Hells.* There was no way I could've filtered what I'd said. What had I said to make her ask that question? All it would've taken was one wrong sentence and my cover would've been blown.

"And you were saying sorry to your mother. Did something happen?" Still bad, but not as bad as it could've been. *Should I give her the truth?* She was staring at me with these wide eyes. I felt like she would believe any answer I gave, but what would the harm be in telling the truth just this once?

"I left my family to become a servant the day I turned thirteen and broke their hearts." The Princess' eyes that were once filled with open curiosity clouded with sympathy. I didn't need her sympathy. I did what had to be done, and I would do a thousand more times if I had to. "A drought was killing the family farm and I wanted to help."

Too many nights I had awoken to Mama and Papa crying over how they were going to support the five of us. Too many times we had to eat the rotting, dried remains of what was left of our family farm. I couldn't sit while my parents tried to get us through it when I knew there was something I could do to help.

"And your parents agreed to this?"

I crossed my arms. "I didn't give them much of a choice. They didn't know until they read the note left for them." The note I wrote in the dead of night. I never got the chance to ask them how they'd reacted to it. Another thing I had taken from me.

"I would say I'm glad you're here regardless of the reason, but I'm sorry this is how you ended up here." It wasn't like she had control over the weather. She kept apologizing for everything, as if it could ease any of the heartbreak.

I stood up from my chair, ready to go back to my room. I swallowed the lump beginning to form in my throat, willing my voice to keep steady. I thought I'd be able to think about that day, their blank faces, blood pooling on the weathered hardwood floors, without tears. Clearly, I'd been wrong.

"There's nothing to be sorry about." I started walking, but she ran in front of me and pulled me into a hug. I froze, unsure how to react. She was tall enough that her chin easily rested on top of my head. She was so soft. I couldn't remember the last time I'd received a real hug. Aerilyn knew I wasn't the biggest fan of them, so she'd stopped trying a while ago.

A small tear had managed to slip down my face and I didn't notice until the Princess reached down to wipe it off my cheek. "I don't care. I'm still sorry you had to come here so young." I finally relaxed into the hug and let the feelings I'd kept down for so long come to the surface, burying my face into the crook of her neck.

I pretended like I didn't mind coming here when I was still a child. I pretended like I didn't lie awake some nights thinking of what would've happened if I'd never left them all those years ago. It hurt. It hurt knowing I'd left without even saying goodbye, without a last "I love you".

She pulled away slightly so I could look her in the eye. Our faces were so close it felt like we were sharing the same breath. I'd never noticed the slight gap in between her two front teeth. It made her look friendlier, an imperfection that only added to her overall beauty. Her skin slightly reddened and I realized I had been staring at her mouth for who knew how long. I was the one to finally break away from the embrace and the space around me felt so much colder.

"I know you said one question, but how did you find it in yourself to make that big of a sacrifice?"

I pondered. The need to help the people I love had been ingrained in me for as long as I could remember. There was nothing I needed to find in myself. It was always there. And still was. I struggled to stop small tears from falling.

I looked up into her eyes, open to me, waiting for an answer. I was consumed by the need to answer her. To answer the question I had never been able to answer out loud before. "We all have to make sacrifices sometimes, even if we're the only ones willing to make them. My family was happy, so I say it was worth it." I didn't wait for a response. I went into my room and shut the door. I threw myself onto my bed and let the flow of tears finally be released.

What would my life be like if I hadn't left them all those years ago?

"Where are you, little one?"

Chapter 17

Princess Yorena

I STRETCHED AGAINST THE back of my chair after sitting at my desk for almost three hours. I'd been going through all the incident and violence reports I could find from Faveru and Nitedand, hoping it wasn't as bad as what Chafik's family was saying. It turned out to be so much worse.

Rioters had attacked the border guards. As far as we could tell, no one that was sent into Nitedand had come out. Nitedand had almost become a fortress of a province, a kingdom of its own. Most people who lived near any of Nitedand's borders had been abandoning their homes to flee. Even scarce reports of people fleeing to Croaga were coming in. Knots began to form in my stomach.

Hundreds of families, fleeing the place they'd made their home. No one should have to go through that. They were innocents getting caught in the middle of a battle so much larger than them. I could barely imagine having to flee my only home, unsure if I would ever see it again. And if I did, if it was still standing.

The more I thought about it, the more my head pounded. I pushed away from my desk and laid on my bed. The light from the rising sun warmed my face. It still did nothing to quell the thoughts racing through my head. *Is there about to be a war? Could we prevent it? Who would even be fighting who? What is everyone fighting for?*

It was becoming more and more apparent that we couldn't even keep the palace safe, let alone the entire kingdom. The bell tolled seven times. I groaned. I was supposed to sit through another strategy meeting with the Commander and my parents soon. They seldom let me talk. They only allowed me to sit there as they threw around ideas ranging from absolutely terrible to mildly decent, chiding me if I tried to interject. I was starting to get the feeling that if Ilise were the one strategizing, our problems would've been fixed ages ago.

The conversation we'd had the previous night replayed in my head. The more I learned about her, the more she amazed me. As a child, she already knew how to make the necessary sacrifices for the better. Yet here I was, moping on my bed, about to be late for the meeting. My stomach twisted more. If only she could lend me some of her strength, some of her sureness in what she was doing.

Maybe she could help me. I rose from my bed and walked out of my room. No one else was awake yet, so Ilise must still be in her room. I looked down and realized I was still in my nightgown and barefoot, but it was only Ilise. I hesitated before knocking. *Am I being dumb? Will she think I'm weak to come crawling to her for help?* I pushed the thought to the back of my mind and knocked. I twiddled with the frilly hem of my nightgown until she opened the door, still rubbing the sleep from her puffy eyes. She removed the bonnet covering her hair at the sight of me.

"Did I wake up late?" she yawned. "I was about to start on breakfast."

"No," I said quickly. "Can I come in?" She froze for a second, then opened the door for me. My face was met with a warm breeze from the open window and I looked around her room. It was bare of any decorations except for a princess doll sitting on her perfectly made bed. I pointed to it. "I like your doll," I said. She mumbled something incoherent and sat on the edge of the bed.

I sat on the other edge of the bed, hyper-aware of the fact the mattress was small enough for our knees to touch. I still remembered how it felt to hug her from last night. She'd been unwilling to relax into the hug at first. I think I'd caught her by surprise. And when she stared at my mouth for what felt like a lifetime, I was sure she was going to kiss me. I'd wanted her to. I still wanted her to. "I need your advice," I said, trying to push down thoughts of last night's hug from my mind.

Her brows furrowed as she looked up at me. "Why do you need advice from me?"

"Because you're, most likely, the only one who can help me." She motioned for me to start talking. I took a deep breath. "Lately I've been in and out of constant meetings with my parents and the Commander trying to strategize on how to combat The Progression and Primis Defense Union, and I have no clue what to do. And even when I think I have an idea, it gets shut down almost immediately."

Her face remained blank. "What does that have to do with me?"

"I want to know how you're so sure of yourself." She looked taken aback, almost surprised though I couldn't see why. She never faltered, never second-guessed herself, everything she did had a purpose. It was one of the things I admired most about her.

"Sure of myself?"

I stood from the bed and walked over to the open window. Breathing in the fresh morning summer air.

"Yes. Just last night you were telling me of making sacrifices at such a young age without hesitation. Yet I can't seem to be sure of myself when it comes to helping my kingdom. Or even manage to voice an idea without getting shut down immediately. And I feel as if every time I open my mouth, I'm disappointing my kingdom. What kind of Queen will I be if I can't help my people?" I knew my voice was beginning to waver, but I couldn't bring myself to fix it.

I didn't hear her come up behind me until I felt her hand on my shoulder. The knots in my stomach were replaced with a familiar fluttering that seemed to accompany any touch from Ilise.

"I wasn't sure," she said.

I turned around, meeting her churning eyes. "Then how did you do it?"

A small smile broke onto her face. "I guess I knew it would be better than the alternative in the long run."

I let out a hoarse laugh. Spirits, this girl was so strong. "At least you knew what the alternative would be."

"Do you not?"

Did I know the alternative? It could be a world where Imperium were all-powerful lords over Primis. But would it even get that bad? If anything, the Primis Defense Union was the bigger threat. Especially after they attacked the Heircestrial ball. What would that world look like? Too much was unknown. And everything we *did* know doesn't bode well for Erea.

"How am I supposed to know the alternative if I don't even have ideas to choose between?"

She took a small step closer. "The same way you managed to get both of us out of danger without a second thought, without letting yourself succumb to your fear which is exactly what you are doing now."

I fiddled with the fabric of my dress. Except I was utterly terrified during the attack. It was a miracle, pure luck I'd been able to get us out "I wouldn't say I'm afraid."

She tilted her head. "Aren't you?"

I was, but it didn't need to be said out loud. Too many lives were at stake, and not enough was being done to protect them. I didn't know how. "That night, the only people who would've gotten hurt were the two of us if I'd failed. If I failed now, it would be the entire kingdom that would fall."

"Then you won't fail," she put simply. I removed her hand from my arm and started pacing the room. She leaned against a bed post, arms crossed against her chest.

"You act like it's that simple," I said.

"'Cause, it is," she said, not leaving room for argument.

"No, it is not." There were too many things that could go wrong. I wouldn't be able to live with myself if a decision I made was the reason the kingdom fell. "I don't want to disappoint my parents and my kingdom. What good am I if I can't be the one thing I was made to be? Being a Queen is all I'm good for." It was all I'd ever be good for.

"Stop doing that."

I turned towards her. "Doing what?"

"Overthinking and doubting yourself."

"I am not."

"The tone of your voice would say otherwise." I opened my mouth to respond, but none came. "If you overthink every little thing that could go wrong, you'll be blinded to what could go right." She patted a space beside her on the bed, I sat down. "It's impossible for everything to go right, that's the worst part of being a leader. But if you focus too much on that, then you'll be stopping the good things from happening." Her voice carried a wisdom that was only granted to a select few. I should've known this. I had been in leadership training lessons for as long as I could remember. Yet, only now was I absorbing it.

"That... makes sense."

She nodded. "And while you're at it, try using that 'I'm the boss of you' voice. I'm sure they'll listen to you."

"I do not have that voice."

The corner of her mouth tilted up. "Yeah, and I'm not the stubborn servant who has to make an equally stubborn Princess her breakfast."

I rolled my eyes.

"You know I'm right."

I glanced at the clock against the wall and chose to ignore Ilise's comment. I had to leave for the meeting. "I should go before I'm late." I stood up and walked towards the door, my hand on the handle before I stopped. I hurried back towards Ilise and brought her into an awkward hug, given I was already taller than her and she was still sitting down. She was stiff at first, then I felt her arms go around me, much quicker than last night. She was warming up to me.

"Thank you."

"No problem, Princess." I became very aware of the fact I was only wearing a very thin nightgown and pulled away, my face burning. I started to walk out of the room until Ilise said, "You aren't a disappointment to the kingdom. And every time you try to convince me otherwise, I'll have no choice but to take away the practice daggers." An amused smile returned to my face and a warm feeling filled my chest. "If we all became what we were made to be, our world would be a very boring place. Don't let yourself be put in a box. There's more to you than being Queen."

How I wished for that to be true. But if Ilise thought it was, then I would have to try to prove her right. I waved to her once more before returning to my room, frigid in comparison to Ilise's room. I shivered. I was awake over an hour earlier than Aerilyn typically rose, so I would have to get myself ready. With only ten minutes to dress and arrive at the meeting room, I opened my closet door and pulled out a simple short-sleeved green silk dress that fell right below my knees.

Transitioning to the bathroom, I studied my appearance in the mirror. My hair didn't look too bad. I used my fingers to comb through the tangles and deemed it presentable enough. I picked up my crown, about to place it on my head, before I remembered. I could never wear it again unless I won Heircestrial, something that spiked dread in my stomach. Even after almost two weeks, I found myself reaching for its familiar weight.

I left the apartment and began walking towards the staircase. My head turned at the sound of footsteps behind me and was met with the unwelcome green eyes of Nikos, Oliver trailing behind him. They gave me a friendly wave. Neither of them had a reason to be up this early. Why were they up this early?

"Where are you two off to?"

He strode towards me with his newfound confidence after passing the test. As if he needed any more.

"Well, last time I checked all of us were in the running to become Heir, so it would make sense that *all* of us would be present at the meetings."

I stared at them open-mouthed. "Neither of you have been in attendance for the last two weeks."

He shrugged, a smirk still plastered on his face. "The King invited us to the one being held today."

I gritted my teeth and turned back towards the staircase. Nikos, as usual, dressed more formally than what was required. He wore a pair of black dress pants and a lilac ruffled silk shirt, while Oliver wore less formal beige pants and a simple white tunic.

We arrived at the small meeting room, a boxy room bare except for a wooden table, some chairs to match, and warm candles lining the windowless walls. The only people present were my parents and the Commander. Nikos bowed upon entry, and Oliver followed suit. I immediately took my chair to the left of my mother, the other nominees sitting across from me. My father rose from his chair and clapped his hands together.

"Welcome nominees," he said. "I thought it would be a good idea to have all of you sit in on these meetings. There is no telling which one of you will win." He said that last sentence with a smile, one that didn't reach his eyes. "Feel free to voice your ideas as we talk." He sat back down. Of course, *now* he was letting anyone voice an idea. A few days ago, I had to sit through another lecture on when to and not speak because I decided to say something for once.

"The goal for this morning's meeting is to decide what to do in response to the last attack on the palace." Nikos started to open his mouth, but I spoke first, taking Ilise's advice to heart.

"Well, it is evident that someone from inside the palace had helped them. Otherwise, they never would have gotten even close to getting past the guards always posted outside." My mother nodded approvingly, and my smile widened.

"Are you saying there are spies among us?" the Commander prompted.

"Yes," I said with my chin held high. To stage an attack of that caliber would've been next to impossible to do alone. Even the one at the summer ball should've been impossible.

"But we have not hired any new staff in the last few months. Whoever they may be would have to have been here for a while," the Commander said. The thought sent a chill up my spine. A few months could be enough time to learn about every nook and cranny in this palace. When the guards rotate, weaker entrance and exit points, and when certain events happen weeks ahead of the public announcement.

"Do you suggest we interrogate every single staff member in the palace?" Oliver asked.

"No, that would alert whoever it is that we are onto them. It will attract too much attention," Nikos countered.

More arguments broke out on how to find the spy, or spies. News of any investigation would spread through the palace like wildfire and scare away the guilty party. Between gossiping staff and nobles looking for something to entertain themselves, secrets never stayed secrets for long around here.

"How about we search for any proof of communication?" Nikos said.

"Search how? Do you have the magical power to find evidence?" I said. A muscle in his jaw twitched. *Ha.*

"No *Princess*, but you do have a large army of guards at this palace who could search for us." I looked at my mother, and she shrugged.

"I am not sure we are following you, Nominee Nikos," Father said.

He sat back in his chair before explaining. "We just have to summon all of the staff into one area, make sure they are all accounted for, and then have the guards search all of their rooms for any proof of communication with the scum who call themselves the Primis Defense Union."

My jaw tensed. "That would be a complete invasion of privacy," I said through gritted teeth.

Oliver spoke up. "I agree with Yorena. Searching everyone's belongings would be a heinous solution." At least *someone* was thinking straight. The only thing that separated us from the Union and The Progression was our morals. And a forced search would make us no better than either of those organizations.

"Nominee Nikos has proposed the best option we have," the Commander said. "I could have all of the guards we can spare ready to search every room by this evening." I tried speaking up again, but everyone kept speaking over me. Nothing I would say could change their minds. I wanted to find the possible spies more than anyone, but I knew there was a better way to do it, there had to be, I just needed more time to think of one.

"So it is settled, we will summon every staff member into the courtyard and then have all the guards search their rooms," Father said. My stomach bubbled with the desire to scream at everyone in the room. To try and talk sense into them. *"Don't let yourself be put in a box."* I shot up from my chair.

"After they find out about this, and they will, you *will* lose their trust. Which is the last thing we need right now." Mother yanked me back into my chair by my wrist. I huffed.

"That is a necessary risk," she said. I could not believe my ears. How were we supposed to maintain the trust of the whole kingdom if our own staff didn't trust us?

"If you give me some time, I could come up with a different solution," I suggested. Everyone but Oliver ignored me as if I hadn't even spoken. They shot me a sympathetic look.

The Commander stood up from his chair. "We should be ready to go at the eighth bell toll tonight."

"Thank you, Commander." my father said. The Commander gave a slight bow before leaving the room. "Nominee Nikos and Nominee Oliver, you are also free to go."

"Thank you for giving us the honor to help," Nikos said.

I scoffed. Mother's hazel eyes churned with fury. Oliver and Nikos bowed as well. Nikos hurried out but Oliver walked up to me, leaning in close to my ear.

"Just so you know," they whispered, "I'm on your side of this." They walked out without another word, leaving me to my parent's fury.

Father turned to me, his mouth pressed into a hard line and I braced for the worst. "And you, my dear, are not dismissed yet. How many times are we going to have to go over how you are expected to act?"

I slumped in my chair, the stiff back digging into my spine. "But what Nikos is proposing is a blatant invasion of privacy that will end in nothing good for us. And you're wrong for agreeing with him."

Mother slammed her hand on the table. "That is no way to speak to your father, Yorena." I looked into my mother's eyes. I never noticed the fine lines forming around her eyes and on her forehead. I could have sworn they were not there before. They were probably just as, if not more, stressed about this as me.

"Would you rather the alternative?" he said. My mind went back to my conversation with Ilise. She only came to work here because the alternative was worse. The alternative now would be the spy or spies would continue to feed information to the Union, and the attacks would only continue, which would only push us one step closer to the kingdom falling. But if Nikos' plan went south, then we'd lose the trust of the palace staff, and the palace couldn't operate without them. It would be the next step to our destruction.

"If what we decide has consequences as bad as the alternative, how can we say it's the right thing to do?"

Father exhaled and rubbed his forehead. "It is a risk we have to take. When you become Queen, you will understand."

I released an empty laugh. "You hardly seem to care about who wins Heircestrial."

"Of course we care, Yorena," Mother argued. *Lies.*

"Then how come the two of you have done nothing but kiss-up to the other nominees. You didn't even ask how I was doing after I failed the first test. My *servants* were more concerned than my own parents." I sat there, stunned I had spoken to them like that. The slow-building anger I'd pushed down since Heircestrial started was starting to leak out.

"I'm sorry you feel that way," Father said. "We only wanted to help you focus on the next test rather than dwelling on the past." But parents were supposed to be there when something bad happened. They were supposed to be your biggest supporters, not drill sergeants.

"It may feel like we are being cold towards you, but you need to focus on your job of winning Heircestrial and nothing more," he said. He pushed away from the table and left the room, grumbling as he left. Mother placed a hand on my knee, her hazel eyes warm and open to me for the first time in a while.

"We love you Yorena, don't ever doubt that." At that, she left as well.

I was supposed to assert myself and actually help for once, but I couldn't even stop *this* from happening. And I knew my parents said they loved and cared about me, but it was beginning to feel like I was something replaceable to them, so long as they ended up fine. My hands started to shake, and I took a deep breath to calm my nerves. The next test would most likely not be for a few more days. I had time to prepare. Hopefully, Chafik's book could help me know what to expect. My own parents hardly had faith in me, and Nikos was continuing to one-up me in everything.

Now it was my turn.

Chapter 18

Ilise

"**I**T'S A SWORD, NOT a crowbar. Hold it correctly," I said.

The Princess grunted in frustration and dropped the sword, the loud clang reverberating throughout the room. "Having an attitude won't fix your form, pick it up."

She tugged on a stray curl that escaped from its bun as she chewed on her bottom lip. "Sorry," she said softly. I didn't know why she was acting like this. Her skills had gotten better over the last couple weeks, and she was a much faster learner than I gave her credit for. Much faster than I had been. It had taken me almost a full year of bruises and busted knuckles to get to her level.

For the last hour, she had a complete personality change. Yanking at strands of her hair, making mistakes she hadn't made in days, easily frustrated over little things, barely even looking me in the eye. Could it have been because of the meeting she was talking about earlier?

I'd been shocked when she knocked on my door this morning asking for help. I would be the last person to know anything about running a kingdom, yet she still trusted me to help her. I didn't want to think deeper on how that made me feel. She trusted me, and I think I was beginning to trust her.

"Is this right?" she asked, holding the sword in front of her. I studied her new grip on the handle.

"Your hands are still too close together." She dropped her arms, almost tearing my tunic as the sharp end plummeted to the ground. *What is her problem?*

"How is this too close? I can control it fine." Ugh. Okay, if she didn't want to actually take my advice, I would show her how she was wrong. I grabbed one of the other practice swords off the wall. It was a long silver sword tapered at the tip with a smooth leather grip. Though the real versions of this sword were typically made from iron, I guess most beginners didn't need to be wielding a blade sharp enough to cut through flesh as if it were nothing but air.

I walked back over to her, and she eyed the sword in my hand as I raised it. She gulped. "What are you doing?" she asked tentatively.

"If you think you have the correct grip, then try to disarm me."

She shrugged. "That should be simple enough."

"Then let's begin." She charged for me first, and I quickly dipped under her first swing. My sword may have been much longer, but I knew how to control it. She slashed out again, striking the very tip of my blade. We became locked in a standstill. I twisted around, pushing against her with all my strength. She stumbled backward a few steps but remained standing. *Nice job, Princess.*

I thought she was getting out whatever was making her so antsy. "Is that all you got?" I taunted. Droplets of sweat dripped down her brow. She was panting but stalked back towards me, eyes more alive than they had been all day.

"Not even close." Before she could strike, I charged towards her with both hands on the sword. She planted her feet, preparing to block me. But I angled my blade so she wouldn't be able to twist the sword enough to block me. I propelled my blade at the very tip of hers, and it clattered to the ground with a loud clang. She let out a small yelp, watching her sword fly from her hands.

"How did you do that?" I picked up the blade and placed it in her hands. I moved her smooth hands so they were farther apart on the grip.

"If your hands are too close together, you lose control and mobility. Don't make me have to raise my sword again."

She curtsied with exaggerated hand motions. "Yes, oh great teacher."

I moved my hand to my hip. "Real cute. I can see you've finally fixed your attitude."

She winced. "Sorry. I've just been stressed after the meeting I had this morning." I felt pulled to her, needing to be closer to her.

"Why?"

She waved her hand. "Nothing you need to worry about."

I shrugged. "Guess that's fair. You worry about everything anyways," I said, trying to bait her into talking.

"I do not."

"You know, every time you say that it proves I'm right." I looked up into her eyes, churning with an emotion I could not decipher. I found my hand moving towards her shoulder. "But seriously, is everything okay?"

She wiggled away from my hand. "Yes, I'm sure." I stared at her, wondering what was wrong with her today. I watched her quickly walk over to the punching dummies. This morning she came into my room at the crack of dawn asking for advice, and now she was acting like she wanted to run as far from me as possible.

But wasn't that what I'd wanted? Was that what I wanted anymore? I thought every minute of my assignment would be worse than being stabbed over and over again. Yet, I found my eyes lingering on her during meals, feeling an urge to pull her into a hug every time I saw her upset, which was quite a lot. Was that completely wrong? She was the daughter of the people who had yet to do anything to change the fact that mine and so many other people's lives were living hells. I wasn't supposed to like her. What were these feelings? The queasiness in my stomach, the urges to comfort her, the way I tried to make her smile. Just to see those damned dimples of hers.

I walked over to the dummy she was practicing on. "I'm not an idiot, something is *clearly* bothering you."

She sighed, continuing to go at the dummy, delivering round after round of forceful punches. "And like I said before, it is none of your concern," she said, her eyes trained at her fists in front of her. Her punches became faster and faster and chunks of material flew off the dummy. Her leg swung in a wide kick, knocking it multiple feet in front of her and it broke into two pieces on the floor. She took a knee as sweat poured down her face, breaths coming in pants.

"Did that make you feel better?" She slumped onto the ground, staring at her hands in front of her.

"No..." I sat across from her.

"Then why don't you talk to me." I scooted closer to her and lifted her head, forcing her to look me in the eye. My hand lingered on her chin for a few more seconds before letting go.

She pressed her mouth into a thin line. "I'm not allowed to tell you."

I snorted. "Since when has that stopped you?" She opened her mouth to speak, but both our heads turned at the sound of paper skidding to a halt.

"I'm supposed to be part of your support system for this absurd Heircestrial thing so you should probably tell me."

Again she opened her mouth to speak but rushed to pick up the delivered message. Her eyes scanned the letter, hands shaking. "I... uh, have to go now. I'll see you later." Before I could say goodbye, she grabbed her crystal and practically ran out the door. Now, something was *definitely* up.

I started picking up the remains of the practice dummy to throw away. If she could do that without her crystal, I couldn't even imagine what she would be like with it on. Couldn't I? During the attack on the Heircestrial ball, I hadn't seen a hint of fear in her eyes. Running straight into the danger, looking like she would kill anyone who dared to touch her. She had never looked more beautiful.

"Maybe she was just nervous about Heircestrial, it's all that's been on everyone's mind anyway," Aerilyn said as she sprawled all over my bed and I braided my hair into a crown. I had asked her what she thought of the Princess' behavior. There had to be something I was missing. If the previous night was any indication, I thought she actually liked me.

Sweat still beaded on my forehead from today's training and I had to change from the long-sleeved uniform, to the summer uniform with a cover-up. It was much thinner than what I would prefer, but I wasn't keen on passing out from the heat.

"Possibly. And she hasn't come back yet from wherever she was summoned," I said.

Aerilyn shuffled to the edges of my bed. "But enough about that, I feel like we haven't talked in a while." I finished my braid and leaned against the bedpost.

"What do you mean, we talk everyday."

She groaned. "Lately, we've only talked at meals since you're always somewhere no one can find you, or with Yorena." Keeping an eye out for any danger in a giant palace didn't exactly leave much time for everything else. But that's how it had always been. Why was she having a problem with it now? I felt like Aerilyn said the Princess' name with a hint of malice, but it was too subtle for me to tell.

"Are you jealous that the Princess has been spending more time with me or something?" I joked. Aerilyn's face told me she didn't find it very funny. Was she actually jealous? I had been spending more time with the Princess lately, but that was only to complete my mission, however, she couldn't know that.

"No, I'm upset that my 'best friend' hasn't been acting like much of a best friend lately." I was trying my best, but there was only so much I could do.

"I've just been busy lately," I said. The simplest lies were always the best ones to use, but that meant they could easily be overused. How many times had I shrugged Aerilyn off claiming I was "busy"? I wouldn't have enough time to think through every instance.

Her face contorted in frustration. "You always say that. But that excuse isn't going to work anymore." What was wrong with her? "The only one of your excuses that's worse than it, is when you say you're 'not a fan of sharing', to avoid telling me anything about yourself."

Is that what she was mad about? It wasn't anything personal, nobody was supposed to know who I truly was. It kept me, and everyone around me safe. "You know plenty about me," I said.

She sat up in the bed, crossing her arms. "All I know is the name of your village, and that your family is gone. I can hardly say I know you."

"Do *not* bring my family into this," I snapped.

She scrambled up from the bed, so mad I could almost see a red tint to her pale skin. "No. You don't get to be upset. Even Mathias has shared more about himself than you have."

I scoffed. "That's only because he has feelings for you."

Aerilyn fisted her dress in her hands, looking up at me with more fury than I'd ever seen in her. "That has nothing to do with this. How am I supposed to call you my best friend when you won't even talk to me?"

I had known from the beginning it would be a bad idea to form any attachments to people here. I'd thought I could handle one friend, and could allow myself to have one person separating me from total isolation. But I guess that was a mistake.

"And I saw you talking to Yorena last night."

I froze.

"How come you told her about your past after knowing her for two weeks when it took me four years to earn it?" I didn't have an answer. The Princess confused me. Sometimes, I felt myself drawn to her. And I could see she truly wanted the best for the kingdom, though she was misguided after living in the palace her whole life. And other times, I found myself disappointed, thinking she knew better than to fall for the lies the crown latches onto. And despite that, I still felt like I could tell her about my past. I wanted her to learn about me. I wanted her to know me, to see me for who I truly was. And I just never felt that way about Aerilyn.

"I don't know," I said finally.

Aerilyn scoffed. "Some best friend you are."

"Then maybe I'm not your best friend," I seethed. Her face softened and tears sprouted in her widened eyes. *Too far Ilise.* She started to back away from me. "Aerilyn, wait," I pleaded. She scrambled out the door, slamming it shut behind her and taking the only friendship I had here with her.

My heart dropped into my stomach. I shouldn't have said that. Why did I say that? Tears sprung in my eyes. How could I have been so heartless towards her? I knew I needed her, yet I pushed her away even farther.

The door knob twisted and I ran towards the door, expecting Aerilyn, but I came face to face with Chafik.

"Are you ok?" he asked. I looked over his shoulder for a head of blonde hair. I needed to apologize. I needed to fix this.

"Have you seen Aerilyn?"

He quirked an eyebrow. "No. She already left with Mathias so I came to get you."

I paused. "Get me for what?"

"We got an air message. All palace staff are being summoned to the courtyard. Apparently, the King and Queen have an announcement for us." I didn't have time for the King and Queen's antics right now. But Chafik didn't give me much of a choice as he grabbed my wrist and pulled me out of the apartment.

Chafik released my hand and I kept pace with him as we hurried down the hall. More staff poured out of rooms, all heading to the courtyard. The corridor became a sea of yellow, our uniforms all blending us together. I hadn't been out there since the Summer Ball as an extensive amount of it had been destroyed. "What do you think this announcement is?" Chafik asked.

"I don't know." An announcement that required all staff in the palace meant something big, but I was too strung up on Aerilyn to think of what it could be about. Would she even forgive me if I tried to fix this? And even if she did forgive me, I wouldn't deserve it.

"Ilise, what's wrong," he asked again.

"I got mad at Aerilyn and said something I shouldn't have." He fell silent after that.

Cool summer air washed over my face as we stepped into the courtyard. The sun was low on the horizon, and stars dotted the dark blue sky. Other staff waited in the courtyard, chatting amongst themselves. The torches that had been destroyed during the wind attack had been replaced. And the trees that had been ripped from the ground had been replaced with a few oak trees. Chafik and I joined Aerilyn and Mathias near the front of the stage. Her head rested on his shoulder and he had an arm wrapped around her waist. If she heard us coming up behind them, she didn't show it.

A hush fell over the crowd as the royal family was led to the stage by a line of guards. My gaze scanned the perimeter of the courtyard as more guards filed in, surrounding us. They must be trying to keep something out... or maybe keep us in. I leaned into Chafik. "Why are there so many guards?" I whispered.

"I don't know. Not exactly comforting," he said. The royals stepped onto the stage. The Queen was decked out in all her royal finery. She wore a floor-length light blue silk gown decorated with swirls of lace. Pearls were strung all around her neck and wrist and her gold crown glinted in the dim light. The King wore a dress uniform with more medals than I could count. There was no way he'd earned a single one of them. The Princess stepped up last, but she never came into the apartment to get ready like she always did. She wore a crimson silk dress that fell right above her knees. Glitter glinted in the long curls of her hair. I noticed she picked at the jeweled belt at her waist. She was nervous.

"Before we begin," the King announced, "We would like to welcome the other Heircestrial nominees—Nikos Vikander and Oliver Li." Every head turned to where the other nominees stepped onto the stage, heads held high, soaking in the smatterings of applause. The fact that they already had the ego of royals made me want to gag. Aerilyn turned her head and I searched her face for any remnants of our argument and found none. She looked happy as always, without so much as puffy eyes. Was I really that insignificant in her life? But maybe that was how I'd treated her without even realizing it.

The Queen began talking next. "In light of recent events, we want to ensure the safety of each and every one of you. And we will not withhold information from you." She paused. *Dramatic much?* "The only way the attack could have happened is if there was a spy living among us. And we will not tolerate this in any way, shape, or form." Whispers spread across the courtyard. A spy? My palms started to feel slick with sweat. *No.* I couldn't be getting caught now. I hadn't completed my job yet. I swallowed nervous gulps.

"And we agreed on a solution that you may not enjoy but it is in the best interest of everyone," the Princess said, her gaze cast downwards. I saw a smirk spread across the face of Nikos as he stepped forward to speak.

"All of your rooms will be searched for incriminating evidence. It's nothing personal, just to ensure your safety." Anger rose in the murmurs across the courtyard. Oliver raised their hands in the air, trying to rein in everyone's attention.

"We understand your anger, but we cannot risk another attack. The guards have already been dispatched to all of your rooms," they said.

I stared at the Princess, willing her to look at me. She finally lifted her head and found my eyes. *Why?* She set her mouth into a hard line and quickly looked away. Aerilyn and Mathias finally turned around to face us. "This is absolutely ridiculous," Chafik spat, his face pinched. Mathias' expression remained calm.

"This is a complete invasion of our privacy," Aerilyn said purposely not looking at me. And it was. In all the years I'd been here, they hadn't thought to pull something like this. Now I felt lucky that none of the letters had been getting through to me. And I burned the ones I received after I read them, destroying any evidence against me.

The crowd grew loud in an uproar. "Last time I checked, our contract didn't include random room checks," Aerilyn said.

"I guess we missed that part," Mathias joked. We all stared at him.

"Not the time my friend, not the time," Chafik said as he patted Mathias on the shoulder. I tuned out Chafik and Aerilyn's complaints as my gaze flickered back to the guards posted around us. All of them placed their hand on the hilt of the swords sheathed at their hips, like they were expecting us to attack them at any second. My traitorous eyes wandered back towards the stage. Looks of pure satisfaction were plastered on Nikos' face. Oliver's face however, matched the Princess'—pure guilt.

One group of guards returned, broadswords already in hand. The courtyard fell silent at the sight of them. The air was thick with stillness. "We have found the spy," one of them announced. Multiple gasps could be heard across the crowd. The man held up a letter they had already ripped apart. He took the note out of the envelope and threw it to the ground.

"My guards found that letter among the apartment's mail." His guards... he must be the Commander. "No useful information was contained in it, but it was a decoy."

A decoy? But I burned all of my letters. Unless one's managed to slip through at exactly the wrong time. My worst fear became a reality. The Commander reached into the secret compartment of the envelope and pulled out the actual letter. He held it in front of the royals' faces. Even from my position, I could see Kass's cramped handwriting. *Hells.*

"Everything contained in this letter pertains to communications with the Primis Defense Union. And this was found in the room of Aerilyn Campos." Multiple sets of eyes landed on her.

"What... I- I am not a spy!" she stammered. Her eyes were wet with the start of tears.

"Lies," the King spat. Everyone around us started to give us a wide berth. I clung to her arm, and took it as a small win when she didn't pull away.

"She isn't a spy. Aerilyn would never do this!" Mathias yelled at the King.

"Stand back unless you want to join her fate," the Queen said.

"Guys just step back, they won't be convinced," she said in a small voice. Tears ran down her face as she pushed us away. The crowd of staff behind us held us away from her as the guards rushed towards her.

My muscles strained, trying to pull myself out of their grip but to no avail. This was all my fault. It should've been me standing where she is. I should've been the one the guards were targeting. I thought all the letters were being stopped by the spymaster. This shouldn't be happening. I felt hot tears roll down my cheeks as I kept screaming her name. The guards formed a circle around her.

I never even got to apologize. The Commander stepped inside the circle. "Aerilyn Campos, you have been found guilty of treason against the crown, and for conspiring with the Primis Defense Union." She let out a ragged breath.

"But I'm not!" she screamed.

"All lies. The punishment for treason is death." He motioned to the guard next to him, and he raised his sword.

"No!" I screamed. No one paid me attention.

The crystal around the guard's neck began to glow white. With his unoccupied hand, he used the air element to keep her still and she was forced to her knees. He stepped multiple feet back from her. Then, he raised his sword and threw with all his strength. The sword spun as it flew through the air straight towards Aerilyn.

I heard the squelch. And saw the spray of blood as it found its target in her chest.

Chapter 19

Ilise

"No!" The noise of the crowd sounded muted as I watched Aerilyn slump onto her side. *She can't be dead because of me. This is all my fault.* I watched her back rise once more before stilling completely. Dead. I fell to my knees and screamed until my throat felt raw. I stared at my hands in front of me, unable to look anymore. Others only watched, horror etched onto their faces.

"She was innocent," Mathias screamed, his voice thick with anger.

"You're all a bunch of monsters," Chafik shouted.

The Commander's polished boots came into my field of vision, clear of blood despite the blood that should be stained into his hands. I slowly looked up into his cold blue eyes, a sneer etched into his features. "She was a traitor to the crown and deserved to die."

I didn't try to hide the breaking in my voice. "She was an innocent girl you killed in cold blood." He kicked dust into my face and turned away from me.

"Imran, dispose of the body." Another soldier clad in a black uniform stepped out of the circle, and I scrambled back from the red glow of her crystal.

"No. Stop, please," I said. I choked on the tears running down my face. She didn't even falter as she raised her hands and formed a blinding ball of flames, growing it to the size of her head. I could feel the heat emitting from it, forming sweat on my brow. She released the ball, and it engulfed Aerilyn's body. My eyes burned from the light, but I couldn't look away. Within seconds she was nothing more than a pile of ash.

"It is done," the Commander said. No. It couldn't be done. Aerilyn couldn't be done.

"Take this as your one and only warning," the King began, "we do not tolerate traitors. All of you are dismissed." The people around me silently filed back into the palace. My legs did not feel like my own. No matter how much I tried, I couldn't get them to move. My eyes were fixed on the pile of ash that used to be my best friend. And no matter how fake it may have been, how many lies it had been built upon, she was my true friend.

Never again would I hear her laugh. Never again would she tease me for something stupid. The letter was meant for me. I should've been the one who was nothing more than a pile of ash. The waterfall of tears kept coming, no matter how hard I tried to stop them. She was just here. How could someone be here one minute and gone the next?

And the last moments I had with her was an argument that pushed her away. I was going to apologize, and I didn't even get to fix my stupid, hotheaded mistake.

She was gone. And I didn't do anything to save her. I was suddenly a kid again, staring at the faces of my family forever frozen in fear. I couldn't do anything then, and I didn't do anything now. Then, I was on my first mission again, in the tight grasp of a Progression member. Instead of Aerilyn's ashes in front of me, it was Val's bruised form. Instead of the palace courtyard, I was in the town square of a now ruined village, buildings scorched beyond recognition. Val had been beaten close to death because of my recklessness, and had been about to pay for it. The Progression member's crystal had glowed red, forever marring my skin in an ugly network of patches. But I deserved it then, and I would deserve it again.

Her body was gone, but I still whispered the sacred words of farewell to whatever may be left of her. "May you be guided away from this world, and lead the Spirits home to you." The quiet whistle of wind was the only response I received.

I lay on the ground, letting the tears fall. I felt as if a piece of my soul had been ripped out of my chest. A strong breeze blew over my face, taking with it Aerilyn's ashes. I cried out as I watched them fly away with the wind. Hopefully the wind would at least carry her ashes somewhere she would like, free of any bugs, out of the scorching Newnina sun. The sound of footsteps filled my ear. I didn't lift my head.

"Ilise," a soft voice said. I looked up to see the Princess standing over me. She rubbed a single tear from her eyes as she knelt beside me. "Let me take you back to the apartment."

I shook my head. If I left this courtyard, it would mean accepting Aerilyn was gone forever. By staying, I could pretend she was still here, I could pretend she was more than ashes flying through the air. "I'm not going to leave you lying on the floor," she said.

I turned to face the other way. "I'd rather stay here." She lifted my head by my chin. Mere inches separated her face from mine and I wanted to get lost in those eyes, and forget everything that had happened. If even just for a moment so I wouldn't have this gut-wrenching feeling for a few minutes. Immediate guilt pulsed through me for having such a thought.

"I cannot even begin to imagine what you are feeling right now. But I do know it won't get better if you insist on laying on the ground out here," the Princess said.

"What about the others?" I said, my voice barely a whisper.

"Mathias and Chafik went back inside and told me they wanted to be alone. Come on." Taking one last glance at what used to be my friend, barely more than a scorched spot on the ground, I let her lift me and walk me back inside. Nobody else lingered as we made our way through the dark halls, and the guards' eyes followed our movements with a creepy amount of attention.

We arrived at the door of the apartment, and the Princess led me to my room. "Do you want to be alone?"

I shook my head.

"Do you want to go to your room?"

I stayed still. I didn't know what I wanted. Nothing could replace the hole Aerilyn had left. "Follow me." She took my hand, and I let her lead me to her room. Her hand was grounding, it felt like the only thing keeping me on my feet.

"Why am I here?" I asked.

She held up one finger. I stepped back as the glow of her crystal brighten. She placed her hands on the armoire and grunted as she pushed it to the side. Behind it was a seam in the wall, in the shape of a door. It must have been another secret tunnel. She pushed on the wall and the door opened with a loud creak. She lit the burnt-out torch hanging on the wall and retook my hand, leading me through the dark tunnel.

"Where are you taking me?" She glanced back at me.

"You will see."

"Why are there so many tunnels?" Goosebumps rose on my arms as the secret door closed behind us with a deafening slam.

"In case of emergency. Almost every room in the palace has an entrance." Cobwebs occupied almost every corner, and half-rotted wood beams creaked, as if the ceiling was about to collapse. Our steps made footprints on the dusty floor, and I held my nose to keep the dust from flying into my nose. We took a sharp left and stood in front of a small wooden door. She handed me the torch to hold as she grabbed the key hanging on the wall.

The door opened with a click, and we entered another dim room. Moonlight poured in from the large windows. With a few flicks of her hand, the Princess lit all the candles scattered around the room. The white walls were decorated with floral gold foil. Old instruments were massed in the far corner of the room, along with yellowing sheets of music.

"Was this a music room?" I felt the heat from her body as she came up behind me.

"Yes. I found it a few years ago when I was wandering through the tunnels. Occasionally I come back as an escape since it's closed off from the rest of the palace." I sat down on one of the couches next to the windows and coughed as dust puffed up from the fabric. The Princess joined me.

"I know there's no way for me to make you feel better, but I thought this might help." The back of my eyes began to burn again. The Princess pulled me into a hug and held me there, stroking the top of my head.

"It's happened again," I said in a weak voice. I felt her warm breath against my ear.

"What do you mean again?"

Only this time it was under the guise of fake justice for a cowardly crown. "There's something I've never told anyone. But I did tell part of it to Aerilyn." Her breath caught for a second.

"What?"

"My family has been dead for years." Dead. I never did enjoy that word. It felt too accidental, as if there was nothing that could've been done to prevent it. But there was nothing accidental about my family's deaths.

"But you said..."

"I know. I couldn't face telling anyone the truth."

"What happened?"

What hadn't happened? Memories of when I first arrived at my smoldering village resurfaced. One would think there were only so many ways to kill someone, but no, The Progression disproved that quickly. Some were simply scorched, some looked like they'd been drowned and then burned, some were impaled, some bodies were separated from their heads, and some had been crushed by crumbling buildings.

And then there was my family. It was almost as if The Progression wanted to taunt me.

At first glance, they could've been alive, but the pool of blood they laid in was indication enough. Along with the chilling feeling of their blood-drained skin, the pale brown of their skin, and their open, unseeing eyes. But I didn't say any of that. I simply said, "They were killed in an attack on my village when I was fourteen."

"I'm so sorry. I can't even imagine."

"Sometimes I still have nightmares where I see their dead faces, haunting me. They were completely defenseless against the attackers. Just like Aerilyn was. And now another person I love has been ripped away from me."

The Princess was silent for a long moment. "Ilise... I don't even know what to say.. I wish there was something I could have done."

A grim thought came to my mind. It was true. I couldn't do anything to save Aerilyn, but the Princess could have. She could have convinced them not to kill her, or to not do the room searches in the first place. Anger flared in my chest. Part of me knew it was unfair to cast all the blame on the Princess, but she was the one with the power. I wasn't, and I never would be.

"Why didn't you do anything then?" I choked out.

Her shoulders dropped. "Nothing I could say would be a real reason why." The back of my throat burned as the anger settled into my belly.

"Whose idea was it?" I seethed.

"Nikos." My head snapped up. *Him?* Even for our sakes, she couldn't manage to keep that cocky Progression member from signing Aerilyn's death warrant.

"Why didn't you stop him? He isn't Heir, he has no power. Did you just sit there as they planned to kill an innocent person?"

She flinched at my words; I didn't care. "I tried. But they wouldn't listen to reason." *They wouldn't listen.* She was supposed to make them listen.

"Is that supposed to be a valid excuse?"

She gaped at me. "I'm not making excuses for myself. Of course, I feel horrible for what happened but I can't change it now." That didn't matter. She was the Princess of the whole kingdom, yet shutting down the mad ideas of one man seemed impossible to her. What's the point of being one of the most powerful people if you weren't going to use it?

I wiggled out of her embrace. Being that close to her felt like being burned all over again. I stood in front of her, my hands in tight fists. "Stop it," I said through gritted teeth.

"Stop what?"

"Stop acting so calm. Stop acting as if we didn't just watch one of us get killed because of a bunch of paranoid Imperium with a spirit-complex."

She shot up from the couch and moved closer to me. "Then how do you want me to act Ilise, huh? There's nothing in the world I would want more than for Aerilyn to be standing with us."

I narrowed my eyes as I leaned closer her.

"Keep her name out of your mouth. I've never had the choice to stop something horrible from happening, but you did. I never get to choose to ignore all the people hurting around me and relax in my fancy palace where I can get anything I want at the snap of my fingers, but you do. You had the power to prevent this and did *nothing*." Anger flashed in her eyes, gone as quickly as it came.

"You call her innocent. But then why did she have a letter from the Primis Defense Union in her room? If she were innocent, the guards wouldn't have found anything." I bit my tongue to prevent myself from blowing my cover right then. The fire deep in my belly grew hotter, an unending inferno.

"What about The Progression? Nikos proudly hung up a Progression flag in his room yet the guards saw that as perfectly fine," I said, packing as much venom in my voice as I could muster.

"The Progression is less dangerous." *Less dangerous?*

"You are full of it," I spat.

"Last time I checked the worst thing The Progression did was spray paint a wall. The Primis Defense Union attacked a ball and killed half the guests."

"Bullshit." She moved her face only a few inches from mine. Golden light churned in the sea of her eyes, her brows furrowed.

"You were there. You saw them. One of them almost killed you, in fact."

"How do you know it wasn't The Progression trying to cover their tracks." A muscle in her jaw twitched. The Progression were the ones who killed half the ballroom, and almost killed me, yet they suffered none of the consequences. Imperium never suffered the consequences. It was always Primis people, always us, and no one seemed to care. Not the crown, not The Progression, and not most of the Imperium in this spiritsdamned kingdom.

"Because The Progression isn't the one with a track record of attacking innocent people." I'd thought she was better than this, with the possibility to be a better ruler than her parents. But I was wrong, I never should have put faith in her.

"You sure about that? Who do you think burned my village to the ground? Who do you think killed my whole family without any care?"

She tsked. "Sure they did," she said sarcastically.

"You want more proof? I'll show you more proof." I stepped back from her and began unbuttoning my cover-up. I'd kept my arms hidden for years, never to be seen by a single soul. But now felt like as good a time as ever to let them be seen. They were always a reminder of what happened when I failed. Now they would tell the Princess the full story.

"What are you doing?" The Princess asked as she crossed her arms over her chest.

"Giving you proof." I finally undid the last button and pulled off the cover-up. I bared my arms to her and watched her face twist in horror as she took in the scars on my arms. Multiple patches of skin healed a shade of brown much darker than my own, and other parts maintained an unnatural shine, extending up to my shoulder. But it didn't even show her the extent of the damage. Parts of my arm had to stay wrapped in bandages so I wouldn't damage the skin more.

She gulped. "Who did this to you?" An emotion I couldn't decipher flickered in her eyes.

"The Progression. When they attacked a defenseless village for no reason other than because of their hate."

Her eyes widened. "I—" I cut her off before she could continue.

"Aw, are you upset I proved you wrong? That maybe the people who want to return the kingdom to a time when Letita's twisted ideals were favored are more dangerous? A world where people like me are treated like dirt, and Imperium like you walk all over us. Is that what you want?"

She flinched. *Good.* "Is this what you consider 'less dangerous'? What will it take for you to get it through your overinflated head that maybe you're wrong."

She stared at me in silence. "Oh, so now you're quie—"

The same stabbing pain I felt in my chest days prior shot through me, and I cried out as I fell to the ground clutching my chest. The Princess rushed to my side. "Ilise, are you okay?" she said in a panicked voice.

My breathing became rapid, still barely giving me enough air. The sounds around me became muffled again. As if my head was underwater, and my attempts of surfacing were futile.

"I know you're here. You can't hide from me forever. You are mine," the toneless voice said. It didn't sound like the Princess.

"Get out of my head," I screamed, yanking at my hair.

"Who's in your head? Ilise, I'm right here." Her voice echoed loudly in my head, a shock from her muffled voice moments prior. I covered my ear at the sound.

I felt her stroking my cheek and slowly, the world sounded clearer again, and the pain in my chest stopped. I started gasping for breath as the beat of my heart slowed. "What was that?" she asked.

I looked up into the Princess' eyes, wide with fear and worry. I could have sworn I saw a wet line going down her cheek. I pushed her off of me and stumbled back up to my feet. Stars danced in my vision for a few seconds before clearing.

"Don't touch me."

She put her hands in the air and took a few steps back from me. "Well I'm sorry for worrying about you dropping onto the floor mid-sentence. It's not like I was a few minutes from watching you die last week."

I narrowed my eyes and pursed my lips. "Was that your attempt at making a jab at me, 'cause it was quite pathetic."

She scoffed. I felt her stare wander back to the scars on my arms. My face felt hot as I quickly put the cover-up back on myself. "I have nothing left to say to you," I said.

I turned to leave the room, but the Princess gripped my arm, pulling me closer to her. This close to her, she towered over me, my face inches from hers. Her breath warmed my cheeks.

"Ilise please, I'm trying to understand," she said, her gold-flecked eyes tearing. Did she think she could lull me with tears, that I would run back into her arms and forgive her for spitting on everything I've worked for my entire life.

I ripped my arm from hers and with nothing left to say, I stormed back through the tunnels. I didn't have a torch to light my way, but I still remembered the way back to her room. At least, I was pretty sure I did. I couldn't explain how I knew this was the right door to use. I almost felt a pull towards it. It felt right, and I always trusted my gut. As long as I wasn't around *her*.

I grabbed the key for the door in front of me and it opened with a creak into another dim room. *This doesn't look like the Princess' room.* Two yellow chairs and a coffee table sat in the center of the room, and moonlight from the small window gave the room a ghastly glow. It must have been one of the rooms we rarely used in the palace. I coughed as another puff of dust was released once I closed the door.

I didn't think I somehow went to another floor, so I should be able to get back to my room from here. A door lined with more gold foil was on the other side of the room. I tested the knob, and it was locked. Using one of the pins in my hair, I maneuvered it in the lock until I heard the soft click. Glancing around, I was back in another dim hallway. It looked the same as my apartment. This couldn't be… was I in one of the nominee's rooms? The only sound I could hear was the pounding of my own heart.

My hands shook as I closed the door as quietly as possible and walked towards the door to get out. The third floor had at least twenty apartments. There was no way I could have been unlucky enough to end up in one of *their* rooms.

"How much longer do we have to stay here?" a soft voice said. I froze. My ear strained to determine which direction the sound came from. Pressing myself against the wall, I kept walking towards the front door. Peering around the corner of the wall, I saw two figures.

One of them lit a match, and their faces were illuminated. Nikos and Oliver, just my luck. My heart burned with anger upon seeing their faces. I should have left the moment I saw them. But the last two weeks had been an information desert. Staying for a little longer wouldn't hurt. My inability to be a useful spy ended up with Aerilyn being killed. There wasn't much I had left to lose.

I took off my shoes but left on my socks to diminish the sound of my footsteps. Both of them turned to face the window, away from me. As quietly as possible, I ran behind the counter, my body shaking with the effort to control my breathing. I crawled to the edge of the counter to face the two of them.

"We won't have to be here much longer," Oliver said. Were they backing out of Heircestrial?

"When will they be here?" Nikos said, twirling a fountain pen in his hand.

"Within a couple weeks. With the palace on the lookout for the Primis Defense Union, they won't see us coming." See who?

Nikos rolled his eyes. "As if they wouldn't notice a giant army heading straight for the palace."

Oliver's eyes narrowed. "Are you really going to argue with me right now? Your job is still not done here."

"You think I don't know that?" Nikos snapped.

"I will say, you have been doing a great job lately. Now you have to keep it up for a little longer." A frightening smile spread across their face. "And if you don't, well, I think you know what happens" Nikos' hands tightened into fists.

I *knew* something was up with those two. There was not one doubt in my mind they were with The Progression. But knowing this was true didn't make me feel any better... it only made things so much more complicated. A chilling realization crept over me. It was *them* who helped stage the attack at both balls. It was *them* who prompted the royals to do something *drastic.* Spirits, I hated being right sometimes.

Chapter 20

Ilise

The back of my eyes burned once again. Aerilyn would still be alive if they'd never come here.

"I know what happens, you don't have to remind me," Nikos seethed.

Oliver let out a deep, chilling laugh. "Oh, but it's so fun to see your expression when I do." I almost thought he was about to strangle Oliver right then. Instead, he stalked off back towards the hallway. I pressed myself against the cabinet so there was no chance he would see me. I'd been focusing my energy on the wrong person. Nikos was merely a pawn while Oliver controlled him in the background.

As his footsteps receded, I let out a small breath. I couldn't stay in this prison any longer, Kass and the others needed to be warned. If a Progression *army* was coming for the palace, they might not be prepared. No one knew how large it was, it could be bigger than the amount of guards the palace had. And if the palace lost... all would be lost.

I'd have to leave tonight if I was to make decent time. Swiping a horse from the stables wouldn't be too tricky at this hour. And if timed correctly, I could make it to the base in a few days, given my inexperience on horseback. And that would give us a little more than a week to gather and mobilize enough people to stop The Progression once and for all. And I would handle the leader on my own.

The front door opened, and every muscle in my body tensed. Tiny hairs all over me began to stand up. Slowly, I peered back around the edge and saw a figure walk in, covered with floor-length black robes. *Who is this?*

"Oliver, I trust you've told Nikos the wonderful news," said a dark, melodic voice. That voice... I knew that voice. But where had I heard it before? I shuffled closer to the edge, my ears straining to listen. The voice had an ancient and entrancing quality to it.

"Of course. And when will you learn to knock, Imogen?"

The figure waved her hand. "He'll be fine. He knows the consequences for disobedience." Consequences? The figure, Imogen, removed her hood. It was an old woman. Her coiled gray hair was pulled into a low ponytail that fell right below her shoulders. And the candlelight made her wrinkled, coppery skin glow. But the air around her felt weird, almost heavy.

As my eyes adjusted more to the dim light, something glinted around her neck. Well, multiple things. I fought to not empty the contents of my stomach as what I was seeing came into focus. Five crystals hung around her neck. Blue, white, red, green, and purplish black.

A sorceress.

"Have you been able to locate her yet?" Oliver asked. Locate who?

"I've felt her energy around the palace, but I have not found her yet."

Oliver pressed their mouth into a thin line. "We need her for *your* plan to work correctly." Since when did Council sorcerers work with The Progression? They stopped only a foot in front of the sorceress. "And *you* promised to find her by now."

The sorceress' mouth curled into a sneer. "And *you* seem to be forgetting which one of us could reduce you to mere ash."

Oliver gulped and stepped back. I had to get out of here, but Imogen was blocking my only way out. Going back through the tunnels would probably land me in another wrong room, and I would be dead the instant they saw me leaving.

The sorceress grew unnaturally still. "What is it?" Oliver asked.

"She's close." *Spirits. How does she know I'm here?*

"Close as in this room close, close as in this palace close, or close as in this kingdom close? 'Cause, it seems you don't know."

"Close as in shut your mouth so I can find her before I imbed you into a tree close." They slumped back into the chair and let out a melodramatic sigh. "Sighing does not count as shutting your mouth."

They responded with a vulgar gesture, and she gave them a warning look. Her head whipped around, and I pressed myself against the cabinet again. I'd gotten too comfortable in this palace. Not even a dagger was hidden under my shirt. I'd been too upset to remember to grab one before we left for the courtyard. My heart began to race again as the sound of her footsteps increased. I couldn't get away from a sorceress and an Imperium with my bare hands. How could I have been so stupid?

The sorceress' steps grew in volume, and I was running out of options. I quietly opened the cabinet behind me, praying for there to be something sharp. Inside were multiple sets of pots and pans. Another tool caught my eye and I could have cried tears of joy. I pulled it out to examine what it was, and my victories were short-lived. In my hand was a bent whisk. *Spirits help me.* But it was better than nothing.

The metal prongs of the whisk pressed into my hand as I clutched it. I unscrewed the rubber handle to reveal the blunt metal end. "Where are you, little one," the sorceress crooned.

I felt a physical jolt as the pieces fell into place. Was this the voice I'd been hearing all this time? "I know you're here somewhere," she said.

Her footsteps receded around the edge of the counter. "A sneaky little one, aren't you." Against my better judgment, I turned my head towards her voice and bright violet eyes stared back at me. "Put down your pathetic excuse for a weapon, and I'll go easy on you."

I spit in her direction.

She shrugged. "Hard way it is then.

Four of the crystals began to glow. I sprang to my feet and leapt on top of the counter. Oliver shot up from their chair, their mouth curled into a snarl as their crystal glowed sky blue. "Silly little girl." Imogen knocked me in the chest with a strong gust of air. I fell onto my back but sprang back onto my feet before Imogen could stop me.

Oliver was on me within seconds. I dipped under their first swing and returned one of my own towards their chest. They jumped back with shocking speed. I had almost forgotten that in addition to power over the elements, Imperium also got a boost of strength. *Can one thing go right today?* Oliver hurled a giant ball of water into my face. I staggered as I choked on the water, and they held the ball around my face. My lungs burned, crying for me to take in a deep breath. They released the water, and I plummeted to the ground with it. Black spots lingered in my vision.

"You didn't have to almost drown her."

"She's under control, isn't she?" they said with a smile. The sorceress stalked towards me and my time was running out. By some miracle, I could still feel the whisk in my hand. Keeping my gaze locked on hers, I flipped it so the blunt metal end of the handle faced her. She knelt beside me.

"I've finally found you my little one," she said as she stroked my cheek. I leaned in closer to her and tightened my grip on the whisk.

"Burn in hells," I whispered. Before she could react, I stabbed the end of the whisk into one of her eyes. She cried out in pain as blood gushed down her face. Both of them froze in shock while I sprinted towards the door.

"Go after her!" Oliver chased me, not far behind. I slipped out of the room. Oliver was slowed down slightly by the door, so I used the time to remove my socks. No longer hindered by the threat of slipping, I bolted down the dark hall. Oliver's footsteps grew louder behind me.

I dared to look back and saw the blue light of their crystal. With the replenished strength, they sped up, gaining on me quickly. "Guards, stop her immediately," they yelled. Three guards rounded the corner to respond to Oliver's call.

"Stop in the name of the crown," the first guard ordered.

"Over my dead body," I said.

His lips turned into a chilling smile. "That can be arranged."

I feigned right to avoid the swing of the first guard's sword. Then, I shot my leg out, aiming for his stomach. He leapt backward into the wall and used it to come back at me. I stepped on his foot with all my weight, and he yelped. I snatched the sword from his hands as his grip loosened and slammed the hilt of the sword to his head. He collapsed into a pile at my feet.

Adrenaline coursed through my veins. "Anyone else wanna play?" Another one of the guards charged me and I leapt out of the reach of his swing. I rushed him, ready to slash out, but he pulled another dagger from his belt, swinging out across my face. Warm blood trickled down my cheek, but I couldn't falter for even a second. Using his momentum against him, I grabbed his arm holding the dagger and twisted it until he cried out. The dagger fell to the ground with a loud clang.

The guard raised his leg and caught me in the stomach. Pain blossomed across my abdomen, and I fell to my knees. Crawling on the ground, I picked up the dagger and embedded it into the guard's thigh. He let out a string of violent curses. I whirled at the sound of pounding footsteps behind me. Oliver was coming after me again. Pushing the injured guard to the ground, I darted towards the staircase. I quickly immobilized the last guard with a quick kick to the groin and hacking the sword into his leg too. I winced at the sound of his scream. There was no time for being clean. I needed to escape. Now.

I risked a glance back and saw Oliver was quickly gaining on me. I wouldn't be able to outrun them. The only way to get away was to remove their crystal so they couldn't use it against me. I skidded to a stop and turned to face them. My stomach pounded from the kick, and I was sure it would bruise later, but I gritted my teeth to keep my head in the fight in front of me.

Oliver smiled as they also skidded to a stop, sending a chill down my spine. "Just give up now, there's no running from me."

I raised my sword. "Not a chance."

They shrugged. "Your loss." Within seconds their crystal was a bright blue, and they rushed towards me. I twirled around to avoid their grasp at the last minute. "Playing hard to get are you," they chuckled. They launched another ball of water towards my head. *I am not almost drowning again.* I dropped to the floor and the water splashed on the floor behind me. Springing to my feet, I swung the sword in an arc and nicked the side of their face. They brushed away the trail of blood. "Cute," they sneered.

Quicker than my eyes could track, they clasped their hands around my neck, lifting me into the air. The spots in my vision returned. I punched them in the eye, and it did nothing to lessen their hold. My lungs screamed for air. "Surrender now. Imogen didn't say I had to bring you back conscious."

I writhed against their grip on my neck, but they held firm. I slowly moved my hand to hold the blade of the sword. Blood gushed out new cuts formed by the sharp edge and with the last of my strength, I cut the necklace holding their crystal.

Surprise flickered across their face, quickly replaced by anger. I shot my knee upwards, and they grunted as it hit them in the chest. Their grip slackened, and I twisted myself out of their grip. "I warned you," I said with a smile, dangling their crystal necklace in front of their face. I rammed the hilt of the sword down on their head, knocking them unconscious. I sucked in lungfuls of blood-scented air, ceasing the headache that had been forming.

I scanned the hallway one last time. Every guard, plus Oliver, was passed out. Every point of pain shot through me like lightning. My stomach throbbed, and every cut I had gained stung like fire. I blinked back tears. Imogen wouldn't stay down for long, and neither would these guards. But it would be hard to leave the palace in my current condition.

I stole the boots off the smallest guard instead of having to get to Hexia barefoot. They were slightly too big, but usable. Then, I swiped the extra daggers and sheaths off the guards' belts. I took three total, two strapped to my thighs and one at my hip. Not sparing another second, I hurried to the staircase. Thankfully, it was empty. The stables were on the first floor, but of course, on the opposite side of where the stairs would leave me.

I arrived on the first floor and listened for the sound of footsteps. The only sound was my own racing heart and erratic breathing. I sprinted down the long corridor, my stolen boots echoing in the empty space. I turned right and burst through the door to the stables. One of the young farmhands eyed me suspiciously, but he averted his gaze at the sight of my weapons. And the blood coating my clothes.

"Hey," I called. He stiffened. "Can you saddle up one of those horses?" His hands shook as he looked up into my eyes. He couldn't have been older than fifteen. Not much older than I had been when I'd first arrived here. If only younger me could see where that fateful day landed me.

"Why should I listen to you?" he said in a shaky voice.

I unsheathed one of my daggers, pointing it at him. "I won't ask again. And hand me one of those cloaks hanging on the wall while you're at it." He quickly nodded and ran to retrieve the reins of a medium-sized, black and white spotted steed. He then handed me the reins and fetched a saddle. He buckled it on for me, and I hoisted myself onto the horse. I pet their mane so they wouldn't get too startled. The boy handed me one of the brown cloaks hanging on the wall. It smelled like horse manure and grass, but it would hide my face for the time being.

"Her name is Daisy." I saw a small tear escape his eyes as he opened the doors for me to leave, and I felt a tiny crack form in my heart. I didn't want this kid to be punished for giving me this horse. "I did what you wanted, please go."

"Thank you. And if someone gets mad at you, blame it on me. My name is Ilise Obrien." A small smile of gratitude formed on his face as I turned away. It didn't get rid of the guilt that settled like a stone in my stomach, but it lessened it. I would never forgive myself if he was punished over me.

I gave Daisy's reins a shake, squeezing her sides between my calves, and she trotted off. I hadn't been on a horse since the time Val had forced me to learn how to ride one, and it felt great. Not sparing a backward glance, the moment I was out of the market square, we picked up speed, away from the palace, away from my prison.

Chapter 21

Yorena

"**S**HE DID WHAT?" I said in disbelief. Nikos nodded solemnly in response. I'd spent half the night cursing myself for making Ilise run out. And of all the things I thought might happen because of it, an emergency meeting hadn't been one of them.

"She attacked Oliver, one of the council sorcerers, and three guards who are now stuck in the infirmary. In addition to stealing a horse to escape," he said. I crossed my arms. Ilise would never have done that unless they attacked her first.

"Ilise would never have attacked people unprovoked."

He waved a finger in my face. "Well, clearly you don't know your servant that well. Imogen's eye is probably damaged for the rest of her life and Oliver is sporting a black eye and cuts all over their face," he said with a frown.

Imogen was a sorceress, her eye would heal fine. But Oliver wouldn't have done something to her to deserve an attack. Multiple bandages were placed over their cuts, and they slumped in their chair. Their good eye stared at an invisible point in the center of the circular table. Defeated; haunted.

"Is all of this true, Oliver?" I asked.

They blinked up at me and sighed. "Unfortunately. She looked upset and when I checked to see if she was ok, she attacked me. The guards came to help, but she turned their weapons against them. It was terrifying." A single tear slid down their pale cheek. Ilise could have been downplaying her abilities, waiting for the moment she could attack. But I didn't want to believe it. I wouldn't—I couldn't.

The Commander walked into the room with a thin parchment clenched in his fist, and he dipped into a deep bow before taking his seat. "Well," Father began, "do you know where she went?"

The Commander sighed. "No, Your Majesty. But I do have a report from one of the farmhands who was working late last night." Oh no. He slid the parchment in front of my father.

"He said a tall girl with curly hair named Ilise Obrien pointed a dagger at him and ordered him to hand over one of the horses. He said she went towards the market square, but I highly doubt she's anywhere close by now. And he mentioned she had at least three visible daggers, there's no telling what else she had."

Threatening someone, attacking multiple people, stealing weapons? None of that sounded like the Ilise I knew. But after last night, I didn't think I ever truly knew her. The pure rage and heartbreak in her voice was something I'd never seen in her. My heart ached at the thought of the burn scars she had shown me. How could someone be so cruel to another human? Her rage and tear-choked words still echoed in my mind. *"Is this what you consider less dangerous?"*

"We need to find her and punish her for not only attacking multiple people, but her response can only mean she was also a spy for the Primis Defense Union," Oliver said. "She even stole my crystal so I could barely defend myself." *Oh, Ilise.*

"Rest assured Oliver, we will spread the message across the kingdom, calling for her arrest. We will not rest until the traitor is captured and executed."

I didn't care what she *allegedly* did. Ilise was not to blame for this. I didn't know much about her, clearly, but I knew for a fact she only fought when necessary. Even during the attack on the ball, she only attacked anyone who tried to hurt us. But it didn't stop doubts from forming in my head. She was always quick to try and defend the Primis Defense Union, and she repeatedly said Aerilyn was innocent. Was she the spy all along? Was the letter meant for her, and Aerilyn happened to pick it up?

Heads turned at the sound of the door opening and Kieron stepped into the room. He bowed to my parents before moving to stand behind the Commander. *Kieron. Surely he'll help me convince them this is all a big misunderstanding.*

"Lieutenant Flores, have you come back with the information I asked for?" the Commander said. My father tapped his fingers on the table expectantly. Kieron looked at me for a quick moment and I could see the words etched into his storming gray eyes. *I'm sorry.* My heart sank. I would find no allies here.

"One of my squads and I asked around the market square and the surrounding town if any of them had seen a girl matching Ilise's description last night."

"Why were you assigned to do it?" I asked.

He turned his head towards me. "Because we're all young and would draw less attention to ourselves than a full platoon." I forced myself to bite my tongue before I filled the room with any more malice. "The only information we found pertaining to her whereabouts is from one woman who was taking a nighttime walk and saw her riding northwest towards the exit road in quite a hurry."

What could be northwest of here? Unless she was going to Lasaintbo to go into hiding, or to live the rest of her days in one of the little farming villages scattered across Newnina.

"Do you think she will try to sail into Pamu or Banauri?" Mother asked.

"Unlikely," Kieron responded. "The witness said she had no visible supplies on her. And unless she somehow snagged a boatload of coin, she won't get far before having to stop."

"And then we can catch her and bring her back here," Mother said.

Kieron nodded, his face grim.

"Are you sure she was a spy?" I asked. Everyone stared me down, and Nikos very visibly rolled his eyes. "If you roll your eyes one more time they might get stuck in your head."

"Yorena," Mother chided.

I locked gazes with the Commander. "Your Highness, the same night we execute someone for being a spy is the same day she pulls this. I highly doubt it's a mere coincidence."

"But the Ilise I know would never do this."

Father slammed his hand on the table, I jumped. "Clearly your *attachment* to the traitor is clouding your judgment. If you are going to fight us on every decision you are dismissed."

"But Father—"

Mother shut me down with a wave of her hand. "You are dismissed," she said, not leaving room for argument.

I pushed away from the table and stormed out of the room. The guards outside the door eyed me suspiciously but said nothing as I rushed past them.

I spun around at the sound of quick footsteps behind me. "What do you want, Kieron?" He jogged up to me. "You knew Ilise was my servant... and my friend. Yet you still went out to find and arrest her!"

"You can't possibly be upset with me for following orders," he said.

"She was my friend and you stood by while they basically planned her demise." Guards patrolling the corridor stole sneaky glances at my outburst. Kieron's eyes darted towards the guard before he responded.

"She's nothing more than a traitor and it's not my place to go against the Commander," he shot back. Not even for me?

I moved within inches of his face, close enough to see the growing stubble on his chin. We were the same height, and I stared into his eyes, my hands curling into fists. "I know Ilise, she would never do something like that unless someone was after her."

Kieron lowered his voice as another guard walked past. "And why would a sorceress, Oliver, and three guards be after her?" I stepped back and tapped my foot, waiting for him to continue. He caved, waiting for me to answer him. "Because she was a spy?" he offered.

I refused to believe it. Ilise hated unnecessary violence. My mind once again went back to our conversation last night. Well, less of a conversation and more of her yelling at me. She had claimed The Progression to be the true perpetrator of everything that has happened recently. But was that not something a spy for the Union would say? Did it make what she said any less true?

Kieron sighed. "I'm worried about you, Yorena."

I started to walk away. "There's nothing for you to worry about."

He grabbed my arm before I could make it far. His face softened. "I can tell you're conflicted about what's true or not, but try not to make yourself the enemy. I felt the energy in that room. Everyone was one more comment away from throwing you out on your heels."

A weak laugh escaped me. "As if that was not what they just did."

He shrugged, one side of his mouth turning up into a lopsided grin. "They didn't technically throw you out, they just told you to leave," he said.

"Because those two things are so different."

"Flores," the Commander called. I looked back at his face, a sneer coming through his usual impassive expression. Kieron nodded in his direction.

"Guess I gotta go now."

I nodded as he went to join the Commander.

The Commander never used to interrupt one of my conversations, even if it was only Kieron. I was the Princess, and therefore ranked above him when it came to power. The only thing worse he could've done was speak out of turn to my parents. Had I already lost his respect?

I scurried back to the staircase to get back to the third floor. Every servant I passed immediately focused their gaze on the floor the moment they saw me and a sick ball of shame formed in my stomach. I'd lost their respect too. They couldn't even bear to look at me.

I arrived at my room and threw open the door. Mathias and Chafik looked up at me from the kitchen. Chafik appeared to have attempted to make lunch in Ilise's absence judging from the plates of thinly sliced meats and cheeses.

"What's got you so upset?" Mathias said flatly as he sipped on his water. I felt like he still blamed me for Aerilyn's execution. Chafik, at least, has still been kind towards me. He looked up at me with slight concern in his eyes.

"Ilise is gone," I said. Saying it out loud made it seem final. I'd never even wanted to voice it to myself.

Mathias finally looked up at me.

"She's what?" Chafik said.

"She fled last night after…" Mathias' hands curled into fists as I trailed off. I gulped. "She fled last night and sent three guards plus one of the council sorcerers to the infirmary in the process."

Mathias scoffed. "That's the least funny story I've heard in a while, now tell us what actually happened."

I crossed my arms over my chest. "I did." Mathias stared at me. "They're about to spread the message to all the provinces to arrest her on sight and have her brought back to the palace."

"Let me guess, to execute her?"

I said nothing. There would be no other fate for her if she was captured. He sighed again and stormed out the door, slamming it shut behind him.

"You'll have to forgive his behavior. He's just upset. We all are."

I put a hand on his shoulder. "It's alright. I can't blame him for taking his anger out on me." Chafik moved to put his cup in the sink. He squeezed the sponge and started washing the dishes. *That used to be Ilise's job too.*

"I'm sure he'll come around eventually."

I nodded. "Hey, how's your family doing? From what I've heard the border situation has only gotten worse." His shoulders sagged slightly as he placed the clean cup in the metal dish drainer.

"They're doing fine. I read their latest letter and they said they've all made it to Ominka. It should be safe there. And they'll go further north into Pria if they have to."

"Ominka is a safe choice. We have not received any reports from there." The word yet hung unspoken in the air. If this continued, nowhere in the kingdom would be safe, not even in the mountains of Pria.

He shook the water off his hands. "I should be going. I have a feeling Ms. Kira won't be in a forgiving mood today if I'm late." No one would be in a forgiving mood after last night.

"Of course, I'll see you later." He waved and walked out the door. I left the kitchen and decided to try and relax my brain in my room. The moment I sagged onto the bed, conflicting thoughts in my head began to scream a dissonant chorus. Was Ilise really a spy? Was I the sole one to blame for Aerilyn's death? Was I losing the power struggle to Nikos? But there was one that kept repeating in my head the most.

Was what I thought was developing between Ilise and me a lie?

It hadn't felt like a lie. I never felt more connected, more seen by another person, until I met her. But how much of it was true? Anytime I asked about her past, she threw up an indestructible wall, one I thought I was finally breaking down. But my actions ended up taking her with it. Maybe if I'd tried harder, fought a little harder to keep them from executing Aerilyn, then perhaps she would still be here. And Mathias wouldn't hate me either. And I wouldn't have dug myself into a deep hole at this point in the competition, one I didn't think I would be able to climb out of.

I must have lay there for over an hour. The sun had moved to a position where it was shining right into my eyes. I sat up from the bed and let out a deep breath. Moping all day wasn't going to fix my problems. I swung open the doors of my armoire and pulled out a pair of black leggings and an old gray tunic. Doing some training would be good for my head. But I found my eyes wandering back to the armoire, or rather, what was behind it. I pushed the wardrobe aside and opened the secret door hidden in the seams of the wall.

It opened without a creak this time. I lit the same burnt-out torch I'd used last night and closed the door behind me. I was thrown into darkness, save for the small area around my torch. I inhaled the stale air of the tunnels as I took the route I knew by heart. To the room that had always been my escape, safe from the prying eyes of everyone in the castle. I took a sharp left and arrived at the small wooden door. I extinguished my torch and picked up the key hanging on the wall. At the sound of the soft click, I opened the door.

Yellow sunlight poured in through the windows. Walking closer to them, I had never particularly dwelt on the fact that they overlooked the castle courtyard. Images from the previous night flashed through my head. The sickening squelch as the sword plunged deep into Aerilyn's chest, Ilise's heartbroken scream as it rose above the voices of everyone else. I didn't think that sound would leave my head for a long time.

I shoved the memories to the back of my mind before they could haunt me further. It was a bad idea to come in here. I would never find peace here again. The only thing it reminded me of was my last moment with Ilise before she fled. I was about to leave the room before I heard the faint sound of shouting from the window.

I raced back over and looked around the courtyard. My eyes were drawn to a whole legion of guards surrounding the door to the gates of the palace. Looking past the gate, my eyes widened at the sight, and I rushed back into the tunnels.

A giant crowd had formed. Growing larger by the second.

Chapter 22

Ilise

MY BACK ACHED, AND I was sure Daisy's legs were just as tired. Every extra mile felt like another round of bruises forming on my tailbone. We rode straight through the night and the sun now washed the green plains in golden light. Stopping for supplies in New Teber would've gotten me captured in minutes. I breathed in the fresh summer air, a drastic difference from the stuffy castle. I never wanted to stay there again.

My goal was to make it to the nearest town before nightfall then I would let myself and Daisy rest and get some supplies before we continue riding towards Hexia. If I remembered correctly, the next town I should arrive at was called Anmia. Anytime we traveled through Newnina, Kass and Val would always let us stop there. It was small but not small enough that our arrival would draw attention.

Unless the palace decided to alert the kingdom about my escape. Hopefully, if they did, news hadn't reached this town yet. I tugged on the reins to slow Daisy's pace to a stop. I hopped off her saddle and let her graze the grass for a quick moment. We both needed a break if we were going to make it to Anmia. I stretched out my back and felt more relieved with every crack. My legs were numb at this point and I shook them, attempting to get some blood flow back into them.

I gazed up in the sky at the sun, now close to being directly above me. We would have to get to Anmia quickly. The cloak would get too heavy and too suspicious to wear in this heat, but it was the only thing covering my still blood-stained servant uniform and concealing my daggers. And the cuts on my face would be suspicious enough. While Daisy continued to graze, I started rummaging through the pockets on the saddle.

I could forget about getting supplies without any coin. If it was a big town, I might have been able to get away with stealing a few things, but I would get caught within seconds in Anmia. Palace horses were used by traveling soldiers, so at least one of them could've left money behind. I found nothing but scraps of paper in the pockets on Daisy's right saddlebag. As I walked over to her right side, she tried walking away. "Daisy, you can't walk away."

She squealed. "There's nothing there except swaying grass, calm down!" I kept petting her neck until she calmed down.

Finally, she let me look through the pockets on the left side. I found a few silvers in the first one and about a dozen coppers in the second. It should be enough to get me some new clothes and a small amount of food I would have to ration. I shook the coins in front of Daisy's left eye. "Looks like I'll be able to get some food and clothes, maybe a room to rest for a few hours."

She nickered. "I guess I'll get you a treat if there is anything left over."

I put my foot in the stirrup and hoisted myself back onto the saddle. I gave the reins a shake, and we started riding to Anmia. We rode for almost three hours before the town came into view. I didn't try pushing her any faster; I didn't need an exhausted horse to worry about. And neither my back nor my butt could stand riding at a faster pace. Sweat managed to seep through all of my clothes and I felt as if I'd been submerged in a boiling lake.

The sun beat down on me, and I pulled the hood of my cloak down. It did almost nothing to cool me. Sweat dripped down the tip of my nose. Despite that, my eyes struggled to stay open and my limbs became nothing more than deadweights. It'd been over a day since I last slept. The palace had made me soft, I should still have enough energy left in me.

I gave Daisy's sides a gentle nudge with my heels so we could get to the town and rest as quickly as possible. She protested but eventually, as my nudges became more like kicks, gave in to my command. We reached the town's main road. Others trotted past on their horses, all of them waving politely as they passed. Sun-bleached orange and yellow houses and businesses lined the streets. To my right, a woman sold flowers from her cart. Another man was calling for anyone willing to buy his small, black, animal wood carvings. I strained my neck to look over the road full of other horse riders for anyone selling clothes. The streets were nowhere near wide enough for all the foot traffic. It took much longer than it needed to to weave through the other townspeople.

On the far end of the street, I saw a short woman selling clothes. Patternless tunics, soft leggings, and cloaks covered the small stand. Many of them appeared to have been hand-stitched. We weaved our way to the clothes stand. Hopping down, I tied Daisy's reigns to a post near the stand next to a trough of cold water. I walked over to the woman, and her smile broadened.

"Hello sweetie," she beamed, "what can I do for you today?" She was an older woman, and her almost white hair was cut into a short afro. Despite her age, a bright spark lived in her deep brown eyes, full of life. Her eyes scanned over my face, taking in all the cuts, but she said nothing. I fought the urge to pull up my hood, but it would only be more suspicious.

"I just need some clothes, preferably ones that are easy to move in. I have a long journey ahead of me." She nodded and rummaged through her stacks of clothes. Multiple pairs of trousers and patterned dresses fell to the dirt behind the stand before she pulled out a pair of thin black leggings and a short-sleeved gray tunic.

"Will this work? I think these will be breathable enough." I took them in my hands and felt the material. The cotton was thin, possibly too thin to survive a trek through the wilderness, but it would last me the rest of the way to Hexia.

"These will be perfect, how much do I owe you?"

"One silver and three coppers will do." I handed the woman her coin and took the clothes.

"Thank you, ma'am," I said as I started walking back towards Daisy.

"You're welcome! Do you need anything else?" I walked back up to her stand. It'd been years since I'd last step foot in here, and I hardly remembered where anything was.

"Do you know of an inn I could stay at for a few hours? And a stand to get some food and water." She pointed down the other side of the road.

"There should be a food seller a few stands down, and the inn is close. Take a right at the small side road after the food stand and walk down until you see the bright yellow building, that's the inn."

I repeated the directions to myself. "Thank you."

"You're welcome, sweetheart."

I petted Daisy's mane and hoisted myself back onto the saddle, her hair burning to the touch. Hopefully, the inn would have space for her to rest in the shade. I gently nudged her side and guided her to the food seller the old woman pointed out. Hordes of people pushed past us as we worked our way through the crowd. Children ran through gaps in the crowd, splashing each other with buckets of cold water. Other people worked through the crowd with sheep and chickens guided with rope.

I was hit with the smell of a warm barn. Four goats squeezed their way past us, the scent spreading quickly along the dense road. It was so wildly different from the empty palace, and I loved it. There was no one telling me what to do with every second of my day, no guards watching my every mood. Just pure chaos and disorder. A line of runaway chickens sprinted in front of me, a frantic man with rope chasing after them.

In a flurry of feathers, I finally saw the man selling food and jumped off Daisy's back, tying her to a nearby post. The man was sold all kinds of summer crops. Vibrant bell peppers, berries dripping with juice, vines of tomatoes, bunches of bananas, apples, and fuzzy peaches covered the small stand. I felt a small amount of victory when my eyes landed on a pile of dried meat. *Just what I needed.*

He met my eyes as I walked up to the counter of his stand. "Welcome, ma'am. What can I interest you in today?" he said in a raspy voice. I played with the coins in my cloak pocket.

"I need some dried meat and a canteen of water."

"Of course." He wrapped two small handfuls of dried meat into a cloth, and grabbed one metal canteen of water. "That will be one silver and six coppers." I looked at the rest of his stock. Daisy had been working hard since last night. She deserved a treat.

"Do you think I could also get one of those apples?" He picked up the ripe fruit and placed it on the counter.

"Your total is now seven coppers and a silver."

I winced. Hopefully, two coppers and a silver would be enough for the inn. I handed the man the coin and collected my food and water.

I waved to him and walked back to Daisy. I fed her the apple, earning a grateful nicker in response. "You're welcome, Daisy," I said, giving her nose a scratch. Packing the food and water in the saddle pockets, I hoisted myself onto the saddle. I nudged her side and steered her right, down the side road. The buildings cast a shadow over the alley, granting me a small reprieve from the heat.

Less people traveled on this road than the main one. The only stands around were one man selling hand-hammered rings and another selling more clothes. At the very end of the alley, I spotted the bright yellow building. It was hard to miss, every other building around it was only one story, and the inn rose a full three stories over the surrounding buildings.

As we neared the front door, a small wooden structure came into view. I leaned in closer to Daisy's ear. "You see that girl, they have a nice little stable for you to rest in."

She neighed loudly. An older lady with streaks of silver through her curly brown hair walked out the door of the inn, waving to me.

"Welcome to the Anmia Inn, my name is Miranda. How long are you staying with us?" I hopped down from the stable and took Daisy by the reins.

"I only need a room until the evening, then I'll be back on my way."

She took Daisy's reins. "You sure?"

I nodded.

"Rocco, get this horse in the stable and give her some food and water." A small child with sun-kissed skin and a dusting of freckles rushed out from the side of the inn.

"Yes ma'am." Before the young boy took her reins and led her into the stable, I retrieved my new clothes from the saddle pockets and my canteen of water. Once I stepped away from Daisy, I waved goodbye to the boy as he took her to the stable, jingling the dwindling coin in my pocket.

"How much do I owe you?"

Miranda waved her hands. "You're staying for less than one night, no charge for you."

"Are you sure?"

"Yes, yes. Now follow me." Wow, people were much nicer around here. From my experience, people who I'd just met that were nice to me always wanted something from me. The part of me that still held some hope for people knew Miranda probably wasn't one of them, but it still unnerved me. I wondered how quickly that kindness would leave once the palace issued the order for my arrest.

Miranda led me into the inn, and immediate relief washed over me. The lobby was empty, save another man napping at the desk. Both of the side walls were filled with windows, brightening the dirt-caked maroon carpet. Same as the outside, the walls were a bright yellow, and a few plants were scattered around the room. Miranda walked behind the desk and handed me a slightly rusted key. "Here's room on the second floor. Take the staircase over there and turn left."

I smiled at her. "Thank you, Miranda."

She waved goodbye. "You're welcome, honey. And if you get hungry, the dinner spread will be ready around five."

I walked to the staircase Miranda pointed to. It was narrowed and enclosed, with only a tiny window every few feet. A majority Primis village didn't get the luxury of keeping torches lit all the time.

Turning left on the second-floor landing, I found the room number matching my key. I put the key in the lock, and the door swung open. It was surprisingly spacious. A full-size bed with yellow pillows and blankets was pushed against the far wall, right next to a small dresser.

A window to the right and above the bed lit up the room, allowing me to see the tiny flowers covering the green wallpaper. And to the left, I spotted another door. Pushing it open, I found a private bathroom already stocked with soap, buckets of water, and towels. *Now this is luxury.*

Immediately, I threw my cloak, daggers, and food onto the bed and ran into the bathroom. I peeled off my sweat and blood-stained clothes, throwing them into the corner. The bandage wrapping my arm was beginning to sting again after not changing it, but I didn't have anything to re-wrap it with. I would have to keep it on until I got to base.

My arms trembled as I lifted the buckets into the metal tub. Then, I lowered myself into the cold water, grabbing the soap on the edge of the tub. The water turned red and brown as I scrubbed the past day away from my skin, not stopping until my skin stung. I washed away some of the dirt and grime off the bandage on my arm, subsiding some of the burn.

I wrapped myself in the towel and grimaced as I picked up the same undergarments I'd been wearing for almost the past two days. Then, I wiggled into the new leggings and my tunic. Clean of the trials the past day, I left the bathroom and flopped on the creaky bed.

Glimpsing at the small clock on the wall, it was only one o'clock. Dinner wouldn't be served for another four hours. I should sleep now, and eat dinner here so I didn't waste my rations, and then sleep until the sun went down. I moved all my supplies and my cloak on top of the dresser to make room for myself, and sat back down on the bed, wincing as I accidentally sit on my daggers. I'd almost forgotten to put them back on. I strapped two of them to my thighs and sheathed the third at my hip.

Despite my eyes feeling heavier than bricks of lead, sleep did not find me. Outside, I could keep all my thoughts at bay with the distraction of the task in front of me. Now, nothing but the ticking of the clock had a chance of drowning out the noise in my head now. I tried willing away the images replaying in my mind. It was futile. Behind my eyes, all I saw was Aerilyn slumping to the ground and the slight rise in her back as she took her last breath. The Princess acted as if she had no power. No power to keep my best friend alive. No power to make the rest of the royals see reason. She stayed silent, and Aerilyn had to pay for it.

This wasn't the first time something like this had happened. It was like I was fifteen again, when I'd almost gotten one of my friends killed. A Progression member had wanted his fellow members' crystals back after I stole them. I'd brought upon his wrath. He'd held Val in a chokehold, almost killing him. And he'd refused to let him go until I gave him the crystals back. But I'd taken the crystals from two women trying to kill the families in the Primis village. Why wouldn't I have taken them? In the eyes of my younger self, I'd done the right thing. But I hadn't learned you couldn't save everyone. After I'd given them back, he'd survived and got out mostly unscathed. The scars on my arm worked as a reminder of how my actions tend to hurt others around me.

But this time was different. Aerilyn was dead, and I couldn't bring her back. No matter how much I wished I could go back in time and put myself in her position.

I wiped the tears streaming down my face. Crying wouldn't bring her back. Nothing would ever bring her back. But I could avenge her as I planned to do for my family. Before I got... distracted. By the lightness of the Princess' laugh. The way her dimples shone through the few times she showed her real smile. I felt a tug in my chest. No. I shouldn't be thinking like that. The thought of her should make me angry. It was supposed to keep my need for revenge alive.

I jumped at the sound of someone banging on my door. I waited for them to announce their name, but they only slammed their fist into the door harder in response. I sat up to answer the door and froze as I scanned outside one of the windows. Outside the window to my right, standing in front of the door to the inn, were two men in black uniforms. I looked closer, and my eyes widened; they were in guard uniforms, ones with a crest stitched in gold over their chests.

The royal crest.

I muttered a curse while I quietly threw on my cloak and fumbled with the clasp as the banging grew louder. I stuffed as much of my food and my water into the pockets of the cloak, praying nothing would fall out from my running. The only way out was jumping out the window over the bed; none of the guards were surrounding the bottom. I paced the room, trying to think of a way to give myself time to make the jump.

I flinched at another loud knock. The guard would barge in any second, but I needed more time. Scanning the room, the only thing I could push against the door was the wooden dresser. I grunted as I moved the dresser in front of the door. It took most of my strength, but I managed to position it in front of the door. Using one of my daggers, I began cutting the thin glass of the window. Breaking it would only attract the attention of the guards. I cut around the edges of the window and quietly placed the glass on the bed.

A soft click sounded behind me. *They have a key.* Looking back, the guard at my door was worming his arm through the crack in the door. Each second, he pushed the dresser farther away from the door. "Stop in the name of the crown! You are under arrest!"

I tilted my head as I smiled at him. He removed his arm from the door to grab one of his daggers, aiming it at me. "You'll have to catch me first." I jumped out the window just as his dagger landed in the wall where my hand had just been.

Struggling to stifle my scream, I landed in the hard dirt below. My ankle twisted at an unnatural angle before I could roll to soften my fall. Perhaps jumping out a second-story window was not the best idea. The deep voices of the guards grew closer. Scrambling to stand up, I ignored the sharp slices of pain and ran around the other corner. Flattened against the wall, I peered around the corner to watch the guards scan the area. They left at the sound of the third guard's voice.

Luckily, this side of the inn was where the stables were. Looking for any more guards, I pushed off the wall and limped into the stable, my ankle throbbing with every footfall. I found Daisy taking a nap at the far end. Hurrying to her side, I scratched her neck until she woke up. "Sorry girl, but we have to leave now."

I stuffed my canteen and dried meat that miraculously stayed in my pocket into the saddle pockets and hoisted myself onto the saddle. I tugged the reins and left the stable. Forgetting to look before leaving, my eyes met with one of the guards. "Stop right there," he ordered. *Hells.* I yanked on her reins and made her run in the opposite direction. People dove out of Daisy's way, and we were able to get through the main road.

An arrow whizzed past, nicking my ear. I turned my head and saw one of the guards on horseback with a bow in his hands. *They want me dead, don't they?* Warm blood trickled from the small cut.

My hand flew to the dagger at my hip, gripping it hard. I wouldn't be able to escape while trying to avoid arrows. I twisted myself so I faced the archer and just as he raised his bow again, I flung the dagger at him, embedding it into his shoulder. He fell off his horse from the impact, with his bow far from reach.

As I turned forward, I jerked the reins, forcing Daisy to halt. Two guards stood in front of me with two children crying in their grip.

"Turn yourself in and we won't hurt them," the bigger guard said. The emerald crystal around his neck swayed in the breeze, a silent warning. Tears and snot tumbled down the girl's tanned face.

"All we would have to say is these kids helped you by attacking us," the second guard said. "And no one would bat an eye when we punish them." These kids couldn't have been older than ten, and yet the guards were willing to hurt them to get to me.

"You're both bluffing. You wouldn't hurt them," I said. My hands gripped the reins so hard they were beginning to go numb. The second guard gripped the petrified boy tighter, his crystal glowing a bright cerulean. But these were children! They couldn't hurt them.

"It would be in their best interest for you to not question us," the first guard said in a low voice. "Nobody will miss a couple of Primis children anyways." A pit formed in my stomach. If the kids were Imperium, the guards wouldn't use them. If they were Imperium the guards would be protecting them instead of using them as pawns. Despite having barely eaten anything, I fought the urge to vomit.

Thick roots sprouted from the ground at the first guard's command, breaking through the cobblestone and wrapping around the little girl. She shook with terror as the branches stopped just above her shoulders. "Stop!" the boy screamed. "Leave my sister alone! Help us!" His screams were futile. No one would go against the guards, it was a death sentence.

"So what'll it be?" the second guard asked. Both of them wore a smug grin, certain they would be taking me in. But I needed to get to Hexia, two kids weren't enough for me to go back to the palace. The guards had to still be bluffing. But even I knew I was lying to myself. I couldn't go back there. I wouldn't.

Ignoring the sour taste coating my tongue and the potent guilt in my heart, I said, in a cracking voice, "I will never go with you." The first guard shrugged and the branches squeezed the little girl, her face turning red.

"No!" me and the boy screamed. I couldn't watch this. I kicked Daisy's side and tugged the reins in the opposite direction. I grimaced as the boy's scream echoed through the alleyways, echoing in my ears, my heart, my mind, my soul.

We picked up pace on the exit road, cobblestone flying under Daisy's hooves. Two kids died because of me. Not by my actions, but by my cowardice. Hot tears rolled down my cheeks, not slowing until we were out of the town.

I just needed to not think about it yet. Focus on the task in front of me, become numb to the events of today. Guilt wouldn't be ignored, but I'd been living with it for years. What was a little more?

Most of the land between here and Hexia was grassland. But if I traveled the more inland route, the grass would be high enough to hide me. We managed to escape the village, but I could tell Daisy wouldn't make it very far if I kept up this speed.

Within less than an hour, the grass was high enough for me to slow down. I crouched my head below the grass. Blades kept slapping my face as we trotted through the grass, but it kept me hidden. And the less time wasted trying to run from guards, the more time I would have to prepare for the palace infiltration.

After an hour of traveling, I wanted to drop. I pulled the reins backward and squeezed her sides, signaling to halt, and hopped off the saddle. I patted her neck and let her rest. We both needed it. Traveling at night would be better anyways. I raised the hood of my cloak to protect my face from the sun and took out the canteen and a small amount of the dried meat. Unbearable saltiness filled my mouth as I took a bite, but it quelled the growing rumbling of my stomach. After hours plagued with exhaustion, I laid down in the dirt. Every ache and pain in my body hit me all at once. But after only a few minutes after closing my eyes, a dreamless sleep finally found me.

Chapter 23

Yorena

N OT BOTHERING WITH LIGHTING a torch, I dashed into the secret tunnels, the door closing with an echoing slam behind me. I opened the door to enter my room and ran out of the apartment. Guards assigned to this floor rushed past me, bolting for any staircase they could find. I had never seen anything like it. That mob of people must've been at least half the population of New Teber. A door opened behind me.

"What is going on out there?" Nikos grumbled. Both him and Oliver walked out of their rooms. I guess the meeting had ended soon after I left.

"No clue, but we should get down there."

The corner of his lip turned up. "So now you want to admit we're on the same playing field." I didn't have time for this.

"Are you going to stand there and gloat or are you going to follow me outside and see what the problem is?"

He put a finger to his chin as if he were actually weighing the options. "I can do both." With no time to argue, I ran towards the staircase, Oliver and Nikos trailing close behind.

"Aren't the guards handling them?" Oliver said.

"We are all competing to be the heir, once we are the monarch, going out there when events like this happen will be our duty," I said.

Nikos scoffed. "You talk a lot about what it's like to be the monarch yet you're the one who seems to be upsetting everyone in the palace." I halted before passing through the door to the stairs. I wouldn't be upsetting everyone if he hadn't come up with the idea that killed Aerilyn and made me lose Ilise. I wouldn't be upsetting everyone if my parents would focus more on my kingdom instead of basically giving the nominees more power than I had.

"Do you want me to throw you down these stairs?" I said, staring Nikos down.

"Leave her alone, Nikos," Oliver said. I took a deep breath and went down the stairs without another word.

If Nikos wanted to make my life difficult, then so be it. But we couldn't waste more time arguing, anything else I said would only add fuel to the fire. At least Oliver wasn't being an egotistical jerk. And they were practically the only one in the palace that didn't hate, or have disappointment in me besides Kieron. We arrived on the first-floor landing and turned right to head into the courtyard.

I thought about what could have gathered a crowd that large and angry, and recalled an event from my history lessons. The last time a mob had tried to storm the palace was right before Anora Schaefer's coronation. Those who were against the rebellion she'd led were trying to deny her claim to the throne. Half the guards were still loyal to the ideals of Letita and didn't try to stop the mob. Most of the first and second floors were destroyed, and it took hours for them to root out the last of them. It was one of the main reasons they built the tunnels in the first place, in case it ever happened again.

But what would the people be angry about now? Unless... "Uh oh," I said. The three of us stopped in front of the doors to the courtyard, already blocked by a squad of guards.

"Are you saying uh oh to the guards, or something else?" Oliver asked.

"Both." I waved them towards the door to one of the servant's hallways. I opened the door, and the few servants milling around immediately put their heads down upon seeing us walking past. "They must have found out about last night."

Nikos groaned.

"You could try to sound a little concerned," I said, failing to keep the panic out of my voice.

"What could a group of Primis do? The guards should be able to control them," Oliver said. Something about Oliver's tone set off warning bells in my head. Just because they were powerless didn't mean they were weak.

"True... but I don't think the guards particularly enjoy having to control an angry mob," I said. We arrived at the door leading to the courtyard. Nikos interrupted me before I could open it.

"Not to insult your intelligence, Princess—" I cut him off.

"Is that not what you have been doing every thirty seconds?" I gritted out.

"Well yes, but if the crowd is mad at the decision *we* made, then how would seeing our faces calm them down?"

I leaned against the door frame. The palms of my hand became slick with sweat. "First, *I* was not the one who wanted to go through with it. Second, if they hear a statement from *us*, they might calm down." He leaned down slightly to meet my eyes. They were greener than vials of poison and I could feel them burning right through me.

"Then why don't you open the door. Or are you afraid this will go up in flames? Like everything else you've done." My hands curled into shaking fists as I turned away from him. Of course I was terrified this would end badly. I'd already thought of thirty ways this could go wrong, but I was the Princess, this was my kingdom, and it needed help. We were in the middle of a crisis; one would think he would stop spitting his venom in my face.

"Can we just open the door?" Oliver said.

Nikos clapped his hands together. "Wonderful idea. Princess, if you don't mind." I looked back to sneer at him before opening the door, and my face was hit with a blast of hot air. A sea of black and gold stood in front of the gilded gate, guards rushing out every door of the palace.

"Your Highness, nominees," one of the guards said as he started to push us back towards the door. I stared past the guard's shoulders, but another line of guards blocked me from seeing anything. "You shouldn't be out here. Get back into the palace," he ordered. I wiggled out of his grip.

"We want to talk to them and see if we can calm them down," I said.

Nikos stepped in front of me. "Correction, *she* wants to do it and managed to drag the two of us along." I narrowed my eyes at him, his mouth curved into another annoying smirk. He was the one who wanted to be King so bad, and this was part of being a monarch. Yet, my parents hadn't bothered to come outside, leaving me to fix this. How was *I* the nominee they were disappointed in? This was *their* job.

The guard looked towards the gate and then back at us. He pointed towards the right guard tower, already filled with archers. "Go to that tower to talk to the mob, the archers should be enough protection."

"Thank you." I hurried towards the tower stairs. The sound of the mob's outcries became deafeningly loud in my ears.

I opened the door to the tower and walked up the twisting staircase, the sounds of shouting muffled by the thick, tan stone walls. "Could you hurry up, I don't want to be here for the entirety of Heircestrial," Nikos said.

"Can you please shut your mouth for just one minute?" Oliver groaned.

We arrived at the top of the tower and pushed open the door. Archers marched along the top of the palace walls, arrows notched. My neck strained to find a guard with a white crystal. "What are you looking for?" Nikos asked, leaning against the back wall.

"Looking for a guard with an air crystal so they can carry my voice over the crowd." I saw one marching towards our tower.

"Hey, you!"

He jogged at my call. "Yes, Your Highness?" I pointed to the still growing crowd. I needed to get them to calm down quickly. These were my people, they loved me. They would listen to me, they had to.

"I want to talk to the people, can you carry my voice for me?" He nodded and stood next to me as I looked out over the mob. Dread settled low in my stomach, my breakfast threatening to make an appearance. I clutched the ledge as tight as my fingers would allow. *What if this doesn't work?* No. I pushed every doubt into the deepest crevices of my mind where they couldn't rear their ugly heads. Oliver placed a reassuring hand on my shoulder, giving it a gentle squeeze and offering a soft smile.

"I'm right here with you," they said. Ilise's words echoed in my mind. *"It would be impossible for everything to go right."* I repeated them to myself as I released my grip on the ledge. My hands still shook so I hid them behind my back.

"Attention everyone!" My voice echoed over the land as the guard carried it through the air. The mob fell silent, turning their attention towards me. "Tell me what your grievances are. We can solve this like the civilized people we are." A boy that looked to be around my age stepped forward, and the crowd retreated slightly for him. The boy stood before one of the guards guarding the gate, his lanky figure small compared to the guard. He waved his hand at the nearest guard, and the guard's crystal began to glow a brilliant white.

He angled his head up to me, and chestnut brown waves of hair fell back from his face, his mouth pressed into a hard line. "My name is Eloi, and we've heard from various sources that you have unjustly executed one of the palace servants because you *thought* she was a spy," he spat. I opened my mouth to speak, but he cut me off. "And you didn't even let her try to defend herself from your accusations. She didn't deserve to die, you tyrant. She wasn't even an Imperium, yet you treated her like she was a dangerous criminal." The guard's hand inched closer to the hilt of his sword at Eloi's tone.

"We gave her the chance to defend herself, but she had no evidence to prove she wasn't a spy. We're not tyrants here. I didn't want her to die, but the evidence pointed towards her. And the guards would've been gentler if she didn't resist when they first tried to arrest her," I said. I didn't think I calmed them down. Various voices began to scream at me, along with the boy.

"Stop trying to downplay what you've done," Eloi yelled, "you killed her, she didn't just die."

I gaped. I wasn't trying to downplay it. What did they want me to say? That I had to force myself to remain still out of fear of being disregarded, *again*? That I had to make myself keep my eyes open, to ensure it was ingrained in my memory. That I knew a letter was nowhere near enough evidence no matter how much I told myself it was, as if the lie would ease even a small fraction of my guilt. Hot tears welled in my eyes, but I restrained myself from letting them fall. This wasn't about me. I wasn't the one who had someone like me killed.

"It's not my fault, please calm yourselves. If I could change what happened, I would," I said, my voice cracking on every word.

Oliver leaned in close to my ear. "Let's give them a minute" We didn't have a minute. I was losing more of the people's trust with every wasted second.

"Do either of you have something better to say?" I asked. Nikos let out a laugh, and my gaze slid to him. "Does it bring you joy to see me mess up?" He had no idea how it felt to watch everything I'd worked for slip through my fingers like water.

"Immensely. And considering it looks like all of New Teber wants your head on a stake, I don't think we can do anything."

I leaned over the edge of the tower, looking down at the crowd. They had gone back to screaming at me, cursing the palace, demanding for my parents to come outside. None of them tried to approach the guards besides the one boy, yet all of them moved their hands to the hilt of their swords. I crouched down on the ground and covered my ears to muffle their chants.

"So we're hiding now?" Nikos said, trying to bait me. My only idea turned out to only worsen the situation.

"I am trying to think. I highly doubt my parents will be coming outside anytime soon. Nor would I want them to, I think it would only make the crowd angrier." Both of them sat down beside me, leaning against the wall.

"Well maybe we could offer them your head on a stake, I think they'd like that," Nikos said.

"If you make one more comment I just might put *your* head on a stake. And cook it slowly over a fire." The image brought me an infinitely small amount of joy.

"Aw, it's sweet you think that scared me."

I glared at him.

"Archers! Ready you bows," someone barked. I scrambled up from the floor, panicking as every archer on this side of the wall nocked and drew their bows. They couldn't shoot arrows at them. Sure, they were angry, and rightfully so, but they were peaceful. There was no reason to shoot at them.

"What are you doing? The crowd is not being violent," I said to the closest archer. The archer didn't turn to me as he responded.

"We have orders directly from the King." No. He wouldn't.

"Please, don't shoot at them. It will only make things worse," I pleaded. Getting shot by an arrow at this height would kill someone. Protesting injustice didn't warrant death.

"Sorry Your Highness, but orders are orders." I ran back into the tower and leaned as far over the side as I could. I waved my hands, begging everyone to leave.

"Leave now! They are about to shoot at you! I can't stop them!" No one heard my voice over the noise of their rising chants.

"Down with the crown! Down with the crown! Down with the crown!"

"Maybe you should step back from the ledge," Oliver said. I did not step back. A whistle sounded in the distance, and the first archer let his arrow loose.

"Agh!" Eloi screamed. I gaped in horror at the arrow going through his bicep. Bright red blood gushed out of the wound. Protesters surrounding him tried to stanch the bleeding, but it only flowed faster with every press on his arm. My stomach twisted at every one of his screams.

"Return to your homes," another archer ordered, "Or else we are on strict orders to release all of the arrows." None of them turned to leave. More gathered closer to the front gate. People must have summoned others from town. They needed to leave, *now.*

"Listen to them, please!" Nobody acknowledged that they heard me. They marched closer and closer to the front gate as guards pushed back against the front line of the crowd. People shied away from their swords, but still refused to back down.

I pleaded to the archer to let them go, but he only shook his head solemnly. "Archers! Fire!"

"No!" I screamed. Arrows pelted everyone in the crowd. Eloi dropped to his knees and fell face-first into the grass, an iron-tipped arrow protruding out the back of his head. I fought back another wave of nausea.

More people fell to the ground as they were struck down by the continuing waves of arrows. Tears dripped down my face at the sight of the carnage. Those who were still standing helped drag the injured away from the gates. Protesters near the back scurried away from the arrows as quickly as they could. Within minutes the entire crowd had retreated into the town.

I slid down the wall of the tower, hiding my face in my hands. Looking up, Oliver's expression of disbelief matched my own, and Nikos slid down an impassive mask over his face. Without another word, I ran past the other nominees, back down the tower stairs. I stormed past the guard trying to stop me. I hadn't realized my crystal was glowing, fueled by my anger.

That was unnecessary, disgraceful, and every other negative adjective my clouded head couldn't think of. My parents only further damaged our relationship with the people, and killed innocents in the process. Nothing they could say would ever be enough to justify the destruction I beheld. Nothing.

Out of the summer heat, goosebumps rose on my arms. There was only one place my parents would be, somewhere they could hide from the "threat" of our people. I ran to the staircase and bounded down the stairs to the underground floor. At the same time the tunnels were built, a panic room was installed, built to house the royals for as long as we needed to hide from danger. Only this time, it was a danger we created.

Two burly guards were stationed in front of the door and stiffened when I approached. "Open the doors. Now," I ordered. They exchanged slightly nervous glances. My parents were the ones who should be nervous.

"Your Highness, these doors remain closed until we are told the threat is gone."

I fisted my hands. "The 'threat' is gone. I will not tell you again, open the doors," I seethed.

He gulped. "Apologies, Your Highness." They both bowed and twisted open the lock on the door.

Both my parents sat on the plush couch at the back of the room. I'd never been in this room before. While the walls were gray concrete, it was decorated with fine furnishings. Plush couches and chairs were all pushed to the back corner, and yellow carpets were scattered across the floors. Crates filled with food were stacked on the left wall, covered in dust.

Not sparing another second, I stormed towards them. "Yorena, calm down," Mother said as she reached to smooth down my hair. I slapped her hand away.

"What were you guys thinking? Firing on innocent people was not the answer. And innocent Primis people at that. How could they have possibly defended themselves?"

Father shifted in his seat. "They were a threat to everyone in this palace and it was the only way to get them to leave." I gaped at him. This was not who we were. Or at least it wasn't who I was.

"They were peaceful. None of them tried to attack the guards, or banged on the gates. All they were doing was demanding the two of you make up for what you did to Aerilyn, to admit you were in the wrong, and make sure it never happened again."

Father's face darkened. "You will not speak to your mother and I like that. What's done is done."

I could not believe what I was hearing. Our royal line was built with equality in mind. Yet every day, the divide already wreaking havoc on our kingdom continued to widen. What was the point of Anora's revolution if we were just going to continue to go backward. I turned to leave but decided to ask them one last thing.

"Was it necessary for you to kill Aerilyn?"

Mother scoffed. "I thought we were done with this conversation," she said, shooting me glare. I used every ounce of my willpower to not shrink under her gaze.

"I asked you a question. Was it necessary?"

Father leaned forward on the couch. "Every decision we make as King and Queen is necessary." I stepped closer to him.

"But if we had waited before killing her, she could have been innocent."

My parents grimaced. "I know that look." They avoided my gaze. They were hiding something. "What did you do?" Mother opened her mouth and then promptly shut it. "Say it," I spat. Mother ran her finger through the curls of her hair. Father's expression hardened.

"The letter we found in her room might not have been for her," he said. All my muscles felt weak. "The letter was in a stack of mail that must have been for everyone in the apartment. It may very well have been for that Ilise girl." I shook my head at them. Mother reached her hand out for me.

Her death was for nothing. Aerilyn never should've died.

"Yorena." I ran out of the room before she could continue.

I forced open the door of the training room. It barely closed before I screamed, with every emotion weighing me down.

Chapter 24

Ilise

A PULSING ACHE AWOKE me from my brief sleep. I groaned as I sat myself up. Small streams of moonlight broke through the high grass and insects buzzed in the distance. I touched my tender ankle and winced. It had swollen from my jump, most likely sprained. Taking short breaths, I pushed myself onto my feet. Jumping out of a two-story window hadn't been the best idea, but it'd allowed me to escape.

Hopping on my good ankle, I edged over to Daisy. She woke up and nuzzled my pockets, no doubt in search of another apple. "Sorry girl, later," I murmured. "We need to keep moving." My still tired muscles protested at the effort, sweat already beading my brow.

After a few tries, I hoisted myself onto the saddle and gently kicked her side. We continued through the tall grass. The only sound beside Daisy's footsteps was the loud chirping from the crickets. I leaned over, digging my hand into one of the saddlebags, and pulled out the dried meat, breaking off half of it. If I was lucky, the rest of the journey would take only a couple of days. And hopefully I would get there before my face was plastered on every poster on every wall in the kingdom, calling for my arrest.

We traveled for a full day and a half at a hard pace before taking a much longer break, walking again the moment the sun went down. I was down to one piece of dried meat, almost all my water was gone, and the Zasen River was still miles away. The last of it I've been sprinkling on Daisy to keep her cool. My stomach cramped at the emptiness.

Daisy and I arrived at the edge of the tall grass and stopped for the night. There was no point in trying to ride until morning; we were both bone-weary. My legs trembled as I slowly slid off the saddle, and she grazed the grass while I carefully settled myself down. My ankle still throbbed and wouldn't stop until I got supplies from the Hexia base. Using one of my daggers, I cut a piece of my tunic to use as a wrap to attempt to keep it in place.

If my guess was right, I was only one day away from the base. One day away from the Union, one day away from starting the preparations for the attack on the palace, one day away from the only family I had left. They might have left me in isolation for five years, but they still cared about me. It was necessary for our goal, no matter how many times I'd cursed them in my head for leaving me there. No matter how much I felt like I'd been abandoned.

But I was just as bad. I'd abandoned those children in Anmia, sentencing them to a painful death because I couldn't get over my stupid fear. I should've turned myself in. My throat and eyes burned as I allowed all the guilt to flow through me. I could've escaped afterwards. Those children did nothing wrong and now they were dead because of me. Why did death always follow me? The hot tears rolled down my face and a quiet sob escaped my mouth. I was even more alone now than before. At least in the palace I had some friends, and whatever me and the Princess were.

I constantly found myself wandering to thoughts of the Princess. The image of her face in my head made my heart clench. I shouldn't be doing that, I shouldn't be feeling this way. She took part in the murder of my best friend, the only person who helped keep me sane while in the palace. But maybe she hadn't been the only one helping me. The Princess was the one person I could be myself around, or as much of myself as I could while being a spy. But she still couldn't save one of the few people I had left in life, the same way I didn't save those kids. A bitter taste flooded my mouth.

I pushed thoughts of both of them into the back of my mind. There was no time to focus on them, I had to rest and prepare myself for the last leg of my journey. The one that would finally put me on my path of revenge. Revenge for my family, revenge for Aerilyn.

Revenge for me.

I wouldn't be robbed of everything I had and sit quietly. I had almost nothing left and I needed to take something back, no matter how small. When I'd first agreed to join the Union, Val had promised me they would help me take revenge. All I had to do was help them, then they would help me. I was finally on the right path to fulfilling my end of the bargain, and I was ready to receive my reward: killing The Progression leader by my own hand.

I spent an hour trying to get comfortable enough to sleep, yet I felt more awake than I had in days, dreading the next day. The grass was poking into skin too much, the buzzing bugs were too loud in my ears, and the air was much too too hot, like unbreathable blanket I couldn't escape from.

I sat up and unsheathed one of my daggers. I couldn't do much about the other things, but there was one thing I could fix. I removed the dirt-caked tie from my hair, matted with grass after days of travel. I took one section and started sawing through it. The clump slowly fell to the ground before getting whisked away by the slight breeze. I got to work on the rest of my hair, and it collected in a pile in my lap. I ran my hand over my newly shorn locks. It was no more than an inch long, and my head felt lighter than it had ever been with the breeze blowing across my head. I wouldn't be able to hide pins in it anymore, but it felt so much more authentic to who I had become.

My head whipped to the sound of something moving through the grass. I unsheathed another dagger and held one in each hand. I hopped onto my good ankle and crouched low in the grass. The sounds came closer to me each second, blood pounding in my ears as I waited.

"We could have gone the other way, you know," a familiar voice said.

"But where's the fun in that?"

"Well Val, considering I have grass in places grass should not be, I could name at least ten more fun routes you could've picked."

I exhaled a breath of relief. I stood up from my crouch on unstable feet, and Val and Kass froze, daggers pointed at me. I quickly put my hands up.

"Guys, it's me," I said. They slowly put their weapons down as they inched closer to me. Their dropped jaws came into view under the dim moonlight.

"Well if it isn't the most wanted criminal in the kingdom," Val said. I hopped over to him and hugged him. It felt like it'd been ages since I'd last seen him. It probably had been. Dark brown stubble dotted his usually clean-shaven face, and he'd cropped his shoulder-length hair to rest just above his ears.

"I missed you too, Val."

He chuckled and released me. Kass held out her hand for me. "Hey, kid. We didn't think you would be this close to the base already." She pulled me into a hug. The moonlight made the tiny scars marring her angular face more severe, and she'd cut her raven-colored hair from when I last saw her, just so it barely brushed her shoulders.

"It's called getting chased out of an inn by the royal guards and having to jump out a second-story window. Really motivates you to move fast."

She let out a breathy laugh and released me. Her green crystal swung on her neck and brought back unwelcome memories from Anmia. I tried to ignore the girl's screaming in my head.

"What're you guys even doing out here?"

Kass sat down and helped me down next to her. "Groups of us at the base have been doing rounds in the areas around the base to find you. We weren't expecting you for another few days after we heard the news from the palace."

Val sat down next to me, wiping dirt from his tanned hands. "And to make sure, you know. That none of the guards came sniffing around here looking for you."

I laughed. "Trust me, I think I lost them back in Anmia." *And much more than they will ever guess.* Kass pointed to my hair and her face broke into a small smile.

"Finally joining the short hair club. Now you gotta convince Orla and Rori to join." A hiccuping laugh escaped me, and with it, a small bubble of joy. I was finally with my people again, someone had my back. The feeling almost felt foreign to me.

"How did you even manage to escape the palace, evade arrest, *and* get this far in only a few days?" Val said. Had it only been a few days? No wonder Kass and Val were so shocked.

"Do you want the short version or the long and gory version?"

A smile finally spread across Val's face. "Long and gory," he said.

I told them the whole story of how I ended up here, from having to fight the guards in the palace after leaving Nikos' room to jumping out the inn window in Anmia. Various emotions passed over their faces as I told the story of the last few days. I felt pride coming from Kass every time I told them of fighting off a royal guard. The only part I didn't tell them was about what I'd overheard Oliver and the sorceress talking about. It would be better to say it all at once to everyone at the base.

I finished talking, and both of them fell silent. "I think I just aged five years listening to that," Val said.

"Then try to imagine how much I feel like I've aged living through it," I said.

Kass pulled me into another hug and I rested my chin on top of her head. "I'm just glad you're okay," she said as she squeezed me tighter.

"If you squeeze me any harder I might not be okay," I said in a strained voice, and she released me.

"There's just one more small thing."

Val groaned. "Let me guess, more bad news?" I nodded, and he gestured for me to continue. I'd been trying to avoid thinking about the voice I'd been hearing. For all I knew, I could be going mad. But Imogen's voice sounded exactly like the voice in my head, and there was no denying she was the voice. And if it wasn't her, who else could it be? She even used the same nickname the voice used for me—little one. Just the thought of the name sent a sickly chill down my spine, as if the way she'd said it was laced with slime.

"I've been hearing this voice calling for me. And every time the voice comes, I feel like I'm being stabbed in the chest. I scared my friend half to death after I passed out in the garden because of it." A sick feeling filled my stomach at one of my last memories of Aerilyn.

Val raised an eyebrow. "A voice?"

"Maybe you were tired and the voice you heard was your friend calling for you after you passed out," Kass said.

"That's what I thought at first but I could still hear her voice in the background." Kass's brow furrowed in confusion. "And it happened *again* the night I fled." Kass and Val shared a look of disbelief.

"Are you certain you weren't hearing a voice and passing out because you were overworking yourself?" Val asked. Unbelievable. If I wanted to stand here and be dismissed I would've talked this out with the Princess.

"Yes. And the first time it happened was right before I went to sleep, but it didn't hurt that time."

The pair shared a look of disbelief. "I hope you realize how ridiculous this sounds," Kass said.

"It's about to get more ridiculous." They both leaned forward, bracing themselves for what I was about to say. "I think one of the Council sorcerers is behind this."

Their jaws dropped. "Why would a Council sorcerer go through all this trouble to get to you?" Kass asked.

I shrugged. "Maybe she wants to read my mind and find out where the Union is." She was with Oliver, so it could be part of their plan.

"Sorcerers can't read minds," Val said. Then why else would she be in my head, trying to find where I was? What did she have to gain by finding me? "Once we get back to base we can ask Cain. He knows a lot about the sorcerers' magic. But as far as I know, reading minds isn't one of their abilities," he said.

Val poked my ankle and I winced. "Have you been walking on this?" I whacked his hand away.

"Only when needed, most of the time I hop on one leg."

His gray eyes flashed with concern. "We should get you back to base." I nodded, and the two of them grabbed my arms to help me up.

"Do you two have horses?"

"Yeah, they're a little ways back." Using Kass as a crutch, I gave Daisy a gentle scratch to wake her up. She made a grunt of complaint as Kass helped me onto the saddle. Poor girl was probably exhausted, but we only had a few more hours to go, then she could rest. Val grabbed her reins and guided her through the grass to their horses.

My stomach rumbled, and I reached into the saddle pocket to eat my last piece of meat. The over-salted rubbery beef made me want to gag, and Kass stopped me before I could eat it. "We have better food in our saddle bags. Hang on," she said.

We arrived at Val and Kass's horses grazing in an empty patch in the tall grass. Val handed me back Daisy's reins and hoisted himself onto his horse. Kass reached into her saddle bag and tossed me a fresh strip of lamb and two apples. One for me, one for Daisy. Daisy gratefully devoured the apple when I handed it to her. And I stuffed my face with the fresh food, licking away the leftover juices and spices. The chef's cooking had never tasted so good. Kass climbed onto her horse's saddle, and Val and Kass rode beside me as we left the high grass.

After a few hours, the sun began to rise over the horizon. Yellow light washed over the landscape. I struggled to keep my eyes open. Multiple times I fell asleep at the reins, and Daisy started to wander away from Kass and Val. After the second time, Kass made me get off Daisy and sit in front of her on her horse, and Val tied Daisy's reins to his horse to keep her from wandering away from us. "How much longer until we get to the base?" I whispered to her as I leaned against her chest, nestling in the comfort.

"If we keep this pace, we should get there before sundown."

I groaned. "Just sit tight," she said.

When the sun was high in the sky, we stopped to take a short break next to a small pond. Kass helped me down and I limped to the pond.

I splashed the lukewarm water on my face, sighing as it helped cool me down. Kass and I were walking back when all her muscles tensed. I looked over at Val to see he was also frozen, on high alert. "What's wro—" Kass shushed me. Val squinted in the distance before his eyes widened.

"I thought you said you lost the guards," he said.

"I thought I did. None of them followed me out of Anmia."

Kass pointed at the figures in the distance. "Then what do you call that?"

I squinted to see what they were talking about. On horseback were three guards charging at full speed towards us. The gold royal crest on their chest shone in the brightly sunlight. "I can't catch a break, can I?"

Val laughed weakly as he unsheathed a dagger and a longsword from his horse. "Nope." I looked to Kass, who also had a dagger and staff in hand. Her crystal glowed forest green as the guards approached.

"You ready?" Kass asked me. I unsheathed two of the daggers I stole from the palace guards.

"Always."

Chapter 25

Princess Yorena

THE DAYS AFTER THE protest blurred in my mind. My parents didn't try to talk to me again, nor did Nikos. Occasionally, Oliver would try to talk to me, but I couldn't let anyone see me like this. Everything was falling apart. Erea, Heircestrial, my life's plan. Most of my time I spent working my anger out in the training room, which was no help in keeping my thoughts off of *her*. I wished I could talk to Ilise. It'd been a week now since she fled. Eventually, another servant had been assigned to take over Aerilyn and Ilise's jobs, but I'd turned them down. It'd felt too much like erasing what had happened to them, what I had allowed to happen to them. Chafik and Mathias split the cleaning workload, and Chafik took over cooking for the three of us. *Three of us. We used to be five.*

I avoided them as much as I could. Seeing them brought my guilt back to the surface. Even now, as I stared at the faded words of Chafik's history book. The candle I lit hours ago was halfway to the stub, it's gentle glow only illuminating the small circle around my desk.

The next test was going to be about diplomacy. After my disaster of an attempt to calm down the protesters, I wasn't feeling confident in my diplomatic abilities. A knock sounded at my door. "Come in," I said. Chafik opened the door holding a plate of steaming food.

"It's past eight o'clock and I don't think you've eaten," he said.

"Is it?" I peeled back one of the drapes on the window and was greeted with the orange light of the setting sun, stars dotting the already purple portions of the sky. Chafik, along with Kieron, had been helping me the past few days, mostly making sure I didn't run myself into the ground. A large part of me felt like I didn't deserve their concern, but it was nice to know I still had friends in the palace.

He set the plate down on the desk, next to the open history book. "You studying up on Heircestrial again?"

I nodded. "I need to be prepared for the next test." I propped up the book on the page of the past nominees. "Almost every nominee who passed the second test became the heir. And they turned out to be some of the better monarchs, even when Letita's ideals were what everyone believed." Granted they'd still been awful, but they were objectively not the worst they could've been.

He shifted beside me. "How hard can diplomacy be anyways?" I looked at him out of the corner of my eye. "What?" he said with a shrug.

"It takes an extraordinary amount of self-control to not snap at the other leaders when it seems they're playing a game of who can ask for the most ridiculous thing possible. And if even one word of what you say sounds accusatory, they'll tear you down."

He snorted. "I deal with Mathias most of the day, and trust me, less than half the stuff he rants about makes sense." Some of the tension left my body as I allowed myself a giggle.

"And judging by Nikos' temper and Oliver's timidness, I think you'll be fine." I turned to face him. His one blue eye glowed in the candlelight as he offered me a reassuring smile. I wanted that to make me feel better, knowing there was at least one person who still had faith in me. But he was only one more person for me to disappoint.

"That's what I told myself last time. And we both know how that turned out."

He patted me on the shoulder before he turned to leave. "What's that phrase people say? Second time's a charm?"

"Technically, it's the third time's a charm."

He shrugged. "Then we'll hope this time it will be the second time's a charm."

I gave a weak laugh as he waved goodbye and closed the door. He left me the bowl of lamb and tomato stew, but my stomach turned at the thought of eating anything. I managed to eat a few bites of the lamb and a few spoonfuls of the broth before a note slid under my door. Abandoning the food, I retrieved the message. The familiar scent of shea butter and lavender wafted from the slip of paper. *Mother.*

I broke the red seal of the note and opened the letter.

Report to the throne room in no less than fifteen minutes. Dress nicely and do your hair; we will be receiving the people. Your fellow nominees will be attending as well, behave.

Love,

Mother

I looked down at what I was wearing. Leggings and an old tunic weren't going to cut it. I pulled myself away from the desk and opened my armoire of dresses. I scanned my eyes over the dresses in almost every shade, some blank, others with lace and stitched floral designs. I settled on a silk dress the color of honey. I changed my clothes and wiggled into the dress, the fabric stopping right above my knees. I ran my fingers through my tangled curls and sighed. Doing my hair was the last thing I wanted to do. Using a hair tie, I pulled it into a low ponytail. Going over myself in the wall mirror once more, I left my room.

"Where are you going?" Mathias asked, not glancing up from his spot on the couch.

"Mother summoned me to the throne room to receive the people and province representatives with the other nominees."

"Have fun," he said in a flat tone. I ignored him and exited the room. Mathias had stopped treating me like poison, but he has shifted to acting indifferent towards me. It almost hurt more than his pure anger, but I guess I couldn't ask any more of him. I passed the extra guards stationed on this floor as I hurried down the hallway. After Ilise left, security increased everywhere in the castle, especially on this floor. There was nowhere one could go and not run into at least a dozen guards.

I arrived at the first floor and turned towards the throne room. A line of people already trailed out the door, and rows of guards lined the people waiting. Many of them tried pushing against each other to get farther up in the line, but they calmed down the moment a guard glared at them. No one was trying to repeat what had happened at the protest. I walked to the two guards in front of the doors. They nodded to me before opening the door.

My parents stared down at me as I walked up to the dais, scrutinizing my attire. Short dresses were usually reserved for more casual events. And at a time like this, painting the image of being unaffected was what I should be doing. But I was tired of pretending. Both of them wore their crowns, the golden vines glinting in the candlelight. Their golden thrones with velvety red cushions were the only pieces of furniture in the throne room. I walked up the stairs to the dais and curtsied to my parents. My throne had been removed from the room. Much like my crown, I wasn't allowed to use it unless I remained the heir. And that was becoming less likely as the days went on.

"Are you going to behave today, or are we going to have a problem?" Father said in a low voice, not moving to look at me.

"Don't worry about me," I said, not sparing them a glance.

"Good," Mother said.

The door swung open, and Nikos and Oliver entered the room. Both of them wore formal black trousers and a white dress shirt. They sauntered up to the dais and stood beside me. "Look who's finally making an appearance," Nikos said.

I ignored his tone. "Nice to see you too, Nikos."

Oliver leaned over Nikos to talk to me. "Is this the second test?"

I shrugged. "Who knows," I said.

"Quiet, nominees," Father ordered. My back stiffened. "You will merely observe unless we tell you otherwise. Guards, open the doors." The guards nodded and opened the gilded doors. They opened with a screech as they scratched against the marble floors.

People filled the throne room, many appearing travel-weary from their trek to the palace. Dirt still streaked their faces and stained their clothes, some dragging their exhausted feet across the floor. They came in from all over the kingdom, from the mountains in Pria to the marshes in Nitedand. Father stood from his throne, instantly hushing whispered conversations.

"Welcome everyone. We hope to hear all of your concerns tonight, but if we run out of time, you may come back tomorrow. Please line up to speak before us," he said. Everyone shuffled into a single file line. A guard waved forward the first person in line, a short Primis woman clothed in a long, beige cotton dress. Her skin turned to a pale brown as she stepped towards the dais, shrinking under my parents' gazes.

She curtsied deeply before standing up again. "Your Majesties, I come from Terdow. As of late, many storms have come through and flooded the roads."

Father nodded. "But roads flood all the time, I fail to see what the problem is."

The woman pulled on a strand of her thick black hair. "Well you see, the roads outside of Terdow are in extremely bad condition, and the flooding has damaged them to the point where we can rarely use them. Carts have been having trouble getting supplies into town for months."

"Did you not take this issue up with the Duke and Duchess of Faveru before traveling all this way?" Mother said.

The woman nodded. "They told me they would need help from the capital to fix all the damaged roads." I stifled a scoff. The Duke and Duchess had plenty of resources to fix the roads. More likely, they were too lazy to deal with it, and felt like making the woman travel all the way here on behalf of the town. Based on her attire, I placed my bets on her being on the poorer side of her town, possibly a farmer or a seamstress. The Duke and Duchess would have dismissed her before she even opened her mouth.

"We will see to it that the roads are fixed," Mother said. The woman curtsied as she muttered her thanks. She left the room, and the next person stepped up. The next hour and a half seemed to move at an agonizingly slow pace. Out of the corner of my eye, I could see Oliver trying to hide their yawns. There were plenty of times I wanted to give my suggestions, but I knew that would only make this night worse.

However, there were multiple parts I couldn't watch. Numerous people had come up, eyes full of hatred. Either from the loss of a loved one during the protest or someone responding to Aerilyn's execution. Those who tried to speak of it were dragged out of the throne room. Some even tried fighting back against the guards, aiming to attack those of us standing on the dais. It took every ounce of self-control I had left to keep my mouth shut, to stop myself from only making the situation worse.

Two hours in, two older men stepped up to the dais. The first one was lanky, with raven, slicked-back hair. And not even the warm candlelight did anything to soften the sharp lines of his pale face. His much shorter companion was almost his complete opposite. His thick black hair fell in waves over his forehead, and the golden brown of his skin glowed warmly. They bowed in unison as they stood before my parents. Mother's fingers drummed on the arm of her throne. *Is she nervous? Impatient? Who are these men?*

"Welcome gentlemen," Father began, "what seems to be the issue."

The first man stood up from his bow. "I am Lord Griffin. I come as a representative for Nitedand." His voice was bone-chilling, feeling as if it was crawling over my skin.

The second man raised his head. "And I am Lord Amin, I come as a Faveru representative."

"Welcome to the palace, Lords," Mother said, the smile on her mouth strained after two hours of this. I almost felt bad for her—almost.

"Your Majesties, I'm sure you know of the problems with the border we share. We're requesting an order for which province shall be responsible for controlling it and cleaning up the whole...debacle," Lord Griffin said. He spoke again before either of my parents could. This was about to be a headache. "Those of us in Nitedand would prefer if Faveru would be in charge of fixing it. Our people are merely speaking their minds, but the *Faveru* border guards keep trying to prevent it."

Lord Amin narrowed his eyes as he turned to Lord Griffin. "'Speaking their minds' you say. I don't know how you do things in Nitedand, but in Faveru, 'speaking their minds' does not mean leaving a path of destruction in their wake."

Lord Griffin waved a finger in his face. Lord Amin smacked it away, eliciting gasps from others in the line. I peered at Nikos, spotting an amused smile at the two Lords' bickering. A muscle in Lord Griffin's jaw twitched. "There would not *be* any destruction if your province was not so quick to interfere," Lord Griffin said.

Father raised his hand, silencing their bickering. "I think this would be a wonderful issue for our nominees to help you with." He looked back at the three of us and waved us closer. Nikos brushed past me to be at my father's side while Oliver stayed next to me.

"We hope we will be of help to you, gentlemen," Nikos said. No one said anything to him about not using their correct titles.

Oliver stepped closer to the edge of the dais. "Is this not supposed to be a reception to the people? Were you two not able to come before the King and Queen at another time?" I suppressed a small smile. Oliver didn't know a thing about ruling a kingdom, this was how things worked.

"This reception is for everyone Nominee Li," Lord Amin said.

"That it is," I said. "I'm sure you two will be willing to compromise on the solution."

Lord Griffin's mouth curled into a sneer. "Your Highness, why should we compromise when it is obviously the fault of *one person's* province." The two lords began to quarrel with one another once again. Mother stared at me, the order clear in her eyes—*fix it*. I ran the fabric of my dress through my fingers.

As I opened my mouth, Nikos spoke. "Lords, this is not the time for incessant arguing. You will be quiet so we can decide who will be responsible." They ignored him, their voices rising, echoing across the room. Neither of them were willing to listen for more than a few seconds at a time. I'd thought Nikos was bad, but these two were on another level. And who could blame them? I had to force myself to not look at any more of the reports from the border. They only stressed me out more than I already was. And neither of the lords wanted to have to solve the problem between their two provinces.

"Gentlemen," Father said, his voice a clear warning. They ignored him as well. I felt the last string of my already thinning patience snap.

"Lords!" I yelled. *Hells. I probably shouldn't have done that.*

Every head in the room turned to me, finally quieting the two lords. *Well, I guess it technically worked.* I took a deep breath, steeling myself against whatever excuses they might come up with to disagree with me.

"Now that I have your attention, I think I have a solution we can all agree on. Yelling at each other is not going to solve this." Everyone on the dais raised a skeptical eyebrow. "Since neither of you want to compromise on a solution, I think the palace should send guards to control the violence and help clean up the destruction. That way neither of your provinces has to do anything."

The two lords considered me for a moment before nodding their heads. The palace hadn't been doing enough before, and starting now was better than not at all.

"I think that is a fine idea, Your Highness," Lord Amin said. He fixed his gaze upon my parents. "Would the palace be willing to do that, Your Majesties?" A rare, proud smile spread across my mother's face. It was almost funny how I'd spent most of my life craving that smile. But now that I'd earned it, I felt nothing. No burst of pride, no feelings of satisfaction. Just nothing.

"Of course, Lords. We will dispatch the soldiers within the week." Soldiers? Soldiers were different from guards. Guards were more preventative, while soldiers were better suited for battles. It was a small difference, but it was an important one. My heart, which had allowed itself to grow full of hope a moment before, sank. What if I had just made a grave mistake? I just hoped they wouldn't force them to repeat the actions from the protest a few days ago, and that I didn't just unleash groups of killing machines into Faveru and Nitedand.

The air became thick. Goosebumps rose along my arms as a chill traveled down my spine. Everyone else in the room looked equally uncomfortable. The gilded doors of the throne room were thrust open by a powerful gust of air and six robed figures strode into the room, the center one's white crystal still glowing. *The Council.* The mostly Primis crowd shuddered as the sorcerers gilded past.

"Hello, Imogen," Father said with a smile that did not reach his eyes. "While you are honored guests of the palace, it does not mean you can barge in whenever it pleases you."

The coils of her gray hair fell into her face as she bowed. "I apologize, Your Majesty, but we have come to announce who has passed the second test." Murmurs filled the room.

"This was a test?" Oliver asked. Imogen walked to the dais. The two lords practically jumped back from her.

"Yes, Nominee Li. This was the diplomacy test, and you and Nominee Vikander failed." A look of plain disbelief flashed across Nikos' face.

"But on the last test you told us it was happening before we began," he argued.

Imogen waved a finger in his face. "Yes, but that one required directions. In the beginning, I said you would get no prior warnings of when the tests would happen."

I looked back to smile at him and took a step towards Imogen. "Does that mean I passed?"

"Yes, Your Highness. Congratulations." A wave of relief flowed through me as I heard the words. I may have passed, but at what cost? The relief was soon supplanted by worry: would my so-called solution result in more senseless deaths?

"In that case," Mother began, "we are dismissing you, nominees. We will finish up here." I curtsied to my parents before rushing out the doors. Nikos and Oliver trailed after me, their shoulders sunken.

"There's still one more test, don't get too cocky yet," Nikos sneered.

"Then you better step up your game," I said. He stormed out of the room.

"Congratulations, Yorena," Oliver said with a sad smile. They may be my competitor, but I still felt bad for them.

"Don't worry Oliver, there's still another test," I said, attempting to console them. "Only time will tell which one of us will win."

Their face lifted ever so slightly. "Indeed."

Chapter 26

Ilise

The grooves of the dagger dug into my palms as the guards stalked closer to our horses. "Would it be too much to ask you to stay back for once?" Val said. I hopped down from my horse. The adrenaline already running through my veins numbed the pain of my ankle, and I knew I would regret using it later.

"Not a chance."

He sighed. I followed Kass and Val as they walked towards the guards. Their broadswords gleamed as they unsheathed them.

"This'll be fun," Kass said.

"I think we have very different ideas of fun," Val said.

I glanced down at the small weapon still sheathed to Kass's thigh. "What's that?" She looked down at it and smiled.

"A last resort."

The guards halted their horses and jumped off. We braced for an attack, holding up our daggers. Every muscle in my body tensed, my feet ready to evade at a moment's notice. They stopped a few feet in front of us, eyes fixed on me. It was an unsettling combination with the smile that was spreading across their faces, no doubt because the crown put a hefty bounty on my head. The largest one stepped closer to us, his green crystal already glowing brighter than the blazing sun. "Ilise Obrien, you have been charged with treason. Do not resist arrest, we don't have to bring you back conscious."

I lowered my dagger, stepping closer to them, and Kass grabbed my arm, pleading with her eyes. I shook out of her grip and whispered, "*Trust me.*" Her grip tightened on her weapons as I walked away from her. They looked at each other in confusion as I stopped in front of the first guard. I stood close enough to see the black stubble dotting his chin as I looked at him directly in his dark eyes. The small amount of food I ate threatened to make an appearance, and I prayed my voice came out steady as I said to the first guard, "Your friends in Anmia must not have told you." His brow furrowed. Before he could react, I planted my hands on his shoulders and kneed him in the groin. He fell to the ground, moaning in pain. "I will never go back."

Kass and Val rushed the other two as they drew their weapons. The man I kneed wrapped his hand around my injured ankle, yanking me to the ground. I stifled my wince and tears welled in my eyes. "You're gonna pay for that," he sneered. I used my other leg to kick him across his face, an audible crack accompanying his grunt as I hit him directly on the nose.

"That's what the last one said." His crystal glowed again as fresh blood gushed from his nose. The ground beneath me shook as I tried to force myself onto my feet. The unsteadiness of the land and my ankle caused me to fall onto my back. The Earth Imperium guard waved his sword in an arc. Using both my daggers, I blocked him just before it could land in my chest. Our blades were caught in a standstill. Most of his body weight rested on my knees, pinning me to the ground.

After days of little to no food, my muscles shook with the effort to block him. The only sounds were my blood pounding in my ears and my erratic breaths. I twisted my neck to Kass and Val, both locked in intense combat with the other guards. I wouldn't be able to hold this man off for long, my muscles grew more fatigued with every passing second.

Pushing against his sword was impossible. Not only was it larger than both my daggers, but he had much more upper body strength than I did. It was like I was trying to push against a stone wall. But size-wise, we weren't that far apart. I scanned his body for any other weak spots to exploit. Tears stung my eyes as the blade edged closer to my chest, a smile forming on the guard's face as my limited energy continued to diminish.

A small part of me in the back of my mind wanted to accept defeat, the part of me that wanted to stay home and suffer with the rest of my family instead of going to the palace alone, the part of me that would trade places with Aerilyn or those kids in a heartbeat. No. I couldn't let those thoughts see the light of day, lest I wanted the last five years to be in vain.

My legs suddenly felt lighter. The guard was putting more of his weight on his legs as he pushed his sword down on me. He must've been a newer guard, everyone knew not to make that mistake, it left a vital part of your body open for attack—my attack. The cold iron of his blade kissed my neck and a trickle of blood slid down my sweat-slicked skin, the crimson liquid dripping onto the grass.

"I warned you," he said in a low voice. I shuffled the leg with my uninjured ankle out from under him as his weight lifted off my knee.

"And I warned you too," I whispered. I drove the heel of my foot into his side, right in the ribs. He rolled off me with a wheeze, and I scrambled to my feet. My victory was short-lived as the guard pushed himself back onto his feet, blood still dripping from his nose as he stalked towards me. I twirled my daggers between my fingers. "Ready for round two?" I said.

He roared as he charged me. Sloppily, he swung his sword in my direction, and I deflected it with the blade of my dagger and pivoted, knocking the sword out of his hands. He rushed towards me, arms outstretched. I ducked low to the ground, nearly getting caught in his grip. His momentum forced him several feet away from me.

My head turned at the sound of Kass' pained grunt. She was curled into a fetal position underneath the other guard. No crystal was visible over his clothes, and cuts marred across his brown, chiseled face. Planting one of my feet back, I took one dagger in both my hands. I threw it with all the strength I had left, and it soared through the air. A sickening squelch sounded as it buried into the center of the guard's back.

The air was knocked out of my lungs and I face-planted into the blood-stained grass, biting down on my tongue. The metallic taste of blood filled my mouth. The guard planted his boot on my back, pressing me into the dirt. My lungs ached from lack of air. "Shouldn't have gotten so cocky, traitor," he sneered. I tried moving my arms, but they felt no better than two useless noodles. My energy was spent. I was so close to making it back to base, so close to alerting everyone what was about to happen to this kingdom. Black spots danced in my vision.

Before I could pass out, the weight was lifted off my back. I pushed myself up with my hands as I gasped for breath. Air filled my lungs, and the black spots disappeared. Val stood above the knocked out guard. "You're welcome," he said.

"Thanks," I wheezed. Val abandoned the guard and rushed to my side. Using him as a support, I stood back up. Several large cuts marred his face and neck, and blood was matted into the waves of his hair, but he looked okay overall. Whose blood, I wasn't sure.

Empty of adrenaline, and energy, I felt every point of pain at once. More tears sprung from my eyes with every step we took. My ankle throbbed more than ever, pounding like another heartbeat. My body felt full of never-ending electric heat. Kass jogged up to us, leaving another passed-out guard in her wake.

"Is everyone okay?" she asked.

Val nodded.

"Peachy," I said through gritted teeth. Kass winced as she looked over at me. She favored one side as she limped towards us.

"We need to get you into the infirmary," she said as she twiddled with the green crystal at her neck. "I can't use my crystal to heal, it's almost spent. There's only enough power left to get us into the base."

So that's why she was still limping. Most of the time, she healed herself with her crystal after battles; there was no reason to let herself suffer. I absently nodded as Val picked me up and sat me on the saddle of Kass's horse. She climbed up behind me, and I leaned back into her.

"We shouldn't be too much farther from the base," she said.

"I think I broke my back, and my legs, and my arms," I said.

"If you broke your back, you wouldn't have been able to move. As for the other things, you'll get patched up soon."

I laughed weakly. "Try and take a nap or something, kid."

I leaned further into her, easing the pain in my back. "I'm not a kid anymore."

She snorted. "True, but I don't feel like coming up with another nickname for you."

We arrived in Hexia just as the sky turned orange and pink. The cobble-stone streets were almost empty of people, the weathered tan stone of the village a welcome image. A light breeze blew across my face, carrying the spiced scent of food vendor carts and fresh pine. We stopped in the stables, the smell of hay and horse dung chasing away the decadent smells of food. Kass hopped down from the horse before helping me down before Val rushed to both our sides to help us limp away from the village.

"Can't we ride the horses to the base and then you take them back to the stable?" I whined. We had to keep the base a good distance away from the town in case of guards and the thought of making the trek made me want to collapse.

"It's not that far of a walk, we'll be there by the time the moon rises," he said. I groaned. "And we don't need to attract attention by riding back and forth."

We traveled in silence for an hour, slowed down by our injuries. Crickets and other bugs chirped as the moon rose. Our pace slowed to no more than a shuffle, but I wasn't complaining. It felt nice to be outside and not running for my life for once. I was the one to break the silence. "So what have you guys been up to while I've been gone?"

Val sighed. "Not enough and too much all at the same time." I moved my hand to his shoulder; it was barely strong enough to count as a hit.

"Why are you talking like a poet?" Kass said.

He shrugged. "It makes things more interesting."

She scoffed, a small smile playing on her lips. "Since Mr. Poetry doesn't feel like telling you, I guess I will. Half of our spies we had in The Progression ranks haven't been returning any of our messages. And we can't even tell if they're getting them."

"Maybe it's a similar situation to what was happening in the palace. The Spymaster was intercepting every letter that came in the mail," I said.

"That's what we assume," Val said. "But we can still glean enough information to guess which villages they'll try to strike next. So we've been pretty busy preparing."

I nodded. I still remembered the times I helped defend villages as if they were yesterday. Though the scars were long healed. At least the visible ones.

"Did you guys notice how poorly trained those guards were?" I asked.

"And here I was thinking I was just that good at fighting," Val said. I laughed and winced as a sharp stab of pain went through my ribs and back.

"The one I was fighting basically left all his weak spots open to me. Even the guards who chased me in Anmia were easy to get away from." *Maybe because I let them kill two innocent children to save myself,* two more on the list of people dead because of me. "I was almost depleted of energy, I shouldn't have lasted as long as I did."

"Or maybe you're stronger than you think," Kass mused. I opened my mouth to respond but tripped on a stone hidden in the grass. Kass stumbled to the ground with me.

"Considering a rock was all it took to knock me down, I disagree," I said. Val let out a deep chuckle and helped both of us up.

"But why would the monarchs send severely under trained guards to capture someone wanted for treason?" Kass said. I thought back to the last few days I was in the palace. More guards had lined the hallways than usual, and even more were near entrances. It was a miracle I was even able to escape when I did.

"Maybe because all the trained ones are stuck lining the hallways. Security in the palace has probably doubled."

"Then how did you get out?" Val asked. We stopped walking.

"Guess they didn't feel like guarding the stables too." He rubbed the stubble on his chin.

"Is it because of all the recent attacks?" he asked. I eased myself down, grateful for a short break.

"Probably."

Val outstretched his hand for me; I grumbled as I took it. "We're here so you don't have to grumble like a ninety-year-old man." I squinted at the ground in the dim moonlight.

"Where's the door?" I asked. Kass limped to my side and crouched down into a section of weeds.

"I grew some extra weeds around this whole area to cover the door more," Kass said. Vivid green light glowed from the crystal around Kass's neck. She grunted with effort, a light layer of sweat forming on her brow. I looked back to Val, a tiny spark of concern in his eyes.

The ground under our feet rumbled as the dirt door revealed itself. Kass's crystal stopped glowing, and she gasped for breath. "Are you okay?" I said, my voice cracking.

"I'm fine kid, I just need some food and rest." Her arms trembled as she pushed herself off the ground. She needed a new crystal, fast. The dark dirt staircase opened to us. "And a new crystal wouldn't hurt."

"Ladies first," Val said with a smile. I stumbled down the stairs, not even needing torchlight to know where I was going. I reached the bottom of the stairs and limped to the metal door. I knocked three times, six, and then two more times.

I heard the click of the lock a few seconds later. Kass' hand rested on my shoulder as she caught up to me. "Why... are you going... so fast?" Kass said between gasps. The door creaked open and Orla's honey-brown eyes widened as she took me in.

"Ilise?" I crouched low and threw myself into her arms.

"I missed you so much," I said. Her blonde bob had grown midway down her back, but aside from that she looked the same as when I left. Though the gentle glow her skin once had was gone, probably from being stuck in Nitedand for so long, making her freckles stand out more than ever. She broke off the hug, eyes darting across my face.

"You look like shit, I'll help you to the infirmary."

Kass limped to us. "That's okay, I'll just limp there," she said. Orla laughed and took Kass' hands to help us.

"And Kass, I didn't tell you guys everything. I wanted to wait and tell the whole base at once." Kass turned her head to me, her shoulders drooped.

"I thought you already told us the worst of it."

I shook my head.

"Trust me, you're gonna need a nice bottle of ale after I tell you."

Chapter 27

Princess Yorena

"Congrats on passing the test Ms. Yorena," Chafik said as he pulled me into a quick hug.

Mathias walked towards the two of us. He stopped with his hands in his pockets before he said, "I would pay my life's savings to see Nikos' face," a hint of a smile returning to his face, finally looking at me fully. It felt more rewarding than the proud smile my mother gave me and I hoped this meant he was starting to forgive me.

"I can promise you, it was the most satisfying thing I have ever seen." Chafik set out a platter of chopped fruits for a snack. I popped a piece of watermelon into my mouth, sweet juice coating my tongue.

"I told you the phrase was 'second time's the charm," Chafik said with a mouthful of cantaloupe.

Mathias let out a low chuckle. "That still isn't the phrase," he said.

"When I win Heircestrial, my first decree will be to make that the phrase," I said.

Mathias wolfed down a handful of grapes as he raised an eyebrow at me. "Don't you have to be a Queen to make a decree?" he said. I grabbed another piece of cantaloupe.

"The winner of Heircestrial gets to make one decree. Even if they aren't the monarch yet."

"If I won Heircestrial, I would decree that violin playing is illegal after nine," Chafik said with a pointed look toward Mathias.

"You just don't know talent when you see it," he retorted.

I snorted.

"What would you decree if you win, Ms. Yorena?" I had not thought about it. Ever since Nitedand and Ominka put forth nominees, I'd only been focused on winning. It'd seemed pointless to spend my thinking of what to do after when I wasn't even sure if the crown would be mine anymore. I walked over to the window, overlooking the lights of the town beyond the wall spreading out below like a dazzling cobweb, full of life. Lives that could change for better or worse depending on who won.

"Oh great, you made her get all philosophical," Mathias said, throwing a grape at Chafik.

"You better eat that," Chafik said. Mathias retrieved the grape from the floor and popped it in his mouth, not breaking from his gaze.

"You guys are unbelievable," I said.

I left them in the kitchen, quarreling over something, my snack settled easier in my stomach. But Chafik's question still nagged me. The only thing I'd been focused on was keeping Nikos and Oliver off the throne. I didn't even know what would happen if either of them won. I could easily see that Nikos would be horrible between his over-inflated ego and the idea of his superiority he's conjured in his mind. Allowing him to win would be the beginning of another dark age.

But what if Oliver were to win? They couldn't possibly be worse than Nikos. They had a kind heart that would serve them well as the monarch, but after the last test it was clear they had no idea about what being a ruler was like. They could learn, but my parents would have to stay on the throne longer to prepare them. And Erea was in too much of a mess for my parents or I to be focused on training them to be monarch.

I pulled down my dress, the fabric pooling in a puddle of honey-colored silk at my feet, and retrieved my nightgown from my bed. I glanced at my bed; the silk sheets didn't entice me enough to enter. Foregoing my slippers, I left my room. The boys looked up from where they rested on the couches. "Where are you going?' Chafik asked as he perked his head up from its lazy position.

"I don't know." I didn't think I could go to sleep now if I tried. "But I'll be back."

I left the apartment and the moonlit hallway was empty save for the guards pacing up and down the halls. None of them paid me any attention as I hurried down the stairs. The stuffiness of the palace hit me all at once. The hallways were suddenly too narrow, the air was too thick, and the sound of marching guard boots was much too loud. I needed to be free of these walls, and allow myself to breathe. I knew exactly where to go. I didn't want to be stopped by the guards, questioning where I was going as if I was an intruder. Most of the servants would have retired to their rooms by now, so I used the small wooden door to the servant hallways that were almost as extensive as the secret tunnels.

Luckily, no one was using them. I reached the end of a hallway, a slow breeze washing over my face as I walked out into the garden, stars dotting the cloudless sky. I lazily walked past the rows of flowers, inhaling the fresh scent of every one. The loud thoughts in my head quieted down for once. Now I could see why Ilise loved the garden so much. My stomach cramped at the thought.

I had to stop thinking about her. About the amount of comfort her calloused hand brought me with every touch, the way she didn't treat me like I was a brainless child, no matter how much she denied it. The way she could manage to make me laugh even in the moments I wanted to tear out my hair. The way she made me feel like I could be... me, without any expectations I had to live up to.

But she couldn't help me anymore, and thinking about her would only bring more unnecessary pain and guilt. I may have passed one test, but it didn't guarantee I would pass the next one or even that I would be a good ruler if I *were* to win. Since I was old enough to walk, my parents, every tutor, and citizen has told me of the greatness of the Schaefer line, constantly raising the bar to an impossible level.

From stories about my great great grandma Vera and how she'd established the stable relations we had today with Pamu, Banauri, and Croaga. And the memory of my great grandpa Avnet and how he'd redrew the province lines in a way that made everyone happy—a feat thought to be impossible. To even the repeated tales about how Anora Schaefer had led the revolution. How could I ever come close to them?

I weaved through the rows of rose bushes lining the winding trees, grown tall enough to reach my shoulders. A tiny bluebird perched itself on my shoulder, chirping softly into my ear. I held out my finger to it, and it jumped on. "Why hello there little bird, are you on a distraction walk too?" The bird chirped and turned its head. "I suppose you can't answer me." The bird squawked and flapped its wings in my face, flying away into the night. I spit out stray feathers that fell from the bird. Wonder what could have startled it so.

Goosebumps and the hairs on my neck rose, contrary to the warm air. "Quite late for a walk, is it not?" a musical voice said behind me. A small yelp escaped my lips at the sound of the voice. I whipped around and was met with sharp golden eyes. The figure was draped in navy robes that hovered just above the ground. *A sorcerer.* Slowly, I increased the space between us. The moonlight made his bronze skin glow and deepened the sharp lines of his face, and streaks of silver cut through black hair that fell to his shoulders.

"Hello?" I said. He bowed before me, black velvet robes fluttering around him in the breeze. He came up from the bow and, eyes so bright they almost glowed, stared back at me. I forced myself not to look away.

"I was hoping to talk to you, Your Highness. My name is Ahn, I am one of the council sorcerers." I let out a nervous laugh.

"Yeah, I could tell by your...." I pointed to his eyes, "your eyes there. And the, you know, the robes."

His face remained impassive.

"Would you care to walk with me?" he asked. I opened my mouth and then promptly shut it. No, I didn't want to walk with the sorcerer but refusing him would be rude. Noticing my hesitation, he placed a soft hand on my shoulder and led me out of the garden. I flinched away from him, and he moved his hand to a fist at his side. We walked in heavy silence into the small grove of peach trees, just past the garden. Fallen fruits littered the grass, perfuming the air with their rotting scent. Ahn stopped in front of the largest, and most likely oldest, tree. The trunk rose high above all the others, so much so it was almost obnoxious. He stared at it, not speaking to me for several moments.

I jumped as he started speaking. "This tree has risen so far above the rest," he said, pointing to the tree next to us.

I tilted my head as I faced him. "Um... I guess so."

He clasped his hands in front of him. "But I bet it started out much smaller than all the others. I don't think anyone would have expected it to grow above them, nor do I think anyone wanted it to. We could all learn a few things from this tree."

I started pacing around the tree, running my finger along the rough bark. "Did you seek me out to speak in riddles?"

White teeth flashed as the corner of his mouth turned up in a smile. "No, Your Highness, but I did come for an actual reason."

"And what is that?"

He looked around the grove, for what, I did not know. And it was at that moment when I noticed just how quiet the garden had become. No birds chirped, no bugs buzzed or swarmed the rotting fruit as they so often did, and even the crickets had ceased their chirping. Ahn stepped closer to me, leaving only a foot of space between us.

My back stiffened as he leaned close to my ear. "I'm only able to tell you this once." I steeled my eyes forward. His eyes scanned the grove one last time.

"What are you looking for?" He waved for me to stop talking.

"I don't want them listening," he whispered. The silence went on for what felt like years until he led us to the small wooden bench. I brushed off a peach that had fallen onto it and sat down next to the sorcerer.

His golden-eyed gaze bore into mine, my finger twirled through the fabric of my nightgown. I hated being this close to sorcerers, but whatever he was about to tell me felt important. "You cannot trust Imogen...or any of the other council sorcerers for that matter."

I raised an eyebrow. "You're a council sorcerer. Does that mean I can't trust what you're telling me right now?" He shook his head.

"After tonight, probably not." I opened my mouth to question him, but he frantically waved his hand again. "Heircestrial has been a ploy to distract the kingdom. Imogen has been working with one of the nominees."

I narrowed my gaze to thin slits. *A distraction?* "Nikos?" I offered.

Ahn stilled and stared off behind me. I turned to see what he was looking at, only darkness and the empty grove laid behind me. Nikos was the most plausible person to be helping her. Between what he first said at brunch about disagreeing with the Schaefer line, and about the flag Ili—, *she* saw in his room, it was likely Imogen allied with him because of ties to The Progression.

"Possibly," he said, still staring.

"What've they been distracting us from?"

He rubbed his hands together, almost as if he were nervous. "I am no longer sure." What? How could he not be sure? It was as if Ahn had changed to multiple different people in a matter of minutes. I'd already known Nikos was up to something. But Imogen? The only reason the Council of Sorcerers oversaw Heircestrial was because it would be pointless if they interfered since their predicament wouldn't change regardless of who was on the throne. Nothing he said was making sense.

"Ahn?" I waved my hand in front of his face; he remained a cold statue. I wasn't sure he even remembered I was here.

He began talking again, still staring at an invisible object. "Imogen grew up in a very different world than we do now." How old were the sorcerers anyways? "If you're wondering how old she is, she is thousands of years old. We sorcerers can live for unknown amounts of time. I am only seven-hundred-years-old." *Seven hundred years?* No wonder he lacked the same wrinkles as Imogen. He looked like he could be no older than fifty.

"You need to be much like the peach tree. Unassuming at first, and then grow to be above all the others. It used everything it had to get where it is today. Others may see weakness in you, but what they see as weakness may be your greatest strength."

I stood from the bench as I felt my frustration rising. "Can you stop talking in riddles for one minute and tell me what you need to say?" His lips parted slightly as he continued to stare. A vein in his neck protruded as if he was fighting against something to speak.

"I will not recall this conversation," he said in a strained voice, his bronze skin taking on a reddish tint. "Heed my advice, for it will be the only warning you get before it's..." he began to mumble and shook with the effort to speak, his eyes were wide with what I guessed to be terror, "before it's too late—" he broke off with a gasp. I took tentative steps back from him and the glowing purple crystal around his neck. I was ready to run, run before he could manipulate my soul, but the glowing died. Ahn looked around, startled when he laid eyes on me. "Hello there, Your Highness," he said in his musical voice. "Quite late for a walk, is it not?"

I froze, my brow furrowed. "You were talking to me. Not even twenty seconds ago."

He tilted his head, confused. "I do not recall even coming out here." I nodded my head slowly, backing away from him. "Have a nice night, Your Highness." I mumbled my response as I continued to back away from him. Once he turned around, I broke into a run back into the main garden.

Sticks and small rocks stabbed my bare feet, but I didn't stop to pick them out. I ran past the rows of flowers and back into the servant hallway, the door slamming behind me. That was officially the weirdest interaction I'd ever had with anyone. When he first came up to me, he'd been as he was now. Kind, welcoming, at least by sorcerer standards. But then he grew scared of something that made him nervous, something that may have caused him to forget the entire conversation. My feet padded across the stone floor as I walked up the dark staircase.

So Nikos was helping Imogen with Heircestrial, and it was only a distraction. But a distraction from what? What could be terrifying enough to scare a seven hundred-year-old sorcerer? And his soul crystal glowed as if he was going to use it on me, yet I had not felt what had been described as a dark caress on my soul. The feeling of falling into a bottomless pit and then watching yourself change before your eyes, unable to do anything but watch. Who or what would have the power to erase a sorcerer's memory? I arrived at the door to my apartment, the boys had retired to their rooms. And it made me wonder, what else could this mysterious force have changed? Who else had they snared into their control?

Chapter 28

Ilise

"Can't the infirmary wait?" I said as Orla led Kass and I into the small room.

"I will not have you passing out in the hallway over something you can tell us later," she scolded. I didn't travel all this way to get herded into a dingy infirmary. Dust kicked up into my nostrils as I dragged my feet through the dark hall. Most would've called it dirty or musty, but to me, it was home. And being dragged to the infirmary wouldn't do anything to help save it.

Orla guided both of us to the small cots in the room and the nurse rushed in, her once white tunic a swirl of gray and brown. Yasmin, the nurse, diagnosed Kass with a bruised rib and me with two bruised ribs, a sprained ankle, and dehydration. As if the latter were not obvious. Yasmin and Orla mixed healing salves for me and Kass while we laid down on two of the three cots. I could feel the weariness settling deep in my bones, urging me to rest. Yet the only thing keeping me still was constant deadly glares from Yasmin. The woman was small, but even scarier than Ms. Kira had been.

I sighed with relief as the icy paste was spread on my torso and back, rosemary and lemon filling my nose. Yasmin then wrapped my ankle with bandages to keep it in place to heal, and replaced the bandage on my arm, stained completely brown from my journey. She also brought in a new crystal for Kass.

"I better not see you walking on this foot for at least a couple of weeks, Ilise," Yasmin said sternly. The long waves of her brown hair tickled my leg. I looked down as she wrapped my ankle, meeting her hazel eyes. "Oh who am I kidding, you'll probably start running laps around the base by tomorrow."

I chuckled, then winced as a stabbing pain went through my ribs. "You know me," I grimaced.

She stood up from the floor, rubbing leftover salve on her black leather leggings.

"Orla, can you help them back to their rooms when they're ready? I'll have someone bring food to them." Orla nodded, and Yasmin walked into the hall, closing the door behind her.

"Believe it or not, the infirmary in the palace was very similar to ours," I looked around the room. "You know, minus the pure rock walls."

Orla laughed, the bubbly sound echoing in the room.

I started to sit up to grab the water, and Orla rushed over and guided me back down. "You have two bruised ribs, sit still for a day. At least *pretend* you're listening to Yasmin."

I snorted. We both knew I never listened to Yasmin.

"Since you're already yapping again," Kass began, "you mind telling us what was so important you had to wait until we got back?" I turned my head to face her. She already sat up on her cot, sipping on a glass of water. The cuts on her face and arms were freshly bandaged. Her movements were stiffened, hindered by the tight bandages.

"I want to tell everyone on base at once."

Kass set herself down on the ground and limped to a wooden crutch leaning against the wall. "I'll tell Val and the others to gather everyone. Shouldn't take more than a few minutes."

Orla helped me down from the cot and handed me a pair of crutches to use. I winced as the uneven wood dug into my armpits, but at least the salve had almost gotten rid of the pain in my back.

People I hadn't seen in years greeted me with smiles and hugs as I slowly made my way to the main room. There was the small group of people my age: Amaya, Khadija, and Joel. The Primis triplets hadn't joined until I was sixteen, so I'd never gotten much of a chance to get to know them. I passed by Zaynab, one of our chefs. He could make a meal out of anything you gave him, and it *still* managed to taste good. And even Malachi, who never seemed to show any emotion other than nonchalance, shot me a grin as I hobbled past. I'd missed this, just being able to walk through the halls and see some friendly faces, a place where people actually knew who I was.

When I arrived, a crowd was already gathered around the small stone stage, parting for me to walk up. Applause and pats on the shoulder welcomed me back, echoing loudly against the high rock ceilings. Kass, Val, and Rori all waited for me on the stage. Rori's freckled face brightened as they laid eyes on me.

I set my crutches on the stage and hopped with my good foot to get up. Val handed me my crutches, and I stood beside the three of them. Rori pulled me into a tight hug. "Didn't expect to see you again so soon," they said as they broke away. Their fiery hair had been cut, so it just brushed their chin.

"Neither did I," I said.

Cain weaved through the crowd to stand in the front. "Everyone is here," he said. I nodded to him. Positioning myself in front of the group, the crowd's eye fell on me. My stomach twisted in nervousness, but these people were my family, I had no reason to be nervous. I took a deep breath and began speaking.

"Hey everyone, I know you're all wondering why I've returned from the palace early," I laughed softly, "and wanted for treason." There were a few quiet chuckles and from the crowd, Cain gestured for me to continue. "While my cover at the palace is blown, I was able to find out something that may mean the end of our mission. In..." I looked at Val. "How long has it been since I escaped?" He counted on his fingers.

"Close to a week," he guessed with a shrug. *I've already lost a week.* That gave us almost no time to prepare other bases to help us, but we still had to try.

"In a little more than a week, The Progression plans to take over the palace, and in turn, Erea." Gasps sounded across the room. I think I even heard the loud thud of someone fainting.

"They what?" my friends onstage yelled.

"Are you sure? Even The Progression wouldn't be stupid enough to try that," Rori said.

I held up my hand, silencing the crowd.

"I overheard this in a conversation between one of the council sorcerers and one of the nominees. I guess they've been planning this since they arrived in New Teber." Val raked his hand through the brown waves of his hair.

"Which nominee and which sorcerer?" Kass asked. Expectant gazes came from everyone in the crowd.

"The nominee, surprisingly, was Oliver Li. I'm pretty sure the other nominee, Nikos, is still involved. And the sorceress Oliver was talking with was named Imogen." Cain's warm brown skin blanched at the mention of her name. Overlapping voices rose in the cavern, and Val clapped his hands to gain everyone's attention.

"We'll discuss a plan. All squad members report to the meeting room in two minutes. Dismissed." The crowd dispersed, the squad leaders leaving for the meeting room.

Cain hopped onto the stage. "Are you sure the sorceress' name is Imogen?" he said with wide eyes.

"Cain, you look like a ghost," Rori said as they patted his large shoulder. Cain's expression remained frozen in silent terror.

"Cain, what's so bad about Imogen?" I said. Everyone leaned into him, waiting for an answer.

"She's one of the most powerful sorceresses to ever live. And she's thousands of years old. All the sorcerers, not just the Council, have to obey what she says. So if Imogen is with The Progression..."

Kass finished for him, "Then all the sorcerers are with The Progression."

Rori helped me down from the stage as we followed Val to the meeting room. "But can't they go against her? They're all still very powerful, what could she possibly hold over their heads to make them obey her?" I said. Val held open the meeting room door for all of us.

"A skilled sorcerer knows the soul better than they know themselves. With the right tweaks, they can control *anyone*," Cain explained. The dim torchlight of the room made his expression even more grave.

My stomach turned sour. Did that mean Imogen *was* the voice I was hearing? But manipulating the soul to the point of mind control and talking to me in my head were two different things, were they not? I took a seat between Kass and Orla at the long table that took up most of the room. All fifty squad leaders were already seated. Rori stood at the front with Val, and their white crystal already glowed, ready to carry their voices over the expanse of the room.

"Squad leaders," Val said, his carried voice silencing the small conversations around the room. "Defending the palace, and this kingdom, against The Progression is already a near-impossible task, but now we have to keep in mind the Council of Sorcerers will most likely also be against us. The floor is open to any suggestions." A Primis boy around Kass' age stood from his chair. His bright blue eyes looked around the room before speaking.

"Why don't we invade the palace first?" he said.

Val's brow furrowed. "What do mean, Erik?"

"Why don't we have a decent-sized group of people to pose as guards in the palace so they can help the rest of us get in? Then when The Progression comes, we'll have an army ready for them." It wasn't a bad idea. But it would be almost impossible to get a group of five people into the palace, let alone an entire army and more. Hells, getting even one person in would be difficult.

"It's a decent idea, but we don't know what security at the palace looks like right now," Val said. He looked at me, the silent question in his eyes. I stood up from my chair. Many of the squad leaders locked their eyes on the bloodstains still covering my clothes.

"The palace security increased after The Progression launched an attack on the Heircestrial ball, pretending to be us." A chorus of voices rose.

"They did what?" one girl yelled.

"No one told us this happened!" another boy said.

"Our relations with the crown were already strained," Rori said, rubbing their eyes.

"You mean our already non-existent relations?" Cain interjected.

"And now any chance we had of getting the crown to work with us is gone," Kass finished.

Val raised his hands, quieting the room once more, and waved for me to continue talking. I gave them all the short version of what had happened at the ball. The figures dressed in black attacking everyone in the room, how probably half the guests were killed, and how not even the palace guards had been able to fend them off. I even told them how I had to keep the Princess safe. I chose to ignore the fluttering feeling I felt thinking of when I had to hold her hand to get through the room.

"I have to admit, they're smarter than we give them credit for,"another squad leader said.

"Yeah, they made us public enemy number one so they could plan their final attack on the palace," Orla said.

"So anyway, almost every entrance and exit is guarded all day and night, and even in the hallways, more guards have been assigned to make rounds. And I highly doubt they'll leave the stables unguarded after my escape."

Val rubbed the stubble on his chin. "Either we have to find an unknown entrance into the palace, or we'll need to think of a different solution. We might have to plan to arrive with an army on the same day as The Progression."

One of the other squad leaders stood up, an older woman. A giant scar was crossed over her permanently closed eye.

"That would give us more time to prepare and gather forces from the other bases." Val considered her. It was a decent plan, but arriving at the same time as The Progression meant there was no room for error. *And it means I won't have time to sneak away and kill the leader.*

"Is everyone in agreement to make that plan A?" Val asked. Everyone in the room nodded. "Okay. Osain, Anika, Fergus, Abbi and Esme." The five of them rose from their seats. "I need you five to spread the message to the bases in other provinces, but stay out of Nitedand. Everyone else, go tell your squads the plan, we need to be ready to mobilize in two days at the latest. And if anyone has any other suggestions, please let us know. You're dismissed."

All the squad leaders shuffled out of the room, leaving me, Kass, Rori, Orla, Cain, and Val. "Are there any more surprises you need to tell us?" Rori said, already rubbing their temples. I felt a headache coming on myself.

"Not a surprise per se, but more of an observation." Everyone settled in a chair closer to me.

"I'm not even twenty-five, yet I feel like I'm aging with every bit of news you tell us," Val grumbled.

"Val and Kass can back me up here, but on the way here we had to fend off a group of three guards. And they were so untrained in combat, it didn't make sense they would send them after someone wanted for treason." Especially considering they believed the Union organized the Heircestrial ball attack. They would've wanted to send guards skilled enough to be on par with those figures. These guards I could've beaten even three years ago.

"And what does that have to do with anything?" Cain said.

"Wouldn't it make sense that this means they've hired more guards? And they're keeping all the more trained ones in the palace. So if we were to invade, we would have to make sure everyone going has about as much experience as a well-seasoned guard," I said.

"I wish that didn't make sense," Cain said. It was the only logical reason.

"You and me both," Rori responded.

"We'll start intensifying everyone's training starting now. That'll give us a couple days to train them and pack for the trip," Orla said as she stood to leave. She said "trip" as if we were going on a nice vacation. Before leaving, she pointed her finger and narrowed her gaze at me. "I better not see you there." Kass snorted as Orla started walking out. "You either Kass."

Rori waved to me before following Orla out the door. "Cain?" I said. "Is it possible for a sorcerer to become like a... a voice in your head?"

He clasped his hand together and stared at the wall for a few moments. "As far as I know, no. And I know quite a lot," he said with a smile. Kass rolled her eyes. "Why do you ask?"

"Lately I've been hearing this voice call for me, searching for me. And whenever it happens, I get a sharp pain in my chest. The first time it happened I passed out in the middle of the garden."

Everyone in the room stiffened. "I know more about sorcerers than any non-sorcerer, and nowhere in any text has it ever been said, or even alluded to sorcerers being able to do that." But Imogen's voice sounded too similar to the voice in my head. Or was that just what I wanted to believe?

"But you said the most powerful sorcerers could basically control someone's mind," I said.

"But that would require them to have at least been near you once. And from everything you've told us, you started hearing the voice before you were ever near Imogen," Cain said.

Then who's been speaking to me? I knew I wasn't going crazy, but it being Imogen made the most sense. The voice called me "little one", the same as Imogen did. But it could be one of the other sorcerers. Maybe one of the other five was as powerful as Imogen.

Val clapped his hands together. "Let's get some food, then we can talk more." He helped Kass and I onto our crutches, and we left for the kitchen. After today, the real work would begin. If it would be enough, it was impossible to tell.

Chapter 29

Princess Yorena

"So what I'm hearing is, a sorcerer came up to you in the middle of the night, spoke in riddles, gave you an ominous warning about Imogen, and then forgot the entire conversation a few seconds later?" Kieron recalled. He was assigned to this corridor, and I marched the hall with him. I could barely sleep for more than a few minutes at a time last night after running into Ahn. The more I tried to dissect what he was saying, the more confused I got.

What reason would Imogen have for interfering with Heircestrial? And why would she enlist Nikos for help? Of all people. My first idea was that Nikos was the one ordering Imogen around, because a sorceress had no reason to care about Heircestrial. Nikos was the one with a Progression flag in his room, which meant he could be a member. But our informants would've uncovered that when we first investigated Nikos and Oliver. Sorcerers lived on their own, basically as a nation of their own up in Mount Bachport. I sincerely doubted they would be *this* involved in our politics.

But what would Nikos be holding over her head to make her cooperate? "Correct," I said. He tapped his finger against the hilt of his sword, thinking.

"Are you one hundred percent sure it wasn't just a nightmare? 'Cause, that is the creepiest thing I've heard in a while."

I side-eyed him. "I wasn't having a nightmare. There's dirt on my floor I tracked in from last night. And I never met Ahn before last night. Unless sorcerers have the power to insert themselves into people's dreams."

Kieron nodded to another guard passing us. "You'd never know. I put those guys up there with the archives on creepiness levels." *The Archives.* I halted my walking. Kieron looked back, waiting for me to unglue my feet to the floor.

"Oh no, you have that look," he groaned.

"What look?" He wrapped his hand around my wrist, pulling me back to his side.

"The 'I'm about to drag Kieron to help me with my stupid idea that makes him question his life choices' look.'" I crossed my arms.

"Ha ha, very funny," I said flatly.

"This idea doesn't require you to do anything but listen."

He sighed. "Fine." We turned back the other way once we reached the window.

"Remember when we went into the archives and found those empty pamphlets about Heircestrial." He nodded. "What if one of the nominees took the real ones and replaced them with the fake ones?"

He rubbed the growing stubble on his chin.

"But they were old, the ink could've faded after sitting on a shelf for so long."

"But if Ahn was telling the truth, then I was set up." We turned around again at the end of the hall. "I wouldn't know anything if not for Chafik's history obsession."

"Your entire theory is based on the word of a riddle talking sorcerer and your paranoia." He wasn't getting it. I wasn't paranoid. Paranoia meant I was worried over nothing, suspicious of everything and everyone. My theory may be based on little information, but it was still based on *something.*

"If I wanted someone to call me paranoid every five seconds, I would've talked this out with Mathias."

Kieron pressed his mouth into a thin line, locking his gaze forward. "You need to stop reading so much into this. If the sorcerer was acting as weird as you said he was, then you can't trust his word, not on something as big as this. What you're suggesting undermines thousands of years of tradition and trust between us and the sorcerers." Maybe he was right, Ahn wasn't someone I would call the most trustworthy, but it didn't mean what he warned me about was false. And who was I to ignore a warning from a seven hundred-year-old sorcerer? "And maybe you shouldn't trust someone who tells you to be like a peach tree," Kieron said after a while.

I elbowed his side. "To be fair his exact words were 'we could all learn something from this tree'. He didn't tell me to *be* a tree, he told me to learn *from* the tree." Kieron flapped his hand, mimicking me. I smacked it away. "If you're just going to mock me, I will take my leave." He placed his hand on his heart, shifting his face into a dramatic frown.

"Oh, what will I do without my best friend yapping about riddle-speaking sorcerers and peach trees?" I fought the urge to throw a small ball of fire at his head and instead, turned away from him to go back to my room, annoyance gnawing at me. How much proof would

I need for him to believe me? Ahn seemed trustworthy enough, at least until he forgot the entire conversation. It wasn't like I had many other people who were as willing to help as he was.

Midday light streamed in from the windows, and my nose wrinkled at the smell of rotting fruit from the night before. The scent would have permeated the room if I threw them out, so I burnt them to a crisp, replacing the rotten fruit smell with an eye-watering smokiness. I pushed the charred fruit remains into the trash and opened a window to eliminate the smoke. I inhaled the flower-scented warm breeze as it blew across my face.

"What died in here?" Mathias said as he walked in with Chafik.

"You guys left the fruit out from last night, and charred fruit smells a lot better than rotten fruit. And I'm frustrated, so I felt like burning something." A small smile formed on his freckled face.

"Is it already lunchtime?" I asked, flopping onto the couch.

"Yes. And we think Nikos is in one of his moods," Chafik said. I perked up my head, brow furrowed.

"Define mood."

Chafik rubbed the back of his neck. "We passed by him in the hallway while he was ranting about something. I don't know, but his crystal was glowing the whole time, and then he ran downstairs to Spirits knows where.

I groaned. I didn't need to deal with him today. "As long as everyone takes that as a hint to leave him alone, then it's nothing to worry about." Mathias slumped in the armchair beside me, resting his head on the pillow.

"Chafik, it's your turn to make lunch."

Chafik walked into the kitchen. "Yeah yeah, I'm going." My fingers fiddled with the fabric of my cotton leggings, and my foot tapped erratically, mimicking my racing thoughts. Eating lunch hardly sounded appetizing. I stood up from the couch, walking towards the door.

"Where are you going?" Mathias said, taking my spot on the couch.

"I need to get rid of some of my energy, I'll be back." He gave a small salute, and I left the apartment.

"Don't burn down the palace," he called, his voice faint now. Kieron was no longer guarding the hall. He must have rotated with the other guards. I didn't have a particular destination in my mind, but it was as if my feet knew where I was going before I realized where I was going.

I found myself on the ground floor of the palace, walking towards the training room. My knuckles itched at the thought of using the punching dummy. As if it would also punch away my problems. I froze outside the door, my ear straining to hear the sounds coming from inside the room. I creaked open the door, peeking through the gap, and Nikos' shirtless back entered my field of vision, drenched in sweat. I opened the door more, and he turned around from the punching dummy panting, and somehow still managed to frown at me.

"If you are going to take over my training room, at least put on a shirt."

His frown deepened. "It's not your room, it's everyone's training room," he said flatly. I rested my crystal on the table next to him as I weaved my hair into a thick braid.

"You could have used the training rooms the guards use." He returned to using the practice dummy, hammering it with his fists.

"Unlike you, I don't need the company of a guard every day. I prefer the privacy of this room, but clearly it isn't as private as I thought."

I steeled myself. Fine, if he wanted to share this room, I could do that. I crossed the room to the wall of practice weapons and grabbed three of the small throwing knives, tucking them into the waistband of my leggings. Nikos watched me out of the corner of his eye; I met his gaze. "What?

Does the act of me grabbing knives annoy you as well?" He shook his head and returned to the dummy.

I walked to the other side of the room, armed with the knives. I pushed the target out of its corner, dust coating my hands whenever I touched it, and pushed it as far from Nikos as I could in the small room and stepped back. I spread my feet apart to ground myself, and I imagined that Ilise was right behind me, teaching me how to throw knives for the first time.

I'd had to beg her to let me even touch the weapons, and she'd deemed I had the least chance of hurting myself with the throwing knives. It'd taken hours of her alternating between barking orders and gentle encouragement to get me to even hit the target at all, and another few days before they hit anywhere close to the middle. My chest warmed at the image of her proud face. It was rarer than the times I heard her laugh.

I forced myself out of the memories, she was gone, and I would never see her again. *At least I hope so.* I exhaled slowly, training my eyes on the target in front of me, and squared my shoulders towards it. The rest of my body relaxed in preparation. I drew my arm back like an archer would the bow string, pointing the sharp tip of the blade to the ceiling. I threw my arm forward, letting the knife slice through the air. It did a full spin before sinking into the soft cotton close to the middle of the target.

"Wow you managed not to kill both of us with your little toy," Nikos said, having abandoned the dummy. I ignored him and stepped back farther for the next throw. I planted my feet again and let the blade free, watching it fly through the air, plunging in the center. "I guess that Ilise did teach you something. Maybe when they capture her I can get a few tips," he moved right in front of me, I lifted my chin slightly to meet his eyes. "You know... before they execute her."

Yup. Nikos was definitely the nominee Imogen was working with. No one else had more of an open excitement over the prospect of Ilise's execution. Anger simmered in my blood, demanding release, but I gritted my teeth instead. *No one* threatened Ilise.

Before I knew it, my last throwing knife was in my hand, tip pointed towards Nikos. "You keep her name out of your filthy mouth." He stepped back from the knife in my hand, a sinister smile spreading across his face as he leaned against the wall across from me.

"Do you really think a little knife is enough to scare me?" I flung the knife towards him and with a loud thunk, it stuck out from the wall, mere inches from his head. He flinched for a second, my smile grew.

"Do you still think it is just a 'little toy'?" I said.

The door opened, Oliver entered the room. "Nikos, I need your help with something," they said.

"I'm not in the mood," he grumbled. Oliver's face fell, unamused. They clasped their hands in front of them, waiting for Nikos to come with them.

"It'll only take a minute, I promise."

Nikos turned to them, sneering. "Well it appears I don't have a minute," he said, irritated.

"Can you get your shirt and come with me, please. I don't have time for this," Oliver said. Why was Nikos so reluctant to go with them? They were asking politely, there was no reason to be so dismissive with them.

"If you can't help me, then I'll just ask Daeva later," Oliver said with a tilt of their chin. Who? Nikos' eyes widened as he grabbed his shirt, grumbling something unintelligible.

"Daeva?" I repeated.

Nikos whirled on me. "Say that again and you won't have a tongue." He left the room with Oliver, the door closing with a slam. Who was Daeva? I waited a few minutes before grabbing my crystal and walking back up the stairs. Daeva was definitely a Nitedand name. But how would one name elicit such a reaction from Nikos? The more information I got, the more confusing it got. I rubbed my temples, already feeling a headache coming on.

I arrived back in the apartment, and Chafik greeted me with a smile. "Hi Ms. Yorena, I made you a plate for lunch." I nodded absently, still trying to decipher what I'd witnessed. "Are you okay?" he asked.

"I wish I knew."

Chapter 30

Ilise

"WHAT DO YOU MEAN I won't be going?" I said. Val sat on the floor in front of my bed, and the dim torchlight flickered in the small room. He came in with a new splint for my ankle so I could walk without the annoying crutches I was already planning to ditch after a day. I now saw it was only a ploy to keep me from getting too upset. A decent effort, but not enough to calm the quiet anger flowing through my veins.

"You're injured," he put simply.

"I've sprained my ankle before and you've never told me to sit and do nothing. I can still train, I'll be careful." Val bit his lip. I crossed my arms. There was something he wasn't telling me, but I couldn't think of another reason he could come up with. "Spit it out, Val. I know there's something else. I'm not a little kid anymore." He stared at me before responding.

"We've all been talking, and think there's a bit of a... conflict of interest."

I raised an eyebrow. "A conflict of interest?"

"You've always had this need for revenge for your family. And after what happened at the palace..." A stab of pain went through me. "We can't be one hundred percent sure you'll be focused on the mission if you come." I hadn't worked this hard to be taken out now. I had to go, I needed to go. If I'd known I would get barred by Val, I would've just gone with the guards.

"You haven't even given me the chance. Don't take me out yet, please," I said. Val's eyes softened, and he groaned.

I held up my hands, pleading. I couldn't be forced to stay here while everyone went on a suicide mission to stop The Progression. That'd been my mission since I arrived here as nothing more than a traumatized child, too scared to have done anything but stare at the blank, pale faces of her family while their blood pooled on the floor. It was my job to make sure no one ever went through that again. He caved with a groan. "You get one chance," he said. I limped to the floor and pulled him into a hug.

"Thank you thank you thank you," I said. Val awkwardly patted my back, and I pulled away from him.

"And how about this, if you can stick to the mission, we'll leave The Progression leader for you." For me? It was like seeing the light at the end of the tunnel. After all these years, I would finally get my hands on the person who made my, and so many others', lives a living hell.

"But if I, or anyone else, get the indication that you're thinking of not sticking to the plan when we leave, you're getting pulled out," he said.

"Yes sir." I gave a mock salute and the corner of his mouth quirked up. An unintelligible emotion flickered through his gray eyes as he fisted his hands before standing to leave.

"Rori will retrieve to help you train with your bad ankle."

I flopped onto my bed. "Got it."

He gave me one last glance. "And if you run into Yasmin, *try* to not make it obvious that you're training. I'd rather not have to deal with her scolding me."

He closed the door, leaving me alone. I couldn't believe they thought I would do something dumb. Every move we made, good or bad, meant life or death. But I didn't have the best track record, so they were justified. I should be resting, but it's not like I felt like sleeping much anymore. The only times my head was quiet was when we were discussing the strategy for the mission. And I'd yet to learn how to fight without wanting to gnaw my foot and ankle off.

And we all remembered what happened the last time I went on a mission without their permission. I was only fifteen, barely trained, and I slipped into one of the carts they were using to ride to Balquet. I'd only known about the mission because I spied on their meetings. There wasn't much else to do anyway, and it's what made them choose me for the spy job in the palace.

A knock sounded from the door. "Come in," I said. Bright red hair appeared in my peripheral.

"Are you just sitting here doing nothing?" Rori said.

"Not nothing. I'm healing my ankle like I was told," I said as I stretched out on the stiff bed.

"Well do you feel like doing something?"

I turned to face them. "Does that something involve going against Yasmin's orders?"

They pretended to study their nails. "Possibly."

My face spread into a grin. "Let's go." I swung my legs over the bed and followed Rori out the door. The splint did nothing to help my limp, but it was better than the crutches. People waved to us as we passed them in the hall. I kept an extra eye peeled for Yasmin, but relaxed as she appeared to be busy somewhere else.

We arrived in the main room of the base. Multiple squads were already training with daggers and longswords, the clanging of swords echoing in the large cavern. A squad of Air Imperium were practicing attacks requiring them to launch the other person at the attacker, and a squad of Earth Imperium were fighting with vines they grew instead of swords. Rori pulled me away from them into an unfamiliar dim hallway. "I've never gone this way before," I said.

"We don't usually use the rooms back here for anything but storage. But they should suffice so I can help you fight with your injury." They retrieved a key from a loose rock in the wall and unlocked the door. Both of us had to push for it to open, stuck from lack of use.

Rori struck a match and lit all of the torches. The room was about three times the size of my room, and the ceilings were much higher. Boxes of clothes and other supplies lined the far wall, and a few mats were scattered across the floor. "Expect to see a lot of these four walls," they said. Rori's crystal glowed white as they whirled all the dust into one corner. I wiped away the pieces that managed to get in my eyes.

"Could I get a warning to close my eyes next time?" I said. Rori let out a belly laugh.

They sat down in the middle of the floor, legs crossed. I sat in front of them. "Is sitting down part of training? If so, I think I'm good to go." Rori tilted their mouth in a smile, but it didn't reach their eyes.

"I need to talk to you about something first."

I leaned back onto my hands. "Is this about how some of you think I'm gonna go off and get revenge when we go on the mission?"

Rori considered me for a moment. "To be fair, when you first joined us, all you wanted was revenge. We can all see the need is still there. But that's not what I wanted to talk to you about."

"Explain," I said.

"You've been distracted ever since you got back from the palace. And I'd be distracted too, after all you had to endure." I looked down and picked at my nails. "But you've been showing signs of a different kind of distraction."

I tilted my head. "I don't have the energy to read between the lines. Just spit it out."

They leaned in closer. "Your mind is on someone who's still in the palace." Someone else? The image of one person flashed through my mind. The springy curls of her hair, the dimples I'd only been able to see only a few times. The way my chest tightened to think about her bubbly laugh. And the phantom touch of her hand whenever we were alone, the way I craved it despite myself.

I scratched the top of my head, hair newly cut to less than an inch long. "I have no idea what you're talking about."

A smirk played across their face. "Do you not see the dopey look on your face?" I forced a blank mask. "I wish I could have it painted so we can always remember the time Ilise fancied someone."

"I don't *fancy* anyone. And who would you suggest I had feelings for?" They tilted their head forward, their response clear on their face. *You know exactly who I'm talking about.*

I stood up from the floor. "Are we going to train or are you just gonna interrogate me?" They stood up.

"We'll train once you confess." We started circling each other.

"Confess what exactly? 'Cause, you're spewing randomness." They let out an exasperated sigh.

"Don't make me say her name before you. If you're to go on this mission I need to know she won't distract you." I stopped pacing and locked my gaze with theirs. *How do they know about her?*

"Everyone thinks I'm distracted from our mission, but I'm not." They stepped closer.

"Just because that's what you tell yourself doesn't make it true."

My face darkened. "I don't care about the Princess in that way, and I never will. She's everything I am supposed to hate." A satisfied smirk formed on Rori's face.

"Oh, so you *do* know who I'm talking about." They continued to circle me.

"Are you happy now, can we train please?"

They nodded slowly. "Mhm. And see, that wasn't so hard was it?" I narrowed my eyes on them. "Will you forgive me if I let you have my dessert at dinner?"

I crossed my arms.

"Fine," I grumbled.

I forced myself to limp to the mess hall. I hadn't been working my muscles as much as a spy, and only a few hours of training with Rori was enough to make every movement hurt. Orla waved to me from the table where the rest of the group was already seated. I lifted my chin at her and limped over. Cain clapped me on the back and let me take his seat on the bench beside Kass. "I'll get you a plate. You're walking slower than a hundred-year-old man," he said. I gave him a vulgar gesture and settled into my seat.

"I take it you enjoyed your first day of training," Orla said as she shoveled soup into her mouth.

"I wouldn't say 'enjoyed'," I said, shooting daggers at Rori.

"What'd I do?" they said with a mouthful of food. I stifled a wince as I shifted in my seat. Miraculously, everything except my ankle felt like it had a second heartbeat. Not exactly what I had in mind when Val said they would help me train without hurting my ankle more.

"You're so small, yet you kick so damn hard. My bruises have bruises."

They waved their hand. "I didn't kick you that hard. And the guards at the palace probably kick and punch at least three times harder." Cain dropped a tray of soup and hard bread in front of me. I mumbled my thanks.

"That may be true, but I'm out of practice." I shoveled a spoonful of the vegetable soup into my mouth and melted as spiced flavors danced on my tongue. All the food at the palace was muted, lacking the spice that was found everywhere else in the kingdom. My mouth tingled more with every bite.

"Aren't you the one who begged Val to let you train?" Kass said, failing to stifle her laugh.

"Training and getting my behind handed to me are two *very* different things." Rori failed to stifle their giggle.

"Jokes aside, we have an update on the palace entrances," Val said. I looked up from my bowl, wiping broth from my face.

"How?" I said.

"You weren't the only permanent spy in the palace."

"What?"

My spoon clattered on the wooden table. I wasn't alone? I could've had people around me who understood what our life was like, and they all kept that from me?

"How could you keep this from me? Do you have any idea how lonely it was thinking I was there all alone?" Kass placed a hand on my shoulder and I shook it off. They'd kept me in isolation all those years...for nothing.

"You have to understand, we only kept this from you so you could stay focused," Kass said. To hells with staying focused, I almost lost my mind in there.

"We can revisit this later," Val said, "but I still haven't told you about the entrances." I clamped my words down, but the moment we had a chance to relax, we *would* revisit this. Quiet anger still simmered, but I had bigger things to be thinking about.

"After you left, they started coming back here. A few of them filled in the holes on our diagram of all the palace entrances. And some are almost invisible or haven't been used in years."

"Then we could get an army in there as long as we go in small groups to avoid drawing attention," Kass said. Val took a long sip of his drink.

"Correct, but there's still the matter of actually getting to them. Our spies said most of them were blocked by either thick vegetation, or they've been built over." Of course they were. Of course, it wouldn't be as easy as using a less guarded entrance to get inside. And they'll be on the lookout for us after what The Progression pulled.

"Not all of them have gotten back yet, but they should be here by tomorrow if all of them have left by now." So we had to wait one more day until we could finalize the logistics of our plan. We would all leave in small groups a week before The Progression's siege. Most of the groups would be the squads we already have. And groups from all the other bases in the kingdom would be joining us, but we'd have the most numbers. We planned to stay hidden in the lower levels of the palace. Almost no one went down there unless they were going to the archives. Then, we would steal uniforms from the guards so we wouldn't get confused with The Progression during the siege.

Pounding feet echoed off the walls, and our heads turned to two boys running towards us. They looked only a little younger than I was, with dirt caked onto their clothes. Val rose from his chair to greet them, I followed. "Are they the other two spies?" I asked. He nodded. The other spies in the palace were even people my age? I could've had real friends, confidants. I knew it made no sense to be mad at the spies, but that didn't stop me. They didn't have to live in the palace thinking they were alone for five years. Why hadn't they tried to talk to me? Val wouldn't have known if we'd talked to each other here and there.

"Is everything okay?" Val said, concern thickening his voice. They put their hands on their knees, panting.

"We were... running... from the guards," the first one said. My heart dropped into my stomach.

"Guards," Rori repeated. "Did they follow you in?" The second one shrugged.

A strong force shook the ground beneath us, and I fell to my knees. Screams echoed off the stone walls as rock crumbled down from the ceiling. I stumbled up to the wall to stabilize myself. "What's going on?" Orla shouted over the noise as she staggered next to me on the wall.

"Earth Imperium, stabilize the ground!" Kass shouted. Emerald light outshone the torches on the wall as a dozen Earth Imperium tried to stabilize the ground. Kass's face contorted into a grimace with the effort. The shaking subsided after a few moments, and all the Earth Imperium's breaths came in loud pants.

Orla and I helped people stand up and moved some of the rubble out of the way. "Zak, did anyone follow you two?" Val asked the first boy. His green crystal dangled out of his shirt.

"I don't think so." The other boy helped him sit down. "We were in a rush to get inside the door, but I'm pretty sure we covered the entrance again." Rori came up to us.

"You're 'pretty sure'? You need to be more than pretty sure." Val put a hand on their shoulder.

"Calm down Rori, the quake was probably one of the guards trying to make the cave collapse. If we wait it out they might think we're dead, and leave."

Loud thumping echoed from the hallway, and I exchanged a nervous look with Rori and Orla. Val's eyes landed on me, a silent command, *go*. "Rori, Orla, lets go check it out," I said. Orla pulled out a small shining weapon, similar to the one I saw Kass have.

"What are those?" I said.

"Butterfly knives. Just got a shipment of them," she said with an amused smile.

"Ilise, if we get killed this is your fault for making me come," Rori said.

"I'll keep that in mind."

The three of us split off from the crowd, following the thumping. "Be careful," Kass said from her chair, still recovering. I gave her a thumbs-up as we left the mess hall. We walked through the main room and into the entrance hallway, an eerie silence falling over the corridor. We paused, ears straining to listen. My hand strayed to the dagger that I kept sheathed to my thigh. Orla and Rori's crystals began to glow blue and white.

We kept walking until we reached the metal door. Nothing looked to be amiss. "Maybe we were hearing thin—" Orla was cut off as the door flew open with a massive gust of wind, knocking all of us several feet away onto our backs. I winced as pain shot up my spine like lightning.

"Everyone freeze in the name of the crown, an air message has already been dispatched for backup. Resistance is futile," the bulkiest guard said as he pointed the tip of his sword at us. The golden royal crest shone on the breast of their uniforms.

"'They might think we're dead, and leave' he said," Rori mumbled.

Chapter 31

Princess Yorena

I SHUT MYSELF IN my room, lying face down on my silk sheets. Leaving my room meant possibly having to face Nikos. Knowing he was working with Imogen, possibly ordering Imogen around, was something I couldn't have predicted. What did Ahn mean when he'd said Heircestrial was a distraction? If I didn't know what they were planning, anything that could happen would be a surprise. I hated surprises. I hated feeling lost like this. But I just had to weather out this storm for another week, then I would be free of them. *Assuming I won, that is.*

A knock sounded at my door. "Come in," I said, not bothering to look who it was.

"So according to one of your servants," Kieron said as he sprawled himself on my desk chair. "You left during lunch, came back with a dazed look in your eyes, and now you've locked yourself in your room." I rolled to the side of the bed closest to him.

"Who told you that?" He leaned back in the chair.

"I'm on break for an hour and came to check on you. The one with two different colored eyes answered the door while the freckled one tried to burn a hole in the back of my head. It was like he was plotting my downfall after only five seconds of meeting me." I covered my mouth to hide my smile.

"Ay, just because you're moping around doesn't mean you get to laugh at me." I sat up fully.

"That's just Mathias being Mathias. He's harmless." I thought again. "At least I'm ninety percent sure he means no harm." Kieron pressed his mouth into a thin line. "Well you checked on me, I've yet to wither into a pile of stress and self-pity."

Kieron snorted. "I imagined you would be a pile of self-pity while you pointed fingers at everyone saying they were working with sorcerers." A giggle got caught in my throat as sirens sounded from outside the window. Birds flew past the window trying to escape the wailing, feathers floating to ground. "What's happening?" Kieron mumbled. I pushed myself off the bed to look out the window.

Lines of guards marched away from their posts around the gates. "Looks like all the guards are being summoned somewhere," I said. I did a double-take. "Shouldn't you be going too?" He looked down at his uniform, as if forgetting he was a guard.

"Oh right," he said as he ran out the door. I followed close behind him as I raked my fingers through my tangled hair. Chafik and Mathias were already gone, the kitchen freshly cleaned, when we left the apartment. He faced me. "Why're you coming too?"

I picked up my pace to match his. "I want to know what is so urgent that they would call every guard from their post."

The corridor was flooded with a sea of black and gold uniforms, the lines that we saw outside turning into more of a mob as the hall narrowed. "Where are we even going?" I asked. I gripped the edge of Kieron's sleeve to stay close to him.

"The high-pitched siren means we all have to report to the throne room." *The throne room?* The sea of guards thickened as we neared the throne room. I leaned into Kieron's ear so he could hear me over the sound of scuffling boots.

"Let's get to the front," I said. He nodded, and we weaved our way to the front of the crowd. The gilded doors of the throne room were thrown open, the dais empty.

Grumbled complaints from the guards we squeezed past quickly quietened once they saw who I was. Kieron and I arrived at the front of the crowd. The Commander walked onto the dais.

"Silence," he called. A heavy silence filled the room. Clicking heels were the only sound as my parents walked onto the dais. I met their stone-faced expressions as they sat on their thrones, golden crowns glinting in the candlelight. Their eyes narrowed as they met mine.

"Ooo, someone's in trouble," Kieron murmured. I stomped on his foot in response, hard. His face contorted with the effort to remain silent.

Oliver and Nikos walked in from the same door my parents did. *Why did they summon them over me?* I trained my eyes forward. I shouldn't give them the pleasure of seeing how much it bothered me. And at this point, would they even care? My father rose from his throne, glistening gold and silver metals covering his chest. "An air message has arrived from Hexia. An underground base has been discovered not far from the town, housing the Primis Defense Union." *A whole base.* Surprised gasps escaped multiple people's mouths. My thoughts were filled with one girl's face.

My mother also rose from her throne, white tulle pooling at her feet. "We need all of you to be on high alert. If there is one base of that size we have only discovered now, then there is a high possibility there will be more." My parents sat down, and the Commander moved to the center of the dais.

"From this moment, there will be no unauthorized entering or exiting the palace. If any of the rebels were to escape, it can be expected they would attack here. And we will dispatch some of you to help scout out any other hideouts they may have. They are a danger to us and the Kingdom of Erea and need to be eradicated." I looked at Oliver and Nikos, and the corner of Nikos' mouth was turned into a smile. Oliver stared at the Commander with knit brows and a thin mouth. *Do they disagree?* Ilise's words echoed in my mind, *"Is this what you considered less dangerous?"*

Just because there was one base didn't mean there were more, it didn't warrant shutting off the palace from the rest of the kingdom. And these were people we were talking about, human beings. They didn't need to be *eradicated* like they were bugs. I stepped in front of the crowd.

"Why close off the palace, does that not show the kingdom we are afraid of them?" I said. Every pair of eyes landed on me and I lifted my chin slightly higher, refusing to allow the instant regret clawing at my stomach to take over. Kieron nudged my shoulder, I faced him. *What,* I said with my eyes. He shook his head ever so slightly.

"I didn't realize you were a military strategist, Your Highness," the Commander said with a cold smile.

My teeth clenched, but I forced my face to match his cold expression. The face of a Princess. The face of a monarch. "I may not be a strategist, Commander, but this is merely common sense." Kieron fought back a chuckle with a cough.

"Closing off the palace and ridding the kingdom of the rebels is the best course of action," the Commander said. Like a small child, I looked to my parents for assistance, both their faces were nowhere close to being helpful. Father's mouth was even curled into a sneer. *Why would they help me anyway?*

They'd trained me my whole life to be the monarch. Yet, the second I formed my own ideas on how to rule, stopped letting them pull my puppet strings, it was as if they were trying their hardest to undermine me. *I* was the Princess. *I* had the power. I'd already failed my people once, letting them and others continue to walk over me as if I were nothing more than a pebble in the road. I forced my eyes away from my parents, pulling on the mask I'd seen them wear thousands of times.

"I disagree," I said firmly. The Commander looked taken aback, steeling himself a second later, pressing his mouth into a thin smile.

"Your Highness, I don't think you are thinking clearly."

I narrowed my eyes as I crossed my arms. "And why would that be?"

He let out a bone-chilling chuckle. "On the same day, two of your servants were uncovered as spies for those rebels. And you seemed *quite* attached to the traitor who recently escaped."

A few of the guards in the room let out low whistles. I fought against myself to keep my face the same, but beneath my skin, I felt my blood boil. No one would talk about Ilise like that, not if I could help it. "You will not talk down to me as if I am a child. Keeping the people's trust is as important as keeping them safe." A kingdom full of untrusting citizens would be divided, only destined for failure.

"Yorena," Mother warned.

"And how do you know there are no innocent people in that base? Surely the rebels might have a family or children."

"Yorena," Father said louder.

"Imagine if it was the reverse, and we were trying to attack the guard living quarters. The guards are not the only people who live there, there are their families and their children. Are you willing to 'eradicate' them as well? Because if you go through with this we will lose the people's trust forever." *And I will lose Ilise forever.*

My parent's eyes widened, along with the eyes of everyone in the room. I took a deep breath to calm myself down, slipping the cold mask on once again and pulling back the small amount of anger I'd allowed to surface. The Commander clenched his fists so tight I could see the whites of his knuckles. Father stood from his throne, jaw clenched.

"What you say may be true, but the sacrifice of a few innocent lives is worth the safety of the kingdom," he said. And just when I thought he was done, he said something to kill the last small ounce of hope I had that my parents still believed in me, even after all of this. After all the years I'd devoted to preparing myself to be the best Queen I could be, one that would earn my place within the great Schaefer line. "You are not the Queen, you are not the one who makes these decisions."

My mouth opened in disbelief. They were genuinely willing to do this, and it would be the worst mistake they could make. "A few lives is worth the price of keeping Erea safe," Mother said. I kept my chin high. I owed them nothing, not even a clue into how their words ripped through me like a sword through water.

"I am still the Princess, I will not be belittled. You're looking at our people as numbers rather than human beings, with lives. Even if some of the people on that base are a danger, it does not mean they all are." They wanted The Progression gone as much as we did, and they were doing more work than we were. And in return we called them rebels and decided to kill them if discovered. *Spirits, what have we done?*

My parents returned to their thrones, staring at me. "Guards, you are dismissed. Your new assignment will be sent to you within the hour." Kieron gave me a sympathetic look before filing out of the room with the rest. The Commander bowed before leaving out the door behind the thrones, leaving only me, my parents, and the other nominees.

"Your behavior has grown more and more unacceptable," Father chided. I went up the dais in long strides, stopping a few feet in front of them.

"You've trained me my whole life to be Queen, yet the moment I have a different opinion from you you act as if I'm nothing more than a common villager."

"What you see as a 'different opinion', could mean risking the stability of this kingdom," Mother said.

"Oh, but when they say something you like, they are the geniuses who would make the best monarchs in history?" I said, gesturing to Oliver and Nikos.

"We are following their example, Princess," Nikos said.

I stormed up to him. "Oh drop the act, you don't care about what happens to this kingdom. You're going to keep making the same bad decisions they're making."

"Enough, Yorena!" Father yelled. His voice echoed off the walls, fanning the fire rising inside me.

"Maybe you should lead by their example, Princess. It might do you some good," Nikos said, his usual bite absent.

"You will not undermine your mother or me in our own throne room, or anywhere for that matter. Your position as the heir is not set in stone, it could be one of those two. So I would keep your mouth shut if I were you, you'll only help the kingdom fall apart more." I studied my father. More gray hairs had sprouted on his head and in the growing stubble on his chin. I knew they hadn't been there a few weeks ago.

I stood before them once more. "The people will find out about this. Dangerous or not, it will kill the small amount of faith they had left in you two. How will that help bring our kingdom together? We'll only tear ourselves apart." I'd never talked to my parents like that before. I'd never tried to lay any claim on the power I knew I had. It was already too late to be claiming it now, but I was the last roadblock between them and total chaos.

"Return to your room, this conversation is over. You are to be confined to your apartment until further notice," Mother said sternly. I gaped at them. After all that, they still dismissed me. What had happened to the caring parents I had memories of? The ones who would have done anything for me or Erea? They wouldn't have sat by while Erea was tearing itself apart. I finally stood up to them to help our kingdom, and I was being locked away because of it.

"You're making the wrong choice, please don't do this." I knew my voice was wavering, but I couldn't let them do this.

"Nominee Li, Nominee Vikander, please walk Yorena back to her room." The two of them stepped off the dais, and I flinched at Nikos' hand on my back.

"We'll take her back, Your Majesties," he said.

They might be sending me back, but they could never turn back from this mistake, just like I couldn't turn back from mine.

Chapter 32

Ilise

THE THREE OF US stared down the guards, or really, the large swords only a foot from our necks. "Stand up slowly and put your hands up," the second one said, a boy about my age. *Why are they sending all the newbies?* I cut Rori a look, and they nodded their head in understanding and muttered a message under their breath, carried away by air. The third guard shot forward at the sight of their glowing crystal.

"I wouldn't do that if I were you," he said with a sneer.

"Are you sure about that buddy?" they said. Before he could lunge for us, Orla hit all three of them with a wave of water, knocking them back several feet. Rori helped me scramble to my feet, dagger already in hand. The guards crouched on the floor, coughing up water. "How'd you summon that much water so quickly?" Rori said in awe.

Orla shrugged. "No clue, but I'm not complaining."

The guards began to push themselves onto their feet. "So what exactly is the plan here?" Rori said while we slowly backed away from the guards.

"Um, I was kind of waiting for you to come up with a plan," I said.

They whipped their head towards me. "Tell me you're joking."

"I'm just a spy, coming up with a plan is you two's job."

"Why don't we just knock them out so they can't hurt anyone?" Orla said.

I shrugged. "Should be easy enough."

"You could have knocked out those guards to save the kids. Like you said, it should be easy enough," the voice said. I gritted my teeth at the guilt clawing at my stomach. Getting past these guards would help me ensure their lives weren't lost in vain. *"Saying it to yourself doesn't make it true."* *Shut up.*

The largest one lunged for Orla and she ducked just as his sword swung across where her neck used to be. *Spirits, they're trying to kill us.* The youngest one charged me, and I spun to avoid their sword, planting my boot into his back. He grunted as the breath was kicked from his lungs. Rori had taught me ways to be lighter on my feet, preventing my ankle from being strained. I skipped back from each of his pathetic attacks with little effort. He whirled on me, aiming for my stomach. I barely leapt back in time and tried to block his swing with my dagger. *Stupid.* His sword knocked it out of my grip. I gulped as I watched it slide across the hallway, too far out of my reach to retrieve. The boy's lips turned up in a triumphant smile.

I crouched to the ground and swept his feet out from under him. Accidentally putting all my weight on my bad ankle, he easily knocked me off balance, swiping me in the side. I cradled my still healing torso, forcing back the stinging tears in my eyes. "Pathetic," he said. The cold metal of his sword touched my neck. I stilled. He pushed it harder into my neck, drawing blood. I kept my eyes on him while I inched my arm closer. "It's a shame, you could be an excellent guard." I gritted my teeth. I didn't intend to make a living out of falsely executing people out of childish fear.

"You know you would do the same if it were a Progression member."

"Get out of my head!"

I gripped the blade of the sword, crimson blood gushing from my hand. Confusion softened the guard's features. I grunted as I pushed against him while I inched my other hand closer to the hilt. I kept my face level as I lightly gripped the hilt of his sword, keeping my eyes on his. "They trained you so poorly," I muttered.

"What?" he said. I pulled the sword out of his hands and he screamed as the blade sliced his hands bloody. I winced.

I elbowed him in the eye, and he rolled off of me, still screaming in pain. It was my turn to hold the sword to his neck. I stood over him, and the eye I didn't hit widened as he eyed the sword. "Please don't," he said, his voice breaking. Guilt pulsed through my heart. He was only a kid, but I couldn't let him endanger anyone here. I took the sword in both hands and rammed the hilt on his head. His muscles relaxed, and I let out a breath of relief to see his chest still rising with breath.

I looked over my shoulder and saw Rori and Orla also knocked out their guards. "Are you guys okay?" I said. Rori nodded.

"A little bruised, a few cuts, but nothing serious,' Orla said. Blood soaked the strands of her blonde hair, but I didn't think it was hers. I tilted my head at the knocked-out guards.

"They look so young," I said.

"Yeah, but we still need to get rid of them," Rori said.

"Where do we put them?" I asked.

Rori clicked their tongue. "We'll leave them here, for now, there's another exit we can all use," they said.

We left the guards where they were and jogged back into the base. "What'd you tell everyone, Rori?" I asked. We pushed past a flurry of people gathering supplies from rooms.

"I told them to pack up as many supplies as they could and get ready to leave. Depending on which town the guards sent their message to, we have less than an hour to a few hours to get out." Dammit. We were supposed to have more than one day to prepare for our siege.

"Where's this other entrance you were talking about?" I asked. Orla jogged faster to match our pace, trying not to get in the way of others. My side and ankle pulsed with each jostling step, but we didn't have time to go slow.

"It's in the back. Down the hallway where you and Rori have been training." Gone with the adrenaline of fighting, I felt every ache in my body. The cut on my palm stung like fire, I clenched my hands into fists against the pain. "We'll all patch ourselves up and then help gather our stuff," Orla said.

We turned the corner into the infirmary. All the cabinets were open and cleared out, save for two bundles of bandages, some water, and a canteen of what I thought to be ale. "At least they left us something," Rori said. Orla helped me wash the blood off my hand and poured the alcohol on it. I gritted my teeth at the sting as she quickly wrapped it in a way I could still somewhat use it. I nodded my thanks and helped Rori and Orla wash and bandage their cuts.

"They already packed the salve I use for pain so your hand will probably start throbbing with pain soon," Orla said.

I let out a weak laugh. Comforting.

We grabbed the leftover bandages and ran out of the infirmary. Val and Kass waited for us in the main room, and others were packing supplies into bags for each of us to carry. Kass had already changed into her leather mission suit, armed to the teeth, and Val had already strapped his weapons to his suit.

Kass handed me another suit. The smooth leather was sewn into a simple jumpsuit with endless pockets and sheaths for weapons. "I kept forgetting to give this to you," she said.

Excitement filled me as I beheld the suit. I always wanted my own, but my job never required one.

"You can freak out over it later, get it on and arm yourself. A bag's already packed for you." We've had to change clothes in front of each other for years, so it didn't bother me as I threw off my leggings and tunic. The leather of the suit felt smooth and cool against my skin as I slipped it on. I zipped the front and limped to the weapons wall. Most of them had already been grabbed, but I managed to get three more daggers and a metal staff. I sheathed the daggers to my hips and thighs and strapped the staff to my back.

Val ran up to me and chucked a bag at me, and it fell to the ground. "You can't just throw a heavy bag at me with no warning," I said. The corner of his mouth tilted up, then vanished in a second.

"We'll all meet at the second exit in fifteen minutes. All the families will leave first, followed by everyone else. You'll leave last with me, Kass, Rori, Orla, and Cain."

I nodded. "I'll help round people up," I said. Val gave me a thumbs up before running off.

I ran through the halls, opening the doors to all the rooms. "Time to go. Families first," I called. People acknowledged me with a head tilt before sprinting to the exit, bags in tow, some carrying younger kids in their arms. I hated they had to be dragged into this, no child should have to be carried through a half-crumbling cave because they would be killed by mere association.

We always had monthly lessons on how to escape in under thirty minutes if needed, a simple drill we never thought we would have to use. It was a frighteningly surreal experience to actually go through with it.

The lines of people going to the exit thinned out after ten minutes. All the rooms I checked were empty, and I met the rest of my group in the main cavern. They all waited with their bags ready to go. "Took you long enough," Cain said.

"I was making sure all the rooms were empty."

Val held up his hand, his face set. "All the squads are going to different bases in Newnina and the Slandslina Forest." That was good. They may have pushed us out of our home, but we were still ready enough to risk our lives to save theirs. "The six of us will head to a base closer to New Teber, the original plan will still be in effect."

Dirt rained down from the ceiling as the floor shook. "They must already be here," I said.

"Let's move out," Val yelled over the shaking. We stumbled into the hallway, struggling to balance with our bags strapped to us. Orla yelped at a piece of rock falling directly behind her.

"They're trying to bring the whole place down," Kass said. The rumbling grew with every passing second. Metal support beams bowed under the weight of the crumbling rock.

"They'll kill all of us!" Orla cried.

"Now is not the time to panic, let's go," Val said. We reached the end of the dark hall, the falling dirt extinguishing the few torches we had here. Another metal door swung open, leading into a dirt-lined passageway. "This way guys," Val said. I walked in after Rori, holding onto their bag to keep from tripping in the dark.

"You can hold my bag, but please don't put *all* your weight on it."

I forced myself to carry more of my weight and my bag's, and my already tired muscles screamed in protest. "Sorry."

We marched slowly through the passage, and eventually, the rumbling stopped. We must have gotten far enough away from the guards who were attacking us. My feet dragged across the floor. It felt like we'd gone for miles already, yet the tunnel seemed to go on forever. I could barely see Rori in front of me the farther we got from the base, the darkness falling over us like a heavy cloak.

"How much longer?" Orla asked as if she could read my mind.

"It's only been like ten minutes," Kass said. "How long did you think it's been?"

"Well it's kinda hard to tell when the only thing we can see is a bunch of dirt," I said. Cain snorted behind me.

"The way out is about three miles from the base, we made it this long to make sure we would be safe if someone ever found us," Val said. They could have done two miles instead of three. Or at least given us some light. Our heads turned at the sound of more rumbling behind us.

"I thought we were too far to feel anything anymore," Orla said. I shrugged. Val stopped the line moving in front of us.

"Why are we stopping?" Rori said. My ears strained to listen to what was happening to the base behind us. I heard rock crumble and crash to the ground, echoing down the passage. A long, heavy silence followed as a familiar lost feeling came crashing down on me. Suddenly I was fourteen again, and I was staring at a destroyed Demessa.

Rubble was all I could see in my mind's eye, the broken bodies of my fellow townspeople littering the ground. Dust and soot floated in the air and some buildings still smoldered. Almost nothing was recognizable from when I'd left. All that was left was a pitiful memory of what had once lived.

"Did they just?" I said.

"Collapse the base," Kass finished for me. I couldn't believe it. All those years, all the memories of that place, wiped away as if it was nothing. From the first time I was able to defeat Kass in a match and we had a nice dinner to celebrate, with delicacies we almost never had at the base. And the night Rori and I had spent playing pranks on Val with the wind because we were bored. And the first memory I had here, arriving with Kass as a traumatized, heartbroken child and she convinced them to let me stay. All of it, gone. Tears ran down my dirt-streaked face. My second home, gone just like the first.

"We need to keep going," Val said in a quiet voice. Our line started moving again, carrying a heavy silence. I still couldn't wrap my head around the fact they wanted us dead. They'd already killed my family, Aerilyn, and now they wanted us to join them. Meanwhile, The Progression killed half the people in the palace ballroom and countless villages' populations, yet they got to run free. They didn't have to walk through dark tunnels to stay alive. They didn't have to constantly fight back guards who would want nothing more than to see you dead. They didn't have their hearts shattered because you put faith in someone to finally help, and they let you down. I dug my nails into the bandages wrapping my hands.

Small beams of light shone a few yards in front of us. Finally, we were going to be above ground. My muscles strained as we trekked up the incline. "We're almost there guys," Val said from up the line. After a few more grueling minutes of hiking up, warm summer air hit my face. Rori held out their hand to help me up the last step of the ladder. Cain was the last to exit the hole and shut the hatch behind him. It wasn't like he needed to close it, there was nothing left for anyone to discover but rubble.

The Zasen River rushed past the empty grass plains we arrived on. I couldn't even see Hexia from here. Good. If anyone came from there we still had time to move. "So what do we do now?" Orla asked.

Val dropped his bag onto the grass. "Now we rest for a few minutes and then start the walk to the next base."

I lugged my bag onto the ground and sat down next to Val. Everyone else settled into a circle, staring at each other.

"Our home is gone," Orla said finally.

"They wanted us dead," Kass said. Rori picked at the grass.

"Our home may be gone," I said as I crushed dirt into a fine powder, "but we can still save everyone else's. We need to ensure this happens to *no one* else."

Chapter 33

Princess Yorena

"I'm sure it wasn't as bad as you're making out to be," Chafik said as he rubbed my shoulder. Oliver and Nikos had escorted me to my room, followed by two other guards, and I knew one stood guard stood watch outside the door. I guess my parents weren't taking any more chances with me. I buried my face in the pillow.

"I embarrassed myself in front of the entire royal guard and got dismissed like a child after being reprimanded," I said in a muffled voice. I turned my head to him; he was wincing.

"Ok, so maybe it was that bad." I groaned as I buried myself farther into the couch, as if I could hide from my own shame and failure. My ears perked up at the sound of the door opening and closing. Footsteps grew louder until they stopped right next to me.

"What happened this time?" Mathias asked in a soft voice.

"I got thrown out of the throne room because I tried to stop them from killing a bunch of people." I made room for him on the couch.

"Well, when you put it like that it does sound like an absolute train wreck," he said. I threw the pillow at him, and Chafik moved onto the floor.

"Why are you on the floor?" I said.

"I don't wanna be caught in the crossfire of your wrath. And this one doesn't know when to shut up."

Mathias gasped dramatically. "But then the world would not be blessed with the sound of my voice."

"The problem isn't your massive ego Mathias, the problem is that my parents are going to kill that entire base and any others they find." Both their eyes widened.

"What base?" Chafik asked. I quickly told them about the Union base that was found and the plan for it. They went through varying levels of shock as I also retold the events that happened in the throne room. The base would be destroyed by now if they had any soldiers near Hexia. *Spirits, please let Ilise be okay.* There was no telling if that was where she ran off to, but I whispered the prayer anyways. To the Spirits no one had heard from in thousands of years.

I was desperate.

"How could they just decide to kill all of them off?" Mathias seethed.

I shook my head. "I don't know. But when I tried to appeal to their morality, it backfired. Horribly." Mathias stormed into his room, and Chafik took his place on the couch.

"Don't take his reaction personally, it's how he deals with things." I nodded. After weeks of living with him, that was becoming more clear. Hells, I wanted to do the same thing. But I couldn't, I had to pull myself together.

"I need to fix this," I said.

"How are you gonna do that?" I crossed my legs and pondered for a minute, staring out the window. Trees swayed in the lazy wind in the distance. *Trees. Peach trees. It used everything it had to get where it is today.* Ahn had told me to be like the tall peach tree. He'd said it used everything it had to grow as much as it did, and now I realized he wanted me to do the same.

"Peach trees," I said finally. Chafik blinked at me.

"Peach trees? Are you going to bribe them with peaches or something?" I left the couch, at last having an idea. "Where are you going?" I paused halfway to my room and turned my head towards him.

"I'm going to listen to a half-crazy sorcerer and be a peach tree."

I did not wait for a response and hurried into my room, locking the door behind me. Ahn had told me I needed to use all the resources I possessed. The ones I had before are long gone now, but there was still one. The guard outside the apartment would stop me in a heartbeat, so I opted to use the tunnels. I grunted as I pushed my armoire to the side, revealing the hidden passage. I opened the near-invisible and headed into the dark tunnels.

Spiders and other bugs skittered past as I hurried down the corridor, my shoes echoing in the empty space. I only had to walk a few yards before turning right, and reaching my destination.

A rusted key lay in the torch dish. I put it in the lock and walked into the small sitting room. Muffled light streamed in through the curtains on the window, and two dusty yellow armchairs sat in the center of the room. After closing the secret door, I crossed the room to another door and walked into the apartment hallway. Was this the creepiest thing I'd ever done? Possibly. But it was worth avoiding the guard.

I walked into the living room and almost made a surprised Oliver fall out of their chair.

"How did you get in here?" they said.

"I have my ways," I said. "I need your help."

"Help with what exactly?" they said. Their eyes darted around the room as if someone else would emerge from the shadows. I sat down on the couch across from them.

They took a long, slow sip of water as I said, "I need your help to stop my parents and the Commander from destroying this kingdom."

They choked and water flew from their mouth in shock.

"I agree that their decision was wrong, but we can't go against the monarchs *and* the Commander," they said. I stood from the couch, moving closer to them.

"But if we don't do something, who will?"

They shrugged. "Maybe Erea is just beyond repair at this point."

Beyond repair? Erea was not beyond repair. If we acted now, we would be able to fix it. It was only a matter of time before the cracks in the seams turned into large fractures. I pushed myself up from the couch. "Erea is not beyond repair. Why would you say that?" They looked around the room as if someone was hiding in the corner. They chugged their glass before grabbing my elbow and pulling me down the hall. "Where are you—" They shushed me.

They pushed me into the sitting room I came in through, locking the door behind us. I gulped. "Why are we here?" Dampened light streamed in through the curtains, casting a yellow glow over the room. I ran a finger along the table, coating my finger in gray dust.

Oliver walked around the whole room, still looking for some invisible object. *Just like Ahn was.* "What are you looking for? I do not think anyone could be hiding in here." They finally turned to me, brown eyes wide.

"You don't know that." I blinked at them. They were acting nearly identical to Ahn. Did they know about Imogen and Nikos too? Or was there something else scaring them. I never thought of Oliver to be the most fearless person, but this level of suspicion was something else entirely.

They met my eyes. "What I say to you cannot be repeated."

I nodded. "That's the same thing Ahn said to me."

They looked taken aback.

"You met Ahn?"

"Yes. And he was acting the same way you are now, looking over your shoulder when nothing is there," I said. "Did you talk to him too?"

They nodded. "Something is always there, always watching."

I was getting more confused by the second. "Just tell me what in four hells is going on and what it has to do with the wellbeing of our kingdom." They motioned to the chairs, and I coughed at the puff of dust that was released when I sat down.

"Imogen is trying to take over the kingdom and she's very close to doing it." My jaw dropped. *Take over the kingdom. So that's why she's using Heircestrial as a distraction.* What could she gain from overtaking Erea? Our kingdom was doing fine before she started messing with it. "And I think she's waiting for your servant to return."

"So when Ahn said Heircestrial was a distraction," I said, "she was just finding an excuse to get into the palace." I rubbed my temples. "Why does she need Ilise?"

They shrugged. "I haven't been able to figure it out yet."

"And how do I know you aren't lying?" The corner of their mouth tilted up into a small smile.

"Weeks of following Nikos around has turned out to be quite rewarding." So I was right, Nikos was the nominee Ahn was talking about. But why was one Progression member so important?

"And you thought I was the creepy one for sneaking in here," I said.

"Also, Nikos' father is the leader of The Progression." I stilled. Leader of The Progression? The same people who hurt Ilise *multiple* times? The same people who attacked the palace. I clenched my teeth, reigning myself in.

I took a deep breath before speaking again. "How did you find that out?" I said through still cleaned teeth.

"We were in his room a couple days ago when a letter arrived for him. And he didn't make much of an effort to hide it from me after he was done reading it. It was signed as 'Your father and leader', and the whole letter was talking about The Progression. If his father isn't the leader then I don't know who is. Also, all of the latest attacks on the palace were from The Progression. They just put so much useful information in their letters." The attacks weren't from the Union? No wonder he was working with Imogen. The son of the leader could be considered royalty within The Progression, one of the most powerful people.

"What are we going to do?"

They rubbed their face and sighed. "Against Imogen, not much. But Nikos has one weakness. Daeva," they said. That name. The same name they used the other day.

"Who is Daeva? You said her name when we were in the training room."

"The letter mentioned this Daeva girl, so I did a little digging in his room while he was gone. And I found a portrait and another letter."

They left their chair and walked out the door. My brow furrowed. A minute later, they returned with a small painting in hand. They locked the door again and handed me the painting. It pictured Nikos with his forest-green eyes and blond hair, but he was smiling, actually smiling. In such a way, he almost looked kind and inviting. His arms were around the shoulders of a girl. She had wavy brown hair so long it ended past the frame of the painting. Her hazel eyes glowed brightly with her gap-toothed smile. She had the same pale skin as everyone in Nitedand had, though hers had a moonly glow to it. "Who is she?" I handed them back the painting.

"I think she was his lover back in Nitedand, and there was a love note in the back of the frame." How anyone could love a monster like that, I couldn't figure out. But at least this shows Nikos had a heart, however small it may be. However, we couldn't use this as leverage firstly because it was immoral to use this innocent girl against him, secondly because she was probably all the way in Nitedand. We wouldn't be able to reach her even if we wanted to.

Oliver's head whipped towards the door as if they heard something. They grabbed me by the wrist and started pulling me back towards the door. I planted my feet into the floor when we got back to the living room.

"What are you doing?" I said as I tried to wrench myself from their grip.

"I heard something, we can't talk anymore. But if I find out more information, you'll be the first to know." Their eyes were wide in fear, their hands shaking. "You should go before someone hears you."

I hurried to the sitting room and back through the tunnels. For once, I was not more confused from when I started, but it still did not make sense. What would Imogen gain from taking over Erea? I pushed open the tunnel door into my room.

The thing that made the least sense was Ilise. What would a sorceress need her for? I mean, she was the most amazing person I'd ever met. I would give anything to have her back in my life, even if she hated me. But I didn't want her back if it meant she would be used as a pawn.

Oliver and I would need to figure out a plan. The more feasible way to go would be to take down Nikos first, but aside from Daeva, he didn't have any other weaknesses. I hoped Oliver could find something, because this was beginning to look hopeless.

Chapter 34

Ilise

V AL MADE US TAKE the long way to the next base, meaning we had to go through the Slandslina Forest to cover ourselves. My ankle threatened to give out, so Rori and Cain alternated between carrying my bag. It was a miracle I found the will to keep going, but the taste for revenge was a good motivator. It got me into an uneasy rhythm.

If I took a few more steps, I was closer to avenging all the people I'd lost. By climbing up this hill, I would finally make The Progression pay, and I would make everyone who let them roam free pay. If I picked my way across the crossed tree roots, I would ensure that no one else would lose their homes like I had mine, twice. By not begging Val for a break, even though I knew he would give me one, I was even closer to stopping the suffering of people like me. People whose only crime was not being born a certain way, a way some thought was inferior. I would show them all *exactly* who they'd been calling inferior.

The searing heat was finally leaving as the sun dipped below the horizon. We made it almost halfway to the next base before we stopped for the night. The moon was high above our heads, doing nothing to illuminate the dense forest. It took us a while to find a somewhat clear space to rest amongst the gnarled tree roots.

Cain handed me my bag to get some food, and I settled on one of the strips of dried meat. The chewy saltiness was a welcome taste in my mouth, and I chased it down with a few swigs from my canteen. "So how much longer until we get to the other base?" Orla said.

"If we start again at dawn, we should be there by the end of the day tomorrow. It's less than half a day's ride from New Teber," Kass said. That would make it much easier for us when the siege happens. Even if the people at the base weren't ready to help us yet.

"Do the people at the other base know we're coming?" I asked.

"I sent an air message the moment we surfaced. As long as no one intercepted it, they should've received it by now," Rori said. After news of what happened to the Hexia base, security around the other bases would increase. And a run-in with a fully armed squad was the last thing we needed right now.

"How many people are in this base anyways?" I said. Kass took another bite of her dried meat.

"This one is smaller. I think it's less than fifty." Fifty wouldn't be enough to protect the palace. Fifty wouldn't be enough for me to slip away to find Imogen or the Progression leader. I realized this was exactly what Val thought I would do, but things were different now. I needed to play dirty if I wanted to even come close to defeating them.

Having a small base was the best we could do. Most other bases weren't as close to the palace, too much of a security risk. And if something went wrong when we started infiltrating the palace, backup wouldn't come for several days. "But a lot of the higher-ups are already there planning the smaller details of the mission... and what to do after," Val said.

*After. W*hen after would be, I couldn't tell. Dread made the meat sit uncomfortably in my stomach. I stood up and brushed off the dirt from my suit. "I'm gonna do some recon," I said.

"Stay close," was all Val said. I limped my way across the thick forest floor. I was sure blisters were forming on my feet inside of my boots, but the pain kept me grounded, kept me from spiraling. I found a large boulder and settled onto it.

A cacophony of crickets and cicadas filled my eardrums. Despite my efforts, I found my thoughts back on my destroyed second home. It was as if destruction followed me. My family, my village, Aerilyn, and now the Hexia base. Maybe I never should've come back. The guards wouldn't have been looking for me, they wouldn't have been chasing the other two spies to find me. And maybe, just maybe, the base would still be standing. And we wouldn't be out in the forest, having to stay hidden from guards to avoid getting killed.

I uncurled my non-bandaged fist, leaving behind crescent moon in-dentions in my palm. As much as I blamed The Progression and the royals, this was just as much my fault. Branches snapped behind me, my body tensed. My hand was immediately on my dagger until Kass' thin figure came into view, and I released my tensed shoulders.

"At least I know your reflexes aren't totally gone," she said flatly. I let out an empty laugh. "Why are you sitting here brooding on a boulder?" she said. I turned back around, away from her.

"I'm not brooding, I'm thinking. There's a difference."

She stepped closer. "Oh?" We waited in silence for several long sec-onds. I couldn't face her. "Are you going to tell me what's wrong or are we just gonna stand here in silence?" I hopped down from the boulder and breezed past her—or as much as I could with my limp—and headed back to our camp. "Your communication skills are top-notch," she said.

I continued stepping over the tree roots towards the camp. Kass followed close behind. "You've been in a sour mood all day, even more than Val. And that's saying *a lot*." A ghost of a smile tried to break through on my face.

"If I hadn't come back," I started. A thick ball formed in the back of my throat before I could finish.

"If you hadn't come back, what?"

I took a deep breath. "If I hadn't come back, those guards wouldn't have come and destroyed the base."

Kass groaned. "Look kid, I know you like to blame yourself for things, but this isn't your fault."

I stopped walking and faced her. "How is it not?" I said, my voice cracking more with every second. Kass pressed her lips together.

"They would have found out about us eventually. And they were following those other two spies, not you." She wasn't getting it, but how could she. I knew she had suffered as much as, if not more so, in her twenty-two years of life, but none of it was her fault. She didn't have a cloud of death following her, touching all the people she cared about most.

"If I never tried to come back, the guards wouldn't have been that close to the base in the first place." I stormed off without waiting for her response. My ankle throbbed in protest as I picked up my pace, but I ignored it. A throbbing ankle was nothing compared to what I'd brought down on my friends. *"Your friends that allowed you to believe you were alone for five years?"*

The beginnings of a headache started at the back of my head. Of course they were my friends. More so than this voice at least. The lie still stung, but it would fade with time, unlike so much else in my life.

I arrived back at the camp a few minutes later. Kass had somehow beaten me back and was now asleep, using her hand as a pillow. Everyone, save Val, was also asleep. I walked up to where he was seated on the stump of a fallen tree. "How was your 'recon'?" he asked softly.

"It was fine," I mumbled. "Area looks secure."

"I'm taking first watch for tonight. Get some rest, we're leaving as soon as the sun starts to rise." I nodded and found my bag to rest my head next to Rori. They stirred as I laid down next to them, I stilled. They settled down after a few seconds, and I relaxed. I focused on the sound of chirping birds and the rustling of leaves in the slow breeze for my lullaby. I nodded off into what I thought would be a dreamless sleep.

I was surrounded by darkness. My hands felt for the weapons I was sure I had strapped to myself minutes before, but my hands were met with nothing but the smooth leather of my suit. I squinted my eyes, looking for anything to pinpoint where I was, and saw nothing. I stood up from the ground, my boots echoing loudly. "Hello?" I called. The hairs on the back of my neck and arms rose in the dense silence. The air was a tangible heaviness, like I was trying to walk through honey. I started forward into the blackness. I gasped in surprise as I continued forward, pain-free. My ankle was throbbing earlier. It couldn't have healed that quickly. I felt something tickle the back of my neck. I jumped.

It felt as if a spear went through my chest. I fell to the ground, clutching my chest. "This can't be happening now," I whispered as my heartbeat pounded in my ears. "Whoever you are, please stop torturing me," I whimpered. I curled into a fetal position when the pain did not subside. But who was I kidding, this could have been what Aerilyn felt. Or at least what she felt for the last few seconds she had until I saw the light blink out of her eyes. I let the tears fall for the first time in a while.

Colorful shadows curled around me. Orange, red, white, and purple swirled at my feet. What were these? I moved my hand through them, grasping at empty air. I tried to blow them away, but more of them appeared. They felt warm as they covered my body, like a blanket and a hug all in one.

"Oh come on now child, there is no reason to cry," a smooth voice said. I flinched and scanned my surroundings, shadows wrapping around me like ropes. I squinted my eyes as a bright light filled the empty space around me. An old woman in deep purple robes appeared in front of me. The coils of her gray hair were tied back into a ponytail, and familiar violet eyes stared at me.

Imogen.

"So it was you. Who's been speaking in my head?" I said.

The sorceress nodded. "I have been trying to contact you since I felt your soul close by," she said as she settled down beside me. I tried to move away, but my body refused to obey as the shadows tightened around me. "We are inside of your soul, you cannot do anything unless I allow it. Those colorful shadows that curled around you were aspects of your soul, it's what us sorcerers manipulate." The pain in my chest subsided but was replaced by a crushing sense of fear. I couldn't move and didn't even know where I was. How could you be inside a soul?

I bit my tongue to keep myself from wanting to indulge in the violence coursing through my veins. Imogen released her grip on my movements ever so slightly, the shadows' grip turning from suffocating back to their earlier warm caress. "How are you able to pull me into my soul, or even talk to me in the first place?" Her lips turned up into a grin.

"It would be much less fun if I told you everything now. But I will tell you that I cannot do this with everyone, you're special." Special?

"Let me go," was all I said. Her laugh chilled my blood.

"I will, but I have something to tell you first." She leaned in closer to me, violet eyes staring right through me. "If you are not back at the palace in three days, I will have no choice but to punish your little 'friends', or maybe the Princess you care about so dearly." No.

"I don't care about the Princess."

Imogen cackled. "I can see your soul, you can't deny what is so clear."

I clenched my jaw. "I don't care what you think. Don't lay a hand on them, or else," I said in a low voice. Imogen's smile vanished from her face, the five crystals around her neck glowed.

"I would suggest you don't threaten me." I gulped but forced myself from wanting to shrink. "You blame yourself for the deaths of everyone around you, don't be responsible for any more." The darkness flashed hues of orange, red, and white before I could think of another response. I was flung away from her still smirking face.

"Ilise," Kass shouted. I opened my eyes as I felt Kass shaking me.

"I'm awake, I'm awake. Stop shaking me." Kass removed her hands from my shoulders and let me sit up. The sun was starting to rise, a few stars still visible in the blue and black sky. I looked around at my friends all staring at me, worry etched in their features. "What's wrong?" I asked.

"You were screaming for help in your sleep and thrashing around." *It was only a dream?*

Memories of Imogen and my dream flashed through my mind. I saw my soul again, Imogen's sharp eyes staring at me as she kept me still with whatever magic she used to pull me in, the ultimatum she gave me before I woke up. I clasped my hand over my mouth and ran to the nearest bush to vomit. Rori came over and rubbed my back as I emptied the contents of my stomach.

I looked at all of them over my shoulder. "Are you okay?" Val said. I wiped my mouth and brushed the dirt off of me as I stood up.

"I'll be fine. Just a bad dream."

"That must have been some dream then," Cain said. I strapped my staff back onto my back and picked up my bag.

"I'm ready to go now," I said. Val raised an eyebrow.

"Are you sure, we can wait a little longer until you're ready—"

"I said I'm ready," I said, cutting him off. He shrugged and led the rest of the trek to the base.

I couldn't go to the base with them. Imogen might not know the exact location we were, but I wasn't about to take any chances with their lives. *Or the Princess'.* I let myself stray to the back of the line. Once they got to the base, I would not be there. My destination was the palace, and I wasn't going to let anyone stop me.

CHAPTER 35

PRINCESS YORENA

TWO DAYS OF PLANNING, two days of being locked in my room, trying to think of a way to stop Imogen. Two separate times I had tried going back to Oliver's room, and both times they didn't have any new information. I wanted to do more than just sit here, I wanted to trust that Oliver would be able to find something we can use as leverage. But we couldn't go into this blindly, too much was at stake. The kingdom, the crown, Ilise. I rubbed the weariness from my eyes as I watched the rain patter my window, dark clouds overcast as far as I could see.

When I wasn't thinking of unachievable ideas of how to go against them, I was questioning why they were even trying to take over the kingdom. Erea had been prosperous since the moment the Schaefer line began, and crowning the son of The Progression leader would throw us backward.

It made me think back to the years when I still had tutors for everything, especially history. The years during and right after Anora Schaefer's reign were known as the golden ages. Constant conflicts had cost the lives of so many Primis in an attempt to start the revolution. It was like they *wanted* this kingdom to fall apart.

I turned my head to the window, watching raindrops streak down the window. More guards than ever marched along the top of the palace walls despite shutting the gates until further notice. Last night Kieron had stopped by my room to say goodbye. His company had been dispatched to Ominka to look for more bases. Ominka was one of the more peaceful provinces, I hoped there weren't any bases there. News had already returned to the palace that the base near Hexia was destroyed by a group of Earth Imperium guards. I nearly cried from relief to hear everyone had already escaped before the cave in.

And that was the base Ilise had last been spotted at. But now I didn't care where she was, as long as she was nowhere near here. No matter how much I thought about it, Imogen and Nikos needing Ilise made zero sense. She grew up in a small village for the first part of her life, and then worked as a servant and then, a spy. A spy for the one group of people who were willing to stand up to her and The Progression. I wish I had seen that earlier. She was the least likely person to help them with their plans.

I pushed away from my desk and crossed the room. What was I going to do? Going up against a sorceress and an entire extremist group would be impossible alone. An empty laugh escaped me. Of course, now was the time I needed Ilise, but I would do anything to keep her away. Staring out the window would solve nothing. I'd been locked in my room for two days. I needed release.

I changed out of the old day dress I'd been wearing long enough for it to smell into a pair of leggings and tunic and tied back my hair as I walked into the tunnels. Thunder shook the walls and I lit a torch to light my way. My feet pounded down the hallway and staircase. Might as well train instead of sitting in a dark room moping. Spirits knew it was only a matter of time before I would need it.

I unlocked the door to the training room and lit the torches lining the walls. Thankfully, it was empty. I removed my crystal and immediately headed to a practice dummy with chunks of it missing. Nikos must have been here earlier. I struggled to lug it to the middle of the room. I spread my feet and began to work on my punches. It helped to imagine it was Imogen or Nikos' face.

Pain sparked across my knuckles, I welcomed it. Bits of the dummy flew off as I continued to hammer it. Sweat dripped down my face and into my eyes. The sound of my pounding heart grew louder than the thunder outside. I stepped back from the dummy to start on my kicks. I was mid-swing when the sound of dripping water caught my attention. This room was completely underground. I shouldn't be able to hear any of the rain from outside.

I gulped in large breaths to calm my heart again. The tiredness was soon replaced by an unsettling sense of awareness. I stilled, listening for the sound again. *Drip drip.* I whipped my head towards the door, stalking towards it. Sweat started to form on my palms. *Is it Imogen? Or Nikos?* I drifted to the small table I had left my crystal, closing my hand around it.

Drip drip. I twirled around again. How was the sound coming from the opposite side of the room now? I clasped my crystal necklace back around my neck. "Hello?" I called. Silence. "I would advise against attacking me," I paused, "you'll live to regret it."

A gloved hand brushed my neck, ripping my crystal right off. I flailed my hands around to grab onto whoever was in the room. I felt the rugged leather of a guard uniform before the cold kiss of a blade touched my neck. I froze. "I'm not going to hurt you, I just need your help," a soft voice said. I knew that voice. It was the voice that visited me in my dreams, the one that had become my internal monologue whenever I felt defeated.

"Ilise?"

Chapter 36

Ilise

I T HAD BEEN SURPRISINGLY easy to slip away once we arrived at the base. Far from any towns, the head of the base led us underground. Val immediately went to meet with the higher-ups, and the others went to eat or rest. Meanwhile, I had taken it as my chance to slip away before they could try to stop me. News of guards looking for me was a good enough reason for the base leader to let me go. She'd shown me the base's back entrance and sent me off. I'd left everything in the room I was supposed to share with Rori, except for my daggers and staff still strapped to my back. Despite the trials of the last few days, my ankle had healed enough for the pain to subside.

The tunnel had surfaced right in front of the Leekrina River. Just my luck, the sky began down-pouring as soon as I left. Water had managed to seep through the tight leather of my mission suit and into my boots. Mud caked them and the whole bottom of my leg. But it provided me with enough cover to hide my face, and enough cover to join a procession of soldiers heading for New Teber. Their feet dragged across the muddy road. I had followed them to the palace, keeping close to trees and shrubbery.

Just outside of New Teber, they'd stopped to rest, and I made my move. The smallest one stepped into the trees, trying to find cover from the rain. Using the thunder to hide my footfalls, I knocked him out using the handle of my dagger in one well-placed swoop. He fell to the ground, and I dragged him farther into the brush. I'd relieved him of his uniform and slipped it on over my mission suit. Security in the palace would be tighter than ever. I'd needed to at least look the part of a guard to get inside.

The procession had started to walk again and I'd fallen in behind them. No one spared me another glance. Not even when we marched through the market square and to the front of the palace gates. The market had been empty of its usual splendor. Many of them might have left because of the rain, but those stands had appeared long abandoned. What'd happened here? I peeked over the shoulders of the guards in front of me as we stopped. One of the guards at the gates was checking everyone's identification papers.

I'd waited until the thunder boomed before slipping away. I'd imitated the marching of the guards pacing around the gates, and they'd nodded to me as I passed. I'd been shocked it was that easy. I'd walked to the opposite side of the wall, to the forgotten entrance we talked about a few days ago. I had to go painfully slow down the hill to avoid slipping and falling into the rushing river below. I'd arrived at the bottom of the hill and whacked away the thick shrubbery with my staff. I reached the door and kicked it down easily, the hinges rusted beyond repair.

I'd shut the door behind me and was plunged into blackness. *Huh, kinda looked like my soul did.* I'd shaken the thought away and continued forward. If my memory of the palace was correct, then this tunnel should be close to the training room. Cobwebs and dust covered my head as I walked down the long tunnel. I arrived in front of a narrow door.

I peeled off the soaked guard clothes, the weight finally off me. I felt along the wall and closed my hands around the metal key. I unlocked the door and opened it so only a sliver of the room was visible. Dim torchlights and rubber mats were the first things I saw, followed by the familiar wall of weapons. Yes, the training room. My stomach dropped at the sound of footsteps, and I froze, not even daring to breathe. Familiar brown curls filled the crack in the door.

Princess. I waited for another boom of thunder before rushing into the room and closing the door behind me.

I watched as she landed punch after punch on the dummy. I paced the walls of the room, not wanting to spook her. *Drip drip.* Her head whipped around, and I pushed myself into the dark corner. Hells, water still dripped from my clothes. I avoided her eyes until she turned to face away and I sprinted towards her. Before she could react, I ripped the necklace off her neck, and pressed my dagger to her throat. Something in me cracked when I heard her small gasp. "Ilise?" she said.

"Hey there, Princess," I said. She exhaled a long breath, and I removed the dagger from her neck, tucking it back into its sheath.

"What are you doing here?" she said in a soft voice. She reached out for me, I backed away. *Focus Ilise.*

"I had to come back and—" She shushed me. I felt her soft hand around my wrist as she led me back towards the door I came in from. We entered the tunnel, and she pulled me through more dark stone hallways than I could count. At some point, we had to climb up a questionable ladder. My wet boots squeaked as I kept slipping on the rungs. "Would it have killed them to put some stairs in here?" I said.

"Guess not," she said dryly. *Going great already.*

We reached the top of the ladder and kept walking until we stopped in front of another wooden door. She grabbed the key on the wall and unlocked the door. The familiar sight of her room brightened the dark. I started to walk inside when she pulled me into the corner by the waist. Every one of my nerves were on fire from her touch, I could feel every point of contact our bodies had. Her arm wrapped around me, her other hand resting lightly on my hip, her warm breath tickling the skin behind my ear. "Wait here," she whispered. She shut the curtains of all the windows before she beckoned me forward. She held out her hand for something.

"What?" I asked.

"My crystal, please?" Oh right, I still had it in my pocket. I placed it in her hand, and she clasped it back around her neck. Every candle in the room instantly sparked to life.

"I need to talk to you," I said. She held up a finger and went into the bathroom. I heard the closing of cabinets before she came back out holding a towel. She draped it over my still soaking shoulders and we both sat on the rug in front of her bed.

"Why are you here?" she said in a pinched voice.

"I'm here to save the people I care about. Too many people have already died because of me."

"No one has died because of you, Ilise." My fingers found the gold necklace I'd kept around my neck since my last day in my village, my eyes trained on the floor. Death was destined to follow me, like a diseased cloud.

"My village, my family, Aerilyn," my voice started to break, "and if I didn't come...the rest of my friends." Her arms wrapped around me, and my head found the space between her neck and shoulder. Against my better judgement, I inhaled her hair's rosy scent, letting myself sink further into the hug.

"None of that was your fault." She gulped. "Especially not Aerilyn. There's not a day that goes by that I don't think about everything I could have done to save her from her fate. But it's not your fault."

I looked up at her, mildly shocked. I could see it in the set of her brow, in the depth of her eyes. *Guilt.* Her breath tickled my ear as she let out a low laugh. "And I know you probably still hate me for not trying hard enough but, after you left I did everything in my power to keep you and the Union safe from harm." I should still be angry at her, but in a matter of a few minutes all of that anger disappeared, replaced with a feeling I'd rather not name.

"Princess—"

She pressed a delicate finger to my lips, silencing me.

"Allow me to finish. I tried to stop my parents from sending the guards to destroy your base. And I've been trying to find allies within the palace to stop Imogen and The Progression. You were right, they were the problem, not the Union."

"Princess."

She shushed me again.

"And after you get dry and I get you some food I'll tell you everything I've managed to uncover. And I cannot put into words how sorry I am for the last few words I said to you." Her hand caressed my arm, where the suit covered my burn scars. Normally I would feel a flush of shame if anyone so much as looked at them, let alone touch them. But something about the Princess' touch made me want her to never stop. I craved it.

"Can I speak now?"

She nodded. I thought carefully about the words I was about to say. I wanted to tell her I didn't hate her, no matter how much I wanted to. But if I told her that, it would be another person's life tied to my decisions. It was better if she didn't know, it was better to keep her where she needed to stay. Arm's length.

"I don't hate you, but don't think that means I like you either." I faltered when I saw her face fall even more. *This is necessary. This is for her own good.* "I don't blame you for what they did to Aerilyn. I know I did the last time we saw each other, but I was upset and you were the closest I could get to screaming at the King and Queen. I came here to help take down Imogen, nothing more."

She chuckled lowly and removed her arms from around me. "I'd expect nothing else from you, Ilise. And trust me, I think I yelled at the two of them enough for the both of us."

Butterflies filled my stomach. Over the time I was gone, I had forgotten how bright the tiny gold flecks in her eyes were. I could see how my words affected her in the droop of her shoulders and how she couldn't quite look me in the eye. But it was necessary to keep her safe. She wouldn't be able to protect herself if she was worried about me. "What was it that you uncovered here?" I asked, trying to distract her from her hurt. She took a deep breath before speaking.

"I learned that Imogen has been using Heircestrial as a distraction. And that she plans to take over the kingdom, with The Progression's help. *And* she can basically control people into doing what she wants."

"How did you find out all of that? I was almost captured after I discovered that same information."

"I've been working with Oliver." *Hells.*

"What?" She recalled the story of her last conversation with Oliver. My blood heated at the mention of their name, and even more so at the fact that she trusted them whole-heartedly. "You can't trust them. They're working with Imogen and Nikos." She stood up from the floor and grabbed one of the blankets off her bed, replacing the towel with it.

While everything they told her was true, they were still the very thing we were going up against. Why would they reveal part of their plan to her?

"What do you mean?" she asked.

"I overheard them talking with Nikos and Imogen the night I fled. They tried to drown me, twice!" Her face fell and she stared at the ground in front of her.

"They tricked me?" she said. I was suddenly glad I had to get here so quickly, there was no telling what trap they might have laid for Yorena.

"Yorena, don't talk to them anymore. They might be luring you into a trap." Her eyes widened as she stared at me.

"What?"

Her face broke into a smile, revealing her dimples. "You called me Yorena."

My face heated. "Oh. That was an accident." Her smile widened.

I stood up from the floor and crossed the room to the window. "How long will you be here?" she asked. I didn't know the answer. I had to give myself over to Imogen tomorrow. Or else Yorena would suffer, and my friends would suffer. She looked happy when she looked at me, but something lurked beneath the surface.

"I don't know. But I won't be here for long." She stood up and paced around me.

"Well, judging by the low set in your shoulders and the fact that none of your smiles have reached your eyes, I think you are going to give yourself over to Imogen," she said. Wow, that was scarily accurate. I tossed the blanket back onto the bed.

"I have to Yorena, more people I love will die if I don't." She took my hands in hers, and I yanked them away.

"But you're the last thing she needs to take over the kingdom. I don't know why exactly, but if you give yourself over, then the whole kingdom will suffer." And I wouldn't force any more people to suffer for my sake.

A lump formed in my throat, and Yorena's face became blurry as tears threatened to fall. "But if I *don't* give myself over, then everyone close to me, everyone I care about will be the ones to suffer."

"Let me help you," she begged. "Don't do this alone." I let out a breath and closed my eyes.

"But yo— more people will get hurt. I only came here to see if you knew more than I did, not to rope you into this." Her soft palm was suddenly on my cheek. I hoped she didn't notice as my face burned by her touch, and the increasing fluttering in my chest.

"Real heartfelt words for someone that supposedly doesn't like me. You try to do everything alone, you act like you can do it all. And I'm sure you would try to save everyone even if it killed you." I flinched. "But you can't do everything yourself, you're not invincible. I can't lose you to this because you decided to go be a martyr."

I let the teardrops fall, and she brushed them away with her thumb. My eyes dropped to her heart-shaped mouth. "Let me fight her with you, please. If it's your fight, then it's my fight too."

I took a breath and closed my eyes. "Ok." Her face brightened as her smile spread across her face. I stepped away from her before she could pull me back under her spell. Her smile tightened, and I tried to ignore the stab of pain it sent through me.

Chapter 37

Princess Yorena

I GAVE ILISE ONE of my spare nightclothes, and she went to bathe. I'd offered to tell one of the boys to heat warm water, but she opted for the cold buckets I'd yet to use. We decided it would be best to wait until tomorrow to start preparing. I knew Ilise told me she wouldn't give herself over to Imogen and let herself be used, but I didn't think she was telling the truth. There was something else on her mind, and she wouldn't tell me what, or why she was still pushing me away. I could tell she felt the same way, at least to some degree, yet she continued to try and distance herself. Unless...she didn't feel the same way and I was scaring her away. Did she? Was I?

A knock sounded at my door. "Come in," I called. Chafik entered the room with a tray of food, lamb stew with fried yams and he placed the stealing tray in front of me, the spiced scents wafting into my nose.

"Dinner is served," he said proudly.

"Thank you." I heard water splash onto the bathroom tile, and the hollow clatter of a bucket being knocked over. I couldn't let Chafik know she was here. I knew neither him nor Mathias would turn her in, but the less people who knew, the better. His head turned towards the bathroom.

"Is there someone in there?" he asked. I forced my face to remain calm, my fingers twiddling with the fabric of my nightgown.

"No, why?" He raised an eyebrow.

"Lies. I heard water. And you always play with the fabric of your clothes when you get nervous." I shook my head and dropped the edge of my nightgown.

"I don't know what you're hearing."

Mathias walked into the room. *Great.* "What's all the commotion about?" I stood up and tried to push them out the door.

"There's no commotion, Chafik is just hearing things." The two boys looked at each other before twin smirks spread across their faces.

"What are you two smirking about?" Mathias wriggled out of my grip, sprawling himself out in my desk chair. I didn't need this right now, and Ilise would be out any second.

"Unless you want to claim that both of us are hearing something coming from the bathroom, it's pretty obvious what we're smirking about," he said. I let out a nervous laugh.

"This is my room, please leave." Chafik flopped down onto my bed. Children. They were actually children.

"Who's in there Ms. Yorena?" he sang.

"Nobody." My heart dropped into my stomach when the bathroom door clicked open. My eyes briefly met with Mathias' before we both rushed the door. Ilise opened the door before I could shut it again. Everyone froze, and the boy's eyes went wide.

My eyes latched onto one of her hands wrapped up in bandages, the slightest bit a red soaking through even after a bath. My chest burned, and my hands were curling into fists of their own accord. *Who hurt her?*

"Ilise?" Chafik said, dumbfounded.

She waved to him. "Hey guys, long time no see." I crossed the space between me and the window to make sure none of the guards' attention was on the room, and promptly shut the curtains.

"Ok, I need all of you to be quiet so we don't draw the attention of the guards outside the window, and the apartment door."

The boys watched Ilise's movements as she moved to the rug in front of the bed as if she would disappear if they took their eyes off her. "I'm not a ghost, you can stop staring at me," she said.

"To be fair, we thought you were either dead or gone forever," Mathias said. Chafik threw one of the pillows at his head.

"We didn't think you were *dead,* we just thought you were never coming back. And if we did see you again, it would be right before they executed you," Chafik said. I flinched at the thought.

"Considering how easy it was to get in here undetected, getting captured is very low on my list of worries," Ilise said as she leaned against the footboard. Mathias laid out on the bed next to Chafik, staring at her. "What are you waiting for?" she asked.

"We expect a full story." She raised an eyebrow.

"You disappear for a few weeks, and come back with no warning after the crown calls for your arrest. There must be a real good reason for you to come back here," Chafik said. "And you know I love a good story."

Ilise smiled, and I wished I could freeze the moment in time to study it. Her smiles were few, and I never wanted to forget that lopsided tilt of her mouth, the way her eyes squinted as if she were staring into the sun. "I'm happy to oblige, considering your idea of interesting is a useless dusty history book that looks older than all of the Council sorcerers," she said. Mathias failed to contain his laugh, and I covered my mouth to hide my smile as I went to sit next to Ilise on the rug, but I thought better of it and sat on the bed next to Chafik.

"My 'dusty history book' was plenty of help when Ms. Yorena needed information on Heircestrial. So it's not *useless.*"

Ilise sighed and told us what happened to her over the last few weeks. From the guards chasing her all the way to Hexia, to her escape from Hexia before it collapsed. A muted spark returned to her eyes whenever she mentioned any of her friends that left the base with her, though she refused to say any of their names. Then she told us how she left them at the other base to come here.

The way she spoke of them, the passion that entered her normally measured voice reminded me of the way I felt for Erea. Now I could tell why she was so resigned to giving herself over to Imogen for their sakes. It was what I would have done for Erea, and, more recently, her.

"But why would you leave your friends to come here if it's so dangerous?" Chafik asked.

"Because they would get hurt if I didn't." Chafik and Mathias looked at each other with matching, confused expressions. "Imogen threatened them, it wasn't a hard decision to make."

Chafik raised an eyebrow. "The ancient sorceress with the purple eyes?"

Ilise nodded.

"But you were nowhere near here, how could she threaten them?" Mathias asked.

I paused. Ilise had never told me how Imogen had contacted her in the first place. She had to have been miles from the palace when she decided to come back. Ilise stared at an invisible object, lost in thought. "Did she send you an air message somehow? Do Air Imperium have a way to send one without knowing where the recipient is?" Chafik asked.

"No, she used a... different method." It was my turn to raise an eyebrow. When she didn't follow up, Mathias got impatient.

"Well don't keep us on the edge of our seats," he said.

She shook herself from her trance. "She pulled me into my soul while I was asleep and talked to me," she said as if it were the most normal thing in the world. We all gaped at her. *Pulled into her soul?*

"Since when could sorcerers do that?" Chafik asked.

Ilise shrugged. "She claimed it only worked over that far of a distance because I'm 'special', whatever that means." How could someone get pulled into their soul? It wasn't a place, it was just a slightly tangible part of ourselves that only sorcerers could manipulate.

Mathias turned to Chafik. "Hey book man, do you have an explanation for this?" he said. Chafik shot him a look then squinted at the ceiling as if it would give him the answers. At this point, I wouldn't be shocked if they appeared there. I thought soul magic only worked when the sorcerer was close to the person whose soul they were controlling, it was the whole reason they mostly stayed in Mount Bachport. Without being close to people, they couldn't change anyone's soul. Could they?

"I can tell you about the history of every single town in every single province, but I don't know the first thing about sorcerers."

Ilise shifted uncomfortably. "That's the thing, nobody does. I can only guess what other powers she has and what she meant by 'I'm special'."

Mathias started to snicker. *Is he really laughing at a time like this?*

"What is it now?" I said.

"Maybe she's actually a sorceress and Imogen's been keeping her a secret to use her as her secret weapon," he said.

Ilise scoffed. "If I was a sorceress, I would've defeated her weeks ago, could've spared myself some effort." It could be possible. I unclasped my fire crystal from my neck and held it out to her. Her eyes widened before she leaned away from it—almost repulsed.

"Try it," I said. The boys leaned closer to us.

"I'd rather not," she said, her eyes not leaving the crystal. Why was she acting so weird? It was just a crystal. Assuming it *did* work, the most she would be able to do would be a tiny spark.

"Come on," Mathias begged. Ilise closed my fist around the crystal, pushing it away from her. Then it dawned on me, the reason she still wore long sleeves no matter the weather, the scars that still marred her beautiful skin. The memory of what they looked like still sent bouts of fury through my veins, knowing someone had hurt her in that way.

I pulled it away and clasped it back on my neck and she let out a breath of relief. "Sorry, I didn't mean to push you." Chafik looked between the two of us.

"I feel like I'm missing something here, but I've heard enough mind-boggling stuff today. I'll see you all tomorrow." He left the room, Mathias followed out behind him. We were finally left alone again.

"So are we going to go to sleep or are we going to plan for tomorrow?" I asked.

"Plan first, then sleep." My eyes strayed to her arms, or more so, what lay underneath.

"Is that the reason you were so nervous around me when we first met?" Her brow furrowed.

"Is what the reason?" I gestured to her arms shrouded in pink silk.

"What The Progression did to you." Her gaze fell to the ground as she nodded.

"But you seemed fine when you yanked it off me earlier." She crossed the room to where her suit was hung in the armoire.

"My suit has gloves. It doesn't bother me as much if I'm not touching them."

"But now's not the time to discuss my childhood trauma. We need to think of a plan to take down Imogen as soon as possible," she said. "Comfortable over there?" she asked as I burrowed myself into the blankets. One of her rare smiles graced her face and I wanted to pretend they were becoming more frequent around me, though she'd already made it clear how she felt about me.

"Very much so. There's plenty of room for two," I said, attempting to bait her. Something flashed in her eyes, gone before I could read it.

"I'll pass," she said as she laid out on the rug in front of the bed. A twinge of hurt scraped against my heart at her rejection. "Idea time," she said.

My mind drew a blank. Imogen was too clever and had too many years of experience on us. She was already stronger than both of us with her five crystals, the two nominees, and the entire Progression.

"We could attempt to trick her into letting her guard down," I said.

Ilise let out a quiet laugh. "And how do you suggest we do that? She's probably fifteen steps ahead of us already. And it won't be long before she senses my presence in the palace." My forehead creased.

"Sense? How does that work? Does she just smell you or something?" She unsuccessfully tried to stifle a laugh. "I know that might be the stupidest thing to come out of my mouth, but I don't hear you explaining it."

"When she visited me in my dream, she said it was possible because she could sense that I was close to the palace. So I assume she'll know where I am very soon." Her eyes darted around the room and her fingers restlessly drummed on the floor. She was afraid. All I wanted was to hold her in my arms until that fear left, but I knew she would only push me away if I tried.

"Then we have to get to her before she gets to you," I said.

She sat up, mischief churning in her brown eyes. "Why don't we use the fact that she probably knows I'm here to our advantage?"

I was getting more confused. "But if she knows you're here, what advantage could we have?"

She started pacing. "We get her and the other nominees in the same room, and we take all of their crystals." I felt the headache starting at the back of my head.

"But what about the control she has over The Progression? I'm assuming the crystal doesn't give her control over all of the members."

"True. But without her crystal, she can't control any of us, *and* she'll be knocked down to the same strength level as us." It finally clicked in my mind.

"And then we can intimidate her into surrendering." She nodded her head. Assuming it was even possible to intimidate someone like Imogen.

"Exactly." It was a good idea, not a plan per se, but it could work if executed correctly.

"Even if we take down Imogen, how will we find every Progression member and make sure they don't wreak any more havoc?" I asked. The corner of her mouth turned up in a grin. "I have a feeling I'm not going to like your answer, am I?" She crossed the room to where her suit was hanging. Her finger ran along the serrated edge of one of her daggers.

"We won't have to find The Progression, they're already coming to us."

My jaw dropped. The Progression is what?

"I overheard Oliver and Imogen talking about an invasion starting in a couple days." The Progression was coming *here*? Most of our guard was scattered looking for Union bases, and none of them were coming back at least for another week. I couldn't lose my home, not to them.

"And how are the two of us going to defend the palace against The Progression? Even with the guards that are left, we're outnumbered." Ilise twirled her dagger through her fingers while I watched in awe. *I need her to teach me how to do that.*

"That's where I come in. I already knew the siege was supposed to happen at the end of this week, and the Union is coming to help."

That was the best news I'd heard all day. Even though the palace wanted to destroy them, they were still planning to come and help defend us. That took another level of bravery. "So we just have to keep Imogen under control until then," I said.

"Exactly." I tilted my head at the girl in front of me.

"When did you have time to think of this?"

She shrugged. "Spend weeks of your life in strategy meetings and you pick up a thing or two. But there's still the matter of how we even get Imogen and nominees into the same room."

It was my turn to smile, Ilise stared at me. "What?" I said. She abandoned her daggers and walked closer to the bed.

"Whenever you get excited, your dimples show." My face felt like it was on fire, but she pretended as if she said nothing. "Go ahead, tell me your idea," she said.

"I call all of them to a brunch claiming it's to celebrate the last week of Heircestrial. We could ask the boys to distract the guards that will be stationed at the door and then we strike." She weighed the idea.

"Good luck convincing them to do that."

I waved a hand. "I'll just tell them to stand outside the door and argue about something stupid. They do it every night anyway." She flopped onto her back laughing, and it sent all sorts of feelings through me. I wished she laughed more. The sound was the same as the sweetest honey tastes, more beautiful than any piece of music I'd ever heard.

"Ok, we have a plan," I said. "Now, we sleep. Tomorrow, we save the kingdom." Ilise returned to her blankets on the rug in response. At that moment I realized, I would do everything I could to protect this girl a few feet in front of me, and I prayed it would be enough.

Chapter 38

Ilise

I DID NOT SLEEP. Yorena quickly fell asleep beside me, her soft snores filling the room, and my body buzzed with restless energy, but it was too early to do anything. I stood up and studied Yorena's sleeping form. I wasn't going to let her get hurt tomorrow, I wasn't going to let anyone get hurt tomorrow. The only person getting hurt was Imogen, and maybe the nominees.

We'd already sent Mathias and Chafik to deliver the invitations to the nominees and Imogen, and now it was a waiting game. Part of me knew our plan was decent enough, even though there were at least a hundred ways it could go wrong. It was half-baked at best. Val and Rori were always the better strategists, but it had to work. The aftermath if it didn't would be too great. But another part of me didn't care about the plan. That sorceress was the reason my family was dead, the reason my village was dead, the reason my best friend was dead. She needed to pay the price, and I was ready to collect. She had a dagger with her name on it, and I needed to be the one wielding it.

The stabbing pain in my chest began again. I crouched on the floor, curling over myself. *Not now.* I forced myself to stay quiet before Yorena woke up. My heartbeat pounded louder than the pattering rain outside the window. My breaths came in short gasps, waiting to be pulled into my soul.

The darkness of her room plunged into a shade of black I didn't think possible. The pain in my chest vanished, and I opened my eyes to the colorful shadows swirling around me.

"I see you've agreed to my deal," Imogen said. I turned to face her wrinkled face, and took a deep breath to keep myself from lashing out at her. The shadows curled around me, waiting to be wielded.

"I haven't agreed to anything," I said, keeping my face a cold mask.

"I know you're here. Nothing you plan will work, I am the one in control." Somehow I preferred her chilling smile to her stone-faced expression. "And considering you show up at the palace soon after I give you my warning, I would say you've accepted." I dug my fingernails into my palms. "Lest you want that little Princess of yours to get hurt. She's more ingrained in your soul than ever." Before she could use the shadows, I sprung forward, my hands reaching for her neck.

"If you touch a single hair on her head, you will pay dearly." She pushed me away as if I were nothing more than an annoying bug. The shadows wrapped around my arms, yanking me back just before I could reach her. Imogen leaned close enough for me to see all the shades of violet in her eyes.

"I've lived thousands of years, girl, you cannot threaten me."

The shadows curled around my torso and squeezed me so tight, it felt like my ribs were about to collapse as blood pounded in my ears. "What... do you... even... need me... for?" I said while gasping for air. A tremor went down my spine when she gave me a full-toothed smile.

"You are going to turn the tables. I have been planning for this your whole life, and I am not letting you walk away from your purpose."

I gritted my teeth. "My purpose is to bring justice to all the people I love that you killed, and send you to the Fire Spirit's hell." She clapped her hands together and released me from the grip of the shadows, making me collapse into a coughing heap.

"Amazing, you're already right where I want you." What?

I blinked, and she was gone as if she had never been there. What did she mean when she said I was right where she wanted me? I scanned the blackness of my surroundings. I hadn't woken up yet, and all I could see was a whole lot of nothing. Did that mean my soul was empty? The colorful shadows swirled around me softly, no longer controlled by Imogen.

The orange and red shadows wrapped up and down my arms while the white one rested on top of my head. What were these things? Imogen said they were aspects of my soul, but did the colors mean something? All of them wrapped around me except for the purple one, laying still at my feet. I kicked it with my barefoot, pain shooting up my leg. It felt like kicking a brick of pure stone. It remained still while the others swirled around me like a tornado. They lifted me into the blinding light growing above, and I closed my eyes as I was sent back into reality.

...

I woke up still on the floor of Yorena's room, and thin beams of light shone through the cracks in the curtain. My head felt like a deadweight. I didn't realize traveling into your soul warranted a headache. It hurt too much to open my eyes beyond thin slits. Yorena stirred and I pushed myself up. The world spun around me as I stood. "Ilise," she said in a sleepy voice. I walked over to the bed and brushed a stray lock of hair from her face, despite my better judgment.

"Good morning," I whispered into her ear. She shifted to face me.

"What time is it?"

I glanced at the clock. "It's already nine-thirty, the brunch is in half an hour." She nodded. "I call the bathroom first," I said. She gave me a sleepy smile before I pulled away. I grabbed my mission suit and weapons from the closet and went into the bathroom. I removed the silk nightshirt and pants and slipped into the mission suit. The cool leather felt as smooth as the silk, and I would never get used to the feeling. I strapped the weapons to their place and tied the staff to my back.

I left the bathroom fully armed. Yorena's back was to me as she buttoned herself into a blue dress. "You can't exactly fight in a dress," I said. She turned around to reveal the rest of her dress. It was a riding dress. The back of the skirt was hemmed so it didn't brush against the floor, and the front was cut like a coat. All sorts of holsters and sheaths lined the pants underneath.

"I've been saving this dress for a special occasion." She twirled with a giggle.

"Okay, you need to go weapon up, and I'll make sure the boys are ready."

She nodded and left out the door to the tunnels. I left her room and pounded on the boys' doors. "Wake up, time to save the kingdom." I heard shuffling feet before both of them opened their doors.

"Why are you so loud?" Mathias said. Chafik frowned as he turned to Mathias.

"Aren't you the one up all hours of the night either singing or playing your violin?" he said.

"Are you saying you didn't enjoy me serenading you?" Mathias said with a bat of his eyelashes.

"I really wish I could throw something at you right now," Chafik said flatly. I crossed my arms as I listened to them argue. At least I knew they would be able to do their jobs.

"Save the banter for when it's your time to distract the guards," I said over them. They rolled their eyes and retreated into their rooms.

I chose to return to Yorena's room, for my stomach was in too many knots to eat anything. I tried to sift through Imogen's words from last night. She claimed I had a purpose, but what could she need me for? She was stronger, smarter, and more skilled than I could ever be. "*You should give up.*" I shook the thought out of my head. If only the cloud of death that seemed to follow me could touch her. I ran my finger along the sharp blade of my dagger. Even if it decided not to touch her, I would make sure it did.

The tunnel door opened behind me. Yorena had armed herself with four throwing knives and a dagger, and she never looked more beautiful. The light curved around her and glinted off the metal of her weapons. But it was her smile. She looked like everything good in the world, one of the few good things I had left in my life.

"Ilise, you're staring." I forced my face back to an indifferent expression. I was sure I looked like an idiot.

"No, I'm not."

"Liar."

"*In more ways than she knew.*"

"*Get out of my head, Imogen.*"

"Where are you going to hide all those weapons?" I asked.

"There are more hidden sheaths in this dress."

The bell tolled ten times outside. "Ready to go?" she asked.

I nodded.

"Time to go, ladies," Mathias called from the hall. Yorena stashed her weapons in all the different folds of her dress. Where did she even get something like this?

Chafik's eyes widened as his eyes landed on me. "You look like you're going to war," he said.

"I am." The three of them left the apartment, and I went into the tunnels.

Yorena was supposed to meet Imogen and the nominees in the royal family's private dining room while I waited outside the secret door until it was time to strike. When I heard the guards go after Chafik and Mathias, I would run out the door and grab Imogen's crystals while Yorena handled the other two. She'd tried to convince me to let her go after Imogen, but I'd rather put my hand in an open flame than let her do that. This was my battle to fight, not hers. *"You'll only fail her and the rest of them."* I ignored her.

I counted the turns Yorena had instructed me to go: three rights, down the ladder, and a left. This passage looked even less used than the others, my footsteps echoing in the empty space. I had to keep my hand on the wall to guide myself without a torch.

I'd imagined this moment a dozen times over, and not one time did it look like this. I was back in my prison of five years, working with Yorena after running from my friends—the only home I had left. An unsettling feeling of indifference washed over me. How did it end up like this?

I reached a wooden door, the hinges long rusted, pressing my ear against it to hear what was going on inside. Only whispers came through. The door and walls were too thick to listen to the hushed conversations happening. A pulling sensation made me want to go inside now and get it over with. It felt as if a cord had been tied around my waist, and I had no choice but to follow its pull. I dug my fingernails into my palms to keep myself still. I only had to wait a few more minutes. A few more minutes, and I could stop all this before it began.

A bitter taste stained the back of my tongue.

"I know you're close little one, come out of hiding." Imogen's voice rang in my head. I guessed being this close to her meant I didn't get any chest pain from her talking.

"But where's the fun in that?" I said. I could feel annoyance coming from her, the buzzing feeling dripping from her words.

"Your little Princess friend is here. If you come out, I won't have to punish her." My fingers itched for the key hanging a few inches away.

"If I come out of hiding, so does a dagger with your name on it." Her laugh was thunderous in my head. My hands curled into fists.

"You're gonna regret laughing." Silence.

"I lost any feelings of regret a long time ago, little one." Unlucky for her, so did I.

Chapter 39

Princess Yorena

"Good morning, Your Highness," Imogen said. We walked in front of the other nominees as I led them to the royal family dining room. It hadn't been used in years, the perfect place for Ilise and I to strike. When I had told my parents about the brunch, they'd deemed it a good enough excuse to allow me to be released from my room. But a guard was to be near me at all times, trailing, watching, waiting for me to snap.

I would have to find a way to get rid of her before I gave Ilise the signal. Or else she may call for backup, and I would end back where I started. And Ilise... I didn't even want to think about what would happen to her. Every one of my nerves were on fire, I could hardly keep my hands still from the energy coursing through me. I could almost see the end, just a few more minutes and this would all be over.

But our victory wasn't guaranteed. There were only two of us and three of them, plus however many guards would try to stop me. But we could do this—we had to. Everything would be fine as long as I didn't panic. I took a few deep breaths to calm down my speeding heart before any of my companions caught wind.

We arrived in front of the oak doors to the dining room. I hoped Ilise didn't get lost on the way to this room, the tunnels were easy to mix up if you weren't familiar with them. My hand grasped the gold door handle, frozen. Maybe there would be a way to give Ilise some more time. I could say the servants didn't serve brunch yet, or I could take a quick detour somewhere.

"Is there something wrong, Your Highness?" Imogen asked. I flashed a fake smile and twisted the handle. *Act normal.*

"Of course not," I said. I would just have to stall inside the room before Imogen or the nominees got too suspicious. Imogen looked me up and down as she passed me into the room. My concealed weapons burned from her gaze, as if she could see right through the thick fabric of my dress.

"Actually, if I may, I would like to take a quick detour," she said. Thank the Spirits. This would give more time for Ilise to get into position, and for me to try and stomp out these nerves.

"Of course," I said. I followed Imogen out of the room and down the staircase. Imogen didn't feel the need for a torch, so I had to drag one hand on the wall as my guide.

We arrived on the first floor and Imogen paused in front of the throne room. Two guards stood on either side of the doors, still statues.

"Is there a particular reason you've taken us here?" Oliver asked. Part of me wanted to pretend Ilise was incorrect when she'd said she overheard Oliver plotting with Imogen. They were kind to me, they even tried to help me fight Imogen and Nikos, but it was all a ruse. The betrayal stung. I should've known it was too good to be true, but I let my desperation get the better of me. Stupid. Stupid. Stupid. They hadn't even dropped the act yet, still believing I trusted them.

Nikos on the other hand was acting... strange. His usual smugness and confidence was nowhere to be found, replaced with an empty look of hopelessness. To most it would look like nothing more than mild disinterest. But I knew the difference, I'd become quite familiar with that face. It was the same one I saw on Ilise. *What's going on?*

"Nominee Nikos, I have a surprise for all of you but it appears I have forgotten it in my quarters," Imogen said. "Would you please fetch it for me?" He gave a tight nod and disappeared back up the staircase. Imogen's strikingly white teeth made an appearance as she smiled. An uneasy feeling swelled in my chest. Just what kind of surprise was she about to deliver?

Chapter 40

Ilise

"Where is this girl?" I said into the tunnel. She should've knocked on the wall by now—my signal to enter the room. But I couldn't hear so much as one footstep coming from the other side of the stone. Maybe she got held up, or Imogen and the nominees were late. I paced the space around the door, tracing my footsteps in the dust. I was itching to get out there. Staying hidden behind a door wasn't going to help save my friends and this kingdom. This was supposed to be a quick fight so the guards wouldn't have much time to stop us.

Yorena had told me about how her parents confined her to her room. It was a miracle she'd even convinced them to let her have this meal, so why was she wasting the already dwindling time we had?

A footstep echoed off the stone walls, and I froze. My hand was immediately on the dagger at my side as I squinted in the darkness. Another echoing step. "Don't come any closer," I called. Nothing but my own voice echoed back to me. I searched for floating dust, the quickest indication of motion, but it all remained undisturbed on the ground. Could I be hearing things?

The hairs on the back rose, every muscle in my body tensed and at the ready. "I'm giving you one last chance," I said. My gloved hands gripped the dagger hilt so hard I wouldn't have been surprised if the leather split open. I couldn't stay here and wait for whatever that sound was. I walked away from the door in the direction of the sound.

It could simply be a mouse that managed to slip through one of the doors, or it could be a settling wood beam. My steps were slow and silent, the only thing marking my path being the swirls of dust around me.

A crash sounded behind me. I whipped around and was immediately blinded. Rough fabric scratched at my face as I thrusted my dagger through the air wildly. "Stop resisting," a voice said. *Have I heard that voice before?* I struggled to remove what I assumed to be a sack off my head. The attacker wrapped the strings around my neck and my head throbbed from the lack of air. I wouldn't be taken down so easily.

I swept my legs behind me and smiled at the grunt in my ear. Without wasting a second, I ripped the sack off my head and threw it to the ground. My attacker staggered up from the floor, a crystal swinging from their neck, though it was too dark to note the color. I charged them, ready to embed my dagger anywhere I could, but they swerved to the side with practiced precision at the last minute.

I stumbled but was able to keep my balance. I swerved back to face them, my blood demanding violence. Where could I stab this person that would hurt the most? Right next to the heart would hurt quite a bit, or maybe in the lower abdomen.

I was offered no warning as pain blossomed across the back of my head. My body was not my own as I slumped to the ground. The last thing I heard before unconsciousness took me was, "Who knew it would be so easy to distract you."

Chapter 41

Princess Yorena

I MOGEN BLEW OPEN THE doors to the throne room and waved us through the doors. Everything appeared to be normal, my parents were absent. Without them there, the thrones were not nearly as intimidating as I always imagined them to be. My skin bristled as I took in the rest of the room. At least a dozen guards were stationed around the room, their eyes tracking our every movement.

We stopped in front of the dais. Last I was here, my parents had banished me to my room for trying to stop them from killing all the bases they found. Again, without them there, the dais seemed so small, just a tiny marble stage. Who knew this plan would lead me right back to where it began?

"You may enter," Imogen said to no one in particular. I looked towards the doors but nobody was coming in. Who was she talking to? The doors behind the dais swung open and a guard walked in with a limp figure in their arms, a burlap sack tied on their head. The figure was clad in a leather suit, dust coating their gloves. Wait, I knew those gloves. Fear and anger spiked through me, I couldn't tell if I would rather cry, or rip her right out of that guard's arms.

They had Ilise.

Another person walked into the dazzling torch light. Nikos stepped next to the guard and Ilise, dirt staining the white sleeves of his tunic. He fiddled with the silver buttons of his navy vest. I had to force my hands to remain calm at my sides.

He captured Ilise, *my* Ilise.

"I found the traitor on the way to your room," Nikos said. His tone was cold, methodical, acting as if he didn't just rip my heart out in front of me. He untied the burlap sack and the guard dropped Ilise. My breath caught in my throat and Oliver shot me a sideways glance.

"What a wonderful surprise," Imogen said. She strode up to the dais and the guard stepped aside. "We have what we need for your third, and final test." Ilise's eyes blinked open and she jumped away from Imogen, but was prevented from moving any further when the guard placed the blade of his sword at her neck. She froze. I found myself moving towards her until Imogen put up a wall of air to block me. My hair blew around my face and tears sprung in my eyes from the cold wind.

"This is the test of loyalty," she continued. Ilise's eyes darted around the room, no doubt looking for a way out. It would be impossible for our plan to work now, there was enough crystal, and manpower, to stop a small army. We stood no chance. She knelt down so she was eye-level with Ilise. Ilise was panting, and her eyes promising violence. "Kill the traitor."

My heart dropped to my stomach, threatening to take me with it. I couldn't kill her, I couldn't *hurt* her. She writhed in the guard's grip.

"I'm gonna kill you," she screamed. The guard around the room placed a hand on the hilt of their sword. Imogen held her hand up and they returned to their previous position.

"No worries guards, the nominees will take care of her." Imogen glided down the dais steps and stood off to the side. "Guards, you are dismissed." Without a word they filed out the door and we were left alone. "Nominees, you may proceed," she said.

Ilise's eye immediately met mine as she stood from the ground. Her finger twitched as she reached for two of the many weapons I was sure she had hidden. Oliver was the first to spring, their crystal glowing a luminous blue. I sprinted after them and tackled them from the back. "What are you doing?" they said, squirming under me.

"I know you're working with her. And you will *not* hurt her," I said in a low voice. My vision partially turned black from a blow to the head. They threw me to the side and continued their pursuit for Ilise. Nikos stood over me, I hadn't even seen him step down from the dais. He was the one who captured her. He was the reason she was used as a pawn for a test. My vision turned red and I sprang onto my feet.

"I know you would like to fight me, but you might want to stop Oliver first," he said blankly. My head whipped around as Oliver formed a sphere of water around Ilise's head. Bubbles rushed from her mouth and her arms flailed wildly, trying to stop them. I wanted to make Nikos pay for this, but revenge wouldn't help her now.

I charged Oliver. I pulled a dagger from one of the holsters and bashed the hilt into their back. The sphere broke and splashed onto the tile. They turned to me, their face turning deadly. Their fist swung at me, aiming straight for my face. I caught their arm with one hand and burnt the skin of their wrist. They cried out and drove their foot into my stomach.

Air rushed from my lungs and I stumbled back. Their crystal activated again and I was ready to counter their attack when Ilise came up behind them wrapped her arm around their neck. Their pale skin quickly turned a bright red. "You really thought you would kill me?" she said into their ear. Silver flashed as she released her arm and replaced it with a dagger.

No. They didn't deserve to be killed for this. "Ilise don't cut their throat," I said. Oliver was frozen in her grip. The back of my head throbbed from Nikos' earlier attack and I could feel the room begin to spin around me as the adrenaline drained from my blood. "Be better than them."

I could see the indecision in her eyes. She sighed and opted to slam the hilt of her dagger down on their head. Oliver slumped to the ground, blood slowly seeping from their scalp.

"Why'd you hit them so hard!"

She shrugged and immediately turned towards Imogen. The sorceress stared at her, arms crossed. Nikos ran up to the dais and lifted Oliver's limp form.

"Consider my lack of involvement my way of helping you," he said before running out the room. *Helping me? Why?*

"Well done, little one," Imogen said with a smile. Ilise stared at her like prey. The plan was to only intimidate Imogen, and if her treatment of Oliver was any clue... she was here to kill. "It was entertaining watching your little Princess try to stop the test."

Imogen charged Ilise.

"NO!" I screamed. I threw up a wall of flames in front of Imogen before she reached Ilise. She chuckled at the flames before walking right through them. *Dang it Yorena, she's immune to fire.* I ran towards the two and Imogen sent a gust of air my way. I was thrown back halfway across the room, the dagger in my hand clattering across the floor. Pain shot through my body from the impact. Black spots swam in my vision. The room sounded underwater, muffled.

I had to get up. I had to help Ilise. Blood trickled from the wound in my now pounding head. I activated my crystal to stave off some of the pain and forced my shaking muscles to work. Flames sparked in my blood as my vision cleared and I beheld Ilise and Imogen.

Sweat and blood dripped down Ilise's cut face, Imogen stalked towards her as she scrambled back. Her weapons all lay scattered across the room. No one hurt Ilise, not on my watch. She had Imogen backing her into the corner, four of her crystals glowing. I sprinted to them, my hand ready to rip the crystals off her neck. Then I felt my strength lessen, the spark I had been using for so long extinguishing. I looked down at my crystal. It was sputtering out. *Hells.* My legs slowed, and my vision blurred once again. I whimpered as the pinpricks of pain from all the attacks I suffered hit me at once. Tears stung in my eyes, but I had to keep going. Ilise's back was glued to the wall while Imogen prowled towards her.

"Last chance, little one," Imogen said. Ilise spat a mouthful of blood in her direction.

"Not a chance." Her eyes met mine briefly before flicking back to Imogen. I threw my depleted crystal at the back of Imogen's head as I rushed to her. Her split-second confusion allowed enough time for me to grasp onto her earth and water crystals. I yanked them off her neck before she had the chance to toss me back. Ilise unstrapped the staff from her back and slammed it into the middle of Imogen's back.

She fell forward, and I swerved to the side as she tried to grab them back. Her fingers just brushed my shoulder. My reflexes were slowing, tiring. "Give those back now!" Imogen screamed. I planted a kick to her middle, and Ilise's staff cracked against Imogen's back. Imogen rolled as she fell to the floor and jumped back up.

"I still have two crystals, don't think you've bested me yet." Ilise reached out her gloved hand and grabbed the fire and air crystals. As she did, Imogen used a hurricane-level force of air to knock both of us into opposite corners of the room. I slammed into the other corner, and my head cracked against the wall. Blood seeped from my scalp. My head felt like an anvil as I lifted it towards Ilise.

She wasn't moving.

She still held Imogen's other two crystals in a tight grip. Imogen knelt as her strength left her. "It's not nice to steal people's crystals, little one," she said in a haunting voice. My heart skipped a beat when I looked back at Ilise as she was slowly dragging her hand to push herself up. I had to keep Imogen's attention off her.

"It's not nice to try and take over other people's kingdom," I said through gritted teeth. The room began to blur as it spun around me, my eyes threatening to close. The darkness of the room was chased away by a growing light, one that brought heat into the room.

I looked at Ilise and saw the crystals glowing.

Both of them.

Flames swirled and spun around her like a tornado filled my vision before the room fell away into blackness.

Chapter 42

Ilise

T HE RUSH OF STRENGTH I felt was unlike anything I'd ever felt before. The heaviness in my limbs disappeared, the pain that shot through me like lightning faded. I peeled my eyes open and saw myself surrounded by swirling fire. Years of fear spiked through me. I curled in on myself to keep myself away from the flames. I couldn't be here. I thought I'd grabbed Imogen's fire crystals. And Yorena would never do this to me. She knew how much I hated fire.

I peeked at the crystals in my hand. My dagger had ripped a large portion of the gloves from gripping it too hard, letting the crystals touch my skin. They were... glowing? My hands shook as I reached out to the flames. They caressed my hands as the colorful shadows did. I didn't feel any heat besides a subtle warmth. *I'm an Imperium?* The tornado of fire moved away from me. I harmlessly slipped out of the middle as it continued to grow, my hands shaking every second the fire touched me. Yorena was knocked out in the corner across the room.

No.

The roar of the flames became deafening. For the first time, Imogen looked upon me without her superiority, her eyes wide as she beheld the swirling inferno. I imagined it moving towards her, and it slowly crept across the room, swallowing the few debris in its path. I pushed it towards her faster. "I told you you would regret laughing," I said.

Despite standing before a fiery death, she grinned. Stark against the heat I felt coursing through my veins, a chill ran through me. "And I told you I lost all feelings of regret a long time ago." I had no warning as I was pulled into the darkness of my soul again. *The purple shadow wrapped around me before I could reach for a weapon. Imogen appeared in front of me and snapped her fingers. The air and fire crystals appeared back on the string holding her soul crystal.*

"Let me go, you monster," I screamed. Imogen sat on the floor in front of me, studying me.

"It's time I told you a story." The orange, red, and white shadows swirled above Imogen's hand as she wielded them. Seconds later, a blue one joined them. "Let me tell you the story of the five Spirits." While part of the purple shadow broke off to join the other four shadows, I tested the ring around me to see if the pressure had lessened. It hadn't.

"At the very beginning of time, before there were Imperium and Primis, lived the five Spirits. Fire, Earth, Air, Water, and the Spirit of Souls." I already knew this story—everyone in the world knew this story. Why was she telling me this now? The shadows danced around each other, forming enormous, human-shaped figures.

"The five Spirits lived in harmony for thousands of years as they oversaw the land of humans. But then one day, a human presented himself before the Fire Spirit. He begged for revenge against a neighboring village that was stealing from him. The Fire Spirit agreed to help and imbued part of themself in the man, and gave him a fire crystal to channel the new power within him, the Spirit's symbols etched into the rock."

"I already know this," I said. She directed another piece of the purple shadow to cover my mouth. My muffled protests went unnoticed.

"He laid waste to the village that was harming his people, and the Fire Spirit never reclaimed that piece of themself, creating the first Fire Imperium. Other people did this with all of the other Spirits, creating the Water, Air, and Earth Imperium. But no one ever came before the Spirit of Souls. As no one trusted the Spirit." Where was she going with this?

"Until one day, a young girl came before the Spirit of Souls. She wanted to influence the people of her village to stop destroying the farmland and resorting to stealing from other villages.

Before the Spirit of Souls could give the girl a piece of themself, the other four Spirits came to intervene. They claimed humans could not be trusted to have power over souls."

I finally blew away the shadow covering my mouth. "I already know what happened next. The Soul Spirit was jealous of how the other four were worshipped and loved by the people after giving their gifts and wanted that for themself. Then they tried to grant the girl power over souls, but when the other four tried to intervene, they accidentally imbued the girl with their power too, creating the very first sorceress."

Imogen smiled at me. "What a smart girl you are." I narrowed my eyes on her.

"Ok, you told me the Imperium creation story, now what does it have to do with me?" Imogen shook her head slowly.

"If you let me finish I would get to the part of the story where the people of the girl's village chased her away because they saw her as untrustworthy, solely because she could control souls. They called her a monster, the same you called me. I am no monster, you just aren't opening your mind to truly listen to me."

"I still don't see the point of you telling me this," I said.

Imogen clicked her tongue. "I thought you were smarter than that. The girl who became the first sorceress and was chased away from her home because of it, was me." The smallest bit of anger made its way into her voice. My jaw dropped. No wonder she looked so much older than the other sorcerers. I thought she was only a thousand, but she must be at least three thousand years old.

"I watched from afar as my village tore itself apart and fell into ruin. When we still ruled as Letita intended, we were prosperous. I will not stand by again."

This sorceress was crazy. I had to stop her; I had to kill her. "I thought you would be able to see things through my eyes. I tried to give you the choice to help me willingly, but you've left me no choice." She prowled around me like a lion waiting to strike.

"So this is what makes me special?" I tracked her with my eyes. "I'm an Imperium that can control two elements? Someone more powerful than most that you want to use as your weapon?"

Her mouth broke into a full-toothed grin. "Precisely. Now you can rule with me and fulfill the role you were meant to fill." I paused. My role?

"Ruling is Yorena's role, not mine." And she would do a damn good job ruling. She stopped pacing and forced me forward.

"Do you remember your parents? Did you look like them at all?" The gold pendant under my suit burned against my skin. I always had a darker coloring than my parents and siblings, but that was normal among families. I thought I had the same nose as my mother. And I had the same rounded face as my father, but the minute details of their faces escaped me. It'd been too long since I last thought of their faces. Thinking of them only ever loosened the little control I had over myself.

"What are you trying to say?" I sneered.

"Yorena is not the Princess, you are."

What.

"No, I'm not." I fought against the purple shadow, and it squeezed me tighter the more I pushed against it. "I was born," my voice started to shake, "I was born in Demessa. My family is not the King and Queen. My family is my parents and Aline and Sam. You're lying." They couldn't be my parents. I couldn't be the product of those awful people.

She crossed her arms impatiently. "Then how do you explain your affinity for fire and air? The King controls fire and the Queen controls air." I didn't want it to make sense, but it did. Imperium could not be born to Primis parents. And my parents had no affinity for an element. Otherwise, our life would have been much, much different. But those people on the throne were not my parents, at least not in the way that mattered.

"Then who are Yorena's parents?"

"Nobody important. They were a pair of very committed Progression members who volunteered their child for my plan." I wanted to vomit. Who could be so heartless and sacrifice their child for a plan like this? The crystal might not have been in my hand anymore, but I still felt the heat in my blood.

"I'm not joining you. Princess or not," I declared. She started laughing... always laughing as if I was some type of joke.

"If only Ahn hadn't stolen you away from us. Then I wouldn't have to fight with you." Who is Ahn? "But I can still force you. That purple shadow is my imprint." I looked down at it. "I put it there to make sure you were a loyal and vengeful person. But clearly, it only made you so stubborn and intent on disobeying me. Changes a sorcerer makes when the person is young enough are permanent." Loyalty? Vengeful?

"It's why I could still contact you through your soul." Her soul crystal glowed a purple so deep it was almost black. Dread filled my stomach.

Everything in my blood screamed at me to run, but I was still strapped in place. "I should have put all my qualities into you in the first place."

No.

More purple shadows filled the space around me and surrounded me. Years of rage, years of resentment filled the space in my head. No. This wasn't who I was.

Yes, it is. You are all of this. You want to return Erea to its rightful glory. You want to rule the kingdom. You need to rule. It is your destiny. *This was my destiny. I must rule Erea. Anyone who stood in my path would be eliminated. They were mere ants, and I had to be the Queen.*

No, you don't. Don't listen to her.

I collapsed in a pile when the shadows disappeared. The blackness was now filled with purple shadows as far as I could see. Imogen held out a wrinkled hand with a fire and air crystal. "Are you ready to join me, Ilise?" I took the crystals and smiled.

"I've never been more ready," I said.

"Time to take back your kingdom."

I grabbed the locket meant for my false parents from under my suit. The last thing I had of them, the last thing I needed to be rid of. I crushed it into a ball of metal in my hands and let it fall to the floor.

Chapter 43

Princess Yorena

SOMETHING DRIPPED ON MY neck. The back of my head pounded. Everything hurt, everything felt bruised. My eyes were still glued shut. I could feel the coarse stone of whatever room I was in, and pieces of gravel dug into my already cut-up cheek. I lifted myself an inch, and fiery pain shot down my spine. I cried out and fell to the floor.

"Ms. Yorena, I advise against trying to move right now," a voice said. I knew that voice. I forced my eyes open and stared at a stone wall. I craned my neck to look around the room. It was quite small, with iron bars covering the one tiny window. *I'm in the dungeons.* Chafik helped me sit against the wall as my eyes slowly adjusted to the dim room. A few blankets that looked older than my parents were thrown haphazardly in the corner with a bucket.

"What happened?" I asked as I rubbed over the painful spot at the back of my head, dried blood stained my fingers when I pulled them away. Mathias paced the small space.

"We were waiting for you to settle into the dining room, but after a while some guards yelled at us for trespassing and we left." Then why were they in here? Trespassing in private areas of the palace hardly warranted being thrown in the dungeon. Everyone knew servants could be nosy sometimes, and they were hardly punished.

"But the weird part is, they didn't apprehend us at first," Chafik said. I winced when my brow furrowed.

"What do you mean?" He sat on the floor next to me.

"When they first caught us they yelled at us for a couple of minutes and almost let us go. But another guard came and told them something, and next thing you know we're getting thrown in here."

What power-hungry person told them to do that? A single beam of light from the window turned orange. *Ilise.* It had to be past seven o'clock by now, and I was still stuck in the dungeons. When I'd fainted, we had the upper hand. How was I still stuck in here? "How long has it been since they threw me in here?"

"I think it's been a few hours," Chafik said.

Mathias stopped pacing and laid on the floor, letting out a dramatic sigh. "Is this what I get for going along with this plan?" he said to no one in particular.

"Hey, she's our friend. Friends help friends," Chafik said. Mathias frowned, unamused.

"Well not when helping that friend lands you in a musty dungeon," he muttered.

"Now is not the time for arguing, we need a plan to get out of here," I said.

I stared at the metal door that kept me from Ilise. It was solid, a door crafted to only be opened by an Earth Imperium. The seams of a slit were the only thing marking the door, but I didn't think they'd delivered any food yet. If I waited until someone came, I might be able to use one of my throwing knives to make them drop something useful. I felt for the weapons I tucked under my dress, and my fingers only met the smooth cotton of the dress. My stomach dropped. *They took my weapons.*

Loud footsteps echoed from down the hall. Mathias and Chafik froze, still as statues. I crawled towards the door, my movements reopening the freshly scabbed over cuts. Warm blood dripped into my mouth. Stone slid against stone as the guard opened the door and stared at me on the floor.

"Get up," he said in a gruff voice. When I did not get up fast enough, he yanked me up by my arm. I cried out, and he cut me look, telling me to be quiet.

I let him half walk and half drag me to the infirmary. I sat on the cot, and Doctor Mendoza worked quietly as she bandaged the wound at the back of my hand, and bandaged all the cuts across my face, neck, and hands. Relief flooded my veins as she spread the healing salve on them. I tried to meet her eyes to ask her what was going on, but it was as if she was purposely avoiding my gaze. The guard tapped his foot impatiently, ready to take me wherever we were going.

"I think that's enough, Doctor." She silently nodded and let him grab me from the cot. His hand gripped my arm hard enough to bruise, even through the thick fabric of my sleeve. She finally met my eyes just before the guard could close the door, and her expression screamed one word.

Run.

"Where are we going?" I asked. He ignored my question and kept pulling me through the halls. The patrolling guards paid the two of us no attention. *What is going on? Has everyone lost their minds?* I bit the inside of my cheek as I pulled against him, slowing us down. "Where are we going?" I asked again. He whirled on me, staring at me in a way that made the blood drain from my face.

"Stop asking questions, I'm under direct orders." He pulled me forward until we reached the gilded doors of the throne room. He threw open the doors and pushed me inside. I stumbled onto the ground.

A pair of dirty black boots stopped in front of me. "What were my orders?" Ilise asked the guard. I shot my head up and almost cried with relief to see she was okay. She was still wearing her suit from earlier and still had all her weapons, even the staff at her back. Her cuts were almost healed over, and my eyes landed on the two crystals hanging around her neck. One orange and one white.

"Ilise," I gasped. She helped me up from the floor and caressed my cheek. My face heated as her soft lips pressed a light kiss to my forehead. I hoped she couldn't feel how much that made my heart speed up.

"Did he hurt you?" she asked. This close to her, I could see something very wrong. New streaks of gold and silver swirled in her eyes from her powers, but jagged purple cracks marred her irises.

"What's wrong with your eyes?" I said.

"I'll tell you later, now answer my question. Did he hurt you?" She said the question with malice, with an anger I had never heard from her before.

"Not that much, he just pulled me a little hard and pushed me in here. There's nothing to worry about." She narrowed her eyes and stalked towards the guard. The guard stood frozen as she approached, his back rigid. Ilise leaned close to his ear.

"What were your orders?" I saw the bob of the guard's throat.

"To bring her to you after taking her to the infirmary. And ensure she was unharmed." Her new air crystal glowed.

"And what did you do?" A single tear escaped the guard's eye. A pang of sympathy went through me, even if he'd dragged me here. Why was Ilise acting like this?

"Do you know what happens when you disobey my direct orders?" she seethed. The guard shook his head, and she let out a slow laugh.

"I think it's time you find out." In the blink of an eye, Ilise threw him across the room with a gust of air and held him to the wall. I ran towards her, clutching her leather sleeve.

"Are you mad! He doesn't deserve this," I yelled. She tilted her head as she looked at me.

"He hurt you. I have to punish him." I pulled on her arm to get her to stop. A web of cracks spread across the wall, identical to the ones from Imogen's attacks.

"Just put him down," I begged. Her lip curled before she reluctantly put him back down. "Thank you."

A faint glow still emitted from her air crystal, one I almost missed." Ilise... what are you doing?" Her lips curved into a sinister smile, and I turned around to look at the guard. His tan skin was turning bright red. "Ilise stop! You're going to kill him!" Blood dripped from the guard's mouth as he brought his hands to his neck. Seconds later, he slumped on the floor, his chest not rising again.

"What is wrong with you?" The glow died down, and Ilise shrugged.

"I can't have guards that disobey me. Especially when it comes to you, Yorena." She reached out for a hug, and I backed away. My heart broke at the flash of pain that went through her cracked eyes.

"What did you even do to him?" I said. I could barely comprehend the scene in front of me.

"Did you know if you form a tight ring of air and make it squeeze the inside of a person's throat, you can kill them with almost no one being able to trace it back to you?"

I slowly backed away from the girl in front of me as bile rose in my throat. Ilise didn't kill people on a whim. This was something I would expect out...out of Imogen. Wait. The purple eyes, the change in personality, and the guards answering to her. No, not her. "Did Imogen get to you?" My voice broke.

"She only showed me what she was trying to do. It's what's best for the kingdom, and I'm going to rule it." I gaped at her.

"What do you mean rule the kingdom? We were supposed to stop Imogen, not join her." She grabbed both my hands, keeping me from leaving.

"Rule with me. You can be my Princess Consort after my coronation." *She has completely lost her mind.*

"Ilise, if you don't stop this right now, I'm going to have to stop you. Even if it breaks my heart." Her expression fell, and she released my hands.

"Are you trying to threaten me?" she said with a cold smile. I forced myself to not shrink under her gaze. I knew she was already stronger than me, but I couldn't allow her to go on like this.

"I don't want to...but yes. You're not yourself. Imogen is controlling you." In the blink of an eye, she moved, so her face was mere inches away from me. *How strong of an Imperium is she?*

"You can't threaten me. I have nothing left to lose. But you, my dear, have everything left to lose. Join me." I tried to sprint away, but she wrapped me in a tight, but surprisingly gentle, ring of air, forcing me to my knees. I fought back a wince.

"You seriously plan to join Imogen and overthrow my parents? Overthrow me?"

"The crown was never meant for you to begin with. And overthrowing your 'parents' won't be a problem. I already took care of them."

I blinked at her. "What do you mean?"

"I delivered them the same justice they delivered to Aerilyn." I wanted to vomit. Aerilyn never should have died the way she did, never should have died at all. But even my parents didn't deserve a death like that. Nobody did.

"You threw swords into their chests and burned them?"

She smiled sweetly, staring down at her new crystals as they sparkled in the candlelight. "I went with a more hands on approach, but yes. And I enjoyed seeing my justice be delivered." They're gone? The last moments I had with them were tense, cold, numb. When was the last time I even told them, I love you? Sure, I'd been frustrated and angry with their lack of belief in me, but we could've fixed it. We could've bonded again. We could've...we could've gone back to how we'd been when I was little. With no Heircestrial, no impending invasion from The Progression, just us. But none of that could happen now. I just saw them yesterday, they were just here this morning.

I thought I knew what grieving felt like when Aerilyn was killed, but that paled in comparison to the empty, yet heart-wrenching feeling in my chest. It was like having a vital part of you ripped out, and you could do nothing but watch the blood flow from the wound. I didn't realize I'd started crying until Ilise reached out to wipe a tear from my cheek.

"She broke you," I said. I refused to believe what I was hearing from the girl I once knew.

"She didn't break me," she said quietly. A smile spread across her lips, one that didn't reach her eyes. "You can't break something that's already been broken thousands of times, and is meant to be broken a thousand times more."

"What do you mean the crown was never mine?" I flinched as her hand caressed my cheek.

"I am the Princess of Erea, we were switched at birth. Your parents gave you up so Imogen could switch us as infants." I stared at her. No. It couldn't be true. I was the Princess. It's what I was born to do. Surely no one could be heartless enough to hand over their child for this insane cause.

"I know it's a lot to take in, but it's true. I was born to be the Princess," she said as she caressed my head. "You were merely acting as my temporary stand-in." I shook my head as I backed away from her. My chest felt empty. The one thing I knew was my purpose was never mine. I was only a pawn to be used and discarded. Everything I've worked for, everything I fought for... was all a lie.

"I'm giving you the opportunity to be my Princess Consort and rule by my side." I had to get out of here. Her face darkened when I refused to answer her. "Do you remember what I said to you the day I was poisoned?" What? When I didn't answer, she stepped closer to me. I squinted at the brilliant shine of her air crystal as she stalked closer.

"I think it's time I give you the translation. And maybe you'll join me after I made up for pushing you away last night. I was scared, and wasn't acting right." She stopped mere inches away from my face, grasping my chin in her hands. I wanted nothing more than to close the small space between us, to pretend Ilise was normal, and hadn't lost her mind. But the purple cracks pained me to look at, a not-so-subtle reminder of who I was dealing with.

"The phrase I said to you was from an old story my false mother found." False mother? How could she say that? Just yesterday she was willing to get herself killed to avenge them, Imogen couldn't have erased everything. "Smile for me, my star. Light the way for I have lost myself to you. To your darkness, beautiful in the way all vicious things are. Your dark side of the star, my star."

A small tear dripped from my eyes. Ilise released my chin, flashing me a sweet smile. "Nikos, take her back to the dungeon. Hopefully, some time in there will help her change her mind." The doors burst open again. Nikos walked in, his face set.

"Right away, Your Majesty," he said in a toneless voice. *Your Majesty?*

"You can't do this Ilise! We were supposed to save the kingdom!" I shouted to her. And I was supposed to save her. She tapped her foot, staring deep into my eyes.

"When the world insists on taking everything from you, stripping you of what gives you life, you have two options: sit there and take it, or steal something back, no matter the means necessary. I've made my choice, now it's time you make yours."

Nikos picked me up by my arm and pulled me out of the room. The doors shut behind me, closing in the stranger that has overtaken Ilise. "Was this your plan all along?" He kept his mouth pressed in a thin line. "Nikos, answer me." He mumbled something I couldn't hear. "What did you say?" He waited until we passed most of the guards in the hallway.

"I'm not taking you back to the dungeon. Your friends that were in there are waiting for me to bring you back." I was taken aback. He was helping me? No, this had to be another trap. But this time I saw it coming, I wouldn't be caught off guard again.

We walked back down to the lowest level of the palace, where the dungeons were. The new guard stationed there let him in with a nod and shut the door behind us. "I thought we weren't going back to the dungeons?" I said, seeing right through his lie.

"The only way out she doesn't know of is through here, be patient." *There's a way out from the dungeons?* We walked to the end of a hall and stood before another stone wall. Nikos' crystal glowed, and he moved the two largest stones in the center of the wall aside. They opened into another dark passageway, cobwebs and dirt lining the walls. *How many secret passages are in this palace?*

He grabbed my hand and closed the opening behind us. We wandered for what felt like an hour until we reached the end. He led me up a ladder and opened the hatch above, the dying evening light of the sun warming my face. He helped me out, and I scanned my surroundings. The Leekrina River rushed by on my left, and the pale palace was blurry in the distance. It wasn't a trap?

"Ms. Yorena," Chafik said. The boys sat under a tree with three bags. I ran to them and pulled both of them into a hug. Surprisingly, Mathias didn't let go immediately.

"I packed a bag for each of you. All filled with necessary supplies and a few crystals for you, Yorena." I was speechless.

"Why are you doing this?" I asked.

He waved his hand. "I'm not telling you. But you can show your thanks by getting out of here and finding the Union. They might help you take down Imogen and get Ilise back to normal." The Union. They were supposed to be coming here in a few days. We might be able to catch them before they get there. "Now go, before the guards realize you're gone."

He climbed back into the tunnel before I could say thank you. "Guess I'm stuck with you guys," Mathias grumbled.

"Where to, Ms. Yorena?" Chafik asked. I watched the sun as it lazily set over the horizon. The sun, the brightest star in the sky. Ilise called me her star. I was supposed to shine bright enough for both of us, protect her from losing herself to Imogen. And I failed. An unfamiliar feeling warmed my stomach. I would get her back, I would make Imogen pay. I've gone from being the next in line for the throne, to my kingdom being torn apart before my eyes. I had to fix this, fix everything that has been undone.

"For now, let's get away from the palace." They followed me as we walked along the river, away from the palace, away from my only home. I told myself something was coming for Erea. I would never have guessed it would be the one person who was helping me stop it.

CHAPTER 44

Ilise

EVERY CHILD DREAMED OF being Queen when they grew up, except for me... now I would live that dream for them. For Erea. And no one was going to get in my way.

Acknowledgments

If you told me two years ago that I would be publishing the first book in a duology before I even graduated high school, I would call you crazy. This book has been one of the few things keeping me sane during the basically year-long quarantine. The first people I want to thank are my parents for supporting me during my journey of writing my first book. I never would have been able to get to this point without them and their support. Next, I want to thank all the authors I've ever read for introducing me to the world of books, my escape for as long as I can remember. Especially the ones who wrote female black main characters I was able to see myself in. Without them, I never would have wanted to recreate that feeling of being seen for others, and truly understand what it meant to be represented. I also want to thank my friend Fabiana for proofreading one of the earlier drafts of this book before I sent it to my editor, even though I gave her a short time limit. Thank you for reading to the end in spite of the amount of question marks I never seemed to type and all the misspellings of my own made-up characters' names and places, love you. I also want to thank my editor Karena for believing in me and helping me make this book the best it could be, and Murphy Rae for this incredible cover. And lastly, I want to thank anyone reading this for taking the time to help support the start of my writing career. Thank you for being willing to take a chance on a teenage author. Thank you to everyone who believed I could publish this book, no matter how much I wanted to scrap the whole project, and doubted myself throughout the whole process.

About Author

Olivia Ocran is a young adult author that lives in Cary, North Carolina. She has been an avid reader for the majority of her life and finally started writing books of her own during the quarantine in 2020. She plans to continue writing through college with aspirations of becoming an English teacher. She intends to create a space where people of diverse groups can see themselves in literature.